BANG

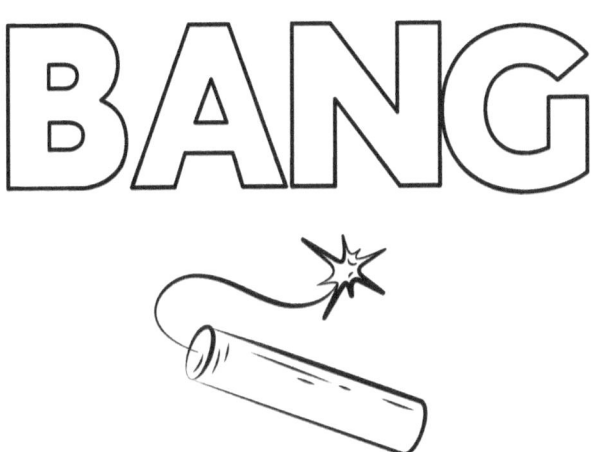

Troublemakers & Heartbreakers

book two

mary cain

cain

BANG

To the Troublemakers

1

Breakup with Boredom

Morgan

MORGAN BLEW A BUBBLE in her gum and tossed her bouncy ball against the wall behind the nurses' station, catching it when it ricocheted.

When she'd decided to become an ER nurse, it'd been under the assumption she'd be dashing from bed to bed saving lives. Turns out, the activity during her shift was rarely that stimulating. Even when the ER was slammed, it never delivered an intense enough adrenaline rush.

She bounced her ball again and Janine, the charge nurse, cleared her throat as she walked up to the station carrying a massive bouquet of pink and peach garden roses, white anemones with black centers, and eucalyptus. Such a lavish arrangement belonged in a wedding, or at least in the lobby of a five-star hotel.

Her bubble popped and she scraped the mangled, sugary residue from her top lip with her teeth. "Who sends flowers to the ER?" The arrangement was gorgeous, but patients didn't stay long enough in this part of the hospital to warrant sending flowers.

"These are for *you.*" Janine plucked the tiny envelope from the clear trident, extended it to her, and smirked. "I should have guessed your funk had to do with a man. At least he has the brains to try to make up for it."

The veteran nurse considered herself more than a supervisor. She knew all there was to know about life and generously doled out free advice to anyone who stood still for more than two seconds.

Morgan's past had enough to unpack to keep Janine busy for ages. A mother who had taken her own life three months after Morgan was born. A father she'd never met. A toxic romantic relationship with a little blackmail mixed in. Oh, and psychological abuse. Couldn't forget about that gem.

But Morgan didn't share her personal life with coworkers. Janine would never know or have the chance to try to fix her.

Not that there was anything to fix. She wasn't broke. Well, financially, she wasn't far from it, but mentally she was in one piece. Sorta. Held together with bobby pins and dental floss but held together.

"There is no man." She snatched the envelope from Janine. There hadn't been for over a year, and the damage that one did was far beyond being smoothed over with flowers.

The funk part was accurate, though. But she only had herself to blame. And maybe her upbringing. Raised by her uncle, a man who could turn the most boring situation into an unforgettable escapade, she'd become accustomed to the extraordinary.

Her current life paled in comparison. Day in and day out, the same boring job, the same people, the same places, the same everything.

Moving to Savannah had started out as an adventure. Then it became a nightmare.

Mixing a romantic relationship and a hustle was the biggest mistake she'd ever made.

But that was all over. She had learned her lesson and cleaned up her act. From here on out, Morgan would live a life free of hustling *and* romance.

"Secret admirer, then." Janine wiggled her penciled in eyebrows.

"They're probably from Logan. My brother is the only guy who has ever sent me flowers." Once she had admitted that out loud, she cringed.

Janine made a sound that expressed—quite clearly—that Morgan was the popcorn hull in her teeth. "Open the damn card."

She ripped open the envelope and pulled out the small card.

I WANT MY BOMB BACK

Her heart raced so fast she got lightheaded. She swallowed hard.

There was no way. Her plot for stealing that bomb had been genius, and she'd pulled it off flawlessly. She might as well have been invisible. Only two people knew she was behind it and neither of them would expose her. Uncle John's fear her talents would be exploited if anyone ever found out about them had taken root early in her childhood. He'd established strict rules to make sure it stayed a secret. The other person was Lucy, the closest thing she had to a mother. She'd never betray Morgan.

"Well?" Janine pressed.

She pocketed the card. "You were right. Secret admirer."

Before Janine had time to squeeze her for information, a patient called for assistance and Morgan jumped to.

She got through the rest of her shift without freaking the absolute fuck out. Or tried to.

Brody Lewis knew *she* had stolen his bomb. Shhiiiiiit.

She'd always been a bit reckless, but she'd never messed around with bombs or the people who made them. Not until Lucy told her what Lewis had planned. She didn't care why or how much he was getting paid, he wasn't going to get away with blowing her childhood home to bits.

Time hadn't been on her side. She'd had to act without doing a thorough background check, but she'd figured he was not someone whose acquaintance she'd want make. Building bombs wasn't a normal skill. A person had to be a little unhinged. It also required a high level of intelligence, which made them even more dangerous.

To her relief, her secret admirer was nowhere in sight when she arrived home.

He probably hadn't been able to find out where she lived. The boat was in her brother's name, and it'd only been a few months since she'd given up her apartment to live on it. Nothing tied her name to this floating residence.

Morgan kicked off her shoes and stretched out on the settee. She pressed her fingers to her temples. Time for damage control. But how? She couldn't involve Logan. Her brother no longer saw her as his spunky little sister who'd never encountered a lock she couldn't pick or a tourist she couldn't con. These days, she was his impulsive little sister who'd messed up royally and who would surely do so again if he didn't keep a close eye on her. He would see this as proof that she couldn't stay out of trouble.

She'd been doing pretty good keeping her hands clean until two weeks ago when Lucy broke the news about Brody Lewis's plan. Stand idly by while some soulless bastard with a knack for making things go *boom* destroyed the only place in the world that made her feel sentimental? Yeah, no. Not her style.

Nor was it her style to get caught. This was a first.

Dented ego aside, Morgan needed to clean up her mess.

The problem? She wasn't sure how to do that if she couldn't figure out where she'd gone wrong. She'd played it over in her head dozens of times and there wasn't a single hole. There was no way he should have been able to trace this back to her.

So, how the hell had he?

2
Absurdly Zen
Morgan

IN THE MORNING, THE situation seemed less dire. Brody Lewis wasn't going to do anything to her. What *could* he do?

Not like he was going to walk into a police station and tell them the bomb he'd built had been stolen. And even if he did, who would believe that Morgan Cash, a registered nurse with zero criminal history—at least, on file—would do something like that?

While tugging her robe on, she strolled into the galley. Drinking her coffee on the back deck while she propped her feet up on the gunwale and read the newspaper was her favorite way to spend a morning.

Of course, there were drawbacks to living aboard. No bathtub, for one. The tiniest makeshift shower imaginable, for two. If the water wasn't calm, forget about using the kitchen.

But until she decided where she'd go next, living aboard the *Gypsy* would do.

The coffee had finished dripping when she reached the counter. Setting the automatic brew feature before bed each night was a kindness to herself she never regretted.

"Mornin'."

She jumped, her pre-caffeine stupor impeding her coordination, causing her to slam her knee against a cabinet. Hissing through the pain, she assessed the man at her dining booth.

He appeared preoccupied by the newspaper in front of him as he took a sip from her favorite mug. The ball cap he wore concealed most of his face, but it didn't matter. It was hard to focus anywhere other than the hulking arms leading to hands so big they made her mug look like it belonged to a child's tea set.

Stunned as though she'd been zapped with a defibrillator, her heart skipped a beat before her pulse rate skyrocketed. "Who the fuck are you?"

His mouth tipped up at the corner, but he continued to stare at the paper. "You didn't like the flowers? I see you didn't bring them home with you."

All the energy she'd put into discounting Brody Lewis as a threat was wasted. There was no talking her anxiety down. Danger was in her kitchen, so indifferent to her presence it was insulting.

Not that she had much of presence to counter his. Being the smallest person in the room wasn't new for her by any stretch, but this guy ate up the tiny galley, his legs so long he could get to her in a half a stride. In these tight confines, he could probably reach out and grab her without getting up.

His aftershave mingled with the aroma of coffee. The woodsy scent that reminded her of a cedar closet did not pair well with her Italian roast. It was like someone drank a gallon of coffee and barfed in one of those preppy stores with low-hung antler chandeliers and black-and-white photos of shirtless models plastered wall-to-wall.

It was truly awful. Disgusting. Not at all the kind of scent that made her want to snuggle up in a flannel blanket, drinking coffee by a window while rain trickled down the glass.

He took another drink from her mug and marked the newspaper with a pen.

She glanced at the paper. A crossword puzzle. For real? A frickin' crossword? Maybe she should direct him to the hammock in the grassy picnic area by the bathhouse. "How did you get in here?"

"You aren't the only one with skills, sweetheart."

Embarrassing. That was the only way to describe him stepping onto her boat without her being aware. The movement caused by his weight should have woken her.

He wasn't anything at all like what she had envisioned. The hair that wasn't hidden by his hat was sandy blond, and his face had seen a razor very recently. Her eyes roamed over exceedingly tan skin, moving to his flannel shirt. A scuffed-up work boot stuck out from under the table. He probably drove a Chevy and chewed on straw.

This was not the kind of guy that built explosives and planted them along the Vegas strip.

No, he was not what she'd expected. And that made him *extra* dangerous.

In six seconds, she could make it to the dock. Running full speed, she could reach her car in another ten, but she would have to grab her purse and dig for her keys. That would slow her down considerably. Her one and only alternative was so odious she could cry. Logan was going to read her the riot act when he learned what she'd done, but first, he'd protect her like a caring big brother.

"Thinking about making a break for it?" Lewis asked, his focus unwavering from his crossword.

"Damn straight," she mumbled, then sprinted up the stairs, through the living room, leapt onto the dock, and ran to the end where Logan's new, shiny yacht, *The Splurge,* floated in all its glitzy, gigantic glory.

She hopped on the back deck and shouted for her brother, then glanced behind her.

Lewis strolled up the dock with his hands in his pockets.

"Morgan?" Logan said as he emerged from inside and met her on the deck, pulling a gray T-shirt over his head. The chaotic, disheveled state of his dark hair and evidence that his face had yet to see a razor today meant she'd interrupted his morning—a morning he'd probably been enjoying with his fiancée. "What's wrong?"

"I'm in trouble." Ugh. She hated saying that. Prior to this, there'd only been one time she'd gotten herself in a mess with the potential to ruin her life, but Logan had found out about it and took it upon himself to fix it. Now, he'd have this to support his argument that she was reckless.

"*Big* trouble," Lewis said. "How's things, Logan?"

Logan pushed her aside and made his way to the stern. "Brody Lewis? What the…"

He stood with his legs braced apart and arms folded across his chest. "Your little sister stole my bang."

He had to be seething about that. There was no way he wasn't. But there was no sign of it. He was so Zen it was absurd.

"You know him?" Morgan asked Logan.

"Yes, I know him," he said, his eyes boring into hers. "What the hell is he talking about, and *where are your clothes?*"

The way he asked the last question, you would have thought she was naked. She checked to make sure her goods weren't exposed and was relieved to see they weren't. She tightened the belt on her robe anyway.

"He was going to blow up the Mermaid. He had to be stopped." She couldn't be the only one bothered by the idea of Lewis destroying the building. Logan had just as many, if not more, memories from the penthouse they'd grown up in.

He rubbed his forehead. His voice was half-bored, half-annoyed when he said, "Morgan, you are giving me a headache and I haven't been awake more than five minutes. You stole a bomb? What. The. Fuck."

It was a stupid thing to do. Brody's target was old and probably ridden with toxic mold, but it would break her heart to see it blown to bits. Carrying out the heist had been the most alive she'd felt in years, though, and given the chance, she'd do it again.

"How do you know him?" she asked, her brain shuffling through possible connections.

"He's Benny Teodori's cousin."

Benny had been friends with Logan a long time. He had spent time around their family and been involved in numerous cons with her brother. But Benny was an outsider and outsiders never knew Morgan had any capabilities. The only way he'd be able to tip off Brody that she'd stolen his bomb was if he'd seen her on camera and recognized her. Not only had she been extra careful to stay out of the range of any lens, but she'd worn a disguise, just in case. The chances Benny had tipped Lewis off were almost zilch.

"Where's my bomb?" Brody asked, sounding only mildly curious.

"I don't have it."

"Couldn't smuggle it on the plane to Savannah?" He smirked and the *oh, you cute little thief* vibes coming off him got under her skin so much she'd have pushed him off the dock if she'd thought she had a shot at succeeding. But he probably wouldn't budge an inch and she'd be the one overboard.

She crossed her arms and glared. She was *not* backing down. All the control in this situation belonged to *her*. Chin up, she said, "It's as good as gone. You might as well forget about it."

"You cost me a lot of money, Cash." Brody shook his head like she was a kid who'd done something naughty yet amusing.

"Logan?" Drew's voice came from inside the cabin. She appeared in a pair of dark green pajamas with white lace around the edges. The bottoms were skimpy shorts, and the top was short-sleeved and buttoned down the front. Unlike Logan's, Drew's hair was tame, held back off her face by a headband, her long auburn locks looking soft as they fell around her shoulders in flawless waves. "What's going on?"

"Sorry, Drew," Morgan said. "I didn't mean to bother you so early."

"Wow," Brody muttered. "Makes sense now."

Logan stepped closer to the back of the yacht deck, his hands fisted and his shoulders tight, like at any moment he was going to spring onto the dock and sock Brody in the nose. "What makes sense?"

"Why you gave up poker."

"I didn't give it up," he snapped, his eyes narrowed. "Stop staring at my fiancée, get the fuck off my dock, and leave my sister alone."

Morgan bit the inside of her lip to hide her smile. Even though she hated conceding to Logan's help, he *did* know how to intimidate. Especially, if you pissed him off by ogling Drew.

"Oh, come on, man. We've always gotten along in the past. Don't let your crazy little sister get in the way of that."

"Crazy?" Morgan shouted. The way he talked about her, as if she was barely worth mentioning, fueled her anger to a new level. "I'll show you crazy."

Logan put out his arm, intersecting her. "What will it cost to build another one?"

"It took me *months* to build that one. I don't have that kind of time."

"Morgan," Logan said in a soothing tone that lost its effectiveness when forced through his clenched teeth. "Where's the bomb? You have to give it back."

Drew's head snapped in her direction, and she pinned Morgan with a wide-eyed stare. "You stole a bomb?"

She nodded. "From a room at the Bellagio."

Thinking about it still made her giddy. If she could bottle that high and take a sip whenever life seemed too boring to endure, she'd have no problems.

"Yeah, good job," Logan said. "If things went so well, then how did Brody find out it was you?"

"You'll have to ask him." She did her best to pull off nonchalant. If he knew how badly it ate her up not knowing how he'd traced the theft back to her, he'd have something to use against her.

They all turned to look at Brody.

He dropped his arms to his sides and tilted his head. "I'm not answering that until I know where my bomb is."

"I guess it's a draw, then." Morgan turned her palms up and shrugged.

"I need coffee." Drew disappeared into the cabin.

Logan took a seat in one of the deck chairs and steepled his fingers across his stomach. "Let's back this up. Morgan, how did you find out what Brody was up to?"

"I'm not revealing my sources," she said, but Brody's voice drowned hers out as he said, "Lucy."

Logan cut his gaze to Brody. "How do you know—" He shook his head and sighed. "She cleans your money. You told her about your plan, and she went right to Morgan with the info."

Brody didn't confirm or deny. He didn't need to. She already knew that part. Lucy had a similar sentimental attachment to the Mermaid, but Morgan didn't really understand it. Lucy had never lived there. Regardless, she'd given her the information and left her to do as she wished.

Or at least, that's what Morgan had thought. When Lucy found out how she'd "taken care of the situation" she'd lost her shit on Morgan. A little bit.

"Now, we know how Morgan found you, but we still don't know how you found her, especially here." Logan raised a finger and did a spinning motion. "I might be inclined to help you…if you tell me who sold out my sister."

She hoped he was just saying that to get Brody to cooperate because if her own flesh and blood meant to help this bastard all hell was going to break loose.

Brody glanced over at the bridge in the distance for a number of seconds while he rubbed the back of his neck. "Lucy."

No.

No. That couldn't be. Short of torture, there was nothing that could get Lucy to give up Morgan's identity or location.

"Bullshit," Logan said.

"I don't go around telling everyone about what I plan to do. Lucy's discretion has never been an issue before, but when she found out what Swiper here did, she fessed up that she'd let it slip."

Swiper? What the fu—

"And told you where to find her?" The scowl Logan wore mirrored Morgan's feelings. Lucy was family. Not blood, but family all the same. The only female role model Morgan had growing up. She *wouldn't* give her up like Brody claimed.

"You're lying."

"Don't believe me. I don't care. I know it was you and I want it back."

"No," she said, dragging the word out because he was as dense as sidewalk chalk.

"Here's what we are going to do," Logan said. "Brody, you are going to go back to…wherever you hang your hat. Cut your losses and get busy on a new project." He turned to her. "You're obviously not going to retire, ever. I give up. Go ahead and pick every pocket in Savannah for all I care, but don't go around stealing explosives for god's sake!"

She huffed and crossed her arms. "Fine."

"Whoa, whoa, whoa." For the first time, Brody's cool seemed to be slipping. "I'm not going to just forget about my bang and leave it in the hands of God only knows who. That's dangerous."

"It's in good hands," Morgan promised with a smile.

"Who hired you to blow up the Mermaid?" Logan asked.

"Look, that's *not* the point. It was a job, Logan, a *job*. I blow that shitty little casino just enough to get it condemned, I get paid, the end."

"Did you know that *shitty little casino* is where Morgan and I grew up? Our uncle moved us into the penthouse when she was a baby. We lived there for ten years," Logan said. "I want to know everything."

Before Brody had a chance to explain, Drew appeared on the deck wearing six-inch heels and a navy sheath dress. Her hair was pulled into a chic twist. It'd have taken Morgan an hour to make that kind of transformation.

"I would really love to stick around and hear this story"—Drew leaned down and kissed Logan—"but I have a busy day ahead of me and I need a latte."

Morgan took a seat as Logan helped Drew step onto the dock.

When she was behind Brody, Drew mouthed, "He's hot," and gave her a thumbs up.

She pointed her finger down her throat. When she glanced back at Brody, he raised an eyebrow at her.

"I make you want to vomit?" A grin stretched across his face.

Logan cleared his throat. "I'm listening, whenever you're ready."

"Uh-uh. That's not how this works. I figured your sister would come running to you, but I honestly believed you'd convince her to do the right thing. I'm out of here."

That was easy. Maybe coming to Logan was the best thing to do after all. Whatever relationship he and Brody had just saved her ass.

As Brody disappeared up the dock, Logan pulled out his pack of cigarettes. He lit two, then handed her one.

"Why would Lucy tell me what he was going to do, knowing I wouldn't let him get away with it, and then rat me out?" She couldn't make sense of it.

"Don't know. He said he's known her for a while, so she knows him well enough to know he wasn't going to hurt you. She probably felt bad she'd cost him the job and was hoping you'd give him the bomb back so he could repurpose it."

Morgan clenched her jaw. She and Lucy were going to have a long chat.

"So, how long is Uncle John supposed to hold onto Brody's bang?"

"He's looking for a buyer right now, but I think I'll tell him to lower the asking price. We need to move that baby fast."

"You're playing with fire," he warned.

"Brody Lewis can't do anything to me."

3
Hostage Reversal
Morgan

MORGAN COULDN'T BELIEVE HER eyes. The *Gypsy* was gone.

Gone.

She peered up the dock to see if there was any movement on *The Splurge*. It didn't look like anyone was home, which meant her brother had probably moored her boat in the channel to teach her a lesson.

"Where is she?" Logan's voice came from behind her, followed by footfalls on the dock.

She turned to face him, not surprised to see Drew at his side. Even though Logan held it against her that last time she'd gotten herself in hot water, he'd dropped everything to come rescue her—which she absolutely did not expect or ask or even want him to do—if he hadn't, he'd never have met Drew. "Why don't you tell me? And while you're at it, why don't you tell me where I'm supposed to sleep tonight?"

He draped his arm around Drew's shoulder and took a drag from his cigarette. As he exhaled, he studied her, squinting as though trying to decide if she was pranking him. "You lost my boat?"

"It's *my* boat now, remember? And no, I did not lose it. Someone moved it."

"It wasn't us," Drew said. "We were out looking at real estate all day. We just got back."

"You're buying a house? You moved an enormous yacht from New

York to Savannah less than a week ago."

"Drew needs a bigger work space. We were looking at commercial properties. So, where the fuck is my boat, sis?"

Morgan pulled her hair out of her ponytail and ran her fingers through it. "You didn't take it. I can think of only one other person with a motive."

"Brody," she and Logan said at the same time.

"That guy that was here this morning?" Drew asked.

"I steal his bomb; he steals my boat. *Cute.*"

Drew laughed and received an icy glare from Logan. "What're you going to do?"

"She's going to give him the bomb in exchange for the *Gypsy*," he said, as if it were the only plausible option.

"The hell I am. It can't be that easy to hide a yacht."

Morgan parked her rental car on the side of a backroad in rural Maryland. Not wasting a second, she grabbed her bag off the passenger seat and twisted her hair into a bun while she waited for her eyes to adjust to the night.

The breeze rustled the leaves in the trees lining the long driveway as she passed beneath them, staying off the gravel to avoid it crunching under her shoes. The house was more than a city block's distance from the road. A shiver ran down her spine as she contemplated all she couldn't see—snakes, raccoons, coyotes…bears? Did they have those in this part of the country?

Not wanting to trigger any motion sensor lights, she crouched beside a tree in the front yard and looked for where they were likely to be mounted. Once she deemed there was no threat of exposure, she crept along the side of the house to the backyard. An old pick-up was parked under a ten-foot pole with an unlit flood light attached to the top. It was far enough from the house that if she was under the porch overhang, it wouldn't detect her. She placed her foot between the railing rungs and hoisted herself up. The soles of her shoes barely made a sound as they landed on the floorboards. The scent of sawdust and fresh stain, and the lack of creaking boards, surprised her. She'd been expecting an old farmhouse. She really needed to stop doing that—expecting things to be a certain way. It had bitten her in the ass more than once lately.

After a thorough inspection, she determined the windows were free of alarm sensors. The lack of security measures disappointed her. She'd psyched herself up for a challenge.

No keypad on the door, or any sign of a home security system whatsoever. Just an old-school doorknob with a regular lock. Using the lock pick set she'd tucked into her waistband, she jimmied the lock in ten seconds.

Breath held, she cracked the door open and slipped inside. There were no bedrooms on the first floor, so she followed the staircase up. At the top, there was an open door to the left, and two closed doors down the right end of the hall. On a hunch, she snuck up to the open door and peeked inside.

It was a spacious bedroom with a king-size bed. In the center, Brody laid there, eyes closed, covers pulled halfway up his chest, which rose and fell. Her pulse kicked up a notch. Lucy might think Brody had enough decency not to harm a woman, but Morgan had miscalculated men's character enough times that she no longer took risks in that area.

She untucked the handcuffs from her waistband and crept closer, eyeing the gap between the headboard and bedpost. Hesitation created vulnerability. She needed to move swiftly. Her breath seized in her lungs as she grabbed his wrist to slap the cuff around it.

Her feet left the floor and she gasped.

Brody pulled her body flush against his and rolled, pinning her under him. Cold metal struck her skin and the clack of the cuff locking around her wrist joined the sounds of rustling as he straddled her. Before she had the chance to escape, he looped the other cuff around the baluster on his headboard and shackled her other wrist.

A sour taste trickled down her throat. This was not good. She yanked her arms but all she managed to do was pinch her skin.

"Ah, Cash, did you really think you were going to get away with that?" His deep voice filled her ear, causing her body to shiver, tighten, and pucker in places she'd hadn't felt so much as a stir in an embarrassingly long time.

"Get off me!" This was *not* happening. Fuckity-fuck-fuck-fuck.

"Quite the compromising position you're in." The sliver of moonlight seeping in through the window cast a shadow across his face that hid his expression, but the amusement in his tone was unmistakable.

She jerked her hips, but his thighs kept hers pinned to the mattress.

Well, this was annoying.

He leaned his face so close to hers she could feel his breath. Surprisingly minty.

Morgan's toes curled. If anyone else had handcuffed her to a headboard, she would be freaking the fuck out. But the only thing she was feeling was pissed—and strangely, a little flustered.

"Where's my bang?" he asked in a husky whisper.

Her chest rose and fell heavily. Oh, brother. She needed to get it together. The man had a sexy voice. Big deal. He had plotted to blow up the Mermaid, stolen the *Gypsy*, and was now holding her hostage.

Morgan ground her teeth together. "Where's my boat?"

He leaned over and flipped on the lamp.

She hissed and squeezed her eyes shut.

"Don't worry, Cash, it's in good hands."

Throwing her words back at her? Okay, *that* unhinged her wrath. Brody Lewis was not going to laugh at her, and he was not going to win this round. Or any round.

His gaze lingered over her stretched out upper body. "This is a good look for you, Cash." He grabbed his phone and held it up.

What a jerk. And apparently, a pervert too.

"Don't you dare."

He snapped the photo anyway. "Don't worry. I'm not going to blackmail you with it. It's for personal use only."

Her nostrils flared. "Delete it."

He ignored her and set his phone on the table. "You're terrible at negotiation, you know that?"

"Screw you, Brody. I didn't come here to make a deal."

The mattress bounced as he got off her. "That's a shame. Okay, well, you sit tight. I'm sure your big brother will be along to rescue you shortly."

She closed her eyes, exhaled, and counted. One. Two. Three. Fo— Damn it! She could count to six-hundred-and-seventy-seven thousand and not be any calmer.

Logan didn't have a clue she'd come to Maryland. She'd called in every favor she had to learn Brody's whereabouts without involving her family. Lucy probably could have answered all her questions about Brody. Even though Morgan wouldn't have shared her plan with her—she wasn't telling *anyone*—she didn't want to risk it getting back to Brody that she'd been asking about him.

She'd managed to uncover enough information about Brody Gabriel Lewis without Lucy's help. Aside from his address, she was relieved to find out that he wasn't married. Not because she gave a shit about his love life, but because it would be super awkward if she'd pulled this stunt while he was sleeping next to someone. Verifying that he lived alone had been trickier. With the help of a friend who made a mint cyber-stalking cheating spouses, she'd found out Brody was single and not looking—or so the absence of even a single online dating profile indicated.

Brody didn't have an address in Nevada. It took some work to find out he owned a substantial amount of farmland in Maryland.

When she opened her eyes, he was across the room pulling jeans over his boxers. His biceps were remarkably sculpted, not to mention tan…a farmer's tan.

Her eyes moved to his face, and she caught him grinning at her.

"Like what you see?"

She shifted her gaze to the window. "Don't be gross."

The combination of his deep brown eyes and the dimple in his cheek would have made her melt, had he not been so infuriating. Drew was right. He was hot. *Really* hot.

And her enemy.

"You know, Cash, I'm impressed at how fast you found me. You've got skills, I'll give you that."

"You have no idea."

As he tugged a dark blue shirt over his head, she relaxed a fraction. He was a lot easier to hate when fully dressed.

"How long will it take you to get out of those cuffs?"

"With the right tool? Less than ten seconds."

Brody perched on the end of the bed. "Tell me where the key is and I'll let you out right now. All you have to do is agree to listen to what I have to say."

"I don't need your help," she told him, notching up her chin. The key was tucked into the interior pocket of her waistband along with her lock pick set. His hands didn't need to go anywhere near there.

"Ah, Cash." He shook his head. "*I* need *your* help. I'll sweeten the pot a little if that's what it takes."

Maneuvering her bound hands, she reached into the bun on top of her head and pulled a bobby pin free. Blindly, she wiggled the pin until it slid into the keyhole. In no time, she'd freed herself from one cuff. Not wanting to draw attention to where her tools were hidden, she used the bobby pin to unlock the second cuff.

"What are you talking about?" she asked as she surveyed the room, determining an escape-attempt was futile. He had already proven he was just as fast—okay, faster—than she was. He'd catch her and probably lock her up again. Scooting back against the headboard, she slid him a bored look. A small part of her was curious to hear his proposition, but he didn't need to know that.

"I worked really hard on that bang. It's my baby. Give it back to me, Cash. I'll tell you where that stupid boat of yours is, and you'll get a million dollars."

"You're going to give me a million dollars?" she asked, voice flat. He must think she was an imbecile to believe he'd give her that much money. Even if the offer turned out to be legit, she wouldn't accept it. Living paycheck to paycheck didn't suck bad enough for her to accept money from this dickwad.

"Not like that. I've got a job in mind. I need someone with your skills. You do this with me, you get exactly what you want, plus a little bonus. I'll even promise not to go anywhere near the Mermaid."

Now, who was crazy? Brody Lewis, that's who. If he thought she would even consider for one second—No. No. *Definitely* no.

"Never gonna happen."

"Why all the venom? It's beginning to hurt my feelings." He put his hand to his chest and looked wounded. "You stole my bomb. Then you broke into my house and tried to cuff me to the headboard—not with the intention of doing anything kinky." Brody leaned back on his elbows. "I think I'm being damned nice to you considering everything, Cash."

Of course, he would leave out the part about him planning to blow up the place where she had taken her first steps. To top it off, he was making fun of her botched attempt at taking him hostage.

"I'm a nurse, Brody. I don't do what you're asking me to do."

He laughed. "You're ridiculous. You've already admitted to breaking into a safe and stealing a bomb."

"I don't care what you believe."

"Think of all the shoes you could buy with a million dollars."

4
Greedy Little Thing
BRODY

"Shoes?" Morgan's voice rose and her face reddened.

Brody hid his smile, knowing he was insulting her and getting a kick out of it. "Isn't that what girls like you are into?"

"You don't know what kind of girl I am," she said cooly, glancing away.

"No, I'm pretty sure I do," he drawled out, stacking his hands behind his head and staring at the ceiling. "I was kidding about the shoes. You're probably more into horsepower and leather seats, chrome and fuel injectors."

Morgan stayed silent.

He turned his head in her direction.

He'd done a little snooping, but not much had turned up on her. A couple sports cars registered to her over the years, including one that had been totaled three weeks after she'd purchased it and was still making monthly payments on. Not a single speeding ticket though. He didn't buy that she'd never been pulled over. Not only was she a highly skilled con artist, but she was fucking gorgeous. Even a seasoned traffic cop would be powerless against that level of sex appeal and deviousness. Only a fool would think she couldn't talk her way out of a ticket.

Her nursing license was legit. Impeccable credit. Everything he had found was superficial. He wanted the dirty deets, but Lucy wouldn't give him anything more than she already had, and there didn't seem to be anyone other than Logan and her uncle that she let close.

"I work alone," she said.

"Yeah, but you're bored. Maybe working with a partner is exactly what you need to find that spark."

"Who said I'm bored?"

"Your internet history. You've been researching what hospitals in the country have the busiest emergency rooms. Read a post called 'Best Jobs for Thrill Seekers.' Oh, and you searched 'what to do when you are bored with your life.'"

She sucked in a big gulp of air. "What are you? A hacker too?"

"Nah, I looked at your phone while you were sleeping."

"I have a passcode."

"And Face I.D."

Morgan lunged for him. He rolled off the bed before she could get her hands around his neck.

He forced himself not to think about how good she looked up on her hands and knees in the center of his bed. In those leggings and that clingy black long-sleeved shirt, little was left to his imagination. She might be a shrimp, but she was a sexy shrimp. She didn't have much in the way of curves. Except for that ass. It was nice and round. Damn, he needed to get his mind off her body. If he got a boner and she noticed, it was not going to help him sway her into working with him.

Morgan was far from what he had expected when he found out a woman had stolen his bomb. He had envisioned tall, dark, and exotic. When he'd looked in on her sleeping on her boat, he'd thought he was in the wrong place at first. Tangled up in those sheets was a mass of pale blond hair and not much else. He figured she was five-foot standing ramrod straight.

Her mouth was what really killed him. Not the sass that spewed from it—although in some twisted way that turned him on too—but the plumpness of her bottom lip and how their color was the exact shade as bubblegum.

She did a swift maneuver resulting in her feet on the floor. The toes of her little black shoes touched his and she jabbed her finger in his chest. "You have a lot of nerve."

He glanced at her finger, then back to her face. Despite their size difference, she wasn't intimidated. Fine by him. He didn't get off on frightening women. "You're going to see that as a good thing when we're partners."

She snorted. "It's *never* happening, Brody."

"That thrill you got from breaking into my hotel room has been haunting you, hasn't it? A little taste to whet your appetite. You want a bigger high than you can achieve on your own. I can give that to you, Cash."

She chewed at her bottom lip, but when his gaze connected with her mouth she stopped. "I want half."

"What?"

"Half, Brody. Partners get half. I know damn well you aren't pulling a heist for two million."

The muscle in his jaw twitched. He shook his head grudgingly. "Fine. Seven and a piece, *if* you tell me where my bang is right now."

"No."

"No? I'm offering you seven-and-a-half-million dollars."

Morgan shrugged. "It's not a sure thing. There's a lot of risk involved. Besides, if I tell you where it is now, you'll go get it, and I'll never see the *Gypsy* again, not to mention the money."

"You're not stupid. I like that about you, Cash."

"Yeah, well, I'm sorry I can't say the same about you."

He laughed from deep down inside his belly. Her dislike for him was kind of hilarious. Brody wasn't a bad guy and he sure as hell wasn't lacking for intelligence, but she'd need to spend a little more time with him to learn that.

"As a show of good faith, I'll tell you where the boat is. Have Logan go check it out. When he reports back with confirmation, you tell me what I want to know."

"And the heist?"

"We can talk about it over breakfast."

"Hell no! I am *not* staying here tonight. No way." She darted around him and headed for the stairs.

Brody had her by the waist before her foot hit the top step. He turned her in his arms and pinned her between the banister and his body. He allowed himself two seconds to soak in how good her body felt against his. Then he pushed that out of his mind because he needed to see her as a business partner and not a beautiful woman who turned him on with her sassy mouth and the fluidity of her movements.

"There aren't any hotels nearby. You either sleep here, or in a cornfield. Call your brother right now and tell him where you are, if he doesn't already know. I packed up some of your clothes from the boat. They're in the room at the end of the hall." He motioned toward the guest room with a nod of his head.

"You went through my things!"

Her outburst didn't faze him. He would have been disappointed if she hadn't reacted so intensely. Poking at her until that sass of hers spilled out was almost as much fun as blowing up watermelons on the Fourth of July.

Leaning in, he brushed his lips against her ear and whispered, "I figured you for a thong girl. I love it when I'm right."

She grasped his shoulders and pulled her head back to meet his gaze, blinking up at him, eyes big and blue.

Brody got sucked in, his train of thought out the window.

And that's when she kneed him in the nuts.

He staggered backward, cupping himself and gasping for air. His eyes watered.

"You deserved that. I'm getting my things and leaving." She headed down the hall.

"Nine," he managed out hoarsely, still doubled over. The pain let go of its chokehold on his lungs and started to subside, but his ego was going to take a lot longer to recover. He needed her cooperation, even if it meant giving her more than she deserved. "Nine million."

She stopped in her tracks. "Ten."

Greedy little thing.

Five million would be enough for him. It would cover the treatments and pay off the existing debt, but it wouldn't leave much for a security net.

"Ten." Without Morgan, he couldn't pull off the job. Multiple small-scale heists would eat up too much of his time. He needed to be at the farm. Keeping it running was all on him now and Brody didn't do failure. "But I want to know where my bang is by tomorrow morning, and I want it in my possession within forty-eight hours."

There was no way he was going to let her call *all* the shots. Letting her think she was the boss to gain her alliance was lower than he was willing stoop.

"Deal. Now, tell me where my boat is."

"Blue Bend Marina. Slip H9." He turned slightly and covered his junk to avoid a second assault.

"You creep! That's literally half a mile from my marina."

He straightened his posture, confident enough space existed between them that he could avoid a second assault, and held his arms out, presenting the obvious. "And yet…you still didn't find it."

She shot him a mean glare, then disappeared into the bedroom at the end of the hall. The sound of something heavy being pushed across the floor drew a sigh from him. Probably the dresser to barricade the door. Breaking into her boat while she was sleeping and the Face I.D. stunt were gonna make gaining her trust a pain.

He went into his room and got back in bed.

The hard part was over.

5
Poached Eggs & Ruffled Feathers
BRODY

BRODY WAS ON HIS third cup of coffee and finishing his daily crossword puzzle when Morgan came downstairs the next morning. He smiled as he took in her outfit—a black mini skirt and a slinky white blouse with a deep V-neck. The clothes were the least revealing out of all the ones he had put in her room.

"Lookin' good."

"Eat your heart out." She sat across from him at the square table in the center of the kitchen. "No pants? Is that your idea of a joke?"

"Yes, as a matter of fact, it is."

He'd thrown together a bag of clothes from a laundry basket, figuring those were her normal wardrobe. That bag was tucked away. The bag in her room was nothing but flimsy dresses, short skirts, thongs, and low-cut blouses. He'd give her the other bag.

Eventually.

Maybe.

"I'm not telling you where your precious bang is until I have some coffee."

He pushed his chair back and stood, then took his mug to the coffee pot. The same mug he had been drinking out of when he'd been on her boat. It was a potbelly shape and olive green with light blue polka dots. Since it had been in the drying rack, he'd guessed it was her favorite.

Nabbing it, knowing it would aggravate her, was too good to pass up.

"You stole my mug," she whispered.

Brody grabbed a mug from the cupboard with Wylie Coyote and the Road Runner on it and filled it with hot coffee. He set it in front of her and winked before turning and lighting the gas stove. "How do you like your eggs?"

"Poached."

He rolled his eyes and turned around. "You would."

"What's that supposed to mean?"

He pulled a pot out of the cabinet and filled it with water. "It would be too easy for you to say you like scrambled eggs."

There wasn't a lot he knew about Morgan Cash, but he'd already figured out the only thing flexible about her was her body. She was more bullheaded than anyone he'd known. Although, he had a feeling she wasn't as oppositional with most people as she'd been with him.

At the metallic flick and snap of a lighter, he spun. She had another thing coming if she thought she was going to smoke in his house.

"What are you doing?"

Morgan took a second drag, blew several smoke rings into the air, then smirked. "What does it look like?"

"Put it out or go outside."

"Umm…no."

The muscle in his jaw twitched. There was a lot he would put up with, but smoking in his house was not going to fly. He walked over and snatched it from her mouth, went out the back door, tossed it onto the ground, and stomped on it. Then he picked up the remnants and strode across the backyard to the barn where he tossed them in the trash bin.

When he got back to the porch, Morgan was standing there, arms crossed, head cocked. "What's that about? I didn't think it was possible to ruffle your feathers."

He walked by her into the house and went to the sink to wash his

hands. She was right. There wasn't much that got under his skin. But she wasn't going to smoke in his house.

"Coffee's good," she said softly.

He glanced over his shoulder.

She'd returned to her chair at the table, her pack of cigarettes nowhere in sight.

"Got a fancy coffee maker as a housewarming present. Grinds the beans and everything."

"How long have you lived here?"

He poured oil into the cast iron skillet. "Four months ago. It took me a year and a half to build it, though."

"*You* built this house?"

"Mostly. I hired contractors for things like the electrical and plumbing." He took the towel off the plate next to the stove and used tongs to transfer the breaded steak into the skillet.

"What's that?"

"Country fried steak."

"Healthy," she said with a roll of her eyes.

"Don't worry, Cash. You'll get some meat on your bones as long as I'm cooking for you. Besides, if you're so worried about your health, you should quit smoking."

"This is the only time you're going to cook for me," she pointed out, ignoring his suggestion.

"Are you going to cook for me the rest of the time, then?"

"What are you talking about, Brody?"

6

Disgust & Detonators
Morgan

As soon as she could, Morgan was getting out of here. The less time she spent with Brody the better. There was no way breakfast was going to become a routine occurrence between them. Not a fucking chance.

"We have a lot of planning to do. I get that the partner thing is new to you, but did you really think you could go back to Savannah, and we would do this all over the phone?"

Morgan felt the color leave her face. "I'm not staying here in the boonies with you."

Brody cracked an egg into the pot of water on the stove and sighed. "I have a farm to run, not to mention, there's a reason I live on one-hundred-twenty acres, Cash."

"Because all of your neighbors moved away as soon as they met you and you got a great deal on the land?"

He threw his head back and laughed. "I like to blow things up, sweetheart. I need the space and privacy."

"Stop calling me sweetheart."

"My point is, I need to be able to…experiment, while we are working out the details. This is the only place I can do that."

"I have a job. I'll get fired if I don't show up for weeks."

"Quit. I bet you're a terrible nurse."

She gasped. "I'm a great nurse, thank you very much."

"Oh yeah?" he drawled. "Maybe we can play nurse and patient." He winked at her over his shoulder.

"You're disgusting." Or at least that's what she was going to keep telling him *and herself* until he gave up flirting with her. This wholesome, clean-cut country boy image of his did not appeal to her. On top of that, she wasn't in the market for a romantic entanglement and if she was, the last person she'd let herself get tangled up with was someone she'd agreed to partner with. So, her stomach needed to quit cartwheeling whenever he winked at her, and her skin could knock it off with the flushing when his voice dropped an octave.

Brody opened his mouth at the same time her phone rang. Not wanting to hear his reasons why she should stay, she went to the porch to take the call.

"Did Logan find it?" Brody asked when she came back in minutes later. He poured thick white gravy over the steak he'd plated and set on the table. Two perfectly poached eggs graced the dish. The space in front of his chair was empty, and no other plates had been dished up.

"Right where you said it was." She took a seat. "Aren't you eating?"

"I've been up for a few hours. Had my breakfast before I went out to harvest the soybeans."

"You harvested soybeans this morning? Who are you?" She cut into the steak and took a bite. Damn it, it was freaking delicious. Was there anything Brody couldn't do well? "By the way, your dog is a terrible guard dog."

While she'd talked to Logan, she'd spotted a yellow lab sleeping under the porch swing. He hadn't even flinched when she called to him, and last night, he had either been MIA, or he simply didn't care if someone broke into his master's house.

His nose scrunched. "He's deaf."

Interesting. She knew very little about dogs, but she did know that excessively loud noises could cause hearing loss in most animals. "Is that your fault?"

Brody laughed. "He was born that way. We seemed like a good fit when I saw him at the shelter."

"It might not bother your dog that you blow shit up, but I don't want to be around for it."

"Oh, come on. I'll let you press the detonator button." He dropped into the chair across the table from her.

"Really?" The rhythm her heart kicked up. As different as they were, they'd both been bitten by the adrenaline-rush bug. Explosives had never interested her, but this was her first time being in the company of an expert. Her gut told her that as dangerous as setting off a bomb could be, Brody wouldn't take risks with her safety. Fucking boy scout.

He leaned forward and heat filled his gaze. "You really want to?"

She shrugged and took another bite.

"When can I get my bang?"

"Is that all you ever think about?" she asked.

"Since it's been missing? Yeah."

"Well, it's in Vegas. How are you going to get it back here?"

"Don't need to. I just need to get it to a secure location."

"It's in a secure location."

"Your Uncle John doesn't know anything about explosives. How is keeping it in his garage safe?"

She dropped her fork. "You've known where it is this whole time? Then, why—"

"I didn't know. You just told me."

Her eyes narrowed. "I hate you."

7
No More Tingles
Morgan

MORGAN WALKED AROUND THE farm while Brody talked to her uncle on the phone. He said it wouldn't be necessary to move the bomb if Uncle John understood how it worked and made sure no one knew about it.

The house was surrounded on three sides by fields and woods on the other. Two of the fields were soybeans and the third looked like corn, although she wasn't entirely sure. This was the first time she'd been to the country.

She'd imagined Brody's house would be surrounded by stinky cows and sheep. There were no livestock anywhere in sight, only lush green plateaus of crops. The air smelled of life flourishing. A breeze picked up and caught her hair, sending wisps dancing around her face.

As much as she disliked Brody, she couldn't deny his land was beautiful. She walked to the front of the yard, the freshly cut grass staining the white rubber toes of her tennis shoes. It was, without question, a man's yard—no flowers, no frills.

Shielding the sun from her eyes, she looked across the road at the gilded fields of hay rolling in the distance. How had she gone her entire life without knowing this kind of beauty?

As she headed to the backyard, Brody's hearing-impaired dog trotted along next to her, brushing her hand and begging for affection. She gave in and squatted, tugging at her skirt to keep from exposing herself. The dog nudged her face with his nose and gave her a lick. She scrunched up her face and wiped the drool from her cheek.

"Thanks," she whispered to the dog and glanced at the porch where Brody still had her phone up to his ear, leaning against a post. No flannel today. Today was jeans and a dark green T-shirt that clung to his muscles. All of them. Chest, shoulders, biceps, abs. When she thought about how he'd pulled her against him when he'd caught her by the stairs, she tingled in a place she didn't want to tingle when thinking about Brody Lewis.

But damn. He was big and strong, and in *control* of every inch of his body. That's why he was so fast, why he'd got on her boat without making a sound or causing the slightest sway. That control hit the top of the sexy meter.

And if he had that much control over *his* body, what would happen if she gave him access to *hers*?

She had to stop her mind from going there. If she was going to work with him, there could be no more tingles.

How had she gone from stealing Brody Lewis's bomb to being his partner? It was a long jump. She wasn't a hundred percent about going along with the heist. Ten million dollars was a lot of money, but there were so many unknowns. She had no idea who they were stealing from, or what they were stealing, for that matter.

Following a trail that led to the back of the property, she lit a cigarette and took a long drag. The dog didn't follow.

"Typical male," she muttered. Once they got what they wanted from you, they fled.

The trail led her through a wooded area, then into a clearing with a small pond in the center. Kayaks and canoes rested on a wooden rack. A pair of Adirondack chairs on the bank across from the water beckoned her.

She stubbed out her cigarette on the ground with her shoe. Just as she was about to make the first stride toward the other side of the pond, someone grabbed her wrist and held tight. She whipped around and

bumped into Brody's broad chest. He'd snuck up on her *again.*

"Let me go."

He released her and shoved his hands into his pockets. "This is my favorite spot in the entire world, Cash. Pick up your trash."

Morgan gritted her teeth and crouched to retrieve the cigarette butt. After shoving it into the cellophane surrounding her pack of cigarettes, she looked up at him. "Happy now?"

"Getting there. Go back to the house."

"Why?"

"This is my spot."

"You never learned to share?" She put her hands on her hips. "Lacking that skill seems like a red flag that you aren't going to make a good partner."

Brody rocked back on his heels and let out an irritated sigh. He glanced around the perimeter of the pond before looking back at her.

"You can stay, but we're going to start making plans. You're going to be nice to me too, got it?"

"Kiss my ass, Brody."

"Don't offer things you don't plan on following through with." He walked past her in the direction of the chairs.

His stride was twice the length of hers, forcing her to jog to catch up.

When they reached the chairs, he motioned for her to take the one on the left.

She considered taking the chair on the right to tick him off but changed her mind.

He stretched out his long legs and adjusted the brim of his ball cap. "Did you bring your EpiPen with you?"

"What?" How did he know she had an EpiPen?

"John told me you're allergic to bees and amoxicillin. He asked me to make sure you have it with you. He also said you have trouble sleeping, so he's going to send me a special lavender blend to mist your pillow with."

Morgan covered her face with her hands and groaned. "He's

ridiculous."

"It's not a bad thing to have someone care about you that much."

She shot him a glance. From investigating him she knew his parents were alive. Background checks—ethical or not—could reveal a lot about a person, but they didn't state if someone had tucked them in each night with a kiss on their forehead, or if they'd spent their childhood seeking approval in vain.

"How'd you sleep last night?" he asked.

After driving twelve hours straight, she should have had no trouble falling asleep, but she'd been acutely aware of Brody being on the other side of that wall. She'd tossed and turned, drifting off as day broke.

"Just so we're clear, if you get anywhere near my pillow, my knee is going to get reacquainted with your crotch."

"You don't have to barricade the door. I promise not to step foot inside your room." He looked over at her, a hint of a smile on his lips. "Unless I'm invited."

He sounded sincere, but believing promises made by men she barely knew was the kind of mistake old Morgan would have made. So was jumping blindly into situations. New-and-improved Morgan knew better. "I need to know all the details," she told him. "Who's the mark?"

"Alexander Gill."

Morgan shot out of her chair. "You're crazy. Just forget about it, Brody. I am not robbing Alexander Gill!"

Gill was one of the richest men in Nevada. A diamond smuggler. He was known for being erratic and merciless.

"You're scared?"

She nodded emphatically. "I'd be stupid if I wasn't."

"Cash, you got in and out of the Bellagio without being seen by a single security camera. You got into my room and stole my bang without leaving a trace. What's the problem?"

"Gill doesn't live at the Bellagio. I have no idea what his house is like, where the cameras are, where his guards are, or what their abilities are. Not to mention you'd be tagging along. It would be like going in blind with a bowling ball tied to my foot."

8
Loud Noise Kink
BRODY

BRODY RESTED BACK IN his chair and tapped his fingers against the armrest. Morgan knew a lot more about capering than he did. She was right. It would be dangerous to go into a high security location she had never been to before.

"What do you suggest we do, Cash?"

"Forget it."

He *tsked*. "Fifteen million worth of untraceable diamonds. I can't forget that."

"Then find another fool. I'm out." She pushed up from the chair.

Before she walked away, he said, "Tell me what you need, and I'll get it. Do you want floor plans marked with the cameras and guard positions?"

"Let me see if I can get this through your thick skull—"

"Hey," he said, cutting her off with a warning tone. "Can we discuss this without slinging insults?"

"You want me to go on a suicide mission. You don't even know what kind of safe he has." She pulled a cigarette out of her pack and stuck it between her lips while she readied her lighter.

Brody snatched it from her mouth. "No smoking here."

She spread her arms wide. "We're outside."

"My spot, my rules."

With a huff, she crossed her arms. "I'd need to be in there several times before I would even think about going in unseen. That isn't possible, so the heist isn't possible, understood?"

"No, I don't understand," he said. "Why can't we go in and get the layout?"

She shook her head. "You think that if we knock on his door, Gill will say, 'Hey, come on in'?"

"He might not invite me in, but I bet he'd invite *you*."

"Why would he do that?"

"Because you're hot."

She shot the meanest glare at him, like he'd called her ugly instead. "I know where you are going with this, and my answer is no."

"Have you ever met Gill?"

"No."

"What about Logan or your uncle, do they know him? Ever been around him?"

"No, we don't associate with scum like him."

Funny that a family of con artists had standards for who they kept company with. From what he'd gleaned from Benny, the Cash family, despite their unique skills, were good people. Morgan and Logan had been straight A students and voted life of the party and most unforgettable in their high school yearbooks, respectively. The Cashes looked after their neighbors and donated time and money to charities and drank hot chocolate with marshmallows while watching Christmas movies.

"Glad to hear it." But he wasn't surprised. Now that he'd learned Lucy was a part of that family, and that she'd helped to raise Morgan and Logan, he didn't have a single concern about whether he could trust her enough to have her as his partner.

"Do you know him?"

He shook his head. "No. We've been in the same room before, once. But I've never spoken to him and I'm sure he didn't notice me."

"How do you know he has fifteen in diamonds in his house?"

"Sorry, sweetheart. Can't disclose that."

"Quit calling me sweetheart!"

He grinned. Getting Morgan riled up was going to be half the fun of this job. *If* he was able to talk her into doing it. She was the best thief he had ever met—not that he had met that many—but the best part was that no one had any idea. To his dismay, this little phantom didn't want to lend him her skills and he couldn't pull it off without her.

So, how to convince her?

The boat was back in her brother's hands, so he didn't have that leverage anymore. There had to be something else she wanted.

"Brody?"

He shook off his thoughts, not even sure how long he had been lost in them. "Huh?"

Morgan chewed on her fingernail. Not being able to light up must be getting to her. Baffling that someone as clever as she was had allowed herself to pick up such a nasty habit. "Where does the bomb come in?"

"What do you mean? We use it to blow his vault. What else would I do with it? Blow up his car for shits and giggles?"

"I can crack a safe. If you find out what kind of vault he has and where he keeps it, I can get into it."

He rubbed his jaw. "So, you're in?"

"No, I didn't say that. I was just wondering, hypothetically, why you would use messy explosives when my way is clean and quiet?"

"I guess you don't need me, do you, Cash?"

"No, I don't need you. And I don't need ten million dollars, either."

Didn't need it, or really even want it. Brody understood the payoff meant something different for her. Her bank account wasn't causing her grief. It was the mundane life she'd gotten stuck in giving her the blues. An addiction like she had didn't have a cure. Her adrenaline fix couldn't be starved.

Brody intended to help her feed it.

"Listen, we're partners. You do what you need to do to get into Gill's house. That part is all up to you. Handle it any way you want. Get a job as his housekeeper, for all I care. While you're doing that, I'm going to be making some sensational bang. If nothing else, we can use it as a diversion, then get into his vault the clean and quiet way, as you put it."

Morgan put her hands on her hips. "I get that you like to blow things up. You probably get hard every time you hear a loud noise, but I know better than to cross Alexander Gill. I'm out."

9
Morally Gray Guts
Morgan

"LOGAN? DREW?" MORGAN STEPPED onto the deck of *The Splurge* and put her hand on the handle of the sliding door to the cabin but froze when she heard rustling and giggling. After counting to ten, she opened the door and looked inside.

Drew stood with her back to Logan, holding her hair out of the way while he zipped her dress.

"It would be nice to come over and find you two playing Monopoly or something once in a while," Morgan muttered. Every time she dropped by, they were either getting dressed or getting undressed.

"We're not any good at Monopoly, and we like to do things we're good at. *Really* good at." Logan wiggled his eyebrows for emphasis.

"Spare me any other information about your sex life, please." She flopped onto a leather chair and rested her head back.

"Was Brody hospitable?" Logan asked.

"You'll never guess what he wanted me to do."

"Work with him," he said oh-so-casually.

"How did you know that?" If he knew something and hadn't shared, she was going to be pissed.

"My guess is he did some digging and found next to nothing on you. Finding out you've been flying under the radar all these years would be like finding gold to Brody. So, what was the job?"

"Alexander Gill."

He whistled. "That caliber of job is way out of your league. Glad you realized that and turned him down."

"Oh, Logan…" Drew closed her eyes and pinched the bridge of her nose. "No."

"I'm not an amateur." Morgan gritted her teeth. He acted as though her skill level was inferior to his, all because he'd bailed her out once. *Once.*

"I didn't say that. The jobs you do are usually on a whim. What Brody has in mind requires extensive planning. The recon alone…" Logan scrubbed his jaw. "Not to mention you aren't a team player."

So not a team player. Ugh. He was right. Although, if she put her mind to it, she could become a fabulous partner. Just not to Brody Lewis.

"I already turned him down, so there's nothing left to talk about."

Morgan left to get ready for her shift at the hospital, determined to psyche herself up for it. She grabbed a pair of scrubs, then plopped on the bed with them folded neatly on her lap.

The void in her soul swelled and throbbed, like an untreated infection. She didn't know who she was anymore. Her job wasn't satisfying. Her social life was lackluster. Her mojo? Long gone.

Logan had a reason to stay in Savannah. Morgan no longer did. Distance would probably be beneficial for them anyway. It would prove to him that she could take care of herself. And it wasn't like they'd never see each other again. If her financial situation improved, she'd have the means to visit all the time.

Her ego nagged at her.

Logan could pick a lock—if he had to. In the fine art of persuasion, he was aces. When it came to recon, he was the best man for the job. But he didn't know how to make himself invisible. He couldn't assess a location and analyze camera angles to find blind spots. Crack a safe? Not happening.

Morgan could do everything her brother could do. *And more.*

It was time for him to acknowledge that.

She wouldn't say she was the superior con artist.

Well, maybe by a smidge.

They'd never gotten caught up in sibling rivalry, and she didn't want to start. She only wanted to be seen as equal.

A change of scenery and the opportunity to pull off a heist so grand it would prove without a doubt she was capable of far more than her brother gave her credit stared her in the face.

Brody got under her skin. *Deep* under her skin. It infuriated her that he'd successfully snuck up on her as many times as he had. The man had held her phone in front of her face to unlock it and she'd slept through it. If Logan ever found that out, she'd never live it down.

But maybe partnering with Brody wouldn't be that awful.

With the size of his farm, he was bound to keep busy tending it. Aside from the times they had to sit down and plot, she probably wouldn't even see him.

The heist was a blank canvas at this point. She could call the shots and make sure things were done *her* way. And that'd be it. She'd retire. Even if she didn't know what she wanted to do with her life, it wasn't being a criminal. The things she typically lifted had already been obtained illegally by someone else, or in the case of Brody's bomb, intended for illegal activities. Except for her diamond earrings. But she didn't feel the least bit guilty about those.

She'd do this job, then quit while she was ahead. Go out on top.

Don't be impulsive. That always gets you in trouble.

She had to think this through before she made up her mind. Needing nicotine, she grabbed her pack of cigarettes and went onto the deck. Halfway through her cigarette, Drew joined her.

"When are you leaving?"

Morgan exhaled a cloud of smoke, being sure to blow it in the opposite direction of Drew. "My shift starts in forty minutes."

She pinned her with a *don't treat me like I'm stupid* look. "You know I'm not talking about that."

Morgan stayed quiet.

"When Logan said you weren't capable of pulling off the heist, it wasn't a dare."

"Did he send you over here to talk me out of it?"

"No. He doesn't realize he provoked you into doing it just to prove you can."

"What did you come over for, then?" she asked, not even trying to hide her annoyance. "To ask me to be a good girl for Logan's sake?"

Drew had never stuck her nose into Morgan's business before. That's not what irked her, though. It was that she'd so easily seen through her. Not only that, but she'd called her on it. It entertained her when Drew challenged Logan about his poor choices. Being the one under her scrutiny wasn't much fun, though.

"If anything, it would be for my sake because I'm the one who will have to soothe him, but no, I'm not going to try to talk you out of it. I came to tell you Logan and I *both* appreciate how talented you are. But it scared him, what happened with Eric. He loves you so much, Morgan."

"I know." She really did. They'd always been extremely close. He loved to claim that they didn't have to pay for therapy because they had each other. Logan could make her laugh until she couldn't breathe. They had more inside jokes than Las Vegas had slot machines. And before she'd met Eric, she'd never kept a single secret from him.

That did it. That made up her mind. Morgan had become someone who kept secrets from her brother and lived in misery but didn't make a move to change it. Well, no more. Time to reclaim her moxie.

"I'm leaving tomorrow. Do me a favor and give me a head start. Don't tell Logan unless he asks."

10
Suspicious as Hell
BRODY

SOMETHING SOFT AND SMOOTH brushed against his stomach. A *clink* brought Brody out of his slumber quick, but not before the cuff clamped around his wrist. His arm hung, suspended from his wrist, dangling from where the other cuff had been secured around the bedpost.

Reaching out, he grasped the narrow hips straddling him with his free hand. He hadn't expected Morgan to return and had gone back to sleeping naked.

He didn't think she had realized that yet.

Taking a ragged breath, he tightened his grip. "Business or pleasure?"

She scoffed. "Don't flatter yourself."

"Mmm…too bad. Want to get off me, then?"

She climbed off and switched on the bedside lamp, then turned back to him, dug a pin from her hair, and set it on his bare chest. "I'll be waiting in the kitchen."

As if she'd forgotten something, she froze in the doorway, then turned. She walked back to the bedside, pulled her phone from her back pocket, and snapped a photo of him. "*Oh*, and don't forget to put on pants."

Brody winced and used his free hand to adjust the sheet around his crotch.

Once the door shut, he grabbed the hairpin and got busy.

He had no idea what he was doing and ended up snapping the hairpin while digging in the keyhole. Too stubborn to call her for help, he fell back asleep. The next time he opened his eyes, he was no longer shackled.

He was sure he had dreamt it all.

Until his eyes settled on the pair of handcuffs on the nightstand.

He groaned. She was much stealthier than him and had probably gotten an eyeful of his goods when she came in to release him of the bondage.

Brody threw on jeans and a T-shirt, then headed downstairs. It was five in the morning—almost time to start on chores.

Morgan sat at the kitchen table, her bare feet propped up on the edge as she tapped away on a laptop. She had let her hair loose of the bun and her blond hair cascaded down her back. She wore all black—pants that were tight as hell and shimmered like they were wet, and a baggy, tattered sweatshirt with a ripped collar that exposed her entire shoulder. No bra strap.

He forbid his dick to react. He needed all his blood flowing to his brain to figure out why she'd come back. She was up to something.

"Have you been up all night?"

"Yep," she took a sip from *her* mug.

"Why are you here?"

He got his Road Runner cup and filled it with piping hot coffee. He was about to turn back to the table when a basket of muffins on the counter caught his eye.

"Breakfast is on the stove. Should still be warm."

She'd made breakfast? For him? Now, he was sure there was a grift playing out and he was the target. He walked over to the stove where a small cast iron skillet covered in tin foil sat in the center of the range.

He peeled the foil back and studied the contents. Looked like scrambled eggs and spinach and…the feta cheese he'd planned to use in a Mediterranean pasta salad recipe he wanted to try. A triangle-shaped piece was missing, and when he cut a slice for himself, he noticed there was a pie-like crust holding it together.

He spotted a small bowl of cut fruit flanking the empty plate and fork she'd left on the counter.

Suspicious as hell.

"Where did the muffins come from?"

"I made them." Her voice was neither snarky nor sweet, and conveyed she had more interest in whatever was on her computer screen than having a conversation.

He carried the plate and bowl of fruit to the table and sat across from her. He watched her, waiting.

She kept typing and clicking.

"Cash." Once her gaze flicked up to his, he continued. "What're you doing here?"

"Just like you said, I'm bored. Looking for a thrill." She closed her computer and pinned him with an emotionless stare. "The split is fifty/fifty. I'm not going in blind. I will take care of how and when. All you have to do is what I tell you to."

"Oh, really? We're partners, but I take orders from you?" He snorted.

"Take it or leave it."

He tapped the tines of his fork against the plate. He needed that money, and he didn't want to work with anyone else. Her unparalleled skills weren't the only reason. It seemed contradictory for a con artist to have unbendable morals, but if he'd learned anything about her, it was that she was a walking paradox.

It intrigued him that she could easily be swimming in riches, but she'd chosen to work. Whether it was ethical concerns that held her back from lining her pockets, or something else, it wasn't lost on him that the demolition of the Mermaid had spurred her into action. A hazardous, crumbling building whose only value was sentimental. She'd put her emotional attachment before her own safety.

Not being drawn to that romanticism was hopeless. She tried to hide her softness, and he'd only seen the tiniest glimpses of it, but knowing it was there was enough. Enough for him to let her think he was motivated by money. It was in everyone's best interests.

"What changed your mind?" he asked.

"I asked around about you. Guess what? No one knows anything about you, aside from that you're some farmer from Maryland who drops into the poker circuit every now and then. That was interesting, but I knew better than to stop there. I started asking about your cousin. Benny disappeared around the same time that four mil' was lifted from three private residences. Whoever was involved in that job used explosives to bust open those safes. Want to know the funny thing?"

Brody gritted his teeth. "What, Cash?"

"The safes were cracked simultaneously. But there wasn't a big bang for any of them. Or even a noticeable one. No one realized they'd been there until at least a half an hour after the fact."

"So?"

She gave him a pointed look. "The technology in your barn doesn't look like any explosives I've seen. Seemed pretty intricate. Designed to be discreet. But what do I know? I'm just a silly girl who likes shoes."

He straightened in his chair. Knowing she'd been in his lab made him feel more exposed than being handcuffed to his headboard while naked. "You've been snooping around?"

"I wanted to know who I'm working with and what they're capable of."

He shook his head. Morgan had seen enough. There was no point in denying anything.

He stabbed at the egg thing on his plate and shoved a forkful into his mouth. He stifled a moan. Fuck that was good. Before he scarfed down the rest, he asked, "What is this?"

"Quiche." Before he had time to tell her how good it was, she said, "Gill is having a party in three weeks. I'm still trying to get my hands on the guest list. I'll take care of the recon. You get busy building what I want."

"And *what* is it you want?"

"I'm not sure yet. If he has the kind of security that I think he does, we have a lot of bases to cover. I'll find out where the central hub is. You take out specific target areas simultaneously."

"I can't do that. It would take out the entire electrical and even then, he's probably got a back-up generator."

"Figure out how to make it work," she said as if the discussion were over, then reopened her computer.

Her attitude killed his appetite. He started to push the plate away, then shook his head and finished eating. No sense letting it get cold. "So, anything else I can do for you, Boss?"

"I want a diversion. Something to get the guards off center, but nothing crazy. It should be subtle."

"You're asking a lot."

Morgan didn't know anything about the technology he toyed with. Yet, she thought she could tell him what she needed and with a snap of her fingers, he would make it happen.

"I'm the one doing the dirty work. Suck it up." She swung her legs off the table and leaned forward with a *go ahead and test me* eyebrow raise.

She was bossier than he'd originally given her credit for.

He was starting to worry she wasn't going to give an inch in any direction. And if that was the case, Brody wasn't sure if this was going to work.

Her gaze dropped to her computer screen. She adjusted her position on the chair and swept her finger over the touchpad.

"Are you going to crash Gill's party?" he asked.

"It's not exactly the kind of party you can crash. I'll have to find someone with an invitation. I just got a copy of the guest list. Hopefully, I'll know one of the names."

"Are you going to find me a date?"

"You aren't going." There was that authority again. This was a partnership and the sooner she accepted that, the better.

"The hell I'm not. I need to see their security technology if you expect me to dismantle it without causing a scene."

"Find your own invitation, then. It's going to be tough enough trying to get myself—" She rested back in her chair, grinning like she'd realized the solution to all her problems. "I found someone on the list I know. Getting into that party isn't going to be any trouble at all."

"Who?" he asked.

"Don't worry about it."

"I get that you are used to working alone, but we're in this together. No withholding information."

Morgan rolled her eyes and took a sip of her coffee. "He's friends with my brother. You might even know him or at least know *of* him. He's a poker player."

"What's his name?"

"Charlie Chao."

Brody shifted on his chair. "I know who he is."

Chao had been rising to the top for the past year. Women salivated over him. They thought he was "nexy" which apparently meant nerdy *and* sexy. Was Morgan into that?

That's none of my business.

"Have you ever gone out with him before?"

Her forehead wrinkled as her eyebrows drew together. "No. Why?"

Brody shrugged. "Will he take you if you ask?"

"Absolutely, but where's the fun in that? I'm going to make him think it was his idea."

"Couldn't we forge an invitation and go as Mr. and Mrs. Peacock or something?" She had connections. A forged invitation would be a piece of cake.

"Our names would have to correspond with the guest list. Even if we used a name off the list, we have no way of knowing who will show up. We can't risk getting caught or drawing attention to ourselves."

Made sense. He wouldn't out-and-out admit it, but she really thought things through.

"Let me see the list. Maybe one of my ex-girlfriends is on there."

"You've never dated anyone from Vegas," she blurted out.

Brody laughed and leaned forward in his chair. "You nosed around in my love life, huh?"

"I needed to be sure there wouldn't be anyone else here when I broke in, even though I figured the chances of you having a girlfriend were basically nonexistent."

"That's funny. Not at all damaging to my ego," he said dryly, even though it didn't bother him. Morgan roasting him amused him. And he liked learning how she got from point A to point B with her planning skills. It was fascinating and informative, even though she probably wasn't aware she'd divulged anything useful. Lucky for her, he had no desire to use it.

"What's on your agenda today?"

"Do some more research on Gill. Go for a run."

"Sounds like fun. I have some stuff I need to get done around here, and then I'll be gone for a while. Can I trust you not to burn the house down?"

"Where are you going?"

"My sister has her learner's permit. I'm taking her to practice driving."

"I forgot you had a little sister."

"Yeah, and she's as much of a trouble magnet as you are. Logan and I probably have matching dents in our skulls from banging them against the wall."

Morgan trying to hold back a smile sent warmth through his chest. It fueled his desire to earn a genuine smile, one that she couldn't escape. "I'll have a stiff drink waiting for you when you get back from the driving lesson."

"It's going to take more than that to bring my blood pressure down." He put his plate in the dishwasher. "After the last time, I had a nightmare that she swerved to miss a squirrel and drove my truck off a bridge. Maybe you can douse me in your uncle's lavender wonder potion to help me sleep peacefully."

Her shoulders shook and the sound of her soft laughter made his chest tight.

Boy, was he in trouble. Feisty and headstrong Morgan was hot. But laughing, unguarded, eyes-sparkling Morgan was irresistible.

11
Goat Grifter
Morgan

MORGAN FOLLOWED BRODY'S DRIVEWAY to the road and lost herself in the beat of her feet. A gentle breeze kept her cool as she broke a sweat. The scenery was a nice change from buildings and traffic. In Savannah, she'd driven to a big park and jogged around the perimeter with her headphones in to drown out the hum of cars zipping by. Not having to dodge people on a sidewalk was great. She didn't see a single car the entire time.

Not needing to stay focused on watching out for obstacles meant her mind was free to wander. And no matter how many times she tried to think about other things, she kept returning to thoughts of her new partner.

Brody wasn't as nauseating or annoying as she'd originally perceived. He didn't seem like he'd been in a bad mood in his entire life. The only time she'd seen him rattled, he'd waited until he'd cooled off before speaking to her. She wasn't used to that.

Uncle John was patient, but he'd raise his voice if he thought he wasn't getting through to her. She and Logan lashed out at each other when they were frustrated, but most siblings did. Lucy had certain buttons that if pushed would unleash a verbal tidal wave.

And then there'd been Eric.

His mood would turn on a dime. Walking away and cooling off wasn't his style. He hadn't hit her, ever, but psychological abuse was his go-to when he felt lousy. Morgan had never known when he'd use her as an emotional punching bag.

Getting along with Brody should be easy enough. Although, she was pretty sure he got too much of a kick out of riling her up to quit.

After her run and a shower, she grew restless at the house by herself and went for a drive, looking for signs of life. Ten miles from the farm, she found it. Leaning into her steering wheel she peered at two-story brick buildings, churches with enormous stained-glass windows and crisp white steeples, storefronts with pottery and hand-knit sweaters displayed in their windows, and a park with a breathtaking bronze fountain. She parallel parked her rental car and went to investigate the series of white tents and long tables inhabiting the inlet street on the other side.

She browsed the wares of the vendors. At the end of the row, she came across a large wire pen with six little goats hovering around a giant white block. The smallest goat pushed his way through the others to get a lick in.

A teenage boy in jeans and a Carhartt T-shirt came up next to her and shoved his hands in his pockets. "They make great pets."

"What are they licking?" she asked.

"A block of salt."

That little one sure was tenacious. The others were bigger and clearly stronger, but he didn't give up. "That's right," Morgan said in a cooing tone. "Don't let the rest of them push you around just because you're smaller."

"Want him?" the kid asked.

This boy reminded her of Brody with his relaxed posture and easy grin.

"Oh, no, thanks. I'm not in the market for a pet."

"I have someone interested in taking four of them, but no one wants the runt. If I don't sell him today my dad is going to make me give him to a guy who trains them to do stunts. He feeds them moldy oats and they don't get proper veterinary care, but we don't have the room to house goats as pets."

This kid was one hell of a salesman.

Morgan angled her head and narrowed her eyes. "Is that true?"

The boy reached in and picked up the baby goat so she could pet him. "It's all true except the part about the moldy oats. I'll give him to you as long as you promise to give him lots of attention."

12
Buster
BRODY

A PAPER NAPKIN WITH BRODY'S name written in big, capitalized letters in black marker covered a plate on the kitchen table. Wary of tricks, he peeked under the napkin and discovered a roast beef sandwich with a pickle and a side of raw carrots and cauliflower.

"I used arsenic in the mayo." Morgan's voice traveled from the archway between the living room and kitchen. "Don't worry, you won't even taste it."

He smirked and opened the fridge. After setting horseradish and a gallon of milk on the table, he grabbed a glass and a bag of potato chips from the pantry. He took the top piece of bread off the sandwich, smeared horseradish on it, piled it high with chips, then replaced the bread. Before taking a bite, he smashed the sandwich, crushing the chips.

"That was considered healthy until you got a hold of it."

Brody swallowed his food and poured himself a glass of milk. "I work hard. I need the calories." He took a long gulp. "You know I was joking about you cooking for me while you stay here, right?"

"Just trying to be nice."

"You want something," he said flatly, dropping the sandwich to his plate.

"I do not. I can be nice, believe it or not."

He stared at her with narrowed eyes while he popped a carrot into his mouth and chewed. Once he'd swallowed, he said, "Nah, I don't buy it. You want something. What is it?"

Morgan sighed and left the room. When she came back, she had a baby pygmy goat in her arms.

He shook his head and took another bite of his sandwich. He had to keep his mouth full to keep from laughing. Once he'd swallowed, he asked, "What are you doing with a goat?"

"I don't know. I kind of got talked into taking him as a pet. He's cute, though, right?"

Not as cute as she was snuggling the damn thing. "He is, but he can't stay in the house. He'll eat everything in sight."

"He can't stay outside. He's a baby." She rubbed her cheek against the goat's head.

"Please, tell me you haven't named him. You're going to have to take him back. You don't know how to care for a goat, and I don't see him living on your boat when you go back to Savannah."

"His name is Buster. Please, let me keep him here for now." She made a pouty face meant to make his resolve crumble and get him to give into her every plea. It would have worked, if having a little sister hadn't conditioned against looks like that one. "I'll figure out what to do with him when I go back."

Brody set his plate in the sink and washed his hands, then walked over to her. He took Buster from her arms and scratched between his eyes. "Where's he going to sleep?"

She perked up. "I hadn't gotten that far yet."

He shook his head, trying like hell to stay irritated—because that was better than the warm, gooey feeling surging through him—and handed the goat back to her.

"I've never had a pet before."

"Never?" Man, he needed to get away from her. Simultaneously feeling sorry for her and wanting to kiss her was messed up.

She shook her head. "We never had a yard for a dog to run in and Uncle John is allergic to cats. We had an aquarium with exotic fish no matter where we lived but it's not like they had names, and we couldn't even pet them."

He let out a deep breath. She was playing him. This pathetic story was meant to gut him, even though it was likely true. Morgan already knew where to swing her axe to bring him to his knees. "I know what you're doing."

Her lips twitched into a smirk. "Yeah, but it's working anyway, isn't it?"

Yes. Damn it.

13
Little Orange Corvette
BRODY

THE NEXT MORNING, BRODY drove the tractor back from the field and idled in front of the barn as Morgan stretched in the yard. The sun had slipped behind the clouds, but it felt twenty degrees warmer. He had never seen running shorts so short. Or a sports bra so skimpy. He supposed she wore it more for cover than support. Her breasts were less than a handful—at least if the hand belonged to him. Maybe a mouthful.

She held her hands high above her head with her face turned toward the sky. The position stretched and bowed her torso, exposing her hip bones.

It made him hard. How could it not?

The minute his cousin found out he was considering working with Morgan, he'd tried to talk him out of it. Benny hadn't seen her since she was younger, but he was certain she'd be more of a distraction than an asset. Now, he understood what Benny meant.

She reached overhead, bending her back until her hands met the ground. One of her feet lifted, toe pointing to the sky. Her other leg followed in a controlled move as her body did an entire revolution, and both feet once again touched the ground.

Seeing her flexibility firsthand was gonna make it hard to behave. He forced himself to look away and drive the tractor into the barn.

Brody managed to immerse himself in changing the tractor's oil until the purr of an engine reached his ears. He exited the barn with Reese at his side, and squinted against the sun, trying to determine if his imagination had gotten the better of him.

Nope. That definitely looked like his brother unfolding himself from a bright orange Corvette. "Nick?"

He met him halfway between the house and barn. "You'll never guess what I saw on the way over here."

Morgan was nowhere to be seen, probably off for her run, so he had a good guess. "A foxy blonde in running shoes and not much else."

His brother's gaze traveled to the car parked next to Brody's truck. His jaw fell slack. "No way. You're shacking up with her?"

"She's my house guest."

The way Nick's face fell, Brody wouldn't be surprised if a tear slipped out. "That sounds boring as fuck."

He gestured at the car in front of his porch steps, where Nick had parked it like an ass. "What are you doing here and where'd you get that?"

Nick grinned and rubbed his hands together. "I made it into the draft."

Blood pulsed loudly in Brody's ears. After four years of college baseball and not being noticed by recruiters, Nick had settled for the minor leagues while working toward a PhD in physics. "You're gonna be in the MLB draft?"

"That's what they tell me."

"And you came home to tell everyone in person?"

"Well, the team that's showing interest in me wanted to fly me in and put me up in a swanky hotel, but I told them my mama would have a fit if I was two hours away and didn't visit, so they rented me that car so I could stay here and drive back and forth."

His mouth fell open. Playing for their home state's team had been his brother's dream since he could talk. Brody's goal had been acceptance into the Naval Academy, but when that had happened, he hadn't been as ecstatic as he was for Nick in this moment.

Brody grabbed him and pulled him into a hug. "I'm proud of you. You've worked hard for this."

"I'd like to think so, but I'm pretty sure the number of followers and how hungry they get for my videos was a bigger factor than my athleticism." He shrugged. It was understandable he'd be a little bummed that the social media profile he'd created as a joke had gotten him noticed, and not his talent on the field.

"Who cares if that's what got you noticed? They don't put players into the draft who can't hold their own. You deserve to be there as much as anyone. Got time for a beer?"

"Hell yes, I want a beer. But just one because I still have to tell Mom and Dad the news." As they walked to the house, Nick asked, "What's the story with your *house guest*?"

"I know her brother. She was in the area and needed a place to stay." He hadn't said anything untrue, but it wasn't the full story.

"How long's she gonna be here?"

"Don't know."

He could feel Nick studying his face. Without glancing over at him, he asked, "What are you looking at?"

"I don't believe you."

"I'm not sleeping with her." He wouldn't tell his brother that he had been fantasizing about it, but he also wasn't going to let him think that something was happening that wasn't.

"No, not that. I don't believe she's a random house guest. Spill."

He grabbed them each a bottle of beer from the fridge and turned to find Nick looking at Buster in his crate. Having a goat in the house was not normal, at least not for Brody, but Nick didn't comment.

Brody took the goat out of the crate and carried him outside, then set him down in the yard so he could nose around.

As he got comfortable in a rocking chair, he debated how much he wanted to tell Nick. His brother knew his fascination with explosives ran a lot deeper than making small homegrown bombs and setting them off in his fields. Even though Nick was aware he and Benny did more than play poker when they went to Vegas, he didn't know the scale of their jobs. He'd have too many questions if he found out how much money Brody had come into—like why it was all gone—and he didn't want his brother to bear that weight. Not while he'd been working on his degree and having the time of his life playing college ball. *Especially* not now that he had a chance to play in the major leagues.

"Her name is Morgan Cash."

"That's all you're gonna give me?" Nick shook his head and twisted the cap off his beer bottle. "You don't trust me anymore, or somethin'?"

"Benny's done. Bianca doesn't want him to take risks now that they've got kids. Morgan's my new partner."

Nick leaned against the railing and crossed one ankle over the other. "What can a cute little thing like that do?"

"That cute little thing got into my room at the Bellagio, stole my bang, and disappeared without being caught on any of the surveillance. Not only is she the best fucking cat burglar I've ever heard of, she was raised by a brilliant con artist—two, actually."

He broke into a wide smile. "Damn. Is she single?"

"Who the hell cares?"

"I do. I need a date to the 4-H dance."

He swallowed the irrational jealousy moving over him like a thundercloud. "I don't think that's her kind of shindig."

"Can I ask her anyway?"

"No." His brother getting involved with Morgan was the worst idea he had ever heard of. He wanted her sharp and focused, not daydreaming about his brother. Not to mention, if anyone was taking her to that damned dance it was going to be Brody.

"Has anyone else met her yet?" Nick asked.

"No. She hasn't been here long."

"You can't keep her all to yourself forever. You know Mom is going to want to cook me a celebratory dinner. Leaving her behind would be rude."

He was about to argue that Morgan wouldn't want to come when she jogged up the driveway.

She froze when she spotted Nick on the porch. Her gaze darted to Brody.

He stood to make the introductions, but Nick pushed by him and extended his hand. "Hi, Morgan. I'm Nick, Brody's brother."

"Nice to meet you." She gave him her hand, but Nick held it without shaking it, grinning at her through lowered lashes with the hint of a crooked smile. Morgan arched her brow at Brody.

He rolled his eyes. Nick acted like an arrogant dipshit whenever a woman was present. He and his brother might share a strong resemblance, but their personalities couldn't be more opposite. Nick was a ham. Pretty early on, he had learned how to coax a smile out of a girl, and once he figured out how to coax one out of her dress, there was no reining him in. Brody would get a real kick out of seeing her take him down a few notches, Morgan Cash style. "You have my permission to fuck his day up. Not that you need it."

Nick frowned and dropped her hand. "What did I do?"

He shook his head at Morgan. "Don't fall for his innocent act. He flirts with anything that moves."

Nick's shoulders slumped and he resumed his perch against the railing, muttering, "That's an exaggeration."

"Beer?" he asked her, lifting his bottle.

She bent to pick up Buster, stopping him from chewing her shoelaces. "No, thanks. I'm going to take a shower and then make a few calls." She glanced at Nick. "Maybe I'll see you around again."

He perked up. "Tonight?"

"I'm sorry?"

Brody groaned.

"Dinner at our parents' house. Brody won't come unless you do."

He made a what-the-fuck face at Nick, but before Morgan turned to look at him, he erased it.

"It's nice of you to offer but—"

Nick put his palms together in front of his face and pouted hardcore. "I'm the worst at keeping secrets. I just know I'm gonna slip and say your name and then our folks are gonna wanna know who Morgan is, and Brody doesn't lie, so he'll tell them and then he'll be in trouble because Mom raised him better than to not invite company to dinner and then she'll go from being mad to sad because she'll think he's embarrassed of her and—"

"Okay, Nick," Brody raised his voice to say. "I think she gets it."

He wasn't wrong, though.

14
The Chip
BRODY

BRODY STOOD OUTSIDE THE guest room and knocked. "Ready, Cash?"

Calling her by last name started out as a way to needle her, but now it was defensive tactic. Seeing her as strictly his business partner with her living with him and doing those sexy as hell stretches in his yard was not easy.

The door swung open. She had on ripped jeans and a T-shirt as thin as tissue paper, and no bra. *That's* what she planned on wearing to his parents' house?

"I'm not going with you," she said matter-of-factly. "I can't leave Buster."

"Look"—he leaned against the doorframe—"I know you don't want to go. The only thing is, my mom called. Nick already told her you were here. Your baby will be fine on his own for a bit."

She shook her head. "I didn't sign on for this."

"What are you afraid of?" Of all her characteristics, shyness wasn't one.

"Nothing. Go away." She tried to close the door on him.

He stuck his foot out to keep it open. "Give me one good reason why you don't want to have dinner with my family."

"Because they're *your family*, Brody. We're business partners, not friends."

"We can be both."

"Hard pass." She tried to close the door again, but between his foot and the hand he'd placed on it, it didn't budge.

He didn't get why she was so resistant, but he had learned Morgan liked to negotiate. "If you come to dinner with my family, I'll owe you, and you can ask me for a favor whenever, no questions asked."

Her brows pulled together. "Like if I need you to blow up something?"

"I'm a man of many talents," he said, lowering his voice and leaning in. "If you ever get yourself in a sticky situation or need back up evening a score, I'm your guy."

She tilted her head and nibbled her lip. "I can call in this chip whenever? No questions asked, you'll do whatever I want?"

"Whatever you want, whenever you want it." In Morgan's world, favors were currency. At least she hadn't already realized there was nothing she could ask of him that he'd say no to. Whether it be tomorrow, or in six months, if Morgan came to him for help, he'd have her back.

Her shoulders fell and she rolled her eyes. "Fine. I need to change."

"Good. I was hoping you weren't going to wear that shirt."

She straightened her posture. "What's wrong with my shirt?"

"I can see your—"

She shoved him out of the door frame and slammed the door in his face.

A good fifteen minutes later, Morgan came out on the porch in a loose-fitting black, sleeveless top with the front tucked into a pair of gray jeans that tapered at the ankle. She'd swapped her running shoes for baby pink, low top Converse sneakers. Her hair was loosely braided over one shoulder and her lips were still that enticing bubblegum color but shimmery.

Brody bit the inside of his lip to stifle the appreciative whistle he knew would aggravate her and risk changing her mind about coming. He picked up Buster who had been under his feet the entire time he'd waited, walked across the yard to a makeshift enclosure he'd made from leftover fencing materials, and set him inside.

"Where did this come from?" she asked.

He tugged on one of the metal posts, making sure it was snug in the ground. "I threw it together this afternoon. It'll do for a few days but it's not super secure. I'll have to come up with something better."

"You built Buster a pen?"

He shrugged. "Ready to go?"

"Brody."

"What? I didn't want him tearing up my house."

She stared up at him. "Thank you."

He nodded and held her gaze for a few seconds, his pulse getting faster and faster. The mask she wore slipped in that moment, the way she said those words so unlike the Morgan he'd come to know.

She glanced at Buster. "Do you think he'll be okay?"

"Baby, he's an animal. He's meant to be outside." He winced and braced for her to scold him for calling her baby. It wasn't intentional. It felt natural, and therefore, slipped out.

She said bye to Buster and walked to his truck, probably letting that one slide because he'd done something nice.

15
There's Gonna Be Biscuits
Morgan

MORGAN DID HER BEST to ignore the butterflies in her stomach as Brody backed his truck out of his driveway. She wasn't the type of girl guys take home to meet their parents. Just ask any of her ex-boyfriends.

It was okay. She got it. Men found her attractive—intriguing, even—but they never trusted her.

That was her fault. She'd been raised to keep anything other than surface details to herself. For Uncle John, cluing anyone in on her talents was a hard no. And he'd been right. The one time she'd revealed her skillset, believing she'd met someone who she didn't need to keep secrets from, she'd been exploited.

But this wasn't like that. Brody wasn't her boyfriend. Just her partner. He wanted certain parts of his life kept hush-hush as much as she did.

"How are you going to explain me staying with you to your family?" she asked.

"That's up to you, Cash. But Nick already knows the truth."

"I thought he couldn't keep a secret?"

"Depends on the stakes. If it's something everyone is better off never knowing, he'll keep his mouth shut. But if it's juicy gossip that is going to get out eventually…not so much."

"He said you don't lie."

"Not to my folks. We'll have to stick as close to the facts as possible and change the subject if they ask too many questions."

Halfway down his driveway, Brody took a hard left onto a dirt lane with a thick line of trees on either side. She'd noticed it when she went for a run, but figured it was a road for his tractor. They bumped along until the trees disappeared and a big farmhouse came into view. There were rows of vegetables planted between the road and the house and an expanse of lush, green grass surrounded the house.

"Your parents live this close?"

Brody smiled and nodded. "I told you."

"You said close by. You didn't say they were your *neighbors*."

He put the truck in park, then twisted his body to face her and put his hand on her headrest. A cloud of aftershave enveloped her. Between the combination of his tantalizing scent, the dimple in his cheek, and his choice to forego a hat and instead comb his hair, it was taxing staying convinced that she didn't find him attractive.

Out of the corner of her eye, she caught him running his gaze over her.

"Do you ever not look sexy as hell?"

A warm knot formed in her core. It wasn't the first time someone had complimented her appearance, but something in the way he said it, like he'd strip her naked right here and now and do things to her that'd make her blush if she let him, garnered a different reaction from her.

"You can't say things like that to me. This"—she gestured between them—"is business only. I don't sleep with my partners."

"Thought you've always worked alone."

She looked back out the windshield. That was basically true. She'd been the only one taking the risks. But not the only one benefiting.

"Cash…did you learn not to mix business and pleasure the hard way?" Was that compassion in his tone? Or was he making fun of her?

"Is that funny to you?"

He flinched and shifted closer to his side of the truck. "No. I didn't actually think you—never mind. We should go in."

The awkwardness radiating off him softened her defensiveness. He opened his door and got out.

She checked her makeup in the mirror, then grabbed her purse, and reached for the handle, but the door opened on its own. Or not. Brody had come around to her side.

"What are you doing?" It wasn't that she didn't know *what* he was doing. It was that she didn't understand *why* he was doing it.

He stepped back, giving her room to get out. "Opening your door."

Morgan swallowed and told herself she didn't like it. "Why?"

He stared at her for a beat. "No one has opened your door for you before?"

"On a date, which this *isn't*. I'm perfectly capable of opening my own door." She needed to establish boundaries. And stick to them.

"Have I ever, in the time we've known each other, indicated that I see you as anything other than capable, if not *more than* capable of most things?" He didn't wait for her answer. "We're going to be spending a lot of time together, so you should know, I'm going to open your door and pull out your chair. I'm going to give you my jacket when you're cold, and if I'm meeting you somewhere, I'll get there first and be waiting for you. If another man disrespects you, I will take him out like the garbage he is. That's who I am, but it's also what you deserve."

Her mouth opened, then shut. Her first impression of Brody—well, besides that he had the physique of a gladiator—had been that he was easygoing and had the composure of twenty Buddhist monks. Rather quickly, she'd learned those traits did not equate to him being a pushover. His assertiveness left her breathless and *curious*.

He raised an eyebrow. "Is that going to be a problem?"

She shook her head.

Brody extended his arm in the direction of the house. "After you." His deep voice stopped her a second before her foot landed on the top porch step. "Cash."

Her jaw clenched at his continued use of her last name, but she managed to relax it before she turned to face him.

His wide, boyish smile blasted her with an unexpected hit of dopamine. "You'll *know* when we're on a date. There won't be any question about it." He made his way around her and held the screen door open.

If she took the bait and pointed out that there was no *when* they were on a date, as his comment implied, he'd succeed in getting the rise out of her he'd been fishing for, so she threw back her shoulders, lifted her chin, and walked past him into the house.

She stopped short, her path blocked by a slender woman with an olive complexion and shiny dark brown hair. An apron covered the front of her floral sundress.

"You must be Morgan." Her eyes shone, like having a guest for dinner was the highlight of her year. "I'm Gia, Brody's mom."

"Morgan Cash." She held out her hand.

Gia wiped her hands on her apron, then shook Morgan's.

"Hey, Mom." Brody leaned in and kissed her on the cheek.

Warmth spread through Morgan, and she gritted her teeth. Stupid ooey-gooey feelings.

"Come on into the kitchen," Gia said, gesturing to follow her as she made her way to the other end of the house and turned right.

Morgan followed with Brody on her heels. At the end of the hall an open archway led into a big kitchen filled with aromas that made her stomach growl. A butcher block island took up the center of the room. Different kinds of vegetables and dry ingredients covered the surface chaotically. A large pot boiled on the stove, steam rising from it, and a cast iron roasting pan took up a good portion of the countertop next to it.

"Is there something I can help with?" Morgan asked.

Gia shoved her hands into oven mitts and lifted the boiling pot, carrying it to the sink to strain the water. "Everything is about done. I'm going to mash these potatoes while the biscuits are in the oven, then we can all sit down."

"I'll mash the potatoes," Brody said. "Relax. Have some wine. I'm sure Morgan would enjoy a glass."

Gia looked at Morgan, her face lifting. "I only have red. A cabernet. Is that okay?"

"Yes. Thank you," she said, even though she didn't drink wine.

While his mom opened a bottle and pulled two glasses from a cupboard, Brody grabbed a little carton of milk and a stick of butter from the fridge.

Morgan shifted on her feet, fidgety from being in an unfamiliar house and having nothing to keep her busy.

As Gia poured the wine, her gaze darted to Morgan several times.

"Mom," Brody said, voice brimming with laughter. "Stop it. You're being weird."

"I'm sorry," she rushed out, red blooming on her cheeks. "Brody didn't tell me—I didn't expect—"

Heat swept through Morgan and her mouth went dry. After only two minutes, she'd made an impression that Gia was embarrassed to put into words. Great.

Gia wrung her hands together. "You're stunning, Morgan, but there's something about you. You're…" She turned her head to address her son. "What word am I looking for?"

He grinned and popped a piece of carrot into his mouth while shrugging.

"You're going to sit there and smile like an idiot while I flounder, Mr. Thesaurus?"

Brody sighed and stared up at the ceiling for a moment. Then his gaze locked on her while he said to his mother, "I think the word you're looking for is *alluring*."

"Yes!" Gia handed her a glass of wine. "That is the perfect word to describe you."

The wink Brody gave her pushed her heart rate from swift to full throttle. Her throat felt thick. She shifted her gaze to the red liquid in her glass.

"Sorry if I'm making you uncomfortable," Gia said. "It's been such a long time since either of the boys had a girl over for dinner."

The buzzing of a handheld electric mixer filled the kitchen as Brody mashed the potatoes.

Gia brought a metal sheet covered in a dish towel from the fridge. She pulled the towel off, revealing a dozen uncooked biscuits and slid them into the oven.

The buzzing stopped and Brody scooped a fluffy mound of potatoes into a serving bowl.

"Everything is ready to go except for the biscuits. They need to be taken out of the oven in eight minutes. I'll be back shortly, if you could make sure the biscuits don't burn," she said to Morgan.

She nodded and smiled, then moved closer to the counter and put the leftover raw vegetables in a basket she found on the opposite counter. She returned the lids to the canisters of the flour and sugar. "Your mom knows we aren't romantically involved, right?"

"I told her." Brody took the basket of vegetables and set them on a chair in the corner, then went to the sink and started scrubbing the pots and pans. "But my parents are the kind of people to believe a man and a woman sleeping under the same roof without something romantic going on is impossible."

"It would be if I was sleeping under that roof," Nick said as he came into the kitchen.

Brody glared at him. "You're a profligate."

"I don't know what that means," Nick said, not sounding so cocky anymore.

Morgan laughed softly. What a fancy way to call his brother a perv.

"Well," he drawled. "I guess Cash knows what it means."

But she didn't know what it meant that his intelligence made her heart flutter. She'd never been drawn to a guy with a high IQ. She didn't want to be. Not if that guy was Brody Lewis.

"I'm just a dumb jock. Cut me some slack."

Continuing to do the dishes, Brody said, "My brother got a full ride to college on an *academic* scholarship. He's a physics major and has made the Dean's list every semester."

Nick actually blushed.

"Is your sister a genius like her brothers?"

Brody shut off the tap and dried his hands on a towel. "I'm not a genius."

"You graduated top of your class at the Naval Academy." She raised an eyebrow to dare him to deny it. "Honors in mechanical engineering and robotics."

"Did you dig up this information about me before or is it an ongoing investigation?" he asked.

"Ongoing, of course. The only thing I couldn't find out is why you didn't go into the field after graduation. Seems strange to do all that work on a degree and then become a farmer."

Brody snagged a bottle of beer from the fridge, opened it, then set it in front of her. He took her glass of wine and dumped it down the drain.

"Why'd you do that?" she asked.

"Because you don't like wine."

"You don't know that."

He crossed his arms and raised an eyebrow. "You haven't taken a single sip."

Well, wasn't he observant? "Maybe I don't like beer, either."

"Maybe you do and you're just being oppositional because you don't know how to handle someone being considerate."

A chill skated down her spine. Diligently taking mental notes of those around her came so natural she didn't even realize she was doing it half the time, but she'd never been in a situation where *she* was the subject of study. Her feelings on it were mixed. On one hand, it was invasive. On the other, his attentiveness to her likes and dislikes wasn't awful.

Nick cleared his throat. "So, Morgan, there's not a woman alive who doesn't salivate over a man in a Navy uniform. How about we get out the photo albums?"

Pictures of Brody in a uniform? She was all over that.

"Hey, Cash," Brody said. "Your biscuits are burning."

Morgan gasped and ran to the oven. The biscuits were dark brown discs, not the light, fluffy towers of goodness they should be. "I had *one* job."

It wasn't like her to get distracted. But the coziness of the kitchen and her curiosity about Brody and his family led her brain on a detour, leaving the biscuits in the dust.

"Damn. The biscuits are the best part of the meal," Nick said.

"Shut up, Nick." Brody grabbed an oven mitt and pulled the tray from the oven. He walked over to the garbage and held the tray at an angle. The biscuits slid in.

"I'm going to throw up," she said, grabbing for the edge of the counter behind her.

Brody moved in front of her and tipped her chin up with his finger. "No one has to know."

Her breathing stopped for a moment as his gaze locked with hers. Her building anxiety halted in its tracks. Why did she believe him? She didn't even know what he meant. Was he going to take the blame?

Gia had asked her to take care of the biscuits. There was no avoiding responsibility. "When there are no biscuits on the dinner table, *everyone* will know."

"There's gonna be biscuits." He let go of her and opened the canister of flour on the island. "Nick, don't let anyone into this kitchen for the next fifteen minutes."

16
Soul Reboot
BRODY

BRODY'S STOMACH CLENCHED AS he led Morgan into the dining room. His father was already situated at the other end of the table, his oxygen tank at his side. No disguising those tubes running from around his ears to his nose. Otherwise, he looked pretty good. His complexion had more color than it had recently, and his copper-with-streaks-of-white hair had been combed. A crisp green-and-white plaid shirt completed his spruced-up look.

Morgan set the basket of replacement biscuits on the table, and he placed the mashed potatoes next to it.

"This is my dad, Theo," he told her. "Dad, this is—"

"Morgan," he said, cutting him off. As a kid, he'd thought his dad's raspy voice sounded cool—like a cowboy. But now, especially since he couldn't get out more than a sentence without needing to catch his breath, it didn't seem so cool. It was hard not to dwell on the inevitability of his dad's condition when it was everywhere Brody looked—whether all the medicine bottles, the oxygen tanks, or even his dad's baseball mitt that had been collecting dust on the bench by the door, a reminder that he'd never have another catch with Nick. "You sure do live up to all the hype. I tell ya, if *I* was twenty years younger, I'd be spending every minute of my time convincing you to be a lot more than my house guest."

"Glad to know being hooked up to an oxygen tank hasn't affected your libido," Brody muttered.

An adorable blush colored Morgan's cheeks. "It's very nice to meet you."

Brody guided her to the opposite end of the table. With a slight nod at the chair he'd pulled out, he waited for her to sit, then scooted her in.

Nick helped their mom carry in the remaining serving dishes.

The loud hum of a diesel engine caught everyone's attention. The slam of a door followed, then footfalls across the porch. The screen door slammed, and there was a clatter, rustling, and then more footfalls up the hallway.

His little sister dashed into the room. Her red hair looked like she'd been in a windstorm, her breathing was heavy, and her face was so flushed, her freckles were barely perceptible. That wasn't the most suspicious part of her appearance, though. Hope had on jeans that were far looser than any he'd seen her wear, and a sweater he'd seen her wear plenty—when it wasn't ninety degrees.

She dropped into a chair and set her napkin on her lap.

Brody cut his eyes to his father to see if he'd picked up on her odd outfit choice, but it was impossible to read him.

His expression was stony as he stared at his teenage daughter.

"Sorry, I'm late," Hope said, staring at her plate. "Madison's piglets got loose, and it took forever to catch the little buggers."

"Was that *Madison's* diesel that dropped you off?" Nick asked.

She shot him a glare. "No. She doesn't have her license. Her brother gave me a ride home."

"You're not allowed to ride in trucks with boys," Theo said. "Not until you're sixteen."

"We can talk about this later. We have company," Gia reminded everyone.

Hope's gaze scanned the room until it landed on Morgan. Her eyes lit up. "Hi."

"Hi," she said. "I'm Morgan. I'm staying at Brody's house for a bit."

Her jaw dropped. "He's allowed to have a girl stay overnight and I can't get a ride home from my friend's brother?"

Brody choked on his water. "I'm eleven years older than you. I don't need permission to have a woman stay at *my* house."

"Dinner is getting cold. Let's say grace." Gia placed her right hand in Theo's and reached for Morgan's on her other side.

When Brody reached for her hand, he was struck by how small and soft it was in comparison to his.

His dad led grace, counting their blessings, which included Morgan's presence and Nick's opportunity to play in the major leagues.

His mom passed the platter of pot roast to Morgan. "What brings you to Maryland?"

"My friend got it in her head that Brody and I would fall madly in love if we met, so she hatched up this crazy scheme to get us together, but it backfired. I won't go into all the details because it's super embarrassing for Brody." She paused to cringe on his behalf. "Anyway, I paid him a little visit so we could square things away. I'd never been to the country before, and it's so beautiful and peaceful here. I realized this is exactly what I needed to reboot my soul. Brody was gracious enough to offer me his spare bedroom, so here I am."

"What was the scheme?" Hope asked.

"Sorry, I'm taking that one to the grave."

Everyone at the table, other than Brody, whined or grumbled. Friend? Was she talking about Lucy? He hadn't even considered she'd been trying to set them up. If Morgan had details about Lucy's plan, she better share.

Wait. Was everything Morgan said true? He went back over it in his head, and unless the part about her finding it beautiful and peaceful here was bullshit, the rest of it was vague, but accurate.

Brody used his fork to split open a biscuit. He absentmindedly spread butter on one of the halves while thinking of the scenic places nearby he could take her.

Then she said something he'd never have expected her to say—especially in front of his family. "And if nothing else, at least I got to see Brody driving a tractor shirtless."

He choked on his biscuit. Christ. He heaved, fighting against the crumbs he'd inhaled. He reached for his glass of water and Nick pounded him on the back. When he was sure he wasn't going to die, he looked at Morgan.

"Whoa, are you okay?" she asked, sounding sincere even though her eyes danced with laughter.

17
The Three of Spades
BRODY

BRODY COULDN'T WAIT TO get Morgan alone. He had a lot of questions.

Once the table had been cleared, she pitched in to pack up leftovers and clean the kitchen, but his father requested a word with him. Brody gritted his teeth and walked next to him at his pace while he wheeled his oxygen tank. He had a good idea what the topic of this lecture was.

With his father in his favorite chair and Brody on the couch with his forearms braced against his thighs, he waited while Theo regulated his breathing.

"I know I'm just an old man who never left the farm, but I'm going to give you some advice, son."

Brody had never discounted his advice. His father wasn't stupid. Neither of his folks were, even though their intelligence probably did get overlooked by outsiders who saw them as simple farmers. "I'm listening."

"Marry that girl."

"Dad." Brody stuck his tongue in his cheek and shook his head.

He was pretty sure his entire family was infatuated with her. She'd entertained them throughout the meal with stories about growing up in Las Vegas.

"You're lucky if you meet a woman like that once in your lifetime, Brody. She's smart as a whip, funny as hell, and if you don't think she's the most beautiful woman you've ever seen, then you better get your eyes checked. What more are you looking for?"

Maybe someone who liked him.

It'd be a waste of time to argue about this. Nothing he could say would convince his father that he and Morgan would never be a couple. Especially not after her little shirtless on the tractor comment.

"What do you want me to do, Dad? Walk up to her and tell her we're getting married?"

"Don't be dense, boy. Never said you weren't going to have to work for it."

"Any other wisdom you'd like to impart?"

"Not at the moment."

He nodded and patted his dad on the shoulder. "Good talk, Pop."

On his way to the kitchen, he pushed his dad's ridiculous advice out of his mind. Although, if he were able to take such a simplistic approach to his opinion of Morgan, he'd probably agree with his dad. If they weren't working together, and if she wasn't bound to get bored dating a farmer, she'd be hard to resist.

His breathing stalled when he reached the entrance to the kitchen.

There she was, leaning over one side of the kitchen island, a deck of cards in her hands. His mother, brother, and sister were on the other side, their attention glued to her. During dinner, Hope had asked if she knew any card tricks, and when Morgan confirmed she did, she begged her to show them one.

Brody leaned against the archway and crossed his arms.

She held up a card in front of Hope. "Is this your card?" The confidence in her voice tugged a smile from him.

Hope's face fell. She shook her head. "No."

"What? Really?" She straightened her posture and looked at the card. "Well, this is embarrassing." She flipped the next card in the deck, then rubbed her forehead. Next, she turned the deck over in her hand and shuffled through it. "Your card *was* the three of spades, yeah?"

His sister nodded.

"This is so weird…" Morgan put the entire deck face up and used her palm to fan them out. "I don't see it." She glanced at the floor around her feet.

Nick picked up the cards one by one, double-checking that the three of spades was truly missing. "It's not here."

She glanced at Brody. "Have you seen a card laying around? The three of spades, to be exact."

He shook his head slowly.

"Are you sure?"

He nodded. Surely, Morgan Cash could pull off a card trick without mucking it up, so what exactly was her game?

"Check your pockets."

Willing to humor her, he shoved his hands into his front pockets, verifying they were empty. Then he slid them into the back pockets. His left hand connected with the sharp edge of something thin and rectangular. He pulled it out and low and behold, there was the three of spades. With his eyebrow arched, he glanced at her.

She bit her lip, but it did nothing to hide her smile. The corners of her mouth lifted and the glint in her eyes danced like blue flames, luring a smile from his own lips.

Brody flung the card onto the island.

"No way," Hope shouted. "How did you do that? He wasn't even in the room."

"And that card was definitely in the deck. I watched Hope put it back in." Nick sounded equally perplexed.

"I don't know how you did it." His mother beamed at Morgan. "But your showmanship is impressive. I really believed you had messed up."

"How did you do it?" Hope asked. "Teach me."

She shook her head and put the three of spades into the deck. "Sorry. No can do."

Hope pouted, and knowing how persistent she could be, Brody cut in before she pulled out the big guns.

He cleared his throat to get Morgan's attention. "Ready?"

She nodded and turned to his mom. "Thank you for having me. Dinner was delicious."

"Come back any time. I'd love to see you again if Brody will share you."

He shook his head, tamping down the urge to insist they were not romantically involved. That sentiment had been stressed enough. His family's refusal to believe it wasn't going to change. No sense wasting his energy.

"Where are you two running off to?" Nick asked with a smirk.

Brody rolled his eyes. "We're going to the hay loft."

"Can I come?" Hope slid off her stool and was two steps from the threshold to the hall when their mother intervened.

"You, young lady, aren't going anywhere. Go upstairs and change out of whatever skimpy outfit you're hiding under those clothes, and then come back down. We're going to have a chat."

Her shoulders slumped, but she did as told, dragging her feet through the hall and up the stairs with a level of drama only a teenager could execute.

"I'm going to finish cleaning up the kitchen, and then talk to Dad for a while," Nick said. "I'll catch up with you later."

Brody saluted him, then swept his hand in the direction of the back door, gesturing for Morgan to lead them out of the house.

She stopped on the porch. "Is the Hayloft the local watering hole?"

"You could call it that, I guess." He smiled, then trotted down the steps.

She followed, but when he walked past his truck, she asked, "Where are you going?"

"To the hay loft."

The barn sat roughly two hundred feet from the house. By the time he reached it, Morgan had caught up with him. He slid the big wooden door open and waited for her to go inside.

"The Hayloft is an actual loft with hay in it?" she asked, as he walked to the light switch.

"Not exactly." The lights came on, illuminating the inside of the building.

Brody couldn't contain his curiosity any longer. "Are you sure Lucy tried to set us up?"

He'd known Lucy for years, and she'd never mentioned Morgan. Whenever he traveled to Las Vegas, he visited her, whether he had business with her or not, and brought her Maryland crabcakes. More often than not, she'd drag him along with her somewhere—a show she had an extra ticket to, a pride fight where she had VIP seating, and even her friend's wedding once. Was it all an interview to see if he was worthy of Morgan?

She fluttered her hand at him, like he'd asked a silly question. "Of course, she did. I can't do anything else right, of course I can't be trusted to choose who I date."

Her gaze wandered around the second floor of the barn. It was a giant open rec room boasting a billiards table, darts, an old cabinet record player, a kitchenette, a cozy seating area with two old couches and three mismatched armchairs. A ping pong table. Shuffleboard. Four arcade games: Pacman, Ms. Pacman, Space Invaders, and Frogger.

"Holy hell." She walked around, scanning the record collection and reading the various signs hung on the walls. "This is badass. How long has it been like this?"

"Started with a dartboard and one ratty couch. Then my folks figured it was a good way to keep us off the roads and out of trouble. Dad and I built the kitchen ourselves, aside from the plumbing. Just kept adding onto it over the years. By the time we were in high school, we had everything except for the pool table. It was here one Christmas morning. Still haven't figured out how Dad got it up here without us knowing, and he refuses to tell me. Just says, 'Santa Claus.'"

She ran her hand along the vinyl covering the billiards table. "Can we play?"

He shot her a crooked grin. "Yeah, we can play."

"Pool, Brody. I'm asking if we can play pool."

"Sure, we can do that…*after* you finish telling me about Lucy's plan."

Her head lolled back, like she'd rather talk about anything else. It gave him an entrancing view of her neck, which flooded his mind with questions of how soft her skin was, and how it tasted. "What do you want to know? She told me your plan so I'd stop you, but I didn't stop you exactly how she'd imagined I would, so she ratted me out."

Lucy had stabbed him in the back too. If she hadn't interfered, he'd be sitting on a hefty pile of dough. It'd taken months to prepare for that job and less than twenty-four hours after he'd told her, his plan was ruined. He should be pissed.

He pulled the cover off the table and tossed it to the side. "How did she think you would go about stopping me?"

Morgan grabbed a pool stick from the rack on the wall and tested its weight and length. "Flutter my eyelashes at you, I guess."

He laughed. "That's not at all your style, is it, Cash?"

She shrugged and swapped the stick for another. "I may have used my charm in the past to pull one over on a mark if the job called for it."

He perched against the arm of a couch, captivated by her movements as she tested the stick. Matchmaking execution might not be Lucy's strongest skill, but she'd done excellent on the selection part. Morgan probably didn't share his opinion on that.

"Wouldn't that have been easier than breaking into my hotel room?"

"Are you saying that I could have sweet talked you out of blowing up the Mermaid?" The laughter in her eyes made him smile.

Could she have? If she'd played the angle about how she'd grown up there…yeah, probably. Brody would like to think he had more backbone than to let a beautiful woman sway him, but Morgan wasn't just any woman, and if she'd been as charismatic as she'd been with his family, it's hard to say what he'd have done.

"We'll never know, will we?" He pushed away from the couch and grabbed the ball rack from under the table. "Do you think Lucy's still scheming? Plan A might not have panned out, but we're going to be spending time together for the foreseeable future. She probably sees that as a stroke of luck."

She leaned the pool stick she'd settled on against the table and fixed him with a look that made him feel like an idiot. "Lucy doesn't want us working together. She had the gall to reprimand me when she found out. Like we'd have ever met if she hadn't been meddling."

"Why doesn't she want you working with me?"

"Don't take it personal. It's nothing against you." She sighed long and drawn out. "She's just bent out of shape because Uncle John found out about her scheme, and he isn't talking to her now."

"I'm sure he'll get over it and forgive her. How long have they been together?"

She squinted and her lips pursed like she'd gotten a taste of something sour. "They're not a couple."

"Oh." He scratched his head.

"They're best friends."

"They've been best friends since you were a baby?"

"Yeah, so?" She wrinkled her nose.

"Neither of them ever married?"

"No, but that doesn't mean anything." Her gaze tracked back and forth across the floorboards. "There's no way they could hide being together for over two decades. That's crazy. Who does that? Why? Why would anyone do that?" Her voice had gone high and panic-filled.

Brody's stomach clenched. Sending Morgan into an anxiety attack wasn't on his agenda. He put his hands on her shoulders. "Breathe. I'm sure they wouldn't have been able to hide it if they were romantically involved."

She nodded. "It's weird that I've never known either of them to be in a relationship, right?"

"Maybe. Your family isn't exactly conventional, though. You know them better than I do, and if you say there's nothing going on between them, I believe you."

"Brody, I am an expert in reading people. I was raised by a con artist. *Literally.* Nothing ever indicated they were anything more than friends. I even begged her to marry Uncle John so she could be my aunt when I was little. I don't remember what they said, but after that, I knew not to bring it up again. It didn't matter that she wasn't my actual aunt, she was there every time—"

He gave her a gentle shake. "Again, breathe. I believe you. You'd know."

"No, I don't know. You've planted the seed of doubt." She shook her head again, as if she could dislodge unwanted thoughts of Lucy and her uncle. "They're both attractive, highly interesting people. They get along. They go on vacations together."

"It's an unusual dynamic, but it's not impossible for a man and woman to be close friends and not be sleeping together. Like us."

She scowled. "We're not close friends."

"We could be…by the time we loot Gill's safe."

Her eye roll told him she didn't see that as a possibility, but he didn't care. All he wanted was to distract her enough to prevent her from hyperventilating over the chance that her uncle and Lucy had been having a secret affair that spanned decades.

18
Hayloft Hysteria
Morgan

MORGAN'S FAMILY WAS DRIVING her crazy. If Uncle John and Lucy were an item, all hell was going to break loose. There was absolutely no reason to hide that from her and Logan.

It wasn't only the possibility of them keeping secrets that got under her skin. Logan thought she was incompetent. Lucy thought she needed a man. Even Uncle John had given Brody instructions for how to care for her, as though she were a child incapable of caring for herself.

"It's embarrassing how much my own family underestimates me," she muttered.

Brody made to grab for the pool balls under the table, stopped, then straightened. "Did you agree to work with me because you're trying to prove yourself to them?"

"Does it matter?"

He shrugged. "Fix a drink while I rack. Beer and soda in the fridge. Liquor in the locked cabinet next to the microwave. Key's stuck to the other side of the light fixture above the sink."

Curious about the key on the light fixture, Morgan walked to the sink. She couldn't reach the fixture, which was a metal pendant hanging from the rafters. She turned to find a stool or chair to stand on and bumped into Brody's chest.

"Forgot you were short." All up in her personal space, he reached for the key, then handed it to her.

She stayed quiet as she accepted it. She couldn't have uttered a word if there'd been one in her head. Brody's nearness left her breathless and speechless.

He only lingered for a second, then grabbed a beer from the fridge and went back by the pool table.

The key was attached to a magnetic keychain. Clever.

The locked cabinet contained a decent selection. Morgan chose a bottle of Jägermeister and snagged two shot glasses from the shelf.

"So," Brody placed the balls into the rack, his big hands able to hold three balls at a time. The texture of his palms was rough—she hated that she knew that, and hated even more that she wondered what they'd feel like on her inner thighs.

Morgan set the bottle and glasses on a side table. "Yes?"

He shrugged and lifted the rack off the balls. "You didn't answer my question. Did you agree to work with me to prove yourself to your family?"

"I'd be lying if I said that I don't want to show Logan I'm far more capable than he realizes. Honestly, if he's not impressed by the Bellagio job, I don't know what *will* impress him. I used to be Morgan, his cute little sister that could pick any lock she encountered, but now I'm Morgan, his reckless, impulsive, screw up of a sister."

"Why? What changed?"

"I'm not answering that."

Brody's eyebrows shot up. "Wow. That bad, huh?"

She handed him one of the two shots she'd poured. "Let's stop talking about my family, huh? What's up with your dad? Does he have a diagnosis?"

He lifted his glass. "Let's make this game interesting. For every ball I sink, I get to ask you a question and you have to answer. If I sink one of my own balls or scratch, you get to ask me a question. And vice versa."

He removed the rack off the balls, leaving them in a tight triangle.

She squinted. "Those are pretty high stakes."

"Okay, fine. We can play for bragging rights. It's going to be a quiet game, though."

She grumbled while she raised her glass. "I'll play, but don't even think about asking anything inappropriate."

He put his palm to his chest. "I would never."

They clinked glasses and tossed back their shots.

Morgan took her time lining up her angle. Even though Brody stayed quiet, the weight of his stare on her made her mind fuzzy and her hands sweaty. She managed a decent break, sinking one ball. "I get to ask my question now, right?"

"Go for it."

"What's wrong with your dad?" Maybe it was none of her business, but she wanted to know. She liked Mr. Lewis. She liked Brody's whole family.

"Emphysema."

"He smoked?"

Brody nodded.

"That's why you got mad at me for smoking in the house?"

"That's another question. But for the record, I didn't get mad at you."

She took another shot but missed. It had been a while since she'd played, and she was rusty. Darts would have been a better choice.

He walked around the table, tilting his head this way and that. Then he backtracked and lined up a shot. The cue ball shot across the felt, bouncing off the side rail. It hit a high ball, making a loud *clack*. It stopped moving and the high ball rolled directly into a corner pocket. Before it had even hit the bottom of the pocket, Brody asked his question. "Did you mean what you said about living here?"

She rubbed her thumb against the ridge where the two pieces of the pool stick joined. "That it's peaceful and beautiful?"

"The part about rebooting your soul."

"Yeah, I meant it. I thought I needed to move to a big, flashy city to find…whatever it is I've been missing from my life. But there's something about this place that makes me feel different. Renewed."

Brody stared at her for a minute with an unreadable expression. Then, he turned to study the table, forehead wrinkled.

A split second before he took his next shot, Morgan added, "I meant it about the tractor too."

19

Pinned Against the Pool Table

BRODY

LEARNING THAT MORGAN APPRECIATED his body provided a nice ego boost but mentioning it right before he took his shot was fucking devious. Of course, he missed.

He glared at her, then poured them each another shot.

"So close." Her tone dripped with mischief.

"Not above playing dirty, I see."

She shrugged, then tipped back her shot glass.

Morgan Cash was the cutest drunk he'd ever seen. Three shots deep, Brody barely felt the effects of the alcohol, but she weighed less than half what he did, so her having to squint one eye while she lined up her shot on the pool table, missing completely, and then *laughing* about it, was not unexpected. But it was adorable.

Brody was in trouble. So much trouble.

Before the cue ball dropped into the pocket, he caught it. "Scratching on the eight ball?" He *tsked*. "I'm disappointed."

Her head lulled slightly to one side, and she snorted. "Join the club."

Her hang up about her family under-appreciating her gave him a weird itchy feeling. They loved her. He'd seen that. But it irritated him that they hadn't done a better job of letting her know they were proud of her.

"What's your favorite food?" he asked.

"That's your question?"

He nodded. Was he curious about whatever she had done to destroy her brother's trust? Absolutely. Was he going to use this opportunity, while she was loose lipped from alcohol, to find out? Nah.

Morgan crossed her arms. "You want to know what my favorite food is? Not how I came to be known as the family fuck up?"

He shook his head. "Favorite food. Spill."

A cute little laugh bubbled over her lips. "Pizza."

Brody raised an eyebrow. Not what he'd have guessed. Maybe sushi or some other exotic cuisine. "Your favorite food is pizza?"

She shoved her hands into the back pockets of her jeans. "Pizza is versatile. There are so many options for toppings, and even sauces, types of crust. I can never get bored with pizza."

He couldn't stop his smile. He liked being wrong about Morgan. Maybe her tastes were simpler than he thought. If so, his plans for tonight were going to be perfect.

"Why are you asking about my favorite food?" she asked, narrowing her eyes.

He walked closer until they were toe-to-toe. "That's a question you didn't earn."

She pressed back against the pool table, her hands braced on the rail, and craned her neck to look at him.

"Maybe I plan on using the information in the future." There was a local place that served specialty pizzas by the slice, and whether she wanted to call it a date or not, he was taking her there.

Morgan swiped her tongue between her lips, moistening them.

It attracted Brody's gaze to her mouth like a heat-seeking missile. He wasn't going to kiss her. But it didn't hurt to know that if he tried, she might not sock him in the nose. She'd let him stay this close to her for this long. So close that his thighs brushed hers.

He put one hand on the rail next to hers and leaned in. Maybe he *was* going to kiss her. Hell.

Her lips parted and damn. Brody didn't know where he wanted to start—that sweet neck of hers, or her rosy lips.

The thud of footsteps on the stairs brought him back to reality.

He cleared his throat and stepped away from her.

Nick's timing was excellent. In another two seconds, Brody would have had his mouth on Morgan.

She'd already drawn a line in the sand about keeping things business-only. Alcohol had corrupted her inhibitions. Sober Morgan would be throwing snark, and she certainly wouldn't have allowed herself to get pinned against the table.

Nick tapped his watch-free wrist. "Ready?"

"Ready for what?" she asked.

"The main event." Brody winked at her.

"I thought this was the main event." She gestured sloppily around the hayloft.

"Nope." He took her pool cue and his and placed them back on the rack. "Come on. We're in charge of the entertainment."

"What the hell does that mean?"

He waggled his eyebrows. "Come find out."

20
Big Bangs
BRODY

BRODY DROVE THEM BACK to his house via the odd tree-lined road that connected his property to his parents'. He wouldn't tell her what they were doing, but he said she should check on Buster and get him settled for the night.

Once she'd done that, she sat on the porch and smoked while he did something in the barn, but he came out before she'd finished. She abruptly lowered the cigarette to her side, feeling guilty for smoking around him. With all the life changes she had going on, maybe it was time to quit.

"I know you smoke, Cash," he said as he carried a large wooden crate from the barn to the porch. "It's kind of pointless to hide it now."

Fair point. She lifted the cigarette and took a drag. "What's in the box?" she asked after exhaling.

"Solid gold bars."

She rolled her eyes, then glared. "Very funny."

The hum of a motor drowned out his chuckle. A weird little vehicle that looked like a cross between a golf cart and a four-wheeler emerged from the dirt lane. It had two seats in the front and a cargo area in the back.

Morgan discreetly stubbed out her cigarette in a small bucket filled with sand that hadn't been there yesterday. She joined Brody in the yard as Nick drove up next to them.

Hope was in the passenger seat.

Brody transferred the crate to the vehicle, then turned to her. "You okay to ride in the back, or do you want to walk?"

"I don't even know where we're going." Morgan walked closer and glanced in the cargo area. There was a cooler and a small stack of firewood. The only place she'd be able to sit would be on the edge, or on top of the crate.

"It's not far."

"Super helpful. Thanks." She smiled at him in the phoniest way.

"We're going to the pond," Hope said, leaning out of the vehicle while holding onto a guitar case.

"Thank you, Hope." She turned to Brody. "I'll ride."

He put his hand out to help her, but she ignored it and put one foot on the back tire and hoisted herself up.

Brody climbed in on the other side and held onto the canopy covering the front of the vehicle.

"Everybody ready?" Once Nick got the go-ahead from everyone, he made a wide turn and drove to the back of the property.

Pieces of her hair came loose from her braid, the wind sweeping them across her face. She reached up to brush them away and made the mistake of looking at Brody.

His stare made her stomach dip. It wasn't even dark yet, but she'd had enough booze that her body was warm and loose. How long until she could escape him? She didn't know how much more she could take without winding up naked beneath him.

The word "hate fuck" came to mind and she grinned.

"What's so funny?" Brody yelled over the noise of the engine.

"Nothing." She shook her head and looked away. She didn't want the reputation of sleeping with every man she worked with. Not that anyone had to find out.

No. Not going there.

If Brody would stop flirting with her, she'd be fine. He didn't seem toxic like the other men she regretted meeting. But then again, none of them did in the beginning.

She wasn't going to repeat her mistakes. No hanky-panky with her partner. It wasn't worth the risk.

The vehicle came to a stop at the edge of the pond farthest from the house.

She hopped out before he had a chance to offer her his hand. She wasn't trying to be independent, just avoiding touching him. The feel of his skin against hers sent shivers down her spine.

Brody unloaded the crate to the ground and crouched next to it. He slid the top off.

Morgan stood over him and looked in. "Fireworks?"

He pulled out a few and stood. "I get turned on by big bangs."

She almost laughed but stopped. "Wait. Are those homemade?"

A grin spread across his face. "You don't think I know what I'm doing?"

"It's fine. We've been doing this since we were kids, and we still have all our original body parts." Nick drove off with Hope, stopping next to the firepit where they unloaded the cooler and firewood.

Brody motioned to the crate. "Stick some of these in the ground. Space them about two feet from each other in a line around this curve." He drew an invisible arc with his finger, then pulled different types of fireworks from the box. Once everything had been set up where he wanted it, he connected each one to several long fuses that all led into one another. "Okay, now, we hang out until show time. It'll be dark enough soon."

"Is this something you guys do a lot?"

He shrugged. "Whenever Nick comes home. It's sort of a little tradition of ours."

She smiled, her mind wandering to Logan and what he might be up to. They had traditions for when they reunited, like when they went home for holidays. Although, their traditions weren't this wholesome.

"Come on." He waved for her to follow him. When they reached the fire pit, Brody offered her one of the Adirondack chairs, then took a seat on an upended log.

"Is Taylor coming?" he asked Nick.

He shook his head but kept his focus on the fire he was building. "She had a date."

"Uh-oh," Hope said.

"And she didn't cancel it to come celebrate the biggest news of your life?" Brody's tone carried an edge, his protectiveness of his brother slicing through his typical easygoing nature.

Nick sighed and ran a hand through his hair. "She doesn't know. I wanted to see the look on her face when I told her."

"Who's Taylor?" Morgan asked.

"His best friend since he was three, who he somehow didn't notice he's attracted to until last year," Brody said. "Now, he's miserable because he feels guilty for being attracted to her, and because he's too chickenshit to tell her."

"It's not like that," Nick said to Morgan. "Not like that at all."

"Do you find her attractive?" she asked.

He blew out a breath and pulled a beer from the cooler.

"Yes, he absolutely does," Hope said in a tone filled with boredom as she opened the guitar case.

"I can acknowledge that she's pretty," Nick said. "But that's it. I only see her as a friend."

"Ever pictured her naked?" Brody asked.

Nick choked on his beer. He wiped his chin, then glared at Brody.

He smirked. "Well, have you?"

Nick scratched the back of his neck and looked around the landscape. "It's a beautiful night, isn't it?"

Morgan snickered along with Brody.

Brody accepted the guitar Hope handed him and settled it across his knee.

"You play the guitar?" She raised her eyebrows. How many talents could one man possess?

"I can, but Hope plays and sings."

Morgan glanced at Nick.

He threw his hands up like he was innocent. "Nope. Not me. No musical talents. I brought champagne though."

"Just as worthy a talent," she said.

As Nick poured them each a plastic cup filled with champagne—except for Hope who only got a half-full cup—Brody strummed the guitar.

Her breath caught when he started singing. Hope wasn't the only one with a good singing voice. Not wanting him to see her reaction, she rid her face of any expression and sipped her champagne.

The song he'd chosen was a fun, summertime tune. Hope jumped in on the chorus and proved she could, in fact, sing. Like *really* sing.

Nick ended up singing during the second verse. His voice wasn't terrible, but not as good as his siblings'.

While they waited for darkness to descend to set off the fireworks, Hope and Brody took turns playing the guitar.

It could be blamed on being tipsy but sitting around a fire with these people put her at ease. The vibe was so cozy, and it was so freaking peaceful here. She could get used to this.

21
You Should Lie
Morgan

"YOUR LITTLE SISTER IS something. I might steal her."

Brody pulled another beer from the cooler, swiping off the cold water and ice coating it. "It wouldn't be much of a hostage situation. She'd help you write the ransom letter."

After the fireworks, Nick took Hope back to the house. When Morgan asked if he was coming back to join them, he got all awkward before saying no. He'd spent the entire fireworks display texting someone—presumably Taylor.

Now, it was just Morgan and Brody. It should be awkward, but it wasn't.

"Maybe I'll dump you and partner up with your sister. With a little training, we could do big things."

He stretched out in his chair and looked over at her. "You could."

"How would you feel about Hope doing something like what we're planning to do when she's older?"

He mused over it. "I think I'm always going to worry about her when I'm not around to protect her. Maybe one day she'll end up with someone I trust to look after her. But one day, like, twenty years from now, you know?"

Morgan snorted. "How realistic of you."

"It's a reasonable expectation."

She rolled her eyes and took a sip of her champagne to hide her smile. Brody was a family man through and through. There had to be some traits of his she'd find repulsive. Had to be.

He groaned. "She's already sneaking around. Not sure doing exactly what, or that I want to know. I know there's no point in trying, but I wish I could get her to see that she's going to look back on this time and wish she'd slowed down."

"I was like that." Morgan winced, memories of her teenage years surfacing. "Fake I.D.s, dating older guys, thinking I was hot shit."

"You might have been right about that last part."

She laughed. "I wasn't always this cool, Brody. It takes years of sleepless nights, bad choices, and heartache to reach this level of badassery." Oh no, why was bantering with him so easy?

It was the drinks and this damn atmosphere messing with her. The campfire, the pond.

"Everything isn't always your fault," he said, his frown unmistakable in the glow of the fire. "Sometimes life just sucks. Other people suck."

Morgan shifted in her chair, not liking the tightness taking over her chest. "I think that's enough getting philosophical for one night. Should we head back to the house?"

"Sure. Let me put out the fire."

Once the fire was out and they'd cleaned up, they walked to the house.

"I feel like I'm going to trip on a tree root or something," she said.

"Better a root than a snake."

She shrieked and moved closer to him, her arm brushing his.

He wrapped his arm around her shoulders, keeping her close. "Come on, city girl, I'll protect you."

Her mind warred between pushing him away and staying right where she was. She could still smell his aftershave but now it was mixed with the scent of campfire, making it even more appealing.

Between the lack of visibility and her compromised state, sticking

close to him turned out to be necessary. Once they got closer to the house, the motion sensor lights kicked on and he let go of her.

"Can I give you some unsolicited advice?" she asked.

"Why not?"

"I know you want to protect Hope from the ugly parts of life, but you can't." She shook her head. "What you can do is make sure she knows you love her unconditionally, so that when she does fuck up, she won't think twice about coming to you to help her fix it."

"Is that how it is with you and Logan?"

She shrugged. "Logan would do anything for me, except shut up about it afterward."

"So, fix her shit, but don't rub her nose in it?"

"*Help* her fix it. Just because she can't fix it on her own, doesn't mean she can't do it with support."

"So, also don't take over?"

"You're getting it." She leaned against the porch post. "Fireworks, champagne, and live music. You sure do know how to show a girl a good time." It was a better date than she'd had in—it wasn't a date.

"Easy. It sounds like you're warming up to me."

She'd gone past warm, and into a climate that'd likely cause her to burn. "I feel like I can trust you, but what do I know?"

He took a step toward her. "You can trust me. You don't need to call in a favor for me to have your back, you've already got it, whenever you need it."

Her pulse kicked up a notch. She swallowed against the tightness in her throat. *It's just a line.* "Then your favor has no value. I want a promise instead."

He chuckled. "Okay. What do you want me to promise?"

"Never lie to me."

Brody put his forearm on the post above her head and leaned closer. "I'll never lie to you."

Time to test the strength of that promise. "Do you want to kiss me?"

He gave a slow nod. But didn't make a move.

"Are you going to?"

Brody slowly shook his head.

"Why not?"

"Because you don't want me to." Morgan opened her mouth, but he took a step back and said, "*You* can lie. You *should* lie. *Please* lie."

22
Ridiculous & Adorable
BRODY

MORGAN PACED THE YARD as though counting square footage when Brody rolled into the driveway the next afternoon. He pulled the new tractor part out of the back of the truck and carried it into the garage. His tool bench was a mess, reminding him he'd told Nick he could borrow a few tools.

He set down the package with the part in it and got busy putting everything back in order. A jar of nails had been knocked over and more tools littered the table than hung on the wall in their respective spots. He gritted his teeth and vowed to get back at him for this.

"What are you doing?" Morgan's voice caused him to jump and drop a wrench, missing his foot by no more than an inch.

"It's not nice to sneak up on people."

"Remember that the next time you do it to me." Her diamond stud earrings caught the light. They had to be the clearest stones he had ever seen of that size. They flickered in the light like chickpea-sized disco balls.

"Are those real?"

Her hand went to her ear. "Yes."

"Did someone give them to you?" Why he so badly wanted her to say no mystified him.

"I gave them to myself." Her eyes twinkled, far more captivating and beautiful than the diamonds.

"Do you think she misses them?"

"Who?"

"The woman you took them from."

Morgan laughed. "I didn't take them from a woman. *He* was a jeweler and he hit on me relentlessly at Bally's. Followed me around all night bragging about the earrings he was traveling with for a diamond expo. I don't usually do that kind of thing, but it was almost too easy. And he deserved it. Grabbed my ass one too many times."

Brody tilted his head and squinted. "What's the acceptable number of times for someone to do that?"

She rolled her eyes. "Do you have time to talk? We need to formulate a plan."

"I know we need to talk but I have to get this part in the tractor. I hope you don't mind me multi-tasking."

With the tools back in their rightful places and his worktable once again clear, he grabbed a wrench and went over to the tractor.

Morgan climbed on the seat and held onto the steering wheel.

"What's the plan, Cash?"

"It's not that easy, *Lewis*."

He chuckled. The fun of Morgan was that she was rarely at a loss for words, especially in response to flippancy. He looked forward to their back and forth.

"Look, the people I've scammed have been…stupid. They didn't see it coming. If Alexander Gill has the kind of loot that you think he does, he's not going to put it in a low-grade hotel safe."

"Obviously."

"This is going to require weeks, if not months, of recon. In the meantime, what are you building me?"

"I'm not building it for *you*." He shook his head as he loosened nuts and bolts.

She sighed dramatically. "Just tell me."

"You know how you have that nifty little GPS device in your car?"

"Uh-huh," she said in a *hurry up and get to the point* voice.

"I'm going to hook tiny micro bombs up to a system kind of like that. You can put them on the cameras and at any time we want, we can set one or all of them off from any distance. There won't be much of a bang or sparks, but each bomb will release enough radiation to short circuit the cameras."

"How?"

Brody glanced up. She seemed genuinely interested in how he would make it work. When he tried to explain the engineering behind his explosives to Benny or Nick their eyes glazed over. Turns out, atoms and nuclei were not scintillating conversation for most people. "Do you know anything about nuclear fission?"

"Only what I remember from science class. It's when an atom splits, right? It produces energy."

He grinned. It was kind of a turn on that he didn't have to spend a half an hour giving her a refresher course on protons, electrons, and neutrons. "Right. Think about when you shoot pool, if the balls are racked tight enough, you'll have a stronger break. Same with a fission bomb. The farther apart the subcritical mass, the less of a reaction. You don't want a big bang, so that requires an implosion-triggered bomb."

He looked to see if she was snoring.

Sitting on his tractor, leaning forward with her elbows propped on her knees, with her two-carat diamond earrings and pink converse tennis shoes, she looked equal parts ridiculous and adorable.

"Can you get me the quarter-inch pear-head ratchet?" he asked.

She slid off the seat and landed on her feet with the grace of a falling leaf. Her fingers wiggled as she moved across his tool bench until she found that particular ratchet.

He turned the ratchet over in his hands, curious as to where Morgan had gained her knowledge of tools.

"You're smart, Brody," she said, leaning her shoulder against the tractor tire. "You could be doing bigger things than stealing diamonds."

"I do something much bigger. I'm a farmer," he said with a grin on his face.

"You must not have always wanted to be, though. You went to the Naval Academy. Pretty ambitious, if you ask me. What happened to change that course?"

"Are you trying to get to know me, Cash?"

"Ew. No."

Brody laughed. "Once I finished school and training, I enlisted. I was on and off aircraft carriers and in labs for a while. Then I found out my dad was in bad shape, so I didn't re-up. I wasn't going to be out in the middle of the ocean while my family struggled to run the farm."

"Where was Nick?"

"In his second year of college, his first season as the starting pitcher for his team."

"You gave up your dream so that Nick could live his."

"Nobody gave up anything. I have a lot more fun playing poker with my dad and I'm never bored around here. There's plenty to keep me busy." Taking over the farm had always been his plan, just not so soon.

"And if you do get bored, there's always plotting a diamond heist to liven things up." The suspicion in her voice sent a flash of shame through him.

He wasn't going to lie to Morgan, but he didn't want to disclose his entire reason for this job. There was getting personal, and then there was compromising the heist. "Do you see a crow-foot socket set over there?"

A minute later, the weight of a box rested on his stomach. He unlatched it, verified it held crow-foot sockets, then looked at her.

"What?"

"Spend a lot of time in the garage growing up?"

She crossed her arms. "My first boyfriend was a motocross rider and a mechanic."

"Of course, he was." He concentrated on his task, irritated as hell over the mental image of Morgan in a garage with some asshole's filthy hands on her.

"What's that supposed to mean?"

He shrugged. "Just seems like the type of guy you'd be into."

"Not anymore. I'm done with men, regardless of type."

"Switching teams?"

"No. I'm committing myself to eternal bachelorettehood."

"What about sex?"

Her eyes widened. "What about it?"

He laughed and rubbed his jaw while he thought about the best way to phrase what he wanted to say. "You don't strike me as a one-night-stand type."

Morgan Cash had the cool girl act down, but he'd seen her drop character. Underneath it all, under the always *down for a good time* façade, was integrity.

She raised an eyebrow. "This is borderline inappropriate. But for your information, I'll be just fine. It's not worth the hassle."

Brody wiped his hands on a rag and stood. "Dang."

"What's that mean?"

"It's supposed to be worth the hassle. It's supposed to be so good you'd put up with someone's irritating habits to keep getting it."

Morgan rolled her eyes. "Irritating habits like cheating?"

His knuckles ached as he squeezed his fists. He didn't want Morgan to see how much rage hearing some dick had cheated on her induced. "Did Logan take care of him, or do I need to?"

"You've met my brother. What do you think?"

"I think he broke a few ribs, at minimum."

"Well, there ya go." She pushed away from the tractor. "If you're done psychoanalyzing me and my sex life, I have better things to do."

Brody's comments about Morgan's preferences in men, and her plans of celibacy had crossed a line. It was unlike him. He mulled over it the rest of the afternoon and when he came in from the field, he marched into the house to apologize.

But his apology would have to wait.

On the kitchen table, she'd left a note. She'd gone to Las Vegas. Her uncle was in the hospital with a possible heart attack. She asked Brody to feed and look after Buster until she returned.

He would have taken her to the airport, and even gone with her, if she'd asked. She'd probably never admitted to needing anyone besides her family. He wondered if she was conditioned to be that way from bad experiences or if it was something her uncle had instilled to protect her.

23
Hospital Hot Seat
Morgan

A PLUMP WOMAN WITH POWDERED sugar on her lips shook a clipboard with a sign-in sheet on it at Morgan as she walked by the nurses' station.

She kept going.

Uncle John had been moved to a regular hospital room, which was a good sign.

"Hello, angel," he said as she entered his room. "You get prettier every day."

With a sigh, she shook her head and wagged her finger. "You should have called me."

Getting the call from Lucy, who knew nothing other than he'd been taken from his condo in an ambulance, was not ideal. The two of them needed to pull their shit together because it was times like this that family needed each other.

"I knew you'd drop everything and come if I did. I'm fine, by the way, so go away."

Morgan huffed. "What does your doctor say? Was it a heart attack?"

"No. Just some chest pains. Nothing to worry about."

She moved to the chair next to his bed, trying to remember a time when Uncle John had been in the hospital, but came up empty. He rarely got sick. Right now, he didn't quite look like himself, though. Not in that hospital gown with his hair messy and scruff on his face. "When are they releasing you?"

"In a few days. The doc wants to get as much money out of me as possible. He's running all sorts of expensive tests." He didn't trust easily, skeptical that those he encountered had ulterior motives. Hmm…maybe that's where she'd learned it from.

"If he's keeping you and running tests, it must be more serious than you're letting on. I'm a nurse, remember? You're not going to get anything over on me this time."

He rested back against his pillow, smoothing the blanket over his lap. "Don't worry about me. I'm going to be fine."

She walked to the table next to the hospital bed and tidied the junk that littered it. Discarded plastic from syringe packages and wrappers from alcohol prep pads. No one had even bothered to put his wallet or keys in the drawer.

"How are things in Maryland?" he asked.

"Fine."

"You like Brody?"

"He's okay." She sat on the edge of his bed and pulled her feet up, sitting crisscross.

"Lucy swears he's beyond reproach."

"About Lucy… You're acting like a child. How long do you plan to go on refusing to see her?"

"It's complicated." His tone expressed that it was an adult matter, and she hadn't graduated from the kiddie table.

"Complicated because you have romantic feelings for each other?" She darted a glance at him but couldn't maintain eye contact. Maybe she wasn't entirely ready to leave the kiddie table.

"She knows how hard I've worked to protect your anonymity. I don't understand how she could give you up to Brody and not see that as a betrayal."

"That doesn't answer my question."

"That's between Lucy and I."

Her shoulders sagged. "Why won't you talk to me about it? What do you have to hide?"

"I'm not hiding anything," he shouted, then covered his face with his hand, tubes running down his arm. His heart monitor beeped frantically.

Great. Scientific proof that her presence was a surefire way to raise Uncle John's blood pressure.

A nurse rushed into the room. Her eyes stayed glued to the monitor as she pulled a blood pressure cuff from the basket on the wall.

Logan appeared out of nowhere. "What's going on?"

"Please wait out in the hallway." The nurse kept her back to them as she checked his vitals.

Uncle John winked at Morgan. "Just a little high blood pressure. I'll be fine, angel." His attention shifted to Logan. "Take your sister to get dinner."

It looked more like Logan was the one with raised blood pressure, but he gestured for her to follow him. On their way out of the hospital, she filled him in on the little bit of info she'd gained since her arrival. He led her to the parking garage and clicked a key fob. A sleek silver BMW flashed its headlights.

"Let me drive." She'd never outgrown begging her big brother to let her play with his toys.

"Fuck no."

"Stingy," she muttered.

He opened the passenger door and grabbed a pack of cigarettes off the seat.

She gave a little shake of her head when he offered her one. "Drew didn't come with you?"

"She wanted to. I told her to stay home. She's on a deadline." He lit his cigarette and leaned against the car. "Where's Lucy?"

"He doesn't want her here."

Logan's eyebrows knit together. "Seriously?"

She nodded. "He sees Lucy outing me to Brody as a betrayal."

He lifted a shoulder. "It borderline is."

If she didn't hold it against Lucy, she didn't see why anyone else should. Nothing bad had happened. Everything was copasetic. "Did you ever wonder if they were more than friends?"

"I mean…I figure they've had to at least gotten drunk and banged once."

Ick. She didn't want to think about that. "Don't put that shit in my head."

He grinned and shrugged. "So, you think what's going on is a lover's spat?"

"Just before you got here, I asked Uncle John about their relationship. He got agitated. That's why his heart monitor went off."

He shoved one hand in his pocket and flicked the ash off his cigarette with the other. "I don't know, Morgan. They're grown-ups. Let them figure it out."

"It wouldn't bother you if they've lied about it since we were kids?"

"If that's the case, I'm sure they had a good reason for keeping it a secret. Does it change anything? They were both there for us whenever we needed it."

Finding out the people you trusted most lied to you should matter. Shouldn't it?

Lucy's condo was two down from Uncle John's. The layout was slightly different, but not by much. The main difference was the decor. John went for sleek and shiny, Lucy liked fluffy and cozy.

Morgan sank into the cloud of a couch in the sunroom and tossed her arm across her eyes. Two sleepless days worrying about her uncle. He was home now. The doctors expected him to be fine. Irritation and frustration had quickly replaced that worry.

Up until Brody mistakenly referred to Uncle John and Lucy as a couple, the possibility hadn't occurred to her. She felt so stupid. Even if it wasn't factual, why hadn't she ever considered it? Probably a weird subconscious coping mechanism to deal with the risk of being let down.

"This reminds me of when you were a teenager and you'd come here to take a nap because you didn't want John to know you'd stayed up all night," Lucy said, her strawberry blond bob swaying as she entered the room.

Morgan lifted her arm from her eyes.

Lucy dropped into one of the velvet armchairs and crossed one leg over the other. She had on white wide-leg pants and a black silk blouse. The way she dressed, the way she carried herself—if Uncle John didn't want her, he was stupid.

She hoped she'd age as gracefully. Maybe never marrying or having kids was the key to avoiding wrinkles and maintaining style. If so, Morgan was on the right path.

"Speaking of Uncle John," she said, "I asked him something when he was in the hospital, and it upset him so much it set off his heart monitor."

"What was that?"

"If you and he were more than friends."

Lucy bristled and examined her fingernails. "I'm sure he told you no."

"Actually, he told me to mind my own fucking business."

She gasped. "John would never talk to you that way."

"It's not a direct quote." Morgan moved into a sitting position and tucked her feet underneath her. "My point is that he refused to give me an answer."

"Ah, so you want *me* to confirm or deny your suspicions?"

"I want to know if you've been hiding a romantic relationship from me my entire life, yes. Is that unreasonable?"

"Morgan," Lucy said softly, "he already told you it wasn't something he wished to discuss with you, so please don't put me in the position of further inciting his anger."

"I don't think he's angry. I think he's hurt. He feels you betrayed him by giving Brody information about me."

"The bottom line is, he's not talking to me, and I'm not sure he ever will again."

"So, you won't talk to me about it?"

Lucy shook her head.

That confirmed there was *something* to talk about. Otherwise, they'd say their relationship was strictly platonic. They would laugh at the absurdity of the suggestion. But neither of them had done so.

"He'll get over it," Morgan said. "He just needs time to work out his feelings and then—"

"It's not only because I told Brody about you," she said. "I know you're curious, and I'm sorry, but I can't fix the damage that's already been done, and I certainly don't want to set the wreckage on fire."

Morgan palmed her forehead. Getting treated like a child who couldn't handle discussing adult problems sucked. This was her life too. And yeah, maybe if something romantic had gone on between them, it wasn't her place to get involved, but damn it, these were her parental figures. She should have been clued in.

She should have been given the chance to be happy about it.

"On the first day of preschool, when all the kids were getting dropped off, I heard them calling the adults with them Mom and Dad." She tried and failed to keep her voice from cracking. "That's when I understood that I didn't have a traditional family, that I didn't have parents."

Uncle John had legally adopted her and Logan before she was six months old. The rock-solid foundation of his relationship with them was built on trust and honesty. He'd never skirted around how he came to be their caregiver, even though it would have been easier.

"Morgan…" Lucy smoothed her fingers over her lips and shook her head. "There's not a father in this world who loves his daughter more than John loves you."

"No, I know that." She stared at the ceiling. "It never bothered me because I believed what I had was better. I could ask you anything, and I knew I'd get nothing less than the truth. But this… I feel like I've been duped, and I can't help wondering if I was wrong all along."

"You weren't wrong. I love you and I will always tell you the truth, but I'm caught in the middle here. This is a line I know better than to cross with John. I might not agree with him, but I understand, so I have to respect his wishes."

"Do you really think I'll be able to forget about it now?"

"I think you should worry about taking care of yourself."

"Right. Because I can't even do that right, can I? Poor little Morgan. What a screw up she is. She's got enough problems of her own."

"Stop being petulant. If I didn't think you could take care of yourself, I wouldn't have sent Brody your way."

"Or you sent him my way because you want him to take care of me."

Lucy pushed up from her seat and came to sit on the end of the couch. "All I want is for you to be happy. Brody is a gentleman and he's…"

Morgan waited, staring at her. "Yes?"

"Handsome."

A laugh-snort escaped her. "I wouldn't phrase it like that, but sure."

"How would you phrase it?" Lucy beamed and the tension between them evaporated, like it'd never been there at all.

"He's hot. You know he's not my type, though."

"That's a good thing."

Morgan stuck her tongue in her cheek and rolled her eyes. It probably was. Didn't matter, though. "I've already told him there's no way anything is happening between us. We're business partners. Nothing more."

"What did he say to that?"

"He agreed."

Lucy tapped her knee. "Because he's respectful. That's a quality you should look for in a man."

She simply shook her head. She could say she wasn't looking for a man until she was blue in the face. It wouldn't make a difference. Lucy had already decided Brody and she were the perfect fit.

Nothing could be further from the truth.

24
Goat-sitting Superstar
BRODY

Tires crunching on gravel lured Brody from the house.

Morgan drove up the driveway in a different car than the one she'd left in.

A smile he had no control over spread across his face. She'd been gone five days, but it seemed longer. The times he'd checked in with her via text message—keeping it short, sending her photos of Buster, trying to be supportive without crossing into bugging her—she'd messaged back promptly, although she had kept her responses brief and to the point.

As glad as he was to have her back, he wished she'd called to give him a heads-up. Oh well. He'd figure out a solution for having two houseguests, but only one guest room.

She unfolded from the car, wearing a white off-the-shoulder top that ended inches before the waistband of her jeans and covered absolutely no part of her shoulders. Giant sunglasses hid her eyes and a good portion of her face. Her long hair cascaded down her back, shiny and pin straight.

He'd missed the view, but not as much as he'd missed their banter.

He met her by the trunk of her car. "I didn't know you'd be back today."

"Is it a problem?" She pulled out a small suitcase.

Brody scratched the back of his head. "Well…"

Her eyes went wide. "Oh, god, do you have company?"

"Yes, but—" Not the kind she'd assumed he had.

"This is awkward. You could have let me know." Her hand flew to her forehead.

"I'm supposed to let you know I'm having company when you aren't here?"

Morgan pouted, her lips looking way too kissable. "No. Whatever you do when I'm not around is none of my business."

"What is it you think I'm doing?" he asked, doing a poor job of concealing his amusement.

"Look, it's fine. I'll just"—she went to put her suitcase back where it'd come from—"go somewhere else."

Ah, hell. As much as he wanted to keep this up and see how jealous she'd get, he didn't want her to think she had to leave, especially when there wasn't any place for her to go.

He took the suitcase from her. "It's Benny. He showed up unannounced. He's over visiting my parents and Nick right now."

"Benny? Your cousin?" She glared at him. "You could have said that."

"I was going to, but you interrupted me, and then went all crazy jealous."

Her eyes seemed bluer when open that wide. Such pretty eyes, it'd be a shame if they popped out of her head. "I'm going to hurt you, Brody."

He smiled and closed the trunk. "So much feistiness in such a small package."

"I'd suggest you sleep with one eye open tonight."

"Why? Going to try to sneak into my bed again?" He winked at her.

"Speaking of sleeping arrangements, how long is Benny staying?"

"Two nights."

"Is he staying in your guest room?"

"No." Because the idea of another man sleeping in her bed didn't sit right with him. "I was going to give him my room and sleep in yours."

She raised an eyebrow. "I'm not sharing a bed with you."

Her tone lacked the revulsion it'd had in the past when he'd suggested anything remotely sexual could happen between them. It'd be bad, though. Bed sharing with someone he was this attracted to but couldn't make a move on would be torturous.

"That's what I'd planned to do before I knew you'd be here. I'll sleep on the couch." He walked to the house carrying her suitcase. He could endure two nights of discomfort if it maintained his sanity.

Morgan caught up with him and blocked his path. "You're too big to sleep on a couch."

"What do you want me to do?"

"I'll sleep on the couch," she said.

"No."

"No?"

"No," he repeated.

She put her palm against his chest and looked up at him through her lashes. "I'll douse it in lavender spray and sleep like a baby."

His mouth curved into a grin. "It's still a no."

"I'll do it anyway. You can't stop me."

She could try. She would not be successful. "You think I can't carry you up the stairs without waking you up?"

"I *know* you can't."

"Well, we're not going to find out because you're sleeping in your bed." Brody maneuvered around her and up the steps.

"You're so stubborn."

"We're both stubborn."

He turned in time to see her mouth go slack.

Having her insult countered by a claim that she had the same vice must be a new experience for her. A line appeared between her eyebrows, then as if she'd accepted defeat, she shrugged and said, "That's fair."

What? He'd been bracing for an argument. Now, he wasn't sure what to do. The sassiness he'd become accustomed to had been turned down a few notches. And he wanted to know why. Her messages had said her uncle's condition wasn't serious, and he doubted she'd have come back otherwise. Something was up with her, though.

"How's John?"

She sucked in a lengthy breath. "Back to his rascally self."

"That's good news."

She nodded, but kept her gaze lowered. The lack of spunk in her temperament bothered him. Was it travel fatigue? Maybe. Instinct nagged at him that it was more than that, though.

"Benny, Nick, and I are going out to dinner. Come with us." He didn't want to leave her here alone if she was going through something. Although, her telling him *what* was going on with her was as likely as finding gold flakes in his cereal.

"I'm not up to it. I'm going to chill with Buster." She walked over to the goat's pen and leaned over the fence, but even on her tiptoes, her arms weren't long enough to grab him.

Brody set her suitcase down and followed. He reached into his shirt pocket, grabbed a generous pinch of sunflower seeds, then dangled his arm inside the pen, palm out. Buster trotted over—more like tripped over his own hooves—and sucked up the seeds like a tiny vacuum. Seizing the opportunity, he scooped him up and handed him to Morgan.

"What did you give him?" she asked.

"Sunflower seeds."

Her gaze swept over him. "Where did you get them?"

He patted his pocket.

"Do you always walk around with sunflower seeds in your pocket?"

"Not usually, no." He took out another pinch and held his hand out to her.

Morgan opened her palm to accept them. She laughed as Buster licked her hand, making short work of eating the seeds.

"He goes nuts for carrots." And beer, but he decided not to tell her about Buster getting a can of beer Nick had left unsupervised. Most of it spilled through the porch boards, so it's not as though he'd gotten drunk.

She narrowed her eyes like she'd caught him doing something worth teasing him mercilessly for. "Have you been playing with him?"

"Of course. I take goat-sitting very seriously." Sure, he could have gotten away with simply feeding him and left him penned up. Brody wasn't heartless, though. It wasn't any trouble to let the little guy nose around in the yard while he sat on the porch in the evenings or spend a few minutes hiding treats to see if he'd find them.

The smile she flashed was a small taste of the side of her he craved. He wanted more than a sample, though. He wanted to put a stick of dynamite into the walls she kept up, despite knowing getting through to her would require finesse and truckloads of patience.

"What's Benny doing here anyway?" She nuzzled her cheek against Buster's head. "Did he change his mind about retirement?"

"Cash, you sound jealous again." And he liked it. The slightest indication she felt possessive over him made him feel like a king.

"I'm your partner now. I want you focused on our job. If he wants in on this, that's a hard no."

"His visit is purely social. He was in New York for his nephew's baptism and decided to come here before heading home. But it's nice to know you don't want to share me."

He waited for her attack—unsure of whether it'd be physical or verbal—but it didn't come. It was almost as though she hadn't heard what he'd said. Her eyebrows pinched together, and she fixed her gaze on his face. If she'd pulled a tiny flashlight from her pocket and shone it in his eyes, he wouldn't have been surprised. "Do you feel okay?"

"I feel great." Maybe a little tired, but that was understandable. He'd gotten up at dawn and worked under the summer sun for hours.

She studied his eyes, then leaned up on her toes and touched the back of her hand to his forehead.

He jerked back as if she'd slapped him. Actually flinched.

"I was just trying to see if you were warm. Why are you so jumpy?"

Good question. He'd like the answer as well. Because up until now, the idea of her touch…he didn't hate it.

"Not warm, Cash. *Hot*." He winked, desperately wanting to divert the conversation. "And anytime you want to feel my heat, I'm game."

"You are *so* ridiculous."

"Doesn't mean you aren't crazy about me," he teased.

"I'm going inside. Have a good time with the boys."

25

All Perceptive & Shit

Morgan

THE SKY SHONE PINK and orange as the sun moved near the horizon. A light breeze cut through the humidity, creating the perfect summer evening.

Morgan sat in the grass on the side of the pond with her legs pulled against her chest. Out here, she could hear herself think. That hadn't been the case in Las Vegas. Uncle John trying to prove he was as fit as a twenty-five-year-old and Lucy wanting to know everything that went on with him, but refusing to ask him herself, had been exhausting.

Movement from where the trail opened to the clearing caught her eye. Her heart lifted, but her response to Brody's presence made her uneasy, so she redirected her attention to the ripples in the pond and locked her emotions in the dungeon of her subconscious.

He sat next to her, so close she turned her head to give him a *what the hell?* look. His ball cap shaded his eyes almost entirely from her view, preventing her from being able to tell whether he'd noticed or not. The little tip at the corners of his mouth said he knew exactly what he was doing, though.

Her gaze dropped. The fabric of his T-shirt strained against his biceps and chest, causing a reaction in her body she didn't welcome. The man could get hit with an ugly stick a few times and still be hot enough to make her wet just by existing in the same space.

"You okay?" he asked.

"I'm fine." She wasn't. All her life, her family had been the one thing she could count on. There were no mysteries. No secrets. That turned out to be a fucking hoax. When everything else in her life was up in the air, or falling to pieces, knowing her family wasn't a source of chaos had been comforting.

Finding out that was an illusion left her spinning without any idea what to grab to gain stability when it was stability she needed most. Seeing Uncle John in the hospital brought forth a realization that inevitably, there'd come a day when she'd no longer have him to turn to.

"Aren't you supposed to be a better liar than that?" He bumped his arm against hers.

To those who could be easily fooled? Absolutely. He, unfortunately, didn't fall into that category. Even worse, she didn't have that unbending desire to hide her feelings from him.

Brody picked up a small stick and tossed it into the water. "Realizing the person who took care of you your whole life isn't invincible is sobering."

"Great, a volunteer therapist," she muttered.

"Yeah, being shown empathy and having someone listen when you need to talk, that's awful stuff." His tone didn't reflect him being irked that he'd offered her compassion and she'd responded with snark. More like he let her shitty mood roll off him, unbothered…expecting it, even.

Accepting emotional support and understanding from outsiders was foreign. Logan had been her confidante, but now that he had a sparkly new relationship, Morgan felt less inclined to drop all her worries in his lap. Her brother deserved to enjoy his happiness without the stress of dealing with her plight.

But she wasn't going to allow Brody to slide into that role. They were business partners. Not friends. It needed to stay that way.

She'd just have to be a big girl and get through this on her own. "Uncle John is stable. It wasn't anything serious."

"But you didn't know that until you got there, did you? You had a six-hour flight for the anxiety to set in."

Six hours on a plane, after a two-hour drive to the airport, and the wait to board the flight. The trip from Maryland to Nevada was the longest trip of her life. When she'd arrived and learned Uncle John hadn't suffered a heart attack, like she'd feared, relief hadn't taken hold. Brody was right. It was easy to ignore his mortality until it smacked her in the face.

Brody knew. He knew because he'd gone through it with his own father. And continued to go through it. The gravity of losing his dad loomed far heavier than hers. Yet here he was, being all perceptive and shit. It felt wrong to be offered his kindness considering the differences in their situations.

"It's getting dark. I'm going back to the house." She pushed herself up from the ground and brushed off her butt.

He stayed where he was, expression still shielded by his hat. "Got it. You're tough."

Morgan took a deep breath. Ugh. Why was she like this? Being his bestie couldn't happen, but she didn't need to be so cold. "Tough, but also a little afraid of creepy-crawlies. Walk back with me?"

Once he'd stood, he smiled at her. "I've got to warn you, there's an even worse pest at the house."

"Benny? I have no problem swatting that gnat."

He laughed. "Let's go, then."

As soon as they got within view of the house, Benny pushed out of his rocking chair. Unlike his cousins, his features were dark and coordinated well with the silk shirt undone one button too many and the gold chains around his neck.

"*Buonasera, bella.* Look at you, all grown up. The last time I saw you—"

"—you got me fired. Save that Italian flirting crap. It doesn't work on me." She stepped onto the porch and glared with all the petulance and rage of a seventeen-year-old who'd had her fake I.D. cut up.

"Still holding that against me, eh?"

Voodoo had been the coolest lounge in Vegas back then, and she'd had the *best* fake. She stared at him, waiting for the apology she deserved.

"You were seventeen. You had no business working in a place like that," he said.

"You had no business making what I do *your* business."

He raised an eyebrow. "I had two options. One, tell your uncle and your brother, so they didn't kill me if they found out I'd seen you there and didn't tell them. Two, I get you fired. So, did I make the right choice?"

As much as she wanted to say no, she understood his loyalty. Back then, Benny and Logan ran cons together, with Uncle John mentoring them. If they'd found out, all hell would have broken loose. They'd have never let her out of their sight after that.

She flashed him a wicked smirk. "They could still find out you didn't tell them."

His face fell, then he turned to Brody. "Is she always this nefarious?"

"Nah, she's usually much worse. Must be tired from traveling."

She winked at Benny and went into the house.

There was a small pizza box on the table. Her stomach growled.

"That's for you." Brody walked around her and tapped the top of the box on his way by.

"You got me pizza?"

"Had to drive fifteen miles in the opposite direction of where we had dinner to get it," Benny muttered as he came inside.

Her gaze flew to Brody.

He shrugged and busied himself with getting a beer from the fridge.

He didn't have to get her dinner. He had, though, and he'd gone out of his way to get her favorite food. Not even just that, but he'd *remembered* what she'd told him her favorite food was. Her last boyfriend couldn't even be bothered to remember that she couldn't have honey because of

her bee allergy. Not that there was any reason to compare Brody to her past boyfriends.

26
Tensies
BRODY

THE SNICKING OF ONE of the doors on the second floor put Brody on alert, but he stayed lying down, his feet hanging over the arm of the couch.

The swish of fabric could barely be heard over the rustling of tree leaves drifting in through the open windows. A tap on his phone screen told him it was one in the morning.

The spring on the screen door squeaked.

He pushed himself up, tugged his jeans over his boxers, and went to the porch.

It was a clear night with enough light from the moon to silhouette Morgan as she leaned against a post, a silky pink robe wrapped around her body. Her hair was unbelievably curly. The drastic change from her normally sleek locks caused him to falter for a second, but he got it together. Assuming these untamed spirals were natural, they matched her personality—wild, unruly, and gorgeous.

"So much for sleeping like a baby. Did you run out of lavender spray?" He swung the door open and joined her on the porch.

She turned, pulled something from her robe pocket and held it up. A pack of cigarettes. "I haven't had one all day, but I always smoke when I can't sleep, so I'm struggling a bit."

"You're trying to quit?" Her bad habits were none of his business. He shouldn't care. If she succeeded in quitting, good for her, and if not, whatever. The level of hopefulness he had going on didn't make sense.

"Yeah, well, I heard it's bad for my health or something like that."

He held the door open and nodded his head toward the inside. "Come on."

"What?"

"Come inside. I have an idea."

She set her pack of cigarettes on the railing and walked past him into the house.

He went into the living room and turned on the lamp, then pulled open the drawer on the end table next to the couch and pulled out a drawstring bag. "Ever play Tensies?"

"Tensies?"

He sat on the floor and dumped the bag. Dice in a variety of colors covered the rug. "We each get ten dice and pick a number and every time we roll, any that land with that number showing, you eliminate. The first person to eliminate all their dice wins. It's fun. Sit down. I'll show you."

She lowered herself to the floor, facing him, her robe only covering one thigh as she sat with her legs crossed.

Keeping his eyes off her smooth skin took every ounce of his discipline.

"Do you, like, have a shirt or something?" she asked.

He glanced at his bare chest. Lot of exposed skin in this room. Good to know he wasn't the only one distracted by it. "You've seen me without my shirt before."

"Actually, I've seen you without *any* clothes."

He cringed as he remembered the night she'd successfully handcuffed him to the bed. "Maybe we should even the score." His gaze drifted to the spot where her robe lapels crossed.

She laughed. "Dream on, country boy."

He leaned over and grabbed his shirt off the end of the couch and tugged it over his head. "Wouldn't want you to be distracted while you're learning a new game."

Morgan snorted. "You're fit, Brody. Should I pretend I haven't noticed?"

"Nah, but you might want to wipe that drool." He tapped a finger on the corner of his mouth.

She tossed a die at him.

It bounced off his chest. His mouth fell open. He put his hand over the spot where it'd nailed him. "Didn't anyone ever teach you to keep your hands, feet, and objects to yourself, Miss Cash?"

"They *tried*."

He grinned. "What color do you want to be?"

She reached for a black die. "I need ten?"

"Yep. All the same color." He sorted out ten green dice from the mix, waited for her to gather hers, then scooped the remaining ones up and transferred them into the bag. "We'll go at the same time on the first roll, but after that, it's a free-for-all. Determine what number you want to go for, pull those to the side, roll again, and repeat."

"Sounds easy enough."

He crushed her the first game. She still had four dice left when he'd finished eliminating his.

"Obviously, you have an advantage. Your hands are twice the size of mine. I can't scoop them up as fast as you can."

He threw his head back and laughed. "You wanna go again?"

"Yes."

"Ready?"

"Brody?"

He glanced up from his handful of dice. "Yeah?"

"I'm sorry for how I was earlier. I didn't..." She stared at the couch and shook her head. "Yes, I'm struggling with accepting that Uncle John is getting older and what that means. I felt guilty for feeling that way when he's going to be fine and..."

"And my dad isn't?"

Her gaze flicked to his. "Yeah."

"There's no need to compare, Cash. It is what it is with my dad. His situation being worse doesn't mean your feelings about John aren't valid, or that we can't commiserate."

She pressed her lips together and nodded. With her hands cupping her dice, she asked, "Ready?"

He beat her the next two games.

"How are you able to deal with your dad's condition so well?" she asked. "Did you go to therapy?"

He snorted. "I'm not so sure that's true—that I'm dealing with it well. But no, I didn't go to therapy. Time is the only thing that has helped me not be bitter about it."

She rolled a die down the length of her palm and fingers, giving it a light flick when it reached the tip of one. It went straight up into the air. She turned her hand over and it landed on the back of her hand. "I can't remember ever seeing Uncle John seriously hurt or even sick. It was…a lot."

"The first time I visited my dad in a hospital, I held it together for about three minutes. Then I made an excuse to leave the room. I got as far as the vending machines before I started hyperventilating."

Her eyes widened. "Brody Lewis? Having an emotional breakdown? Now I've heard everything."

He stared at her for a moment. How did Morgan see him? Sounded like she thought he had some sort of emotional superpower. Either that or he'd given her the impression he was unfeeling. "I'm human, like everybody else."

"I know, but you seem like you've got it all figured out. Like…you can handle whatever life throws at you without breaking a sweat."

He leaned forward and lowered his voice. "Of course, I don't break a sweat. I'm fit."

She rolled her eyes. "Let's play."

Another four games, all losses for her. Her shoulders tensed and her eyebrows furrowed. Brody wasn't going to give her the win. Hell, he wasn't even going to take it easy on her. If she wanted to win, she'd have to earn it.

She scooted until her back hit the armchair, then got up and plopped into it.

"Giving up?" It was hard to believe she'd fold so easily.

"Don't you have to get up early?" She shifted to hang her feet over the arm of the chair.

"Worried about me?" He shook his head. "I'll be fine."

Lack of sleep wore on him, causing a dull ache in his head. But he didn't want her to go upstairs yet. He wasn't going to be able to sleep anyway. While they'd been playing, he'd stolen glances at her, watched her while she made up an excuse for why she'd lost again, studied her while she ran her hands through her curls, and adjusted her robe. And now he wanted her even more than before.

"You should go sleep upstairs." She rested her temple against the chair back. "Were you even able to get any sleep on the couch?"

"It's not that bad."

"You need a decent night's sleep more than I do, and besides, I can sleep in. Go upstairs."

"I like it when you boss me around like that."

"Does that mean you'll do it?"

"No."

She huffed. "I'm not going up there, so the bed is going to go unused."

"Didn't we already establish this conversation had reached a stalemate because we're equally stubborn?"

"I agreed that we're both stubborn. No one ever mentioned anything about equality."

"You're right. You are far more stubborn."

Her eyes fluttered closed as she yawned. "Says the man choosing to sleep on a couch that's too small for it to be remotely comfortable for him." The last few words came quietly. Her breathing changed.

He sat there, staring. Nick had oh-so-helpfully told Benny that Brody was crushing hard on Morgan. And maybe he was. Thanks to Nick's big mouth he'd had to hear it the whole ride back from picking up her pizza. When Benny had asked him what he was going to do about it, he'd told him the truth—the job was more important than his love life.

Confident she was asleep enough that he could move her, he stood. Brody eased her into his arms and headed for the stairs.

"I'm awake," she murmured, her breath warm against his neck.

"Barely."

She tossed her arm over his shoulder and snuggled tighter against him. Her breathing deepened.

He smiled. All bark and no bite.

He couldn't wait to tease her about this tomorrow.

27
The Cash Family Way
Morgan

THE SCENT OF COFFEE hit Morgan as soon as she opened the bedroom door. Her mouth watered. Airport and hospital coffee after tasting Brody's had been brutal.

A light murmur of voices traveled up the stairs from the kitchen.

When she reached the bottom, she found Benny at the table video-chatting…with kids. Little ones.

She stayed out of the view of the camera and crept to the coffee pot. The Road Runner mug sat next to it. It contained a folded piece of paper. Morgan glanced over her shoulder. Benny was saying goodbyes and I love yous.

Keeping her back to him, she unfolded and read the note.

Rematch tonight?

She smiled, folded it, and stuck it in her back pocket. Steam rose from the mug on her way to the table, the aroma reminding her why life was worth living. "You have kids?"

"Four and one more on the way."

Holy crap. She sat and stared at him with wide eyes. "Been *busy*."

His chuckle and the crinkling of his eyes ebbed away a bit of her grudge. "I've been *happy*."

They'd never spent any meaningful amount of time together, and other than the Voodoo incident, she only had one other memory of him.

It'd been before he'd gotten her fired. The lobby at the Mermaid had been decked out with gingerbread houses and heavily trimmed trees. She'd been sitting on a sofa by a fake fireplace, waiting for a boy to pick her up for the Winter Wonderland dance, *for over an hour*. That's when Benny came through, looking for Logan, and spotted her pouting in her red party dress. It didn't take him long to put together what happened, despite her being tight-lipped. He'd handed her the keys to his Camaro—which he said matched the color of her dress exactly—and told her to show up to the party in it and act like the jerk who'd failed to pick her up didn't exist.

"What are you thinking about?" he asked.

"Your Camaro." Especially the way it'd smelled like a cherry Tootsie Pop. And how she'd parked it right in front of the youth center's entrance. How she'd been unable to stop smiling when she'd handed back his keys later that night.

He smiled. "See? I'm a good guy."

Morgan had accepted his keys and advice, but she'd never been able to leave well enough alone, even back then. Flirting with several other boys right in front of the one who'd stood her up hadn't gone over well. At some point, a fist fight broke out. Two days later, she and that boy were back together. And so began a sequence of toxic relationships. Her blindness to red flags wasn't Benny's fault, though.

"Yeah, maybe," she said. Brody wouldn't have worked with him if he wasn't. Alarming, how solidly she believed that.

Though, her family had known Benny a long time and there'd never been bad blood. Not just Logan and Uncle John. Lucy too. He'd been her client for *years*. Maybe he knew something about her relationship with Uncle John—if there'd been one.

"What've you been up to? You left Vegas, huh?" he asked.

"Yep. When's the last time you saw my brother?"

His grin stretched wider. "Evasive. The Cash family way, right?"

"Answering my question with a question isn't evasive?"

He ran a hand through his hair and blew out a breath. "It's been a while, but he called me last week."

She set down her mug and frowned. "About me?"

"He's your brother. He needed assurance that Brody wasn't an axe murderer."

"More like the Unabomber," she said under her breath.

Benny's laugh boomed through the kitchen. "He's a bit less whacked than that."

"I have to feed Buster." She pushed her chair back and slipped on her shoes by the door.

Benny trailed along behind her. "How long have you been here, and you've already got a pet?"

"Don't judge me." She walked to Buster's pen and spotted a gate—a gate that hadn't been there before. Brody must have been making improvements while she was gone. *And* playing with Buster.

She let herself inside the pen and crouched, beckoning him to her.

Benny stood outside the fence and snapped a photo of her with his phone.

She froze with Buster in her arms. "What the fuck are you doing?"

"Sending this to your brother. I'm captioning it 'Green Acres'."

"Did he ask you to check up on me?"

"No. I was within driving distance and haven't seen Nick or Brody in too long. Although, I gotta admit, the chance to see you was too tempting to pass up."

"Why?" She walked out of the pen and waited.

"Curiosity. I figured you're a Cash, so you had the same charisma as the rest of 'em, but they never said anything about your skills. You're a phantom."

"Perks of having a paranoid and overprotective uncle." She walked to the barn. The bag of Buster's food was inside the door, on a shelf. She set him down and poured some into the empty bowl under the shelf. "Did

Logan introduce you to Lucy, or was it the other way around?"

"He introduced me to her. Why?"

She shrugged. "Just curious."

He leaned against the open bay of the barn, his eyebrow raised. "You're not *just curious*. You want to know something. No question about you being a Cash. Logan drives me crazy with this shit."

"What are you talking about?"

"Trying to weasel info out of me instead of asking me directly."

"Sorry. Habit."

"If I fucked you over, I don't know who'd kill me first—Brody or Logan. Ask me, and if I know, I'll give you an answer. No need to be all covert and shit."

Since Uncle John wasn't going to talk, and had Lucy gagged, she might as well do some digging elsewhere. If he got mad, well, he should have answered her questions. "Did you ever get the impression that Uncle John and Lucy were more than friends?"

"I never saw him kiss her or anything, but without a doubt, he puts out the vibe that she's his when they're in the same space."

"He's protective of her. That's just how he is." Either that, or she was in full-on denial. Both Brody and Benny had noticed something. It frustrated her that she and Logan hadn't.

"He's protective of *you.* He's possessive of her. There's a difference."

"I've never picked up on that."

"Why would he act possessive of her toward you? You're not a threat."

Damn it. That made sense. Benny might not be as shallow as she'd originally assumed.

He pushed away from the side of the barn. "Look, I'm not saying they're…you know…but Lucy's one hell of a woman. Being single is a choice for her."

Lucy was strong, independent, and sassy as hell. If she wanted to have a relationship with someone, she wouldn't let Uncle John stop her.

"Why are you asking me about this?"

How much was too much to tell him? She believed he wasn't going to tell anyone about this conversation, but airing her family's dirty laundry didn't feel right. "They're not talking. He says she betrayed him by telling Brody about me."

He waved a hand through the air. "If John met Brody, he'd get it."

"What do you mean?"

"How long were you around Brody before you knew you could trust him?"

"Who says I trust him?"

The way he tilted his head and pursed his lips made her laugh.

She shrugged. "Not long."

"If Lucy had any doubt over whether Brody could be trusted with you, she wouldn't have given you up to him, and I doubt she made the decision to do so lightly. I bet she knew how John would react and did it anyway."

It'd be nice if all it would take to get Uncle John to forgive Lucy was him getting to know Brody. It couldn't be that simple, could it? Then again, it wasn't the craziest thing she'd heard. Logan knew Brody and he seemed much more chill about her partnering up with him than if it were someone else. John was going to want to meet him when they went to Vegas to do recon on Gill's place. If he realized Lucy had only done what she'd done because she was one-hundred percent positive Brody could be trusted, it could set things in motion for them to make up.

If they did make up, though, what would that mean? Would things be how they'd always been, or would they be open about their relationship?

The rumbling of an engine grew louder and louder. She and Benny moved out of the way as Brody drove the tractor into the barn—wearing a shirt, unfortunately. He cut the engine and hopped off.

A haze clouded his normally clear brown eyes. The whites were even a little bloodshot. "You don't feel good, do you?" she asked, following him out of the barn toward the house. "I knew you were getting sick."

"I'm fine."

"You're sick?" Benny asked, sounding horrified.

"I'm just tired. Didn't sleep."

"Let me take your temperature," Morgan said once they'd gone into the house.

"Only if you do it with your tongue." Good to know his dirty mind was still in working order, but the scratchiness of his voice worried her.

It kind of made her tingly too.

Benny snorted.

"Your illness hasn't affected your innuendo game, so that's a good sign," she said.

He turned from the cabinet where he'd grabbed a glass, then stared at her. "I'm not ill."

She walked to him and pressed as far up on her toes as she could to put the back of her hand to his forehead. This time he didn't flinch. "You're burning up."

"Shit," Benny said. "Bianca is eight months pregnant. I can't be going home and getting the entire family sick."

Brody glared over her shoulder at him. "Thanks for the concern."

"He's right," she said. "This is probably viral. You need to quarantine."

"I'm going back out in the field after I rest for a minute." He sat and drank his water.

"No way," she said. "The only place you're going is to bed."

"There's too much to get done to slack off."

"Slack off? You're sick, you big dummy."

Benny chuckled. "Well, I think you're in good hands, so I'm going to get my stuff and get out of here. Hope you feel better, man."

Brody gave him a salute, then pressed the heel of his hand to his forehead. "Fuck."

"You have a fever, Brody. Go lie down in the guest room. I'll take care of you. This is your opportunity to get a taste of your nurse/patient fantasy."

His laugh was half-hearted. "Even though it *kills me* to turn that down, I can't. I have to get back to work."

"Where's Nick? Can't he help you?"

"He already is. He's in the front field helping Hope with the watermelons."

"I'm going to talk to him."

"Cash—" His sneeze practically rocked the house.

"Not sick? Your dog probably heard that sneeze."

He flashed her a weak smile. "I appreciate your concern, but farmers don't get sick days."

"Never?"

He shook his head. "Not during harvest season."

"I'm going to talk to Nick and formulate a plan for taking care of the farm. When I get back, I better find you in bed."

A grin slowly spread across his face, but before he had time to make any sexual references, she said, "Save it, Brody," and walked out the door.

28
Be Back Before You Die
BRODY

COOLNESS BRUSHED BRODY'S FOREHEAD. He blinked himself awake and pushed into a sitting position.

Morgan stood next to the guest room bed, staring at the cold object she had swiped across his forehead. It beeped. "101.4"

"What time is it?" He winced from the dryness in his throat. It burned now that he'd spoken. And he ached from head to toe. Damn, this sucked.

She handed him a glass of water from the nightstand. "Five-thirty. How's your appetite?"

"Non-existent."

"That's what I figured. I'm going to take a quick shower, then Nick and I are making a grocery store run. Need anything before I go?"

Every muscle in Brody's body tensed. Grocery shopping sounded like a couples' activity. Nick wouldn't make a move on her, but that didn't mean Morgan wasn't attracted to him. From what he'd gleaned, she had a type of man she gravitated toward—one that drove a fast car, partied hard, and broke hearts like he was in a smash house.

Nick wasn't out there callously breaking hearts, but his lifestyle was a lot more in line with her preferences than Brody's. And Nick wasn't her partner. No reason for them not to get involved.

Nope. Fuck this.

He didn't like them spending time together without him. Even though

Nick had been nonstop encouraging him to go for it with Morgan, and he knew deep down in his soul his brother would *never* touch her, he didn't want to be stuck in bed, feeling miserable, while Nick made her laugh and bonded with her.

"Why can't Nick go by himself?"

She perched on the edge of the mattress and half-turned toward him, her eyebrows pressed together. "Why do you sound like you're about to have a tantrum?"

Because his brother was playing with his toy. Holy hell, he'd just referred to her as a goddamn toy. It must be the fever making him into a miscreant. He didn't see her that way, not at all, but he still didn't want to share her with Nick.

Which was insecure and stupid on so many levels.

"You said we were going to act out my nurse/patient fantasy," he whined. "You're supposed to be taking care of me, not leaving me here to die."

"You're dramatic when sick, got it." She sucked her bottom lip in, then let it pop back out. "I'm going to the grocery store, not a different country. I'll be back before you die."

"What if I need a sponge bath, though?"

"I'm going to wait to do that until after your catheter insertion." She winked.

He scrunched his nose and shook his head. "I don't like this fantasy anymore. Can I pick a different one?"

She stood. "Go back to sleep, Brody."

He released a long, rumbling groan. "I already slept seven hours."

"We leave for Las Vegas in seventy-two. If you don't give your body the rest it needs, you're going to drag this out and be too sick to go."

Like hell. The next time she got on a plane for Nevada, he was going to be with her.

"Speaking of going to Las Vegas, how come you came back here if it's only for a few days?" Until now, he hadn't realized her return didn't make much sense. He'd been too excited to see her again—like the giddy dipshit he became whenever she was around. But it wasn't very practical to come back here, only to turn around and go back to the same place. In-depth plotting couldn't happen until they got the lay of Gill's house. There were a lot of bases to cover, but at this point, staying in Vegas for three days wouldn't be detrimental to their plan.

"I left in a hurry and didn't pack enough clothes."

"I could have brought you more clothes. I've packed for you before."

She glared at him. "Exactly."

It hurt his throat to laugh, so he suppressed it and took a drink of water. "What do you think I'm going to do, Cash?"

"What do you mean?"

"If you're honest with me. About this, or anything else. Do you think I'll use it against you?"

Her gaze dropped to the floor and stayed there for a few seconds. "Look, Brody, I'm fucked up, okay? I was raised to never share anything about myself with anyone. And the one time I broke that rule, I learned pretty damn fast why Uncle John insisted on it. So, yeah, I'm laconic and jaded."

"Laconic, huh?"

"You're not the only one who knows big words."

"I guess there's no point in asking you what happened to make you that way. I'll just have to assume you came back because you missed me so much that three days without me seemed unbearable." Brody didn't mind getting deep with her, but she wasn't ready for that. So back to teasing her about having the hots for him it was.

The noise she made was half groan, half laugh.

He sniffed and she snagged a tissue from a box on the nightstand and handed it to him. At least his sense of smell was impaired. Smelling her on the sheets and pillowcase would have made it hard to rest. "What if you get sick and have to miss Gill's party?"

"I'm not going to get sick." She walked to the dresser and pulled out folded clothes.

Earlier, she'd been wearing a different outfit. She'd changed into a loose T-shirt that she'd tied at the waist, and a pair of those sexy running shorts. That wasn't what was unusual, though. The unusual part was her being filthy. She had dirt on her clothes, her arms, and her legs. Her curls had come loose from her ponytail so that only half of her hair was pulled up.

He threw the covers off and tossed his legs over the side of the bed. Dizziness struck him and he curled his hands over the side of the mattress and squeezed his eyes shut until it subsided. Once he felt steady enough to stand, he walked over to her.

She still had her back to him, rummaging through drawers.

"What did you do all day?" he asked.

"I helped Hope."

"With farm work?" Now that, he'd like to see. Miss Grace and Glam picking cabbage and stacking hay bales. What a sight.

She spun and put her hand on her hip. "Yes."

A smear of dried mud on her arm caught his attention. He rubbed at it, unsure how he felt about her working on the farm. She wasn't here to do that. Their partnership had nothing to do with the farm. Not directly anyway. "Hope was supposed to pick the ripe watermelons and cantaloupe, then make sure the irrigation systems were working."

"I know. That's what we did."

"You didn't have to help."

"Oh." She pressed a hand to her chest and fluttered her eyelashes. "You're welcome."

He laughed, then started coughing.

"Of all the patients I've had, you and Uncle John are by far the most difficult. Since you're up, you can go get in your own bed. I laundered the linens after Benny left and put them back on."

"You don't have to do all this." He didn't want to take advantage of her staying here by treating her like his maid, or in this case, his personal nurse. Okay, so he did want to treat her like his personal nurse, but in a way she'd enjoy as much as he would.

She gave him a push toward the door. "You didn't have to take care of Buster while I was gone, or bring me pizza, or entertain me when I couldn't sleep."

"Ah, it makes sense now. You're taking care of me because you feel indebted."

"I'm taking care of you because that's what friends do. Can we just leave it at that?" She turned on her heel and marched toward the bathroom.

Brody smiled at the bathroom door she'd shut like he was a serial killer she needed to escape.

Morgan Cash had referred to him as her friend. Did that really happen?

29
Soft, Stupid, and Suffering
Morgan

GROCERY SHOPPING WAS NEVER fun, but it had to be done. Morgan grabbed a bag of carrots from the produce section and turned to put them in the cart, but Nick made a face like she was holding a smelly shoe.

"You do realize Brody has a garden, right? Whatever vegetables you have on your list, you can probably cross off."

She went over the list with Nick, and he was right. Aside from avocados, he claimed Brody had everything else growing at home.

They buzzed through the store, getting ingredients for chicken noodle soup, a few essentials, and decongestant for Brody. In the checkout line, she grabbed a crossword book and tossed it on the belt.

When she looked at Nick, he was grinning at her all goofy.

Morgan put the book back.

He snagged it and returned it to the belt. "You two need to just get it over with."

"Get what over with?"

"Banging."

Her cheeks tingled as they warmed. "Not happening."

"Is there something wrong with my brother?" he asked with a *no one talks shit on my brother* expression and matching stance.

"No—Well, yes. He's my partner. He's off limits."

"He said that?"

"No, I did."

He laughed. "Well, that was pretty stupid of you. I'm sure Brody won't hold you to it, though."

She swatted him with a reusable shopping bag. "Go bag the groceries."

As much as she tried, she couldn't stop dwelling on how everyone around them encouraged her and Brody to be more than friends. What was it that led people to believe they'd be compatible? They were opposites in so many ways.

By the time Nick dropped her at the house, she had a mile-long mental list of the ways she and Brody differed. So many of them were deal breakers, even if she could get past the partners problem.

For one thing, he lived here and she…technically, she lived nowhere. Fuck. Did that make her homeless? Not like *living on the streets* homeless but lacking a permanent address. She'd circle back to that. Another thing, he got up with the sun, and she was basically nocturnal. Their upbringings were vastly different. He'd grown up on a farm, with a traditional set of parents and somewhat normal siblings. She'd been raised by her uncle and Lucy and had to put up with Logan for a brother. Raising kids together would be a nightmare. They'd never agree on anything.

Holy fuck.

Did she just think about having kids with Brody?

That was not in the realm of possibilities. Not at all. Maybe it was time to think about something else. Cooking. She'd focus on that.

It didn't take her long to make herself at home in his kitchen. Soft music floated out from a Bluetooth speaker she'd found on the countertop. With the chicken cooking, she went to the garden to get the carrots, onions, and celery. Pulling up carrots took more effort than she'd expected. Since she hadn't intended to garden, she'd gone out in her dress and now, she was as dirty as she'd been before she'd showered. If she'd thought to take a basket to carry everything in, it wouldn't have been so bad, but instead she'd had to use the skirt of her dress as a pouch.

She looked up from admiring her bounty and there Brody was, standing on the porch in a white T-shirt and faded jeans. No shoes. No hat.

Morgan swallowed. Attractive even when sick. Damn him.

He grabbed a basket from the corner of the porch and held it at a level where she could dump the vegetables from her dress.

"No smart-ass comment?" she asked as she passed by him into the house.

She turned when she reached the table, as he'd still not answered.

His gaze was locked on the tiny, fabric-covered buttons in the middle of her dress that started at her cleavage and ended at her knee, where the dress split.

She played with the top button and swayed a little. "Do you like my dress, Brody?"

His gaze rose to hers, intensifying. He nodded slowly. "If I wasn't sick, you'd be in so much trouble right now."

The reckless side of her considered asking him to elaborate, but he was, in fact, sick. Hot sick. If he'd have actually been her patient, her attraction to him would be considered unethical. Acting on it would result in an automatic termination of her job, and probably her license too. "You should be resting."

"I have been resting, Cash," he said, his voice scratchy and deep, clearly fed up with hearing he needed to rest. He took a step back and rubbed his palm along his jaw.

She slipped away from him and put the vegetables in the sink to rinse. Her mile-long list of reasons why Brody was a bad idea suddenly seemed flimsy. She couldn't find it in her to care that they were all wrong for each other. The buzz he gave her whenever he dropped his voice—or his manners—was like nothing she'd ever experienced.

Brody coughed—a dry cough that sounded worse than it had earlier. She'd never wish illness on him, but it was a good thing there was at least one reason staring her in the face, reminding her she couldn't give in to the lust he stirred. A plan for how she was going to keep boundaries once he recovered jumped to the top of her to-do list. Clearly, complicating their business relationship and a virus weren't enough of a deterrent.

"You should take medicine and push fluids," she said over her shoulder. "There's a box of decongestant by the coffee pot." Maybe it'd make him drowsy, and he'd go back to bed. Where it'd be easier to ignore his sexiness.

"I don't need it."

She turned with a carrot in her hand, the long, bushy green sprouting ends dangling. "Don't act tough. I already know you're a big softy. Besides, refusing to take medicine isn't tough, it's stupid. Why suffer more than you have to?"

"Save those for Buster."

"The medicine?"

"The carrot tops. He'll eat them." Brody walked over, pulled a cutting board from a lower cabinet, and laid it on the countertop.

She scowled. "Were you even listening to me?"

"Yep. I'm soft, stupid, and suffering unnecessarily." He crossed his arms. "Do you degrade all your patients this way?"

"Only the ones who wrote it as a preference on their kink sheet."

"No one gave me one of those sheets. Is it too late to get one?"

She bit into her bottom lip to keep her smile at bay. "We only issue them after a patient takes their medicine."

"I guess I'm stuck with degradation, then. Maybe I can learn to like it. Call me stupid again, but this time pull my hair and slap me around a bit."

Laughter bubbled up in her throat and spilled out. "You're not stupid, but you are suffering unnecessarily."

"That's because my nurse is neglecting me."

She pointed the carrot at him. "Your nurse is trying to take care of you by getting you to take medicine, but you're being resistant. Not to mention, she's making you soup."

"I don't want medicine or soup."

"What do you want, then?"

"That dress." He dropped his arms to his sides and took a step backward, like he was prepared to make a run for it if she came at him. "On the kitchen floor."

30
Hey, Nurse
Morgan

BRODY'S CHEESY LINE ABOUT wanting her dress on the floor shouldn't have done anything other than irritate her.

So, why was she into it?

The boyish charm he exuded while saying it didn't hurt. Or that she trusted he wasn't going to do anything unless she gave him an explicit invitation, and even then, not while sick. Brody was a different breed than the men who'd pursued her in the past. They would have thrown the comment out there and undressed her without waiting for her permission.

And speaking of undressing her, she was pretty sure Brody was doing exactly that in his mind—one button at a time. Which turned her on far more than…than maybe anything ever had.

It took every bit of self-control she possessed not to comply. How would Brody react if she unbuttoned her dress and let it fall to his kitchen floor? Could be he was all talk, but she didn't think so. The unshakeable suspicion that he wouldn't be satisfied with *only* her body kept her from stripping.

That and her ego. She'd sworn she wouldn't budge on the boundaries she'd set for their relationship. Nick might be right that Brody wouldn't hold her to it, but she was too stubborn to fold.

Standing firm wasn't going to be easy, though. She'd never felt as sexy with a man, even decked out in racy lingerie, as she did in this simple dress, standing in Brody's kitchen.

Without him even touching her.

Her nipples pebbled and she regretted not wearing a bra. She turned back to the sink, hoping he hadn't noticed, while knowing that between his intense gaze and the thin fabric there was no way in hell he hadn't. "My dress is staying on, and you're going—I don't actually care where you go, as long as you leave the kitchen."

"Sorry. I shouldn't have said that. I'm not—" He paused for long enough that guilt over allowing him to misinterpret her self-preservation as indignation weighed on her. "You've been clear that there's no possibility of anything happening between us. And I agree we should keep things platonic. This job requires all of our focus, and we can't risk getting distracted."

Hearing someone agree with her had never disappointed her so much. Good thing he couldn't read her thoughts because she'd seem fucking crazy. She ignored him, pretending to concentrate on washing the vegetables, waiting for him to go away.

Brody wasn't done, though.

He came up behind her and braced himself with one hand curled around the counter's edge as he leaned in, his chest brushing against her back. His breath caressed her neck and his voice dropped to that deep, gravelly tone that made her thighs clench. "I'll mind my manners, but if you ever wear this dress again, I'm going to have a real hard time not talking you out of it."

She bowed her head, and her curls, which she hadn't had time to blow dry and straighten, curtained her face, concealing her smile, since she couldn't seem to quell it. Her heart pounded three times the speed of his footsteps as they receded.

Once he'd made it to the top of the steps, she turned and sank to the floor. Oxygen filled her lungs like fire through a forest, burning and consuming. She closed her eyes and fanned herself with a tea towel. If he could work her into a frenzy like this with only words and glances, sex between them would cause her to combust.

By the time the soup was ready, she'd gotten her pulse back to a normal rate and changed out of the dress and into a pair of black sweatpants and a baby pink ribbed tank. She found a serving tray in his pantry and loaded it with a bowl of soup, a glass of water, the box of decongestant, and the crossword book.

Brody's bedroom door was cracked, so she turned her back and pushed it open. Aside from the streak of light pouring in from the hallway, the darkness of the bedroom left her blind. Careful of her steps, she walked to his dresser and set the tray on top. His breathing was deep and even. She eased onto the edge of the mattress. With a light touch, she felt his forehead. Clammy.

He groaned and turned onto his side, curling around her, resting his head on her thigh.

She couldn't help herself from running her fingers through his hair. Seeing a man as big as Brody so vulnerable tugged at her heartstrings. "I'm sorry you feel this way," she whispered.

If she could've made it stop for him, she would, but the only thing she could do was force medicine and fluids. The thermometer was in the other room, but she had no doubt his fever had spiked. "Brody, wake up and take medicine."

When he didn't respond, she switched on his bedside lamp.

He flipped onto his back, tossed his arm across his eyes, and mumbled something.

She went to his bathroom and wet a washcloth with cool water, brought it back out, and draped it across his forehead.

He flinched, then groaned again, and opened his eyes. His voice came out scratchy and lethargic. "Hey, Nurse."

"Hey, Brody. You ready to stop being a stubborn ass and take medicine?"

"What's in it for me?"

"Feeling better."

"Overrated."

Morgan let out an exaggerated sigh. Time for a little tough love. "Fine. Have it your way. I brought you a bowl of soup, eat it if you want. I don't care." She pushed off the bed.

"Morgan." His hand circled her wrist.

She froze, and so did her pulse. He'd said her first name. He'd never done that before. It was always, "Cash," in that lazy drawl he used when he teased her. She fluttered her eyelashes at him. "Oh, so you do know my name."

31
Crosswords & Coercion
BRODY

"Don't go."

Brody sounded pitiful, even to his own ears. Morgan had been kind enough to *try* to take care of him, and he hated that he kept pissing her off. Getting sick rarely happened to him, but when it did, he tended to kick it fast.

"I'll stay if you take some medicine and try to eat something." Her stern tone and crossed arms left no doubt she'd walk out if he didn't.

"Fine. Give me the damn pills." He put his hand out.

She brought a tray from the dresser over to the bed and set it next to him. While she worked on opening the box and the blister pack, she asked, "Why do you always call me Cash?"

"At first, it was an easy way to get under your skin."

She extended her hand and dropped two pills into his palm, then handed him the glass of water from the tray. "Sounds like somewhere along the way, you found a different motivation."

He removed the cold compress and popped the pills into his mouth. Even though he washed them down with water, it still hurt like a bitch to swallow. Hoping that satisfied her, he rested on his pillows. "It was a pathetic attempt at forcing myself to think of you as my partner and not a woman."

Her eyebrows raised and she glanced around, like she was looking for his mind because surely, he'd lost it. "I'm both."

Of course, it didn't make sense to her. It hardly made sense to him. All he knew was if he let go of that last grain of detachment, he'd be a goner.

"Huh. I hadn't noticed," he said and grinned.

"Like you didn't notice the dress I had on earlier?"

Yeah, like that.

Brody glanced away. Avoiding noticing her as a woman may have been the stupidest thing he'd ever attempted. He'd straight fallen on his face.

"For the record, your flirting, or whatever it is, doesn't bother me. Not that I'm encouraging it. I just…it's not creepy or anything."

He turned his head in time to catch her blush. "That's nice to hear."

"I thought you should know I don't think you're a sleazebag," without any pause, she added, "I went to the trouble to make this soup, so you better eat it."

He snorted and accepted the tray she set on his lap. "You're good at this."

"At what?"

"Taking care of people."

"Duh. I'm a nurse."

He pushed the spoon around in the soup. "I doubt your education included coercion or moxie. Did you master that at Lucy Slade U?"

Lucy and Morgan didn't share a resemblance, but he'd spent enough time with Lucy to recognize her brand of bossiness. She had a special softness she only revealed to certain people—probably necessary in her line of work—and Morgan had a similar, but not exact, softness. He liked Morgan's more because she fought it. Keeping it locked up tight was her normal and it seemed to surprise her as much as it did him when it broke loose.

She snatched the crossword book off his tray. "Possibly. Have a pen or pencil?"

"In the nightstand."

He spooned soup into his mouth while she opened the drawer. It probably tasted good to someone whose taste buds weren't on hiatus.

"You have a gun?"

Shit. Yeah, a gun and condoms and god knows what else. What the fuck was he thinking letting her open his nightstand? "Does that bother you?"

"I broke into your house twice. I could have gotten shot."

"I was expecting you the first time. The second time, you did surprise me, but it's not every night I wake up with an attractive woman straddling me, so I figured out it was you pretty quick. You were in no danger of being shot either time. It's not even loaded."

She shut the drawer and crawled onto the bed, near the footboard, and folded her legs in a pretzel-like fashion only she could pull off gracefully. Sometime after he'd come up to bed, she'd changed and put her hair in a ponytail. Her black bra—which she definitely hadn't been wearing earlier—showed through her shirt.

"Lucy said to tell you hi, by the way."

He smiled. "Did John forgive her?"

"Hell no." She huffed. "But I did ask both of them if something was going on between them."

"And?"

"Uncle John refused to talk about it. Lucy wouldn't breathe a word because she didn't want to piss him off more than she already has."

Brody raised an eyebrow. "That basically confirms it, right?"

She shrugged and held the pencil poised over a page in the crossword book. "Five letter word; hoarse."

"Raspy."

Her gaze raised to meet his. "You didn't even have to think about that."

"It was an easy one."

"Mmhmm. Eight letters, second letter R, means set up?"

He set the tray with the soup to the side. He had no appetite and couldn't taste it anyway. He held up both hands. "A." He bent his thumb toward his palm and continued to tick off the letters using his fingers. "R-R-A-N-G-E-D."

She tossed the book at him.

He dodged it. "Hey!"

"Have you already done that one?"

He laughed. "No."

"Your intelligence is annoying."

"So is yours." He didn't really think so, but he wanted to rile her up.

She stretched out on the end of the bed and laid there with her hands folded on her stomach and her legs bent, staring at the ceiling. "I'm nowhere near as smart as you."

"Yeah, because people of average intelligence are capable of what you are."

"That's skill, not intelligence."

"When you stole my bang, did someone tell you how to do it?"

"No."

"You planned and executed a fucking reverse bomb heist—one that I haven't been able to figure out how you accomplished, and not for lack of trying—but you're not brilliant?"

She turned her head to the side and stared at him. "You only think that because you don't know about all the stupid stuff I've done."

"Like what?"

Her attention whipped back to the ceiling. "Like stealing drugs from the hospital."

"What the fuck did you do that for?" Morgan didn't strike him as someone who abused prescription drugs. Hearing she'd done something like that sent tension throughout his already aching body.

"Because my boyfriend told me to."

That *was* pretty fucking stupid. "The same prick who cheated on you?"

She closed her eyes and sucked in her bottom lip.

That was a yes. "What else did he make you do?"

She sat up and scooted off the bed. "He didn't make me do anything. He asked, and I did it."

"Bullshit. You're defiant as hell. I can't see you following anyone blindly."

Here she was opening up, and all he could think about was shattering every bone in her ex's body. That asshole was Morgan's hard lesson. The reason she wouldn't give him a chance.

She walked to the other side of the bed and grabbed the tray's handles. "Well, I did. I don't care if you believe me."

"I don't get it. You were that in love with him that you'd do whatever he wanted?"

"Yes, okay? And I wanted him to love me back so bad that I let him fuck me over again and again. Cheating was the least of it." She turned her head so he couldn't see her face.

"I'm sorry you had to go through that," he said softly.

Her glare stung worse than a slap to the face. "Ever had your heartbroken, Brody?"

"Never got serious enough with anyone to give them my heart."

He was glad Morgan was turning the tables on him. He didn't have any horror stories to tell, but he wanted her to see this door swung both ways. If she wanted to know things about him, all she had to do was ask.

She set the tray on the dresser, then came back to the bed. "Why not?"

Brody leaned closer and looked her directly in the eye. "How do you tell the person you're dating that you build bombs in your barn?"

"That's...a really lame reason for you to be single."

He rested back on his pillows. "I'm serious. That's not even taking into consideration explaining what I use them for."

"Don't tell them, Brody. It's not worth risking them using what they know against you if you get on their bad side."

"I'd like to think I wouldn't be drawn to a woman who'd do something like that."

Morgan snatched the crossword book and stretched across the end of the bed, this time on her stomach. With her ass right there where he couldn't not look at it. "We'd all like to think that we're only attracted to trustworthy and decent people. I hate to break it to you, but it doesn't work like that. Some people are scum and excel at hiding it, but if you want to learn the hard way, Mr. Honesty, be my guest, go put it all out there and find out."

It bothered him that he couldn't protect her from her past, that it was too late to prevent her from learning firsthand how narcissistic and downright malicious people could be. Before darkness breached her light, how much brighter had she shined?

Like a blow to the chest, paralyzing his lungs, the truth hit him. He already knew someone who didn't hold it against him that he had a dangerous and sometimes illegal hobby. Someone he trusted to keep it hush-hush. Someone who understood that part of his life better than anyone else ever would.

Someone he also happened to be extremely attracted to, intellectually and physically.

He ran his hand down his face. Brody wasn't ever going to find a woman that fit his life better. Nor would he find someone he wanted in his bed so much. Even with clothes on. He liked her here, lazing about, ponytail bobbing as she tapped the pencil eraser against her lip.

She kept her nose in the book, unaware of his internal freak out.

His dad was right. Even with her light dimmed, no one would ever outshine Morgan. A romantic relationship ranked low on his priorities scale, but he didn't want to be single forever. The timing was shitty, but he'd never meet another woman like the one in front of him.

Fuck.

He had *just* promised not to make a move on her. Because this job was important and complex. He needed Morgan to pull it off and if he made her mad or uncomfortable, and she refused to work with him, he'd be screwed.

So, they'd do the job.

But after the job…

After the job was over, it would no longer be an obstacle.

By then, the sexual tension between them would be on the verge of igniting.

Sex was the easy part. Getting her to believe they could have a healthy relationship would be a feat. He'd already put a few cracks in her wall, but once they came down, he'd still have to navigate the rubble.

And he'd come clean with her. After the job, it wouldn't matter why he'd done the heist. If she asked before then, he wouldn't lie, but he didn't want to put that pressure on her if it could be avoided.

"Ten letters. First letter N. Means unsure how to react," Morgan said without looking up from the book.

"What?" Sounded like he had a damn frog in his throat. Maybe she'd write it off as him having a sore throat. "Sorry. I wasn't listening."

She repeated herself, speaking slowly. "Ten letters. First letter N. Unsure how to react."

His brain did not want to think about vocabulary. It wanted to calculate how many days, hours, minutes, and seconds until they hit Gill's safe. But that's not where his mind needed to be.

Her lips turned up. "Stumped?"

"Let me see it."

She handed him the book.

He found the clue and the space on the puzzle. And stared at it.

"Nonplussed," she blurted out, then snatched the book back and scrawled the letters.

"This fever is making my brain blurry."

She pushed up and crawled to him.

By some miracle, his jaw didn't drop. His dick jumped, though. The covers hid it, he hoped. Morgan provided way too much material for his fantasy file. If she straddled him like she'd done the night she'd handcuffed him, he'd lose his mind.

She knelt beside him and put her hand to his forehead. "Your fever is going down now that you've taken the medicine."

"I'm trying to make an excuse for my ignorance, and you're ruining it."

Her lips formed an O, then curved into a grin, her eyes shimmering. She moved back to her previous spot, stuck the pencil into the book, and tossed it near the pillows. "We should do something else. I'm not sure your ego can take more of this."

His mind couldn't take any more of it, either. He couldn't stop staring at her.

Her smile was hypnotic. Being the reason for it made him feel like he was responsible for the earth spinning.

"While we're in Vegas, Uncle John wants to meet you."

Brody rested his shoulders against the headboard. "I'm cool with that."

"Palatable," she blurted out and straightened her posture.

He lowered his brow and stared at her.

"The answer to twelve across. To one's liking. The first letter is the P in raspy, and the third letter is the L in nonplussed. It's palatable."

He reached for the book. She was right. He scratched his head. That was a lot to recall without looking at the page. "How…?"

Morgan wilted like someone who'd realized they'd said too much.

"Nineteen across."

She blinked at him, as though expecting him to say more, and spun the ring on her finger.

He couldn't tell if she was playing dumb. Maybe she didn't know what she'd done was far from ordinary. Morgan wasn't stupid though.

Far from it. More likely, she did know and exposing her ability had been a slip-up.

"What's the clue for nineteen across, Morgan?"

"I don't know. You have the book."

"You don't need to see the book, though. You can visualize it without looking, can't you?" That was a nifty skill. And exactly the kind of thing her uncle would tell her to keep to herself.

She scooted to the edge of the bed and smoothed her hands down her thighs. "Visiting hours are over. Get some rest."

"Visiting hours are for visitors. You're my nurse."

"My shift's about over."

"You don't have to hide that kind of thing from me. I'd never use your secrets against you." It bothered him that she hadn't learned that. Yeah, she'd been burned, but Morgan's inability to share her whole self ran deeper. She'd probably been doing it for as long as she'd been able to talk. How did he even begin to undo that level of conditioning?

"Never say never, Brody."

32
Penny Slots
Morgan

MORGAN SWIPED ON DUSTY pink lip gloss and gave herself one last look in the hotel bathroom mirror. With her hair in a high pony—she badly needed a cut—and with her makeup heavier than she'd done it in a while, a more vibrant version of herself stared back at her. The version who'd rarely come home before the sun came up. She'd calmed down a lot since those days, but she hadn't forgotten how to doll herself up for a night out on the town.

It wasn't really a night out on the town, though. Just drinks with a friend. If she didn't get Charlie to invite her to Gill's party, she'd resort to asking him, telling him as little as possible about why she needed to go.

Curious how Brody would receive her outfit, she stepped out of the bathroom. She'd worn a sleeveless black bodysuit, a pair of army green cargo joggers, and black pointed-toe heels. It was sexy, but not too sexy for going out with a guy who might as well be her little brother.

He had his back to her, all the way across the room, facing the window, phone to his ear. "Hope, I'm cool with being a chaperone for the dance, but dress shopping? Can't you order something online? I'll give you my credit card. Buy any dress you want. Shoes, jewelry, whatever—and pay for fast shipping if you need to."

Sounded like something Logan would say. Thankfully, she'd had Lucy to take her shopping. But Hope had a mom, so why wasn't she taking her to find a dress?

None of Morgan's business. Living on the farm made it hard to keep their lives separate, but she needed to do better. Whatever his family had going on didn't concern her.

She slipped back into the bathroom and waited until he'd said goodbye to Hope before coming out.

He glanced up from his phone, then pushed away from the desk near the window he'd perched on and slipped his phone into his pocket. His gaze ran over her from head to toe, but his poker face kept her from guessing what he was thinking.

Her stomach flipped. Did he like her look or prefer her less glammed up?

Wait. She shouldn't be concerned with what he thought. Why was this so hard?

He whistled. "Damn, Cash. You clean up nice."

She suppressed a smile and rolled her eyes, then grabbed her clutch off the bed and opened it. "What are you going to do while I'm gone?"

"Get drunk and play penny slots."

She tucked her clutch under her arm while she put in one of her gold hoop earrings. "That sounds like a good time."

He walked closer, not even being subtle about checking her out. Having her appearance appreciated so blatantly should be offensive, but it wasn't. Not with Brody. Instead, it gave her a nice little self-esteem boost. Knowing he was attracted to the whole package, and not only her body helped. "After you get Chao to ask you out, ditch him and join me."

"It could take all night."

He tilted his head and gave her yet another once-over. "Not with you looking like this."

"He's not into me like that."

Brody reached behind her and gave her ponytail a tug. "I promise you, he finds you attractive."

She put the other earring in and bit back a snarky comment about banging Charlie. "Charlie has spent so much time with Logan over the years, he's practically family. And that is how I know he's had unrequited feelings for the same girl since he was sixteen."

Brody's personality made it impossible to maintain a bland business partner relationship with him. On the flight from Maryland to Las Vegas, he'd been like a kid on his way to a fun-filled vacation. His excitement turned out to be contagious. Once they'd landed, they stopped for lunch, then spent an hour in an arcade having a Skeet-Ball competition.

He'd won. He'd also insisted they redeem their tickets for surprise gifts for each other. His selection for her consisted of a mood ring, a sparkly teal bouncy ball, and a mermaid wand that blew bubbles. She gave him a mini wind-up tractor, a bath bomb—which had gotten a good laugh from him—and a little Las Vegas snow globe filled with glitter and tiny dice.

"You're trying to tell me Chao's celibate?" Brody's laugh boomed off the walls. "His unrequited love didn't seem too important to him at the last poker event I went to. Women hung off him like ornaments on a Christmas tree."

Thirsty women at poker tournaments swarmed Charlie, that was true, but he hated it. She'd never convince Brody of that, though. His arrogance annoyed her. Getting knocked down a notch or two would be good for him.

"Good," Morgan said, shooting him a saucy smile. "If Charlie's gotten over her, we can get sloppy drunk and come back to the room while you're playing slots."

His entire body tensed, and his jaw ticked. "Sure, if you're trying to get him killed."

Her thighs clenched. Heat spread up her neck. What the actual fuck? Did him threatening to murder a close friend turn her on? She needed therapy. Intense therapy. She couldn't help it though, Brody's control slipping was so hot, and pushing him to that point gave her a rush.

Morgan slapped her clutch against his chest. "You're not a killer, Brody."

He, of course, didn't budge.

He might not be a killer, but the menacing vibe he currently had going on worked for him and for a minute or two, she did not mind being the object of his possessiveness.

"Chill, okay? It'll probably take me an hour, but I can't leave right after I accept his invitation, so give me two hours. Then I'll come play slots with you."

After twisting his mouth side to side, his shoulders slumped. He plopped onto the bed, propping himself up with his elbows behind him.

"And get sloppy drunk?" He wiggled his eyebrows, back to his lighthearted self.

She glared, even though getting tipsy and hooking up with him sounded like a way better time than playing penny slots. "What happens in Vegas, stays in Vegas doesn't apply when it's your hometown, so get that out of your head right now."

"Does that mean we can't get married by an Elvis impersonator? I thought you were adventurous."

"Not *that* adventurous."

"Okay, fine, let's go to The Strat and go on the rides."

"You mean voluntarily get dropped a thousand feet?"

He grinned in that boyish way that jacked up her pulse as much as getting a dose of seething, *I'm not joking anymore* Brody.

"That's an awful idea." She grabbed the keycard off the dresser and put it in her purse. "I'm in."

33
If Morgan Wanted To...
Morgan

ON THE WAY TO the casino bar, Morgan spotted Charlie at the Blackjack tables. She hadn't seen him in almost a year. He didn't look like a teenager anymore. He didn't dress like one, either, thank god. He'd swapped his skateboarder style for a more mature look—a pair of dark designer jeans and a gray button down. His black hair hung in his eyes as he bent his head, adding freshly won chips to his stacks.

"Couldn't wait for me?" She slid onto the stool next to his.

He checked his watch, then looked back at the cards being dealt. "I've still got six minutes. This shoe is almost done."

She shifted her gaze to the table. "You've got a gambling problem, you know that?"

He grinned at her. "It's only a problem if you lose more than you win."

Cocky little shit.

A cocktail waitress came to the table and Charlie motioned to Morgan. "Put her drinks on my tab. I'll have another beer."

"Vodka martini." Morgan smiled at the waitress, then turned to Charlie. They'd mentioned playing table gambles in their text exchange. They'd also agreed to meet at the bar. "So, we're not even pretending to meet for a drink? We're diving straight into gambling?"

Charlie won on a double down. "Seems like it."

She laughed and got comfy on her stool, then took out cash to exchange for chips.

"What brings you back?" he asked. "Logan said John was in the hospital?"

"Yeah. But he's fine. I'm going back in a few days." No need to say she'd only arrived today. If he wanted to think she'd been here longer, that worked for her. "I needed to get out for a night bad. Thanks for meeting me."

"I'm only doing it out of pity," he said, deadpan.

She shoved him lightly. "Have you seen Layla lately?"

"It's been a few months. She moved again."

Poor Charlie. He really loved that girl and Morgan was pretty sure she had no idea. As soon as they'd graduated high school, she moved a few states away and ever since, she seemed to relocate every six months.

"All I ever get with her is a few hours here and there. And fuck, Morgan, my mind malfunctions when I'm around her. I'm going to make a mess out of whatever I try to say, so I say nothing."

"And do nothing." She accepted the chips the dealer slid toward her, set out a short stack for a bet, then pulled the rest in front of her. "Let your actions speak for you. *Kiss her.*"

He cleared his throat. "Can we talk about *your* love life now?"

"Nope. Don't got one."

"I don't believe you."

"Why?"

"You're all bubbly and you've got that new relationship glow." He held his hand up and did a circular motion in front of her face.

She batted his hand away. "Your Spidey senses need a tune up."

The last time he'd seen her, she'd been a mess, still nursing her wounds from her breakup with Eric. Her current mood was baseline. It'd just been a while since Charlie experienced it.

"Nah. They're sharper than ever. Maybe not a relationship, but you're crushing on someone."

She sipped the drink she'd just been served and focused on the card game.

"Uh-oh. I touched a nerve."

Yeah, he had. Because damn it, her crush on Brody needed to run its course so she could concentrate on their job. It'd fade faster than normal with them living together. Learning all his bad habits. Seeing him doing mundane tasks as he went about his day to day.

Like driving a tractor…

Splitting firewood…

Holding a baby goat…

Oh, fuck. That was not helping. She lowered her head and covered her face.

"Morgan Cash, flustered? Now, I've seen it all."

She lifted her head and took her turn, then tossed back a healthy gulp of her drink.

"Is *that* how the night is going to go? Because if we're drinking for sport, I'm switching to liquor so I can keep up with you." Charlie sucked down the rest of his beer, then dropped it into the cup holder built into the table.

"It's always such a pleasure catching up with you," she said dryly.

"This is payback for all the times you've grilled me about Layla. So, what's his name? What's his sign?"

"Hey. You got Blackjack," she said and tapped his arm.

"Why don't you want to talk about him? Doesn't he know how you feel?"

She rolled her eyes. If he kept teasing her, his balls were going to pay the price.

"Take your own advice and just kiss him."

The dealer chuckled.

She glared at him, then turned to the dumbass next to her who thought he was a comedian. "I'm not a little bitch like you. If I wanted to, I would."

"Got it. You want *him* to make the first move. It's a little old fashioned, especially for you, but I'm not judging."

"Fuck all the way off, Charlie." This kid. He'd always been snarky. But he'd leveled up.

He laughed so loud that people at the other tables looked their way.

There were very few people she'd feel comfortable walking into Alexander Gill's party with. Charlie was one of them. If all went to plan, he'd never know anything out of the ordinary happened. But…if things got hairy, he had the clout and the contacts to stop whatever Gill would do to her if he caught her.

Once Charlie had gotten his laughing fit under control, he tipped the dealer, then colored-in his chips.

Morgan did the same and dropped the handful of chips into her purse. "Now what?"

"Grab your drink. I've got an idea."

34

Taken Hostage by Evel Knievel Wannabes

Morgan

THE NOSE-BURNING STING OF burnt fuel filled the night air. With all the money Payton Jabara had pulled in from being an absolute idiot, he could have afforded landscaping. He could have easily afforded an in-ground pool with a grotto and deck made from imported Italian stone. Instead, the professional daredevil had a roughly dug pond surrounded by dirt and sand.

Morgan swore under her breath as she navigated pebbles and patches of desert grass in her four-inch heels. A motorbike zoomed by, kicking up dust.

Charlie glanced over at her and smirked without breaking stride.

"I thought you'd never top taking me to get my palm read," Morgan said. "But you've done it." Bringing her to her ex's best friend's house—or compound or whatever the hell Payton called this oasis of insanity—scored eons above going to a sham psychic who told her she'd be betrayed by someone she trusted. What a lame, generic prophecy. People suck, of course she'd be betrayed by someone she trusted. It was only a matter of time.

"You know what? Give me a list of every guy who has gotten into your pants, and next time this won't happen. But send it digitally, okay? I'm not carrying around a thirty-page document every time we hang out."

Morgan grinned and shook her head. Her list wasn't even a half-page long. No bad blood existed between her and Kade, but in addition to being her first, he'd been her palette cleanser between every loser she'd dated. Until Eric. Being all the way on the other side of the country had helped her not fall back into Kade's bed.

Spotlights suspended above the ground illuminated the pond and the water's edge where a crowd gathered, drinking and smoking and being rowdy. In the distance, suited-up figures straddled motorbikes, preparing for their turn to launch themselves up a ramp and across the water with the goal of landing safely on the other side.

A horn pierced the air, gaining everyone's attention. The first rider in line took off, speeding across the dirt and up the ramp. While airborne, his body lost contact with the bike, aside from his hands on the handlebars. He stuck the landing. Everyone cheered.

Charlie elbowed her in the side and nodded in the direction of the rider who'd taken off his helmet. "Look, it's him."

No kidding. Almost as if a neon arrow floated above her head, pointing down and blinking, Kade's gaze shifted to her. A slow smile spread across his face. He hung his helmet off of his handlebar and started toward her.

"He's coming over here," Charlie whispered.

"I can see that. Don't embarrass me. You know what? Just don't say anything. Pretend he's Layla."

Charlie gaped at her. "Nice burn."

And that's why she loved Charlie.

He approached and lifted his pierced eyebrow, asking without words what she was doing here. "Morgan," he said, and smiled in a way she'd once considered charming but now found lackluster. "I haven't seen you in forever."

"I moved to Georgia."

After removing his jacket and tossing it aside, he stretched his shoulders, drawing her attention to the ink covering his forearm. His

T-shirt was missing the sleeves, the holes cut nearly to the hem, exposing his torso and glimpses of unfamiliar tattoos. He'd always been tall and lanky with the kind of lean muscles she favored, but the pull she'd had to him before was absent. "I heard. Tell me you're moving back here." He raised his hands in front of his face and pressed his palms together.

"Just visiting." She thumbed to Charlie. "This is Charlie. Charlie, this is Kade."

They shook hands, then Kade focused back on her. "What brings you here?"

"Payton wants to talk to Charlie about collaborating on a poker run event." Until they'd stepped out of the car, she'd had no idea it was Payton's party. That's what she got for blindly following Charlie.

"What about you?" he asked. "Are you with him or did you come to see me?"

Pretending Charlie was her boyfriend crossed her mind. Without prepping him, he'd probably blow it. Instead of having Kade think she cared enough to lie, she crossed her arms and said, "Neither."

He tilted his head and rubbed his thumb across his bottom lip. "Payton is about to jump. Let's get you two a drink and watch."

Might as well. Charlie wouldn't be able to talk to Payton until after his jump, and only fools turned down free booze.

Kade led them to an enormous pole building with a big overhang that created a roof over a cement pad. Three kegs and a big trough filled with ice was exactly the kind of bar she'd expect from Payton and his gang.

She filled a plastic cup with beer and tried to give off the vibe of being engrossed in the stunts performed over the pond. No one needed to know her heart was slamming in her chest.

A year ago—hell, a couple of months ago—running into Kade would have been a happy development. Tonight, the idea of him touching her made her skin crawl. She wanted to blame her reaction on her disenchantment with men, but a little voice in the back of her mind piped up, pointing out that she didn't feel disenchanted around Brody. *He* didn't make her skin crawl.

Kade stood close and put his hand on the small of her back. His nose brushed her ear as he leaned in to whisper, "Come for a ride with me."

Kinda sad that he was still using the same line. Then again, he probably didn't need to up his game. No need to fix what worked.

She turned and leaned against a post supporting the overhang, effectively forcing him to move his hand. "This place is flush with girls who'd love to go for a ride with you."

He shoved his hands into his pockets. "Look, I've been on my bike all day. I don't really care about going for a ride. I asked because I want to spend time with *you*."

This is where she'd usually melt. Sweet words plus an adrenaline-inducing ride—after that, ending up naked together was only a matter of where and when. The sex had been decent, and their relationship was hands down her healthiest, although, the bar was so low it was underground.

Ultimately, Kade's lifestyle caused her too much stress. His frequent trips to the emergency room took their toll. Caring for other people as a nurse wasn't the same as seeing someone she cared about with horrendous injuries, especially when it happened so often.

"I don't see why we need to go anywhere." She took a sip of her beer, then glanced around, avoiding eye contact.

"Really?" he asked, like he was holding back laughter. "Morgan…"

Charlie walked over, carrying a beer. "Is that Payton?"

Sparks shot out of the ground on the side of the pond vacant of people. On the other side everyone was rowdy, enthusiastically cheering for Payton.

"Yeah," Kade said, stepping out from under the overhang.

She pulled her phone from her clutch and walked closer to record.

The stunt was nothing less than spectacular. Payton soared high through the air, backflipping while holding onto his motorbike.

When he landed, the crowd cheered, and more pyrotechnic displays lit up the night.

Morgan sent the video to Brody, then looked up from her phone in time to witness a rider fail to land his jump.

He fell into the water a split second before his bike landed on him.

"Oh, shit," Kade shouted, then ran to the pond and jumped in the water.

Several people did the same, hurrying to get to the rider who hadn't surfaced.

Panic built in her chest, expanding painfully. Should she call 911? She didn't even know the address or the man's name or age. What if she was the one with the most medical training here?

Two EMTs appeared out of thin air, it seemed. They rushed to the pond. Kade had both his arms hooked under the rider's armpits, hauling him out, then he laid on his back, panting as the EMTs took over.

A woman fell to her knees next to the injured man. Her anguished scream stole Morgan's breath. His ability to move proved him to be alive, but the damage could be extensive. The kind that meant he'd never ride again.

She pulled Charlie off to the side, away from the crowd. "Whenever one of his guys gets hurt, Payton goes to the hospital with them. I don't think you're going to get a chance to talk to him tonight."

More than ever, she didn't want to be here. Not with her past and her could-have-been future staring her in the face.

"Probably not. I'll call for a car."

While he did that, she checked her phone. No response from Brody. By the time she got back to the hotel, it'd be too late to go to The Strat. The rides would be closed. Her shoulders sank, along with her heart. She'd been looking forward to that.

"The car will be here in thirty minutes," he said.

"You just earned yourself a lifetime ban from planning our hangouts."

He ran his hand through his hair. "My bad."

She sent off another text to Brody.

> I've been kidnapped and brought to the desert to watch Evel Knievel wannabes do stunts.

An ambulance that appeared out of nowhere, much like the EMTs had, backed up to the pond. Payton took charge, ordering his guests to give them room to do their jobs.

After the man had been loaded into the ambulance and it had driven off, she checked her phone. Still no response from Brody. Was he playing slots? What if he'd gone to the bar or the table games and met a woman there?

She released a huff. If he wanted to hook up, fine by her. A relationship might not be on Mr. Honesty's radar, but who visited Vegas without it crossing their mind they could get lucky beyond gambling?

Her.

She didn't count, though. She was from here.

The idea of Brody in some woman's hotel room made her stomach knot. She checked again. Still no reply.

"Get left on read?"

Her gaze met with Charlie's. Heat flooded her face. *Busted.*

He smiled and squeezed her shoulder. "He'd have to be a fucking idiot to purposely ignore you. I'm sure he's just busy."

"It's what he's busy doing that I'm concerned about." Ugh. She couldn't believe she was opening up to Charlie like this. "Even though I've repeatedly told him that he and I would not be *getting busy.*"

"Is he a decent guy?"

She nodded. "Super decent."

"And he's told you that he's into you?"

With her lips pressed together, she nodded again.

"Then I doubt he's off fucking someone else." He flicked her forehead. "Stop being stupid."

She rubbed the spot and shot him a dirty look. He was right, though. She was being paranoid. And for no reason. Brody hooking up with a stranger was unlikely, but it wasn't her place to care.

While they waited for their ride and the crowd thinned, they sat on a boulder and drank beer, keeping to themselves. Kade looked around after the ambulance left, but Morgan stayed in the shadows, unable to afford the emotional energy it'd take to deal with his attempt at seduction.

A second after she got settled into the car Charlie had called to pick them up, her phone dinged. Her lips pulled into a smile as she read Brody's name on the screen.

> How much is the ransom?

> > They realized I'm more trouble than I'm worth, so they're letting me go.

> Their loss. My gain.

"Does that smile mean he finally replied?" Charlie asked.

"Can you stop enjoying this?"

"No." He whistled and stacked his hands behind his head, leaning against the headrest.

Her phone buzzed again.

> I'm guessing going to The Strat is out?

> > For tonight

They had two more nights before they flew back to Maryland. Maybe they could squeeze it in.

Having fun with Brody wasn't something she should be invested in right now.

She needed to secure her invitation to Gill's party. That's where her focus needed to be. "Well, that was an interesting evening. What are we doing tomorrow night?"

"I have another party to go to. I'm allowed to bring a guest."

"Whose party?" she asked.

"This guy who invested in the circuit and we're all supposed to kiss his ass or something."

"Alexander Gill? I saw where he's the producer of the televised live events now."

Once she'd discovered Charlie was on Gill's guest list, she'd wanted to know why. Charlie didn't have a ton of friends. He didn't want a ton of friends. And a slimeball like Gill was the last kind of person Charlie would choose for a friend.

"That's him."

"Bet he's got a nice house. And the food will probably be incredible. Free top-shelf drinks. I'm sure it won't be that bad."

"If you come with me, it won't be," Charlie said.

And there it was.

35
The Audit
BRODY

GLASS PRISMS TWINKLED OVERHEAD, backlit to enhance their sparkle and shine. Brody carried his beer and Lucy's cocktail from the bar to where she sat in a cozy nook outfitted with a semi-circular sofa. Behind her, string upon string of clear beads cascaded from the ceiling, curtaining the entire area, creating an opulent atmosphere.

He hadn't seen Morgan since that morning. She'd had to get a dress and her hair done and stuff. He hadn't expected it to take *that* long. Not seeing her before he left to meet Lucy bothered him, so he'd sent a text message telling her where he'd be, hoping she'd stop by for a drink before Chao picked her up for Gill's party.

He handed Lucy her drink, then took a seat next to her.

She always insisted on before-dinner drinks. They had business to discuss—his whole reason for joining Morgan on this trip—but Lucy didn't want to hear a word of it until after a drink.

"How's your dad?" She lifted her glass to her lips and sipped, her gaze locked on him. This is always how it went. She wanted to know what was going on in his life.

Lucy felt like family. They'd talked about everything there was to talk about over the years—or he'd thought they had. Until he'd found out about Morgan. "The same. No better, no worse."

"Has he met Morgan?"

"Yes, and he's enamored with her." Brody chuckled. "He told me to marry her."

Her eyebrow lifted and her lips turned up at the corners. "Are you going to take his advice?"

She must be dying to know what had taken place between them. He didn't know how much, if any, Morgan had told her. Not that there was anything to tell. But Lucy had set them up, and he had some questions about that. "Is that what you want?"

"It doesn't matter what I want. What do you want?" She tilted her head and narrowed her eyes.

He wanted Morgan. But he didn't want to admit that Lucy had been right about them having chemistry.

"I want to pull off this job." He took a long swig of his beer. Tonight was a big night. It was the first step in forming a plan to get into Gill's safe. And it was all up to Morgan. He didn't like it, but he had no way of getting into the party and wasn't stealthy enough to get surveillance photos even if he had.

"Are you sure that you can?" She set her drink on the table and pulled out a little mirror. She checked her face, rubbed her lips together, then slid it back into her purse.

"After tonight, I'll know the answer to that."

Lucy opened her mouth, then shifted her gaze beyond Brody, and shut it.

He turned to see what she was staring at.

Morgan, in a short, midnight blue dress, walked toward them. The slinky fabric glimmered beneath the lights as her body moved. Her hair brushed her shoulders, at least a foot shorter than it had been the last time he'd seen her.

"Hi," she said, looking up at him.

Shit. He'd stood without realizing it. And met her halfway across the room.

"You got your hair cut." *Great.* He'd become so mesmerized by her that he'd lost the connection between his brain and his mouth.

Her fingers connected with the ends of her hair. No wild curls tonight, but it did have waves and she'd pulled some of it into a little ponytail on top of her head, which somehow made her eyes even bigger and bluer. She didn't have much makeup on. Just a little lipstick from what he could see. Her skin looked dewy, the light catching on the angles of her face.

"It looks good. All of you does—I mean—" He squeezed his eyes shut, hoping if he stopped looking at her, his ability to not be an idiot would return. But no, it only made it easier to imagine her underneath him, looking kissable as fuck. He opened his eyes, disappointed in his lack of control over his thoughts.

Her eyes showed laughter but to her credit, she didn't outwardly laugh. "Thank you?"

Several seconds passed with his mind blank. Until tonight, he'd been able to carry a goddamn conversation with her. Now, he'd been reduced to a blubbering idiot. It wasn't only that she was all decked out. Her bright smile and the confidence she carried herself with magnified her beauty.

"Can I say hi to Lucy?" she asked.

He stepped out of her way, then stared as she walked to Lucy and took a seat. Prying his gaze away from her, he scanned the space. She had the attention of more than one person. How many men had salivated over her as she'd passed through the casino?

His chest locked up, and he joined her and Lucy, lowering himself into an armchair next to the sofa. "You're supposed to be flying under the radar."

Both women turned their heads to look at him.

Morgan wrinkled her nose. "I am."

"In that dress?" he asked.

Lucy covered her mouth, but he didn't have the wherewithal to examine why.

She glanced at her dress, then back at him. "What's wrong with it?"

"It's going to attract attention. You're supposed to blend in."

"That's why I dressed for a party at a millionaire's mansion."

Shit. She was right. And it didn't matter about the dress. Morgan would draw attention no matter what.

"I know what I'm doing, Brody."

She had enough baggage about the people close to her doubting her. He wasn't about to add to it. "I know you do."

He'd wanted Morgan to be his partner because he believed she was the best, and he still believed that. She was smart. She wasn't going to take unnecessary risks. And she had a lot more experience in playing a role to get intel than he did. He had no experience in that. He was just the engineer.

He still didn't want her to go. He wanted to say fuck it. Fuck this whole thing. No party. No heist. The only thing he cared about or wanted at this minute was right in front of him. And if he knew any other way of getting the money he needed, he'd call this whole thing off.

"Can I get you a drink?" he asked, remembering his manners.

"I need to stay sober, and I don't have time anyway." She reached across and grabbed his wrist, checking his watch. "I'm meeting Charlie in the lobby in five minutes."

"Please, be careful tonight," Lucy said, pulling her in for a hug and kiss on the cheek.

"I will." Morgan stood and faced Brody. "Walk me out?"

He followed her down the stairs to the main floor of the casino.

She looped her arm through his and tugged him to a corner filled with slot machines but devoid of gamblers. She released her hold on him, then grabbed the strap of her dress and twisted it, exposing gold fabric. "My friend who makes costumes for showgirls made this dress. It's reversible. I'm going to switch it in the bathroom before I snoop around, just in case. If I get caught on camera—not that there's any real chance of that

happening—they won't make the connection between me and the woman in the blue dress that came as Charlie Chao's guest."

"What about your hair?" A lot of women had blond hair, but not the same exact style.

"I'll pin it up."

"Thought of everything, huh?" he asked.

"I hope so."

So did he. The risk of her getting caught weighed heavier on him with each passing second.

"I'll be fine," she said, verifying his worry was written all over his face. "Have fun with Lucy and I'll be back before you know it. Maybe we'll have time for The Strat tonight."

Her attempt to soothe him tugged a smile from his lips. It didn't help *at all*, but he appreciated the effort. With more time, he had no doubt she'd successfully divert his thoughts. She was a master at that.

"I have to go," she said.

He shoved everything he wanted to say to her about being safe deep down.

They stood there, staring at each other, neither of them making a move. A simple spoken goodbye didn't feel right, yet giving her a hug didn't seem to fit the moment. He wanted to do a lot more than hug and if he touched her, he wasn't sure he'd be able to resist kissing her.

"Okay, so..." she said. "I'll see you later."

"Yeah."

She smiled, then turned and walked away.

Brody waited until she'd disappeared, then rejoined Lucy in the lounge.

"I don't think your father is the only one enamored with Morgan." Lucy used her teeth to pull an olive off the skewer that'd been in her martini.

"Nothing's happening between us." He stretched his arms across the back of his chair.

"You're not a liar, so I'm going to guess you're in denial."

"I haven't touched her," he said, forcefully this time.

"Just because you haven't acted on what's happening between you, doesn't mean nothing is happening. It's obvious to anyone with half a brain that you like her."

"Of course, I like her, Lucy." He squeezed his forehead. "You could have told me about her, introduced us in a normal fashion."

"That would have worked for you, but not for her. Morgan is determined to make her own choices—always has been."

"You think you know what's good for her, better than she does, so you trick her into it? Then, you're surprised when she feels disrespected?"

Lucy stared at her lap. "Brody, I risked damaging my relationship with my two favorite people in the world because her happiness is more important to me than my own."

It wasn't that he was ungrateful she'd arranged for them to meet, but Morgan's family's behavior toward her boggled his mind. She was by far smarter than anyone he'd ever met, crazy talented, and from what he could tell, she'd lived her life without incident, aside from one mistake. Not many people could say they'd gone through life without making a bad decision. He bet Lucy couldn't.

He played her words over in his head. "You think I can make her happy?"

"You don't?"

Before this trip to Vegas, he'd thought maybe he had a shot at it. But now, especially after seeing her tonight, he had doubts. She was so damn classy. A woman like her wouldn't be satisfied with a redneck like him. She'd never be content living on the farm long term.

"I don't know, Luce." He sighed and ran his hand through his hair. "It doesn't really matter. She's made it clear nothing can happen between us because we're working together."

"Did she have a reason for that?"

"She thinks it would put us at risk of distraction, and she's right."

"That's the stupidest thing I have ever heard." She shook her head. "Brody, if you two have feelings for each other, they're going to exist whether you act on them or not. *That's* what is going to trip you up."

He froze with his beer bottle at his lips. His stomach clenched. No. No, that couldn't be right. Although, he was having trouble discrediting it with logic. This made his *wait until after the job* plan seem foolish.

"You care about her," Lucy said. "If you're doing a job together, you're going to worry about her, and if you're worried about her, that's going to take away from your bandwidth to stay focused on getting in and out safely."

"I have to do this job, Lucy."

She stared at him for a moment before lowering her gaze. "I know."

"I won't let anything happen to her," he promised.

Her eyes closed as she inhaled deep. The exhale ruffled her bangs. "Do you know about Morgan's mother?"

36
You Do You, Baby
BRODY

BRODY STEERED CLEAR OF talking about biological parents. Morgan had never brought hers up, and he'd rather not discuss his own adoption.

He and Nick may not have started their lives with Theo and Gia Lewis, but they'd had damn good ones thanks to them. They'd kept them together, taught them solid values, and showered them with unconditional love. Whatever could have been didn't matter.

"I know that she died," he said, "but that's it."

"Cassie struggled with postpartum depression. She and John were very close, but he had no idea it was that bad."

A burning sensation settled in the back of his throat. He didn't like where this was going.

"She took her own life?" he asked, keeping the volume of his voice low.

Lucy nodded, but her gaze didn't lift to meet his. "I'd never seen that man fall apart before. Then on top of it, he suddenly was the guardian of two kids. Morgan was only three months old."

Getting blindsided with the responsibility of caring for an infant would be a lot under normal circumstances. Acclimating to it while grieving? No fucking thanks.

"That must have been a shock for both of you." He fought the temptation to ask if she and John were more than friends back then. If Lucy wouldn't talk to Morgan about it, she'd be even less willing to discuss it with him.

"It took some getting used to. Our little insta-family made it impossible to ignore all the family trauma I'd been trying to outrun when I left home at fifteen."

"You ran away?" Her home life must have been awful for her to make that choice at that age—Hope's age. He couldn't imagine his sister out there, having to survive on her own. Lucy was tough, but she shouldn't have had to be. She should have gotten to be a kid.

She swirled her last skewered olive around in her drink. "I ran from one bad situation to another, then spent an embarrassing amount of time trying to claw my way out. But I did, and I met John, and I got my life together. Or at least, I'd thought I had, until a social worker set a three-month-old baby in my arms."

"Let's go sit at the bar." Maybe something stronger to stop his mind from running in too many different directions—worrying over Morgan's safety, shoveling through the shame that popped up with talk of biological parents, and processing the helplessness from learning someone he cared about had endured so much pain.

They slid onto stools at the bar and waited for the bartender to get to them.

"You might not have been prepared," Brody said, "but you did it. You did a bang-up job of it too."

She smiled, it didn't last long. "I screwed up so many times. It never seemed to matter, though. Morgan has the most beautiful soul of anyone I've ever met. But I worried the dark parts of me would leech onto her."

He drew his eyebrows down, no clue where Lucy was going with this.

"There's no one in this world, other than Morgan, that could have gotten me to open those old wounds. Facing my trauma was as painful as experiencing it the first time. But I had her as a reminder that there is good in the world, and it got me through. She taught me what love was, just by being her little self. I'd never survive losing her, Brody." Her voice broke on the last part, and she bent her head, covering her face with her hand.

Lucy's protectiveness didn't come from doubting Morgan's capability, she was just terrified to lose the light in her life. He could relate to that. Unfortunately, this was an either/or situation. Without Morgan, it'd take several jobs and significantly longer to get a hold of the amount of money he needed to keep his own world from crumbling.

Even before this, she'd put herself in dangerous positions. He hadn't introduced her to this career choice—if it could be called that. Trying to change her mind, for no other reason than to soothe Lucy's anxiety would not go over well.

"Family is important to me too." Though he didn't think he needed to remind her. "I don't know what you want from me, Lucy. The bell has already been rung. If you'd told me everything up front, things could have panned out differently, but you didn't. So, here we are."

"I'm aware of the irony. Thank you." She flagged down the bartender and ordered two shots. "It's nothing new. She's an adult now and I've gotten used to standing by, never knowing if I'll get the worst kind of news."

He released a long exhale. "If we pull this off, I'm done. When it's over, I want her in my life. If she wants that too, I'm not going to tell her she has to keep her hands clean, but I won't ask her to do anything dangerous again. I promise."

"What if she's not interested in a life with you?" She lifted her shot glass and looked over the rim at him.

"I'm trying not to think like that." He'd failed to come up with any alternative plans. Begging her? Nah. Trying to persuade her like some pushy, skeevy creep? Not gonna happen. All he could do was cross his fingers and hope his feelings weren't one-sided. "We better get going if we're going to make our reservation."

He paid the tab and spent the next two hours in a dimly lit corner in Lucy's favorite restaurant, talking shop. If all went to plan, he'd require

mary cain

her services more than ever.

After dinner, Brody distracted himself while waiting for Morgan to get back by making calls and walking around. He resisted the urge to send a text, not wanting to distract her, but at midnight, he still hadn't heard a peep. Ten minutes after she hadn't answered his first text, he sent another. At one, he called her, listening to it ring and ring and ring.

Queasiness flooded his stomach and throat. All the holes in their plan, all the things they hadn't talked about, and all the ways she could get hurt, wove into dread. He paced the hotel room, phone in hand, calling her every fifteen minutes. Every time she didn't answer the fear in the pit of his stomach grew tighter.

Unable to stand it any longer, he pulled up a different number in his contacts, but hovered his thumb over the screen. He didn't want to worry Lucy without knowing for sure if there was anything to be worried about, but he didn't have Chao's number. The other option was Logan. Neither thrilled him. At least Lucy was here and aware of Morgan's agenda.

He tapped SEND and closed his eyes.

After the third ring, the tinkling and merriment of a party filled his ear. "Hi, Brody."

He swallowed against a dry throat. Sounded like she was having a good time, and he was about to ruin it. "It's probably nothing, but Morgan hasn't come back and she's not answering my calls or texts."

Lucy sighed into the phone. "Morgan's with me. We're at the rooftop pool and she's had a lot to drink."

"Great," Brody muttered and grabbed his wallet and keycard.

"She said she told you to meet us here."

The door slammed as he left the room. "I had no idea where she was.

I've been freaking out."

"Shit. I'm sorry. We'll sort it out when you get here. You are coming, right?"

"Yes, I'll be there in a few minutes." In the elevator, he checked his phone again to make sure he hadn't missed a call or text from Morgan. Not one.

He forced himself to slow down and think—though, the thoughts that came were far from rational. He'd never wanted to yell at anyone so bad in his life. But he also needed to see with his own eyes that she was okay.

At the doors that led to the rooftop, he paused and took a minute to get his head straight. Blowing up on her would do no good, especially if she was drunk. If he wanted to avoid an argument, he had to pull his shit together.

He walked in feeling calmer. Then he spotted Morgan.

She waded knee-deep on the pool steps of the shallow end while talking to a blond woman sitting on the edge with her legs dangling in the water.

His heart hammered. Seeing her should have brought a sense of relief. Instead, it solidified how much it would suck to never see her again.

She did a little spin and went to take a sip of her drink. Before the straw reached her mouth, her eyes lit up. "Brody! You're here." Her arms flew up, liquid swishing over the rim of her plastic cup. She teetered, lost her footing, and fell off the step, but she managed to stand before going all the way under. Her hair stayed dry except for the ends. The same couldn't be said for her dress.

"Oh, shit," the woman she'd been talking with said. "Are you okay?"

Morgan held up her cup. "I saved my drink."

Brody walked to the edge of the pool and squatted. He shook his head. "Cash, what am I going to do with you?"

Not stay mad at her, that's what. Christ on a cracker, he was defenseless against her when she'd had a couple of drinks. Her getting all smiley and playful was potent.

She prowled up the steps until she was within reach. The sultry licking of her lips didn't help his effort to ward off an erection. "I could provide suggestions, but I'm going to be disappointed if you need them."

He lowered his gaze to where her dress clung to her chest. "Don't worry, my imagination is working fine thanks to this wet dress."

A wicked grin formed on her face. Slowly, she crept up the pool steps. When her intention became clear, he debated on whether to stay dry or let her plaster her body against his.

"Don't." He stood and held up his hand. Staying dry won out, not because getting wet bothered him, but because he'd used all his willpower by not grabbing her when she got close. Full-body contact with her would break him.

She batted her eyelashes. "Don't what?"

Tossing her into the deep end tempted him, but he didn't know how strong of a swimmer she was, or if he was up for starting a war. "If you get me wet, there'll be consequences."

"That's what she said."

Brody pressed his lips together to contain his laugh. Damn it. He shouldn't be so amused by her after what she'd put him through tonight.

"Morgan Cash," Lucy said from behind them, where she rested on a lounge chair, "behave."

"I'm not sure that's a skill she possesses," the woman who'd been sitting on the side of the pool said. She'd moved to stand next to a man sitting on a patio chair next to Lucy's.

"You're one to talk, Kins." Morgan stumbled to a lounge chair and plopped onto it. "By the way, this is Kinsley, and her friend, Easton."

Kinsley looked to be about Morgan's age and Easton was older, but not much. Their clothes screamed money, her in a short black dress that fit like it had been made for her, and him in a dress shirt, slacks, and an expensive watch.

"Kinsley is Lucy's niece." Morgan put effort into making that lie believable, but he saw through it. He couldn't guess her motivation, but right now, he didn't give a shit. "Kinsley, this is my…my…Brody."

He raised an eyebrow. Unexpected, but he didn't hate the label.

Kinsley laughed. "Your Brody?"

"No, I mean, his name is Brody, he's my…um…" She glanced at him. "Are you going to help me out?"

He sat on the chair next to hers, folded his arms, and crossed one ankle over the other. "Nah. I want to see where this is going." She could have called them business partners, but she didn't, so she must have a reason for making up a story about their relationship.

The look she shot him could have burned a hole right through him. "Brody's my patient. I'm his caregiver. No need for concern, though. There's nothing wrong with him physically, it's purely mental. He looks like a capable adult, but the truth is, there's a lot he needs help with."

"Nice," Brody muttered.

"Where have you been?" she asked him after downing the rest of her drink. "Did you get lost? I told you riding the elevator by yourself was more than you could handle. All those buttons must have been overwhelming."

He sighed heavily. "I spent the past few hours pacing the floor, worried about you."

Her forehead wrinkled and she pouted. "Why?"

"Because I couldn't reach you."

"I texted you to meet us here."

His frustration bubbled, the tension from earlier returning to his body. "You must have sent it to the wrong person."

"Where's my bag?" Morgan grabbed the purse from Lucy's outstretched hand and rifled through it. Her phone lit up in her palm. "Oops." She turned the phone so he could see it. "I didn't hit send."

He glanced at the screen, then her face. He couldn't care less about a stupid text she'd failed to send. "I called you ten times. I sent you message after message."

"I forgot to take my phone off silent after I left the party."

"You never checked it that entire time?"

"That might be my fault," Kinsley said. "It's been a few years since I last saw Morgan, and I had a lot to fill her in on. It was also my idea to put our feet in the pool, and you know, phones and water aren't the best of friends."

Chicks before dicks, apparently. Maybe Kinsley was lying through her teeth to protect her. Maybe it was the truth, and she was only sticking up for her. Either way, Brody liked that Morgan had a friend who would do that.

"You should have checked in with me when you left the party."

Morgan flopped back on her lounge. "You didn't answer my text right away the other night. I didn't blow a gasket over it."

He cut his gaze to Lucy and gave her a *please tell me I heard her wrong* scowl. This was payback? "I didn't hear from you for five fucking hours, despite calling you repeatedly. That's not the same as me taking thirty minutes to text you back."

She groaned. "I meant to text you but didn't send it."

"I do that all the time," Kinsley said, nodding.

"See?" Morgan did an exaggerated presentation gesture at Kinsley without moving from her laid out position, then changed her aim and pointed at the colored lights strung around the patio. "Look at those little halos around the lights. So pretty."

He didn't see any halos. "Did you take something at the party?"

"Like drugs?" she asked.

"Yeah, like drugs."

"No." She ran her hands over the wet fabric covering her hips. "I took drugs after the party. Kinsley gave them to me."

"And you can't understand why I worry about you," Lucy muttered under her breath.

"You're such a narc," Kinsley said at a high pitch. "For the record, it was only a small dose of mushrooms, and Easton is my plug, so go after him."

"Who's the narc now?" Easton slung his arm around her waist and pulled her closer.

"Plug?" Lucy asked.

Kinsley turned to her. "It's slang for drug dealer."

"I'm not a drug dealer," Easton said. "But it's Vegas. We're here to have fun, right?"

They might be, but Brody and Morgan were here to work. He didn't even know if she'd been successful on her mission. He couldn't ask in front of everyone.

She deserved to blow off steam, though. Expecting her to come to her hometown and not see friends would be a dick move. Whatever she wanted to do with her spare time was her business. But it felt really shitty to get left out when he wanted to be in on her shenanigans.

She turned to Brody and wrinkled her nose. "Don't be all judgy pants."

"I don't give a shit that you're high, Morgan." He shrugged. "Probably wasn't the best idea to wash the shrooms down with vodka, but you do you, baby."

"It was rum, not vodka," she shot back.

He cracked a smile. It took serious skill to be a goddamn smartass while high *and* drunk.

Lucy stopped in front of Morgan's chair, a pair of sparkly high heels dangling from her fingers. She slid the shoes onto Morgan's feet, then grabbed both her hands and pulled. "Come on, I'll help you get back to your room."

Morgan dug her fancy heels into the patio and pulled her hands from Lucy's. "I'm hanging out with Kinsley."

"Actually," Easton said. "Kinsley needs to be taken back to her room, as well."

Kinsley's mouth dropped open. "Why? I've barely got a buzz."

Easton wrapped his arm around her waist and stared up at her from his chair. "I'd like to go back while you're still sober enough to make decisions."

Understanding dawned on her face. She went to Morgan and gave her an awkward semi-contactless hug to avoid getting wet. "It was so good to see you. Call me next week and let's catch up some more. Maybe we can get together again soon."

"No," Morgan whined as Kinsley returned to Easton's side. "Going back to the room is boring."

Brody moved close to Morgan, then whispered, "Something tells me they're not going to be bored."

She turned, the playfulness in her expression replaced by parted lips and curiosity shining in those blue eyes. Giving her an opportunity to make a comment would be a mistake.

"You will be, though." He winked at her, then grabbed her by her shoulders, turned her, and patted her ass. "Get moving."

She looked over her shoulder at him with raised eyebrows. "Did you just—"

"Party's over, kids," Lucy said and clapped her hands. "Kinsley, it was great to see you. Easton, lovely to meet you." She gave quick hugs, then linked her arm through Morgan's, tugging her toward the doors.

Morgan pulled away. "I can walk on my own just fine."

Three steps later, that proved to be blatantly false. One of her heels wobbled and her leg buckled.

Brody leapt forward. He grabbed her elbow and hip, steadying her.

Once she'd regained balance, she pushed away. "I'm good. I've got this."

"You definitely don't got it, Morgan." Lucy's voice was a blend of exasperated mother and amused, cool aunt.

"Might help if you take off your heels of death," Brody said.

"And walk on casino carpet barefoot?" She shook her head. "Gross."

"I'll carry you."

"Even grosser." Her grin stretched wide. "Just kidding. But it is unnecessary." With that, she took off on unsteady legs, swaying and holding her arms out like she was on a tight rope.

Brody looked at Lucy. "It's like trying to reason with a brick wall."

She patted him on the back. "I know."

They caught up with her and got her onto the elevator.

"How come you didn't tell your friend we're partners?" Brody asked Morgan.

"Because she was protecting you," Lucy answered for her.

She rolled her eyes and leaned into the corner of the elevator car.

"From what?"

"Probably nothing. Being tightlipped is her love language, just like it's John's. It'll feel like she's ashamed of you, but it's how you know you're important to her."

"That's not it," Morgan said and sighed. "You're my partner. Giving you up is giving me up. Kins is cool, but I don't know that guy she's with. I don't take chances with that stuff."

The elevator opened and she strode off.

Brody let Lucy exit ahead of him, then followed.

Several feet ahead, Morgan wobbled on her heels, then started to go down, but caught herself by placing a hand against the wall.

"I've seen enough." He scooped her up and threw her over his shoulder, wincing from the wetness penetrating his shirt.

"Brody," Morgan shrieked. "Put me down."

He turned to Lucy. "I've got it from here."

"Are you sure?" she asked in a voice that said she had zero confidence in him.

"She's half my size. I'm pretty sure I can handle her."

Lucy patted his cheek. "So pretty, but so naïve."

"Hello," Morgan said. "Can you put me down now?"

"No." Brody lifted his chin at Lucy. "I'll check in with you tomorrow."

Once he'd gotten the door unlocked and carried her into the room, Brody set Morgan on her feet in front of him. He'd have tossed her on the bed, but she was wet.

She trailed her hands up his chest and around his neck, then blinked up at him, her eyes bright and blue.

He circled her wrists and with them held in front of her, backed her up against the wall, then pinned them above her head. Keeping his head straight would be a lost cause if she kept touching him. The smell of chlorine clung to her, which wasn't a scent that he'd found pleasant in the past, but it came with the skimpy, soaking-wet dress package, and he was a big fan of that.

"How'd things go tonight at Gill's?" he asked, cutting that line of thinking off before he reached self-inflicted misery status.

Her body bowed away from the wall, but her attempt to free herself lacked oomph. And yet, the smirk she delivered was pure cockiness. "Perfect. I took photos of everything you asked for, and even some video."

It'd have been nice to know that hours ago. This couldn't happen in the future. Weak communication would get them in trouble. "We need to come to an understanding."

"That sounds nice." Her gaze landed on his mouth.

He groaned. She probably wasn't going to remember this, but he was going to say it anyway, because if he didn't get it out, it'd eat at him all night.

"From now on, if you're doing something dangerous, you will check in with me at regular intervals, and when you're done, you're going to let me know you're safe immediately, so I can breathe again." He'd have to edit that before he sprung it on her sober. Tone it down a little. Okay, a lot.

"Oh…Bossy Brody is back. I like him." In that raspy tone, she might as well have whispered in his ear and grabbed his dick.

"Bossy Brody?"

Her cheeks turned pink, and she tried to yank her wrists free, but he held tight. "Don't make a big deal out of it."

Oh, he was going to. She couldn't assign him an alter ego and expect him not to have questions. "Thought you hated being told what to do. Doesn't apply *all* the time, though, does it?"

"Apparently not." She sagged against the wall. "I guess that old saying, 'don't knock it 'til you've tried it' was right."

"Oh, it's news to you too, huh?" *Interesting.* He needed to investigate this further. For science.

Her lips drew into a pout. She nodded.

He loved how the booze washed away her posturing, leaving the flirtatious, agreeable, sweet side of her that she didn't want him to know existed, but her reaction to him immobilizing her and being stern left him flummoxed. If she really wanted him to he'd let her go but any protests she'd made had been halfhearted. And she hadn't kneed him, so that was a plus.

"It's only hot because you're not like that the rest of the time," she said, staring at his chest.

"So, I'm not hot when I'm not being bossy?"

She darted her gaze to his. "Regular Brody is hot too."

"Regular Brody?" His lips twitched. What did that even mean?

"Yeah. I kinda like him too." She held his gaze, so serious.

"Why do you do this to me?" he asked, even though he didn't want an answer. They couldn't talk about any of this until she'd sobered up. Even then, he didn't know how to approach it. Slowly, probably.

"I don't know what you're talking about," she said. "I'm not doing anything."

"That's the problem. You scramble my brain without even trying." He closed his eyes and breathed deep before opening them again. "I'm not going to touch you while you're drunk, so, *maybe* you could be a good girl and stop fucking with me."

Her eyes rounded, and her chest rose. "You want me to be a good girl?"

Ah, fuck. He needed to put her to bed before he lost his damn mind. He let go and moved what he hoped was an adequate amount of space away from her. "Think you can get out of that wet dress on your own without hurting yourself?"

"Let's find out." She walked into the room, grabbed the edge of her dress, and pulled it over her head. The wet fabric made a *plop* on the carpet when she dropped it, leaving her in a thong, shoes, and nothing else.

This was not being a good girl. "Holy fuck, Morgan."

Letting the image of her perky tits get burned into his brain was a terrible idea, but he couldn't look away.

"Are you super impressed that I didn't hurt myself?"

He forced his gaze to meet her eyes and stay there. Only there. "You can't take three steps without face planting. I don't think it's out of line to assume you might need help."

She turned to her suitcase and flipped it open. After rummaging through it, she grabbed a couple pieces of fabric. "I'm going to take a shower. Do you want to help me in there too?"

"No," he croaked.

"Mmm. Didn't think so." She brushed by, clutching her clothes against her chest, and he couldn't stop himself from turning to get a look at her ass.

"Don't lock the door," he called out as she disappeared into the bathroom and his brain resumed function. Breaking it down because she'd fallen or passed out would be the cherry on top of it all.

She ducked her head back out and tossed him a smile that sent a streak of heat down his spine. "I won't even close it."

He gritted his teeth and walked to the desk to empty his pockets. This was hell. For sure. At some point in his life, he'd unknowingly done something reprehensible, and this was the style of torture designed to drive him fucking mad for all eternity.

While she showered, he hung his damp shirt and her wet dress in the closet, keeping his back to the open bathroom door. That glass panel on the shower deflected water. It did nothing to conceal a woman's naked, wet, tantalizing body.

Not closing the door was her way of toying with him and honestly, he'd asked for it. Patting her ass. Carrying her to the room. Telling her to be a good girl. Challenging her ability to undress. Anything that got in the way of her autonomy set her off. His attraction to her was a powerful tool for revenge.

He stretched out on his bed and put massive effort into not thinking about her naked body with soap suds running down it. Despite his trying, he failed.

The shower stopped running. He adjusted himself, hoping she didn't notice his hard-on when she came out. As an excuse to avert his gaze, he picked up his phone and checked his e-mail. More visual stimulation would be his undoing.

Her exit from the bathroom was a lot less wrecking ball than he'd expected—no falling, no knocking things over. His screen went dark, but he continued to stare at it, tracking her movement with his peripheral vision.

She crawled onto her bed and sat in the center.

He pushed up from his bed and went to brush his teeth and talk his dick down. The steamed-up mirror and shower glass only made the images of her wet body more vivid. Her scent filled the bathroom, also not helping his predicament.

After he'd gotten control of his mouth and dick, he came back out and kept his eyes to himself. He sat on the bed and picked his phone up and swiped, opening his crossword puzzle app. Not the same as doing it on paper, but desperate times and what not. He could feel her stare on him, making it even more of a challenge to keep from looking at her.

Second after second passed with her staring at him and him staring at his phone.

The silence stretched so long that he caved and glanced over.

She had on a dayglow green T-shirt, and presumably panties, but he couldn't tell. A frown put a damper on her formerly exuberant face.

"What's up?" he asked.

"Nothing." The word held an unmistakable note of umbrage. She pulled back the covers and crawled closer to the pillows.

He put his phone on the nightstand and swung his legs over the side, facing her. "What happened to the sassy-mouthed girl who flashed me?"

It was like that part of her personality had been powered off.

She shrugged, then laid her head on her pillow. "She won't bother you anymore."

"Morgan, I've never once felt annoyed by you."

"Okay."

He gripped the edge of the mattress until his knuckles throbbed. "You don't believe me?"

"You're too polite to admit you've had enough of me."

Enough? That wasn't even close to true. He wanted more of her. So much more. "What did I do to make you feel that way?"

She snuggled in, pulling the covers to her chin and closing her eyes. "Did you forget that I'm really good at reading people?"

"If you think I'm tired of you, then you're not as good as you think."

That got her attention. Her eyes snapped open, and she sat up. "Yes, I am."

He crossed his arms. "Prove it."

She blinked.

"Let's hear it. What evidence do you have to support your theory?"

"Your attitude changed. Ever since I came out of the bathroom, you've given me the cold shoulder."

He laughed, then released a breath. "I was avoiding looking at you because seeing you naked got me all worked up, and I didn't need any more provocation. What else you got?"

"Just let it go. I know I'm a handful. Exhausting. Hard to love." She laid down and switched the light off.

Brody reached over and switched it on. "You are none of those things, Morgan." Especially the last one, but he'd need to unpack that on his own.

She huffed, threw back the covers, and grabbed a bottle of water from the mini-fridge. "You're right. I'm drunk and being stupid." She uncapped the bottle and took a long drink.

He angled his head. "I don't understand what's going on right now."

She strolled closer to the balcony, running her fingers over the arm of the sofa. "Neither do I. Don't waste your time trying to make sense of me, Brody."

37
Tonight Was Not Cute
Morgan

LIFE WAS SUCH A bitch. Whenever Morgan started to feel like the past was in the past, she got shown in the most emotionally crippling ways that the remnants of her personal history would forever stalk her.

Her ex had left his mark. No matter how hard she tried, she couldn't undo how his abuse had reshaped her mind. He'd get off on knowing that he still took up space in her brain. That his programming seeped into everything good that came into her life.

Like Brody.

Tonight was proof she was permanently damaged. Accusing him of giving her the silent treatment?

He'd never do that. Even if he was sick of her.

Her chest squeezed.

It was all in her head. Her fucked up, always-ruin-everything head.

Brody grabbed a T-shirt from his bag and put it on.

She'd miss his abs and pecs, but it was for the best.

"Still high?" he asked.

"A little. I only took enough to relax me and make things look extra pretty."

"Come here." He walked to the balcony and slid the door open.

"Why?"

"I bet the fountains look extra, extra pretty."

"Aren't you sober?" Maybe he'd had a few drinks, but she didn't think he'd taken psychedelics. Did he even do that kind of thing? He seemed cool enough about her doing them.

"That doesn't mean I can't enjoy the best view in Las Vegas." He crooked his finger. "C'mon."

She stayed put, although she almost instinctively complied. If he said "good girl" again, she'd have to change her panties. The timbre in his voice when he'd said it tied her in knots. She didn't even think he'd meant to say it *like that*.

He dipped his chin and gave her a look that said he intended to get his way. "Does bossy Brody need to come out?"

A burning blush spread across her face. Her and her stupid mouth. Rum always dismantled her filter. "Oh, my god. Can you please forget about that?"

He grinned wide while slowly shaking his head. "Never."

On her way past him to the sliding door, she elbowed him in his stomach, but it hurt her elbow more than it probably did his solid abs.

The colors of the cityscape appeared more vivid, and the rhythm of the fountains captivated her. A breeze cooled her face as she leaned out, looking over the strip. This was so much better than lying in bed overanalyzing.

Brody placed his forearms on the railing, bending, bringing himself closer to her eye level. His stare was far from subtle.

She swiveled her head in his direction. "Yes?"

"I don't know. I like looking at you." He shrugged and grinned. "I like being around you too, in case you didn't pick up on that."

To keep her smile under wraps, she bit into her lip and looked at the boulevard. "Even when I'm a drunken mess?"

"I've never seen you be a drunken mess, so, I wouldn't know." He bumped her shoulder. "But I do think you're cute when you've had a few."

"Tonight was not cute."

"You taking off your dress? I agree, cute is not the word to describe it."

Take rum and add a splash of Brody questioning her competence, and of course, her dress was coming off. Her particular brand of spunk had irritated her ex. If she'd behaved the way she did tonight around Eric, there would have been consequences. Hanging out with Kinsley, getting wet in the pool, taking mushrooms—any fun she had was guaranteed to set him off.

She stepped back from the railing. "If you could never bring that up again, that'd be great."

He chuckled. "Fine. I won't mention it again. But I'm not promising I won't think about it. Often."

A mind-erasing device would be clutch right now. Maybe she could even use it on herself to undo the damage Eric had done with his cruelty.

Brody moved to the cushioned patio sofa, propped his feet up on the ottoman, laid one arm on the armrest, and stretched the other across the back.

"Sorry for ruining your night," she whispered, staring at her electric-blue-painted toes. The night wasn't the only thing she worried she'd ruined. Their relationship was hard to define, but she liked spending time with him too. The possibility of her craziness alienating him made her eyes water.

"Cash…" He dragged out the name and patted the cushion next to him. "The only thing that upset me was not knowing if you were okay. I'm glad you got to see an old friend and have fun."

All she could do was stand there and blink. *Worried about her? Glad she'd had fun with a friend?* Her gut told her it was a trap and to proceed with the utmost caution.

Brody's eyebrows pressed closer together. "Did I say something wrong?"

"You shouldn't have had to take care of me."

"Sit the fuck down." He waited until she'd followed his order. "I didn't take care of you. Mostly because you refused help, but if someone is going to look after you, I want it to be me."

She opened her mouth, then shut it. Outside of her family, she wasn't used to anyone caring about her that much. "I'd hoped to celebrate with you tonight."

"All you had to do was ask. Or"—he cleared his throat—"check your phone."

She turned toward him and pulled her knees to her chest, her bare feet on the cushion between them. "I was avoiding my phone."

"Why?"

"Last night, I kept checking to see if you'd answered my text, thinking really stupid things, and I told myself I wasn't going to put myself through that again, so I looked for ways to distract myself—Kinsley, booze, drugs—I guess it worked because I had no idea how late it had gotten when you finally showed."

"I'd have come if I'd gotten your message."

"I know, and I should have realized that you would let me know if you couldn't. Just like I should have realized that you not answering my text right away last night wasn't to mess with my head, and just like I should have realized you weren't ignoring me as punishment."

Spilling her guts actually made it feel like her insides were churning.

"Ignoring you *as punishment*?" He jammed his hand through his hair. "I wouldn't do that."

"I know, Brody. *I know*. Or I should. My brain does. Until it doesn't." And that was a big problem. Getting blindsided by an uncontrollable trauma response sucked.

"He did that you?" His tone sent a chill down her spine. "Ignored you to punish you?"

No need to verbalize who *he* was. Brody knew enough to make the connection.

"What," he said slowly, his jaw stiff, "did he punish you for?"

"Being me." Telling him this, especially since he was trying so hard to keep his cool, might not be the best idea. He wasn't going to drop it, though. "If we were around other people and I did a card trick, or even if someone asked where I was from and took interest in me growing up here, I'd get the cold shoulder. For hours. Days. He'd never say exactly how I pissed him off, so I had to figure it out by trial and error. Eventually, I realized he hated everything about me."

"He sounds insecure as fuck."

She shrugged. "I stopped trying to figure out why he did the things he did to me a long time ago because I realized there's no reason that will make me feel better about it or make me any less broken."

He grabbed her ankle and tugged, pulling her across the cushion until her ass hit his outer thigh.

"Brody!" She pushed up onto her elbows to keep from being flat on her back.

He draped her legs across his lap. Then he turned to her, as if nothing out of the ordinary had happened. "You're not broken. You had your head fucked with. That's reversible."

"You're dropping a lot of F-bombs."

"Well, I fuckin' like bombs. And I *don't* like what he did to you."

She leaned into the back of the couch, putting her head on the cushion. A headache was beginning to replace her buzz. "You're wrong. It's not reversible."

"I don't believe that."

"You don't want to believe it. That's not the same."

He slid his hand from her ankle to her knee, then up her inner thigh, but stopped before halfway. His big palm warmed her skin while he rubbed in lazy circles with his thumb.

Morgan drew in a shaky breath. Holy hell. How did this feel ten times more erotic than anything she'd ever experienced?

His gaze wandered up her body, settling on her face. "Give me a chance to prove you wrong."

She wanted that. She wanted him to be able to fix it, because she sure as hell hadn't been able to do it herself. But she knew better. There was a greater chance that she'd drag Brody down with her. "What if instead of you fixing me, I break you?"

"You won't."

"I'm really good at ruining things."

"You've already ruined me. No one is ever going to compare to you."

She brushed water from her eye with her knuckle. "That's easy to say now. Wait until I show my crazy."

"I can handle it."

Silence stretched between them, the many sounds of Vegas at night replacing their words. Could he? For the most part, Brody came off as unshakeable. Keeping his cool didn't mean her nonsense wouldn't affect his feelings for her, though.

"Does Lucy know what you went through?" he finally said, but his voice didn't sound right.

She scoffed. "Why would I break her heart like that?"

"I think you should talk to her."

"Why?"

"I want you to feel like you can talk to me about anything, but with this, I think she can help you better than I can."

38
Chameleon
BRODY

SUNLIGHT SNEAKING IN THROUGH a spot where the window blinds didn't quite meet stabbed Brody in the eye. He almost groaned but didn't want to wake Morgan. Brunch with her uncle was today. Sleeping in after the night she'd had would do her good.

He rolled over and looked at her bed. Her perfectly made bed.

The ache of panic hurt his chest. He reached for his phone on the nightstand. His fingers brushed stiff paper. He flipped on the light. The paper was a piece of a tourist pamphlet, about four inches long, and folded in half like a place card.

Check your messages.

That's all it said. He snatched up his phone and woke it up. Nine already? One text message waited from Morgan, but instead of text, it was a link.

He clicked it and his map app popped open. Two seconds later, a little cartoon woman with blond hair appeared with an arrow below her, indicating her location on the map.

It showed her in the hotel, but not exactly where. He switched to his messaging app, but before he could type anything, the door opened.

Morgan walked in, her body silhouetted by the light from the hall for a moment before the door swung shut. "Hey."

"Hey."

She moved through the dark room and set something on the nightstand. The aroma of coffee hit his nose at the same time his eyes adjusted and recognized a drink carrier with two coffee cups in it.

A beautiful woman delivering him coffee in bed? No—*this* beautiful woman bringing him coffee in bed? Yeah, he could get used to that.

Too bad when they got back to the farm, his routine would return to starting his day long before she started hers. Maybe she'd be in his bed when he left it. Last night, they'd left things undefined. He wouldn't have held her to anything she'd agreed to while not one hundred percent sober, but until he had a better understanding of where he stood with her, he'd be antsy.

"Just wake up?" She walked to the balcony and pulled back the blinds.

How long had *she* been up? That was the question. She looked like a goddamn royal about to visit an underprivileged school for a photo op. Rays of sun haloed her figure. Her cream-colored, ass-and-hip hugging skirt ended just past her knees. Her black sleeveless blouse was tucked into the skirt and topped off with a wide tan belt. The crowning touch was a tan felt hat with a brim all the way around. She'd even accessorized with jewelry—a wide gold bangle and hoop earrings.

"Yeah." He sat up. "How long have you been awake?"

"About an hour and a half." She came back around the bed and handed him one of the coffee cups, then took the other for herself.

"I didn't hear you."

"You didn't hear me when I broke into your house, either." She smirked and took a sip of her coffee.

He grinned. "That's not true. The first time, I heard you coming up the stairs."

She shrugged, then sat on the edge of her bed. "I still got into the house without you knowing. Both times."

"You're a badass, Morgan. Is that what you need to hear?"

She nodded vigorously. "Thank you for acknowledging that."

He took a long minute to appreciate the classy, sexy thing she had going on while she looked at her phone, swiping.

Her gaze flicked up. "What?"

"You look nice."

"What's that tone for?"

Pretending he didn't know he'd used any tone would be pointless. The constant alteration of her appearance amused him. "You haven't looked the same twice since we got here."

"It's just clothes and makeup. Chill."

"I've never seen anyone transform themselves into someone new every day, so, no, it's not nothing."

She dressed how she wanted to be seen, and that varied based on who would be seeing her.

"What's your point?"

"You're like a chameleon. It's hot."

"You're into lizards. Got it." She glanced back at her phone like a bored teenager trying to ignore an adult attempting small talk.

Brody chuckled. "We both know I'm into *you*."

She tossed her phone on the bed and put both hands around her coffee cup. "Did you get my message?"

"You're sharing your location with me?" He didn't know how to take that. Giving up that level of privacy went against everything she'd been taught.

"Look, I'm not saying stalk me. It's in case of an emergency. You're not going to need it when we get back to the farm. Unless you want to track me while I'm running. That might not be the worst thing. If I break my ankle or get thrown into the back of a van, you'll be able to find me."

He closed his eyes and shook his head. "I didn't worry about you running before, but I'm going to now."

"That's why I shared my location. If you're ever worried, you'll be able to find out where I am."

"Not if you don't have your phone with you."

"I'm not getting microchipped. This will have to suffice."

He laughed. "What do you remember from last night?"

"I remember you pinning me against the wall." Morgan peeked up from staring at the lid of her cup, a blush dotting her cheeks.

He winced. "Not my finest moment."

"Not your worst, either."

He flexed his hands. They itched to grab her and push her up against that same wall. But this time he didn't plan on talking. "Is that all you remember?"

"No. I remember all of it, including our conversation on the balcony." She set her coffee on the nightstand and paced in front of the beds, tapping the tips of her fingers together in front of her stomach. "Could we put a pin in this until after brunch?"

That's not what he wanted to do. Brody pulled pins. Putting them back in was not his style. He wanted to kiss her. A lot. But what was he going to say? No? Insist they talk about it right this minute?

"We can, but it'd be nice to know why." He grabbed his pants off the end of the bed and pulled them on.

"Because this brunch is giving me anxiety and I can't think about anything else right now."

"You're anxious about having brunch with your uncle? Why?"

"I need him to like you. I'm not nervous about that part, because I know he will, but I'm worried that it's not going to have the effect I want, and then I don't know what I'm going to do."

"Okay," he said calmly, moving to block her, stopping her pacing. "What effect do you want it to have?"

She stared up at him. "I want him to forgive Lucy."

"Baby." He shook his head. "Let them work it out on their own."

"Neither of them is even trying," she whined. If she'd stomped her foot, it wouldn't have surprised him.

"You don't like when they meddle in your life."

"That's true, but right now I don't need you to be the voice of reason." She came at him with pity-me eyes that knocked him off center. "Help me plot to push them back together. You're my partner in crime, literally. You're obligated."

The death grip she had on his critical thinking skills both impressed and embarrassed him. In his entire life, he'd never been able to say he'd follow anyone off a bridge. Until now. "How is your uncle meeting me supposed to get him to forgive her?"

"That's why I'm freaking out. Benny sorta gave me the idea, and it seemed like a good one until this morning. Now, it seems flimsy."

"What's the idea?" If it came from Benny's mind, it was either brilliant or stupid as hell. No in between.

"For him to meet you and get to know you."

"And?"

Her cringe exposed her lack of confidence in her half-baked plan more than her words ever could. "That's it. I told you it was flimsy."

"I don't get it."

"If he meets you, maybe he'll see that Lucy didn't make a mistake."

"No?" His curiosity over how Lucy had concluded that he and Morgan would be a good fit lingered. Replaying all the time he'd spent with Lucy, looking for that one moment when she'd decided he, of all people, was so compatible with Morgan that she'd risk alienating her best friend, hadn't gotten him any closer to an answer.

She shook her head. "You can be trusted. Obviously. I gave you my freaking location."

"But Lucy was trying to set us up. Are you saying she was right about that too?" The need for some type of validation to get him through until after brunch plagued him. She'd let him get away with calling her baby, but it wasn't the first time. And it wasn't enough.

"It's one thing to get him to like you if he thinks we're partners. It's another to get him to like you if he thinks we're together. That's why I want to put a pin in it until after we see him. Then if he asks if anything is going on, you can say no without having to lie."

"Your mind is a strange place, isn't it?" He grinned because he liked it. Watching those wheels turn, knowing she was going to come at him with an off-the-wall scheme, was fascinating. The way she mesmerized him, he'd probably go along with every one of her bad ideas.

She glared at him. "Are you going to help me or not?"

"For the record, I think you should stay out of it, but yes. If you wanna go setting shit on fire, I'll grab the matches and gasoline."

39
The Pin
Morgan

MORGAN DIDN'T KNOW WHAT to do with herself while Brody took a shower. She tried relaxing on the balcony, but relaxation was so far outside of her grasp it was pointless. It took all of twenty seconds to tidy up the room.

She picked up her coffee cup. It was almost empty. Brody had barely touched his. It was still warm.

The sound of running water stopped. Shortly after that, the door to the bathroom opened. Steam drifted out.

She waited, but when he still hadn't come out after a minute, she scooped up his coffee and walked to the bathroom. Cautiously, she peeked inside.

Brody stood in front of the mirror with a towel wrapped around his hips. His eyes caught hers in the reflection. He paused from rubbing shaving cream on his face.

She didn't mean to stare, but damn. All that farm work did *not* hurt his physique. Her heart banged around in her chest. At some point, she was going to have sex with him. Probably. Most likely. She was going to feel that body against hers, be able to touch it.

Wanting something while simultaneously being scared out of her mind to experience it was a new level of mind fuckery. She'd never had nerves like this over the possibility of sex.

She'd been awkwardly lurking in the doorway, taking inventory of the ridges and valleys of his muscles for too long. She moved inside and set his cup on the sink. "I'm going to go get more coffee."

"You can have mine." He finished smearing the shaving cream evenly across his face, then rinsed his hands, and picked up his razor.

The offer sent warm, tingly feelings through her. Giving her his coffee out of sheer kindness was a small gesture, but it felt big. "I wasn't so much going for the coffee as I was to burn off this nervous energy."

"I'll be ready in a couple minutes. We can walk to the restaurant if you want."

She moved his coffee out of the way and hopped up onto the counter.

He turned to her with his eyebrows raised.

"Do you want me to get out?" she asked, suddenly aware that she shouldn't feel so comfortable hanging out in the bathroom with him while he only had on a towel. Yes, she'd seen him naked but…that was *before*.

He focused back on his reflection and ran the razor down his cheek. "Stay. Let's talk about your parent trap. How am I supposed to act around John?"

"Parent trap? Really?" That made it sound juvenile. Maybe it was. Oh well. She wasn't giving up on them working their shit out. They needed to get it together, so they could all go on being their eccentric little family.

He smirked into the mirror. "That's not what this is?"

She ran her finger around the outer rim of his coffee cup lid. "Stop making fun of me. I feel like it's my fault, and when I'm not around, I want to know that they're looking out for each other. I don't care if it's as friends, or if it's more. I just want them back how they were."

"Fine. I'll stop teasing you. I'm down to help, but I don't know what you want me to do."

"You don't need to do anything. Just be yourself."

He shook his head. "That's not a plan."

She groaned. "Yes, it is, there's just no deception involved. I'm trying to put his mind at ease that Lucy didn't throw me into the clutches of a monster."

Finished with one side of his face, Brody rinsed his razor off. "You sure about that?"

The predatory look he gave her made her throat dry. She tried to swallow rather unsuccessfully.

He set down his razor and shifted closer with a grin that sent waves of panic and excitement through her. "Remember last night when you wanted to give me a wet hug?"

"Don't do it." She shifted closer to the edge, prepared to jump down and take off. With nowhere to go and five-inch heels, it was a terrible plan.

"You ought to be careful with who you mess with, Morgan. I'm bigger and faster than you." He swooped in, wrapping his arm around her middle, and pulling her closer.

She squirmed, but the only thing it did was make her hat fall off. Palms against his chest, she pushed, trying to keep him from getting shaving cream on her face or anywhere else. She laughed. "Stop it."

"It's happening." He rubbed his cheek against hers.

She shrieked. It was cool, wet, and it tickled. "Brody! St—" She couldn't even get the word out through her laughter.

He loosened his hold on her and leaned back. With a towel, he gently wiped the shaving cream off her face, then his, before tossing it to the side, never breaking their locked gazes.

Heat shot up Morgan's neck and crept to her face. Her voice wasn't capable of more than a whisper when she said, "The pin, Brody."

His stare lasted a long moment, then he moved away and picked up his razor.

She grabbed her hat and spun it in her hands. "Are you mad?"

"You know I'm not." Even though he tried to keep his tone neutral, there was no hiding his irritation that she'd even ask that. "Though, if that's what you want, you need to stop coming so close."

She scooted off the sink top. "I'll go get that coffee. Want another?"

"I haven't finished this one."

"Right."

The flip of her already knotted stomach caught Morgan by surprise when Brody came around the corner in the casino. She'd distracted herself at the Blackjack table while waiting for him to come down from the room. With her anxiety at full tilt, it was either that or go buy a pack of cigarettes.

If he hadn't grinned at her from across the room, she might not have recognized him. The man sure knew how to wear a suit. The blue color, the fit, the absence of a tie—it all worked.

It was a different look for him, but he was still her Brody. The guy who didn't take his eyes off her as he walked toward her. He was *hers*. At least he could be if she wanted.

And she did. Whether he was in jeans and flannel or dressed like this, she wanted him. She had no idea what was supposed to happen now. What if making it into more ruined it, inevitably leaving them worse than when they'd started?

Her nerves sizzled like live wires. She'd already been having a mini panic attack about introducing Brody to Uncle John. Not knowing what would happen between her and Brody later had compounded her internal freakout.

The dealer signaled for her to make her bet.

Morgan shook her head to communicate she wouldn't be playing another hand, then scooped her chips into her purse.

Brody reached her side as she stood, forcing her to crane her neck to look at him. He held his phone up. A photo of Hope with her arm around Buster's neck and her face next to his graced the screen. "She's taking good care of your baby."

"I have to get her something before we leave to thank her."

"No, you don't."

"I'm *going to.*" Showing her appreciation was a must. It'd also help her feel less guilty about leaving Buster, which she'd done twice in the short time she'd had him. She really missed that cute little guy. She'd never have guessed her very first pet would be a goat.

He shrugged and glanced at her shoes. "You still want to walk there?"

"Yep."

"Five bucks says I have to carry you over my shoulder again."

She slapped his arm. "I'm not going to get drunk at brunch."

"Darn."

"And anyway, I didn't need you to carry me last night." She slipped around him and headed for the exit, knowing he'd catch up to her in a single stride.

"You're welcome for not letting you twist your ankle," he muttered from behind her.

She shook her head and kept walking. Her thoughts pulled her in during the walk to the restaurant, and she stayed quiet, lost in them.

Brody didn't intrude on her silence. Every now and then, his hand brushed hers, and she could feel him glance at her.

Her hat kept the sun off her face and the big, dark lenses of her sunglasses kept her from squinting, but she regretted the decision to walk. The summer heat amplified her minimal hangover. When they reached the Venetian, she was eighty-percent sure she was going to barf, and the ringing of the slot machines in the casino pushed her headache from mild annoyance to major irritation. She needed food and water stat.

As the hostess showed them to their table in the restaurant, she kept her chin up. No one needed to know she didn't feel like a million bucks.

Uncle John stood when they reached the table and pulled her into a hug. The scent of his aftershave, which she normally found soothing, stung her nostrils. "Hi, angel."

She swallowed against her watering mouth. "How are you feeling?"

He let her go and spread his arms wide. "Never been better."

Uncle John was lying about how he felt, but she let it go because she was doing the same thing and the sooner she got a glass of ice water, the better. Although, appearance-wise he looked great, on an emotional level, there was a subtle sense that something weighed on him.

"This is Brody." She swept her arm in her uncle's direction. "Brody, this is Uncle John."

She waited while they shook hands and exchanged pleasantries.

Brody pulled out a chair at the table and motioned for her to sit.

Out of the corner of her eye, she caught her uncle take note as Brody slid her in.

Their server appeared, turned over the glass in front of her, and filled it with chilled water from a pitcher.

Morgan took a long swig while the server filled the men's glasses. When it was just the three of them again, she asked, "Am I going to keep having to make plans with you and Lucy separately when I come home to visit, like some weird custody arrangement, or are you going to get past this?"

Uncle John's posture stiffened. "This is a family matter. We'll talk about it later. No need to make Brody uncomfortable."

"He's not uncomfortable and whatever you're going to say, he's going to hear one way or another."

Brody pushed his chair back a bit. "I can go."

"Don't." She turned back to her uncle. "Why do we have to be like this? Why can't we be normal? I'm so tired of secrecy. It was one thing when you expected me to keep hush-hush about things and I felt like I was on the inside, but now I find out, you've been keeping secrets from me."

His face reddened as his grip tightened on the arm of his chair. "Everything I've ever done is to protect you, Morgan."

The server reappeared with menus, a carafe of coffee, and a pitcher of orange juice.

Brody shot her a questioning look across the table when Uncle John glanced at the menu.

She hadn't planned to pounce on him like that but seeing the empty extra chair at the table for four set her off. Lucy should be here with them.

"Tell me about Maryland," Uncle John said to Brody. "You have a farm? Cows and pigs? That kind of thing?"

"No, just crops. Morgan has a goat, though."

His gaze cut to her. "You have a goat?"

"It's a long story." She opened her menu, then shut it. "How does keeping secrets from me protect me?"

John huffed. "Morgan."

"If you don't tell me, you'll destroy my trust in you, and I'll walk out of here, and things will never be the same between us." The words tumbled out, followed by frustration that she couldn't put the brakes on her mouth whenever this subject crossed her mind.

Despite the menu in front of his face, she caught Brody's frown and him shifting in his chair. She didn't want to make him uncomfortable, but this had gone on long enough. Tomorrow, they'd be leaving Las Vegas. She needed to know.

"You don't want answers to the questions you're asking," Uncle John said.

Brody set down his menu. Her focus was on her uncle, but she was highly aware of his presence and body language. He might feel awkward. He might think this was the worst idea. He might even think she needed psych meds. But he wasn't going to contradict her.

"You don't get to decide what I want. Last chance to come clean, or I'm gone."

Brody nudged her foot under the table.

Her gaze shot to him.

He widened his eyes, silently giving her the message that it might be wise to back off.

"You want to do this? Fine." John signaled for the server and ordered a bloody mary. "Lucy and I were together. A long time ago. Before you were born, we lived together."

Her stomach dropped and it had nothing to do with her nausea, which was only background noise at this point. Even though she'd thought it was a possibility, hearing it from him rocked her world. "At the Mermaid?"

"Yes."

"That's why she didn't want it blown up," she whispered.

Brody's forehead wrinkled. Probably wondering why Lucy hadn't simply asked him not to blow up a building to which she had a sentimental attachment like a freaking normal person.

"So, you broke up before you got custody of Logan and I?"

He offered a tight shake of his head. "No."

"I don't remember her ever living with us."

The server made a quick return with his drink. "Are you ready to order?"

"No," Brody and Uncle John said at the same time.

"Okay, I'll check back in a few."

"She moved out a couple of months after your mom died." John stirred his drink with a stalk of celery. "She didn't want kids or to get married, which I knew before we started living together."

Her eyes widened. "Did you ask her to marry you?"

He nodded, but he wouldn't meet her eyes. "We used to keep Logan a lot. And then you were born and…after Cassie…Lucy helped plan the funeral and took care of you and Logan when my grief made it hard to."

She tried to put herself in his shoes, but it was hard to imagine Logan with kids, and even harder to imagine grieving his death.

"I went through a lot to make adopting you official—getting your dad to relinquish his parental rights, changing all of our names, court hearings. I was worried if something happened to me that you'd be taken away from

Lucy, so I asked her to marry me so we could adopt you together."

Brody covered his face with his hand and muttered something she didn't catch.

She leaned forward in her chair. Her heart thudded with painful force. "And?"

Her uncle winced. "She turned me down, angry that I'd ask when I knew how she felt about it. I told her to forget about getting married but I still wanted her to adopt you and Logan."

Her heart stopped beating. Her eyes dropped to the tablecloth. "And she refused."

It wasn't a question. She didn't need confirmation. Lucy had never had legal guardianship of her or Logan. She didn't have the same last name. On school forms, John had put her down as an extended family member who had permission to sign them out of school and go on field trips.

"We argued about it constantly, and ultimately, couldn't get past it, so we split up. She moved out." As overwhelming as it was to hear, being forced to recount the past had changed his entire demeanor. He kept his head bowed, and the ache in his voice tore at her heart. She didn't know whatever he was hiding was going to be this.

"I didn't see or hear from her for three months. Until one night she got herself in a sticky situation and called me for help. I brought her back to the Mermaid and she stayed the night. The next morning, she watched you while I took Logan to tee ball practice. You took your first steps while I was gone." He chuckled and for the first time during his story, made eye contact. "After that, she stayed for a while. And I'd missed her. So, I took what she offered, but it wasn't enough. I kept getting hung up on her adopting you. I needed the peace of mind of knowing she was your legal guardian, and I didn't understand why she wouldn't give it to me."

The server came back but before she reached the table Brody gestured for her to leave them be. He cleared his throat. "Maybe we should have the rest of this conversation with Lucy present."

He was probably right, but she wasn't here, and Morgan wanted to know everything. She'd waited long enough. Besides, if Uncle John closed back up, she might never get the rest out of him.

She directed her attention at her uncle, keeping her expression blank. If he knew how livid this information made her, he'd likely shut the conversation down. "You clearly came to an agreement on raising us at some point."

"She got her own place, and I said I wouldn't pressure her about getting back together or adopting you as long as she'd stay in your lives."

"And that's it? You've been 'just friends' for twenty years?" she asked.

John sighed. "No. We had moments of weakness. But I was adamant that you and Logan never find out. You'd already lost one mother, and I was worried she'd leave again if I wasn't careful."

Her eyes stung. She blinked, but the fuck if she was going to cry. Not here. She forced her voice to stay even and asked, "Anything else?"

"When you moved to Georgia, I decided I could no longer settle for less. I told her I was done living half in and half out. We were going to tell you."

"I moved to Georgia over two years ago!"

40
Derailed
BRODY

THE HELPLESSNESS THAT OVERCAME Brody while watching Morgan digest her uncle's confession sucked him into a dark place. For the longest moment of his life, he held his breath, waiting for her to fall apart, to break down and let out her pain and torment. But that's not what he witnessed.

Like a wave receding, the emotion disappeared from her face, and she lifted her chin and slid on her sunglasses. She shoved her chair back.

"Morgan," John said, reaching for her hand as she stood.

She snatched it away. As she walked off, she didn't say a word. She held her head high and strolled out of the restaurant like a duchess who'd had a lovely brunch and was onto her next engagement.

John stood and turned to go after her.

"Let her go." Brody's voice held an edge he didn't mean to put there. He grabbed his water glass and took a drink. This was Morgan's uncle. The man who raised her. He wasn't someone Brody should give a black eye.

He scowled. "She's my kid."

Brody nodded, trying to find his calm. John's story painted Lucy in a bad light, and he didn't like that. She'd told him enough the other night for him to know there was more to it.

The compulsion to ask why he didn't tell her Lucy had trauma and worked her way through it *for* Morgan swarmed his mind, but he kept it to himself. John might not even know Lucy had done that. With how this family buried their skeletons, it wouldn't be a shock.

"I know she backed you into a corner, but she's gotta process what you told her," Brody said. "Trying to talk to her right now is likely to make things worse. She needs to cool off."

He sat and stared at the pitcher of orange juice sweating on the table. "You're acting like you know her better than I do. What's going on with you and her?"

"Nothing yet. Probably fuck up my chances if I talk to you about it, though." Brody didn't owe him anything. He should want Morgan's father to like him. That's what she wanted. It's why she'd brought him along. For her sake, he'd maintain a respectful attitude toward John, but it wasn't easy keeping his head cool when he knew she was off on her own, crying—or more likely, screaming and breaking shit.

John rested back in his chair and studied him. "Can't argue with you there. She's never going to tell me anything ever again."

"Shocker," he said dryly. "Keeping secrets from someone their entire life is not the way to build trust. Who'd have thought?"

John's jaw shifted. "I don't want her out there alone while she's this emotional."

Neither did Brody. So, they had that in common, at least. But unlike John, he wouldn't intrude upon her right to space. If she needed him, he'd be there, but the last thing he wanted to do was push her away by forcing his presence on her. Nor would he allow anyone else to get in line ahead of him to comfort her.

Maybe if John knew where she was, he'd settle down.

Brody pulled his phone out. After opening the map app, he located her, then showed him the screen. "She hasn't gone far."

His eyes went wide. "You're tracking her?"

"She sent me her location. I didn't ask for it."

"Morgan is *allowing* you to know her location?" he asked again, as

though rephrasing the question would get him a different answer.

"She can turn it off whenever she wants, but yeah."

John scoffed, then took a long drink of his bloody mary.

"She's fixated on getting you and Lucy to settle your differences. She had this idea that if you met me, you'd see I was a decent person and then you wouldn't have anything to be mad at Lucy for."

"It's not that simple."

"Given the lengths you've gone to in order to keep Morgan hidden, I believe that. You mentioned that you changed your names. How can I protect her without knowing who you're hiding her from and why?"

John rubbed his forehead and sighed. "I changed our last name to Cash after I got her bastard father to sign over his rights. He went to prison before Morgan was born. She's never met him. After what he did to my sister, I don't want him to ever be able to find Morgan."

A sour taste coated his tongue. "Do I want to know?"

He shook his head. "Not unless you like having nightmares. I couldn't prove all the fucked-up shit he did to Cassie without implicating her as his accomplice. In the end, he went down for everything he'd done to everyone else, and he looked like the asshole of the century trying to point the finger at a pregnant woman who'd never even had an overdue library book."

Brody wanted to know what he'd been charged for. When he'd looked into Morgan's background, he hadn't found much about her biological parents, but then again, he wasn't even close to being a detective. If he went to jail before she was born and was still there, it was something major, or several charges combined. "When does he get out?"

"Four or five years, at most. He's not the kind to think twice about tracking down kids he hasn't ever met and upsetting their lives. If he can't find them, he can't do that."

"It'd be harder to find her if she's living on a farm tucked away in rural Maryland." Especially if nothing tied her to living there. He'd have to make sure she didn't get any mail forwarded or leave any other type of paper trail. "What if she wants to meet him?"

"She knows where he is. If she'd wanted to meet him, she'd have done it by now."

A chill crept up his neck. She could have hidden it from him like Brody had when he'd tried to track down his birth parents. But the more he thought about it, he doubted she had any interest in her biological father. Even now, with the upheaval of discovering that her perceived parents had kept secrets from her, he couldn't see her reacting by running to her incarcerated sperm donor.

"How persistent do you think he'll be in finding her?" Brody asked.

"I don't know. Not as persistent as he would be if he knew Morgan is like her mother. Cassie was his golden goose."

John had started telling Morgan early on to hide her gifts. She wasn't cracking safes in diapers or navigating through complex security systems before naptime. There was something else, an advantage she'd demonstrated at a young age. Brody was pretty sure he knew what it was, and it made sense that John would recognize it if his sister shared the trait. "Because she had a photographic memory?"

John's face went stony, the same way Morgan's had before she'd left. "Photographic memories don't exist."

"I've been paying attention. Don't tell me Morgan doesn't have some sort of intellectual superpower." He hoped John didn't interpret that to mean Brody paid *too much* attention to her. Even if it was true.

He shrugged. "I've never taken her for a diagnosis. Like her mother, she's got a strong visual and auditory memory, but what memories get stored requires intention. The more she focuses on something, the more vividly she can recall it."

"Like a book?"

"She can't glance at a page, and instantly read it, nor can she store an entire book in her memory to read later."

"But if she stared at it for a while, she could memorize a single page?" Like the crossword book.

John ran his fingers through his hair. "Yes. Especially if it's something that holds her interest."

Brody checked his phone again. She'd stopped near the Mirage. He wanted to go to her. He wanted to fix this for her, even though he accepted that there wasn't any way to fix it. But that didn't mean he wasn't going to try to make it better.

He sent her a quick text.

Care for some company?

I'm going to go see if she's okay. Letting Lucy know what you told Morgan would be the decent thing to do." He pulled out his wallet and tossed down enough cash to cover the drinks and tip.

John stood. "I need to talk to Morgan first."

"Yeah, well," Brody drawled out, "I only care about what she needs, and I don't think that's it."

"Now, listen—"

"I'm sure she'll reach out when she's ready." Whatever happened with Morgan's relationship with her uncle was up to her. "And, as long as she's cool with it, you're welcome to visit any time."

Unless this derailed them from pulling that pin—and he did *not* feel good about his chances that it hadn't—the guest room would be available.

He didn't look back as he left the restaurant. The only thing he cared about was finding Morgan. Being able to use his phone to locate her sure beat the hell out of pacing the floor, wondering where she was.

According to the map, she wasn't far. Her avatar no longer moved on the screen. He walked, getting closer and closer to where the map showed her position.

She stood under the palms outside of the Mirage, leaning against the railing that surrounded the volcano.

He came up next to her.

She had an unlit cigarette dangling from her fingers.

"Haven't seen you with one of those in a while."

Without a word, she lifted her other hand and revealed a pack. Using her thumb, she flipped back the lid. One cigarette was missing. Otherwise, the pack looked brand new.

"I'm sorry," he said, resisting the insanely strong urge to pull her into his arms. "That was…a lot."

She spun the cigarette like a mini baton. "I don't want to be here anymore."

"We can go back to the room and chill there. Do you want me to get a cab?"

"I don't want to be in Las Vegas, I mean. I want to leave. As soon as possible."

Their flight out wasn't until tomorrow. "Are you sure?"

Morgan nodded and pushed away from the railing.

"Okay. I can do that." Actually, he wasn't sure he could. The chances of getting two seats on a flight at the last minute would be slim. But if he couldn't, he'd figure something else out. "Do you want to see Lucy before we leave?"

She pinched her lips together and shook her head.

41
Flight Response
Morgan

MORGAN OPENED HER PURSE and spotted the pack of cigarettes she'd bought earlier. She plucked them out and dropped them into a nearby trash bin, then gave Brody her I.D. and waited while he dealt with checking them in.

Once they got to security, he handed her boarding pass to her.

"Brody, this says our destination is Tampa."

"I know."

"Why are we going to Florida?"

"Because the soonest I could get us a flight to Baltimore was tomorrow, and you wanted to leave today."

She stared at him, unsure what to say. "You don't live in Florida."

He grinned. "I know that. We're catching a red eye to Baltimore."

"You made your own layover?"

He nudged her along as the line moved. "Sorta. We're going to have six hours to kill."

The buzzing in her purse resumed. She sighed and pulled it out. Uncle John had been calling nonstop. She rejected it, then hastily wiped at a tear that slipped out, trying to catch it before Brody noticed.

His arm came around her. He pulled her into him and rested his chin on the top of her head. They'd both changed into jeans before coming to the airport. He'd put on a plain white T-shirt, and she'd put on a black bandeau and a loose racerback tank top that was so tattered it covered less skin than the bandeau. He ran his hand down her back and settled his hold on her waist, no fabric between the rough texture of his palm and her skin. Unlike last night when he'd run his hand up her thigh, his touch soothed her, and made her feel closer to him, more connected. Right now, he was the *only* person with whom she felt a connection.

She sagged into him. When the line moved, so would she.

He'd tried, gently, to get her to talk more than once when they got back to their hotel room. But she couldn't. Not yet. Everything was too fresh. Too raw.

She didn't think she was even mad at anyone. Everyone had been hurt. Everyone had a reason to feel cheated. Now everyone needed to find a way to heal and move on.

Too tired to do anything but go along with Brody, trusting that at some point he'd get them back to the farm, she let him guide her through the airport. Once their plane had taken off, she rested her head against his shoulder and closed her eyes.

She woke up with Brody smoothing her hair out of her face, telling her they'd be landing soon. Like a zombie, she went through the motions of unboarding, grabbing dinner outside of the airport, and then into a cab—she didn't pay attention to where Brody told the driver to go. The weight of everything that'd happened since she'd stepped foot in Las Vegas suffocated her, leaving no room in her mind for more information.

They got out of the car by a path to the beach.

"You comin'?" The sky beyond Brody glowed orange and pink. The horizon and the dipping sun painted a picturesque background as he stood at the entrance to a path through the dunes.

He'd taken off his shoes, and she did the same, then followed next to him.

White powdery sand warmed the soles of her feet. The sound of the surf and the smell of salty air brought her back to life. The breeze off the ocean blew her hair about and cooled her face.

He walked to a lifeguard chair several feet taller than he was, then turned to face her. "You go up first."

"So you can look at my ass?"

He shrugged. "I'm not ashamed."

Morgan rolled her eyes, dropped her shoes and bag, then climbed up the chair.

Brody pulled himself up the platform and sat next to her on the bench.

"You couldn't get a direct flight home, so you brought me to an entirely different state to watch the sunset?" she asked, not even sure how to feel about that, or why it made her heart beat double time.

"The ocean always helps me clear my head when life gets to be too much. I thought maybe it'd do the same for you. I wish I could take credit for planning to get here right at sunset, but I got lucky with that part."

She turned and leaned against him, studying the horizon.

He wrapped his arm around her. Her world was unraveling, and yet, the ache in her chest was tolerable with him next to her. She wasn't used to people in her life standing quietly by, there for support, not to take over. He hadn't even brought up pulling the pin. A man had never shown her this much patience or understanding. And she'd never felt stronger simply because of one's presence—safer, yes, but not stronger.

"I feel more like me when I'm with you," she said quietly, because that's as high as her voice would go without it cracking. She didn't have to hide parts of who she was. She didn't have to tone down her personality.

His lips brushed her hair as he whispered in her ear. "I know the feeling."

She smiled and relaxed into him. For a while, they watched the sky change colors, the sun disappearing far too fast.

The sounds of the ocean calmed her and helped her mind catch up. She squeezed her eyes shut when the realization of how badly she'd behaved in front of Brody formed. Fighting dirty wasn't a good look, but she'd exhausted the other options. "Turns out I didn't need your gas and matches. I burnt that shit to the ground all on my own."

"Fire requires fuel, heat, and oxygen, and it needs all three to keep burning."

She tried to keep a serious face and focus on the sunset, but it was hard not to smile when he went all science nerd. "Are you giving me a chemistry lesson?"

He laughed. "No, I'm trying to let you know it's not all on you. John and Lucy set the fire, baby. Did you stoke it? Sure. Then, I fed the flames after you left. Some situations are incendiary, and they're going to combust no matter what."

Morgan whipped around to face him. "Fed the flames? What did you do?"

"That plan you had for your uncle to like me? Yeah, uh, I kinda bombed that."

"Bombed?" She snorted. "Really?"

"I was on a roll with figurative language." He winked.

"What did you say to him?" Try as she might, she couldn't imagine Brody making a bad impression on Uncle John—or anyone, for that matter.

"He wanted to go after you, but I spoke up and said he should leave you alone. I don't think he liked that."

She sucked in a sharp breath and widened her eyes. He wouldn't have liked that one bit. "You told him to leave me alone?"

"More like, *advised* him to give you space. And I may have said some other stuff that probably cemented his dislike for me." He winced. The way he said "advised" did not sound at all passive.

"Like what?"

"Uh"—he scratched the back of his head—"I made him tell me why he hides you like he does."

"Okay," she said softly, her mouth going dry.

"I'd already guessed that you had an impressive memory. He confirmed that and filled me in on the situation with your biological father."

"Okay," she repeated. Blood rushed in her ears. Her temples throbbed from her brain's very helpful habit of trying to block out information that was hard to process. He now knew more about her than anyone outside of her family. Her knee-jerk reaction was to freak out, but a voice deep inside her spoke up, asking her why she wouldn't want that?

He put his fingers on her cheek and guided her gaze to his. "I'm not going to use you."

"I know."

"Then why do you look like you've been given a death sentence?"

She shook her head. "It's foreign to me—someone knowing that much about my life. I'm also having trouble wrapping my head around Uncle John sharing information with you."

"I told him I couldn't protect you if I didn't know what I was protecting you from. He doesn't like it, but he knows you're safer with me."

She stood on the platform. "I'm not in danger." She wasn't afraid of her father. She almost said that he couldn't make her do anything, but it'd already been proven that her mind could be twisted in the right hands.

He shifted forward, scooting to the edge of the bench, taking up the space she'd put between them. "When he gets out, do you want him in your life?"

"No. I have no desire to meet him."

"Then, you need to keep being a ghost."

"Oh, so, you're taking over keeping the princess locked in the tower?"

Brody grabbed the back of her thighs and tugged her to him, forcing her to stand between his legs.

She grabbed his shoulders to steady herself, then stood there, staring at him, not even caring that he had her held hostage. There wasn't anywhere she wanted to go. But she didn't want to be treated like a child, either. She was fucking tough and could handle what came her way. With or without Brody.

Her preference would be *with* Brody, though.

Acknowledging that to herself stole her breath.

He stared up at her, his expression soft. "You're not a princess. There is no tower. You're a brilliant woman with the type of skills your bio dad has exploited in the past. I don't know exactly what he did, but people don't get sentenced that much time if they didn't do something major. I want you safe, and if you think I'll back down on that, then you don't know me at all."

"Brody…" Whether she was flustered by his nearness or aggravated by his overbearingness, she didn't know.

"Morgan…" His lips twitched.

She covered her eyes with her hand and groaned. "I can't sit here. I need to do something."

"Build a sandcastle? Skinny dip?"

She peeked between her fingers, then dropped her hand away.

He had his lips pressed together. His eyes shone with laughter. "Which one caught your interest?"

She leaned back, putting whatever distance between them she could, and crossed her arms. "Those can't be my only options."

"They are." He said it so seriously, then stood, swallowing up the remaining space on the platform. He moved an arm loosely around her waist, looking over her shoulder cautiously, probably making sure he didn't push her too close to the edge.

"We don't have shovels," she said.

"Guess that narrows your options even further."

"I'll skinny dip with you," she said as she prepared to escape. "But you have to catch me first."

She dropped down, then swung over the side. No time for the rungs, she jumped backward and landed on her feet in the sand. She didn't wait, knowing the length of her legs compared to his put her at a disadvantage, even if she did run routinely.

In several strides, she hit wet sand and picked up pace, not daring to look over her shoulder.

She'd gotten farther than she'd thought she would when her feet lifted off the sand. She shrieked.

Brody kept her back pressed to his chest, one arm under her breasts, one around her stomach. He walked toward the surf holding her like that.

"No, Brody," she shouted as a wave splashed them. Her pants were going to be soaked.

"When are you going to learn, I'm faster and bigger?" He kept going until the water came to his knees. "Or maybe you wanted to get caught."

"Take me back to shore," she begged between laughter. Him catching her had been inevitable, but that didn't dull the exhilaration that came with challenging him, knowing he'd be good to her when he caught her.

She needed this. To laugh and play with Brody. To have fun and be… free. To remember the girl she'd been.

"Nah. I'm gonna toss you right out to sea." He'd stopped, but he held her against him like a sack of potatoes.

"No, don't," she said, adding extra panic to her voice. "You'll miss me."

"I might consider taking mercy on you. Convince me."

"Brody!" This time she wasn't faking. She didn't believe he'd actually toss her into the ocean, but her jeans were soaked from ankle to thigh and if she got any wetter, she'd be miserable until her clothes dried.

"Convince me, Morgan. Come on, turn on that charm and show me how a master con artist gets out of this situation."

"I don't. If I end up in this position, I'm toast."

He blew a raspberry. "You want me to underestimate you, but I'm not that easy of a mark, baby."

She wiggled against his hold.

"You're not gonna do it that way," he said, mouth to her ear. "Use your words, Morgan."

Her attempt to elbow him in his stomach got her nowhere thanks to his tight hold. "Please."

He chuckled. "Try harder."

She grumbled. After a few beats, she yelled, "Shark!"

He burst into laughter, his body shaking hers since he held her so tightly.

Once he'd calmed down, she glanced over her shoulder at him, and lowered her voice to a sultry whisper. "Pull the pin, Brody."

He froze for a moment. It was enough to give her the opportunity to break through his hold, but once she left his arms, she didn't gain her footing and started to fall. Brody grabbed her by her arm before she hit the water. He swung her up and over his shoulder. "You're devious."

He carried her up to the dry sand and set her on her feet.

The moonlight shadowed his features, making it difficult to read him. Goosebumps broke out on her arms. "Pull it," she said, the *I dare you* implied.

He curled his hand around the back of her neck and then his mouth was on hers.

A buzz ran through her body. She parted her lips, moaning when Brody didn't hesitate to tug the top one between his. As patient as he'd been, she'd not been expecting this kind of kiss. It wasn't rushed. It was demanding, though. And hot. And everything she didn't know a kiss should be.

He grabbed her waist with both hands and lifted her.

She wrapped her arms and legs around him.

The smoothness with which he moved his hands from her waist to her ass was pretty slick. She pressed closer, trying to appease the pulsing ache between her thighs.

Meanwhile, his mouth was doing things to hers that made her rethink her entire kissing history. It could be like this? She'd been robbed.

She melted into him more.

He slowly pulled his lips from hers.

She followed his mouth with her own, not ready for it to end. The beach, the moonlight, the feeling of everything falling away and leaving only them. This was everything. The best she'd felt in the longest time.

A growly, grumble came from his throat. He took over, his tongue stroking hers.

Something deep within her burned, radiating warmth into every part of her body. She trailed her fingers up the back of his neck and into his short hair.

His lips rubbed across hers with such ease, a ripple of amazing sensations traveled through her. Even the light scratch from the shadow of a mustache and beard that'd grown in felt good as he devoured her mouth.

There was no tension left in her body. She was officially a jellyfish. Good thing she was at the beach. If he could do this to her every day, she'd never need a massage or therapy.

He once again pulled his mouth from hers. He had her boosted high enough that her head was above his, resulting in him looking up at her. The moonlight revealed the curve of his lips. A shiver ran through her as he swept her hair away from her ear, his fingers brushing her neck. "I like feeling you go soft in my arms."

Her mouth opened. She didn't have words, though.

"I like how you look after I've kissed you too."

Lightheadedness swarmed her. "How do I look?"

He set her on her feet, then rubbed his thumb across her bottom lip. "Your lips are rosy and swollen." He ran his knuckles up to her cheek. "And your face is flushed." He pressed his forehead to hers, and whispered, "And your eyelids are droopy, like it put you in a daze."

His mouth brushed against hers, sending a wake of warmth through her body.

"You look like you're mine."

42
White Linens, Golden Skin
BRODY

THERE WERE A LOT of things Brody wanted to do to Morgan, but he didn't want to do them in the sand. As painful as it was to hit pause, he'd forced himself.

For the past hour, they'd been sitting in the sand, her back to his chest, his arms wrapped around her. The temperature was warm enough that the breeze felt refreshing, not chilly. At first, he'd kept it together and simply held her. She'd fought it, but thirty seconds of his fingers running up and down her arm had lulled her to sleep.

But now…

Holding her might have been tolerable if she hadn't been so restless. The little noises she made and the friction of her shifting against him drove him mad. He let his hand roam, traveling to her wrist. The softness of her palm as he swept his fingertips across it tempted him to bring it to his mouth to kiss, but he held back.

He lost himself in exploring her body with light touches, intrigued by how she responded to his touch in her sleep. The little sigh she made when he crept his hand under her shirt to the silky and warm skin of her stomach incited his craving for more. Lazily, he worked his way up, his fingers coasting over her ribcage. That's when she bowed away from him and emitted a tiny, barely audible noise that made him harder than anything she'd ever done.

Getting a room crossed his mind, but he wanted more than a few short hours with her before they'd have to go to the airport. When he took her to bed, he wanted to take his time, and stay tangled in her from dusk to dawn. Besides, she was exhausted. Sure, she'd slept on the plane and was half in and half out of sleep now, but that wasn't quality rest. He didn't think she'd slept much last night, if at all.

He swept his thumb in a line under her bra. Yeah, keeping his hands off her was going to be a real problem.

She curled onto her side, tucked her head under his chin and wrapped her arms around him, hugging him with an unintelligible murmur.

Brody lifted her legs and draped them over his thigh, then changed his hold on her, cradling her with one arm. As much as he looked forward to getting her home and seeing what happened when they had all the time and privacy in the world, he wasn't in a rush to end this new, anticipation-filled intimacy.

Before Morgan came into his life, he'd felt heavier. The weight of responsibility never left his shoulders. He still carried it, but having this with Morgan was a reprieve. Sitting in the sand with her while waves crashed, he realized he wanted his life filled with moments like this one. Moments of not caring about anything but her. Smelling her and stroking her smooth skin and feeling lucky she was his.

He continued to sit with her in his arms until it was time to head to the airport. Once they'd recollected their carry-ons, she pulled out a hoodie and put it on. While they waited at the gate, she curled back into his side. He kissed the top of his snuggly little zombie's head.

Even when her eyes weren't closed, she didn't say much, but she didn't seem upset, just worn out. It had been too long since she'd gotten adequate rest. He didn't even know if she'd gotten used to sleeping in the guest room. But he did know she hadn't slept through the night most of the nights she'd spent at the farm. She'd checked on him several times when he was sick—even when she'd thought she was being sneaky so she

wouldn't wake him. Last night, she'd either not slept or not slept much. Even before that, she'd traveled to see her uncle when he'd been in the hospital. She'd been running on turbo for weeks.

When they finally made it back to the farm, he was exhausted, but more than that, he didn't have the heart to keep her from getting into bed by herself and sleeping soundly for as long as her body needed.

He didn't kiss her goodnight.

He couldn't.

She'd be all soft and sweet, and he wouldn't stop until they were naked and sweaty. He hadn't expected her to be so easy to drag into mindless lust, but he'd take it. He couldn't wait to push her over the edge.

Three hours after getting into bed, it almost killed him to drag his ass out. He'd spent too much time away to delay further, though. The forecast called for thunderstorms in the early afternoon, so he needed to make the most of the weather until it turned.

He returned to the house around eleven as thunder rumbled and gray cloaked the sky, sure Morgan would be awake, but the quietness indicated otherwise. He stripped out of his filthy clothes in the laundry room and headed upstairs in his boxers. Once he'd showered and changed into fresh clothes, he knocked softly on her door and slowly turned the handle.

She was under a cloud of fluffy white covers, her blond hair, still wavy like it'd been the day before, poked out, along with half of her face. One arm hung over the side and her leg had escaped from the blankets. Brody didn't see any sign of clothes. Just white linens and golden skin.

He shut the door, even though he wanted to confirm his suspicions about her nakedness.

His workday being cut short on his first day home irritated him a lot more now that he wasn't going to be able to distract himself with her. He made himself lunch and ate it on the porch as the storm picked up, blowing green leaves around, plastering them to his truck and her car.

He didn't even taste his sandwich. Morgan consumed his mind. He wanted to see her. Taste *her*. Touch her. Get her very naked.

Looking for a boredom killer, he grabbed a crossword book and his ukulele and laid in the hammock on the side porch. He got bored with the puzzles and tossed the book onto the porch boards. He absentmindedly plucked at the ukulele for a while, then played a song. Halfway through, he sensed movement and glanced up.

Morgan stood at the bend where the porch wrapped around, wearing a short, frilly dusty-pink nightgown with a beige, baggy sweater hanging off her shoulders, open in the center, the sleeves rolled to her elbows. Her hair was a dead giveaway that she'd spent the last nine hours with her head on a pillow.

He stopped playing.

Maybe his craving for her clouded his objectivity, but he didn't think she could look more beautiful. Even with the sweater hiding her shape, she was sexy as hell. He wet his lips as he thought about kissing her exposed shoulders.

Her cheeks turned rosy. She glanced at the floor. "You play the ukulele too?"

"I get bored if I don't keep my hands busy."

"That's why you build bombs and teach yourself to play instruments. Oh, and the crossword puzzles." She peeked at him.

"There's other things I enjoy doing with my hands." He grinned. "Do you want to get in the hammock?"

She shook her head no, but her lips nearly pulled into a smile. She lowered her head again, probably trying to hide the fact that she was lying through her teeth.

"Yeah, you do. Come on. I'll play, so you don't have to worry about my hands."

"When did I say I was worried about your hands?" She walked closer, taking each step slowly.

He shifted and placed the ukulele on the floor on the opposite side, then turned back to her and crooked his finger. "You talk a big game for such a small person."

Her eyes opened a fraction wider. She moved within his reach. The very second he slipped his hand inside her sweater and grasped her waist, a big splash came from the driveway. The sound of a car engine followed.

Morgan turned and walked back the way she'd come.

He swung his legs over the hammock and got out, standing behind her where she'd stopped.

"Logan," she muttered, then walked to the steps and stood there, arms crossed as the black sports car pulled up next to his truck.

"Big brother coming to check up on you?" Brody asked as he leaned against the post next to her.

"God, he's so annoying."

He laughed, amused at how quickly she'd slipped into petulant little sister mode.

Logan emerged from the car, opened an umbrella, and went around and opened the passenger-side door. He held the umbrella over his fiancée's head as they made their way to the porch.

"What are you doing here?" Morgan asked, moving so Drew could get in out of the rain.

"Uncle John told me what happened. He wanted me to check in with you."

She glared at him. "You could have called."

"Not really my style, is it?" Logan grinned and ducked under the porch roof. He closed the umbrella and leaned it against the railing.

She turned to Drew. "You're a terrible handler. You could have at least given me a heads-up."

"Quit referring to her as my handler." Logan looked his sister up and down, then narrowed his eyes. "It's one in the afternoon. Why are you still in...*that*?"

Brody wanted to laugh, but instead cleared his throat.

"Hi, Brody," Drew said and flashed him a smile.

"Hello." He turned to Logan. "Did you drive here from Savannah?"

He scowled. "We were in New York."

"I got to teach a workshop at my alma mater," Drew threw in, beaming.

"Do you want to come in?" he asked them. "Can I get you something to drink?"

"Oh," Drew drawled out and wiggled her eyebrows at Morgan. "He's got manners."

"I'm good right here." Logan sat in a rocking chair and pulled out a pack of cigarettes.

"You two relax," Morgan said. "We'll make coffee. Do you want anything else? Water?"

"Yes, to water." Drew took the rocking chair next to Logan's.

Brody held the door open for Morgan. He liked how she knew where everything was in his kitchen. But what he liked even more was how she'd assigned them a task *together*. Little Miss *doesn't work well with others* did just fine alongside him. "You good with them being here?"

"If I say I'm not, are you going to make them leave?" She turned her head and searched his face with her gaze.

He ran his hand across her lower back as he moved around her. "If that's what you want."

"As much as I could smack him for showing up unannounced, knowing he dropped whatever he was doing to make sure I was okay makes it hard to stay mad at him."

He pulled extra mugs from the top shelf in the cabinet. "I can go somewhere to give you time with your family."

"You don't need to go anywhere. Maybe let's not advertise this, though." She gestured between them.

"You want to put the pin back in *again*?" Heat crept up his neck. She couldn't seriously be asking him to do that.

"I don't want to, but I think it'd be wise at the moment."

He put his hands on the counter on either side of her and brushed his nose against the soft spot behind her ear. "No."

Her hands, which had been scooping coffee beans from the bag, stopped moving.

He trailed his lips over the shell of her ear. "I can't."

The bag of coffee *thunk*ed as it fell from her grasp. The beans spilled onto the counter. She fumbled to clean them up.

He put his hands over hers to stop her. "I'll make you a deal."

She twisted around and looked up at him. A smile snuck across her lips. "Oh, really?"

"Go change out of this nightie, and I'll keep my hands to myself in front of your brother."

Her eyes shimmered, and too late he realized he'd need to be a lot more specific. None of this gray area nonsense.

"Morgan," he pressed closer, "if you go change into something even more sexy than what you have on right now, I'm going to take it off you and I don't care who is watching."

The fallen look on her face cracked him up. She was outmatched on this. He'd do it if she pushed him, and she knew it.

Fucking hell. If her brother hadn't shown up, he was pretty sure he'd be between her thighs right now, or at least getting to second base in the hammock—*not* agreeing to pretend he wasn't counting the minutes until he could have her all to himself.

He grabbed a fistful of the lacy ruffles covering her thigh and pushed them higher, his palm spreading over her hip as he leaned in to kiss her.

She pushed at his chest and turned her head, leaving him kissing her cheek. "No kissing. Make coffee. I'll go change."

He groaned, then let her go.

As she walked away, he trailed his fingers through the hem of her nightie, frowning when it was no longer within his grasp—when *she* was no longer in his grasp. Hopefully, he could find out how long her brother planned on staying without coming off like he wanted to get rid of him so he could get his sister naked.

43
I.O.U.
BRODY

BRODY LOADED FRESH BEANS into the machine, then cleaned up the spilled ones while it ground them and automatically transferred the grinds to the brew basket. By the time the pot was full, Morgan still hadn't come back downstairs. He killed a few minutes pouring coffee into the mugs. He set them on the table, along with milk and sugar, then invited Drew and Logan to come inside.

He had his cup to his mouth, about to take his first sip when Morgan walked down the stairs.

A short red skirt swished against her thighs. She'd tied her white T-shirt in a knot just above the waistband of her skirt.

What did she think this was, if not sexy? Her hair pulled up like that, those little blond wisps framing her face, and the shininess of her slightly glossed lips led his imagination down a path that was far too wicked for him to go down when they had company.

As if challenging him to make a comment about her outfit in front of her brother, she put a hand on her hip.

"I love that skirt," Drew said, drawing her attention.

"Thanks." She turned back to Brody.

He shook his head and took his coffee out to the porch to prevent his mind running rampant with images of all the different ways he could get under her skirt.

The rain was still coming down but not as hard. He set his mug on the porch railing and perched on it.

Drew and Logan came back out with their coffees and sat in the rockers.

Morgan joined them seconds later. She sat with her back against the post next to the steps and stretched out her legs, crossing one ankle over the other. Even though she was only eight feet away, he didn't care for the separation.

"I called Uncle John an asshole." Logan's gaze slid to Morgan.

She choked on her coffee. "Why?"

Brody hid his smile behind his cup. This was going to be interesting. He'd not put much thought into Logan's relationship with Lucy, but he did know Lucy. She wouldn't have been less of a mom to him than she had been to Morgan.

"Because he's being one."

"Lucy is twenty years older than you," Drew said, straightening in her seat like she'd been hired to be Logan's translator.

"Okay?" Morgan's eyebrows squished together.

"They were kids." Logan shook his head. "Uncle John was a little older, even if not by much, and he might not have thought anything would actually happen, but he did agree to be our guardian if it did. Lucy didn't make any such promises. And she was *twenty* fucking years old, Morgan."

The age part made it messed up without taking into account that Lucy had been struggling with her mental health. Becoming a parent at that age would be hard no matter the circumstances, but it happening in the blink of an eye while the person is already struggling to exist?

The compulsion to tell them was strong. Lucy hadn't sworn him to secrecy, but then, she didn't need to and was aware of that. Brody was torn between being Lucy's confidante or her defender.

"I get it." Morgan shrugged. "But she didn't stay twenty."

"She did *stay*, though," Drew said gently.

"According to Uncle John, she left and only came back when she got in trouble and needed him."

"Do you believe him?" Logan asked, rubbing his jaw.

Brody didn't. No one had asked him, though, and he hadn't participated in the conversation thus far. He hadn't felt the need to. This was Morgan's family, and even though he had a connection to Lucy, in this moment, his role was moral support for Morgan.

"I believe that's how *he* sees it," she said.

Logan squinted at her. "Why are you so calm?"

Brody fought his smile. When Logan wasn't looking, his sister had mellowed out. A little. She'd still start a riot if she cared about something deeply enough.

"I don't know how to feel about it. I mean, it doesn't make me feel good, but…" Her shoulders lifted slightly, then dropped. "There's nothing I can do. It's too late to beg her to adopt us. And I can't fix whatever is broken between her and Uncle John."

"Have you spoke with Lucy?" Drew asked.

"I need more time," she said softly.

"I did."

She whipped her head in Logan's direction. "You talked to Lucy?"

"Fuck yes, I called her."

"And?"

"Uncle John told her before he called me. She was pretty down when I talked to her but she's hanging in there."

"Did she give an excuse?" The way Morgan looked at her brother tugged at his soul. He'd seen that same look from Hope when she asked him something but was afraid to hear the answer. Whatever Logan said next, Brody hoped it wouldn't crush her.

"No, but I didn't give her an opportunity to. I told her I loved her, and that this didn't change anything. I asked her about her life before us."

Morgan huffed. "Can you just tell me what she said instead of dragging it out?"

"No," Logan said, "because you won't call her yourself if I do."

"It's that bad?"

"He means that if he tells you, you won't have a reason to call her," Drew said. "And Morgan, you need to. I think you'll be glad you did, and I also think you owe it to Lucy. She'd never avoid you while you were suffering."

She turned her head sharply, directing her gaze at the rain creating puddles and mud. Her jaw had a tight set to it, like she was clenching her teeth.

"Did you know Lucy ran away from home when she was fifteen?" Brody asked, uneasy with it. But he wanted to give Morgan something to help her see that Lucy hadn't had an easy life before she'd come into theirs. Maybe it'd make her curious to find out more.

Her gaze locked on him. "No. Why do *you* know that?"

Shit. He hadn't considered she might not like that he knew things about Lucy that she didn't. She'd said "why." Not "how'd you find that out," but "why were you told in the first place?"

"She told me when we were in Vegas. Because of her upbringing, she thought she couldn't be a good mother to you. But she never said anything about having the opportunity to adopt you." And that's all he was going to say. Although, he was positive she was going to try to drag more out of him.

"Okay, so, everyone here knows more about her past than I do?" She tossed the coffee in her mug out into the yard, then stood.

"Only because you haven't spoken to her. Well, and before that, because Uncle John wouldn't let her tell us."

Morgan turned her attention to Drew. "Wanna go shopping?"

Shopping? That's where her head was right now? That didn't seem like her.

"Sure," Drew said. "I saw a really cute boutique on the way here. I was going to make Logan stop there when we leave." She turned to him. "You're saved."

"What the fuck am I going to do?" Logan asked.

Oh, fuck. Brody would rather lick a power outlet than spend time alone with the brother of the woman he was into. He had an idea of how it would go, and it wasn't gonna be fun.

"Hang out here? Play cards with Brody or something." Morgan turned her attention to Drew. "I'm going to grab my purse from upstairs. Come see my room."

They disappeared into the house, and Brody and Logan sat in awkward silence, drinking their coffee. Maybe Logan was waiting until the women left to attempt to murder him so there'd be no witnesses. After what seemed like enough time to tour a museum, not a bedroom, they came back out.

"Oh, nice," Drew said, "it stopped raining."

"How long are you going to be?" Logan asked, sounding as though he was in pain.

"Long enough that you should get your ass over here and kiss me goodbye," Drew said, arms crossed.

He grinned and stood, then he crooked his finger at her.

She sauntered over to him and wrapped her arms around his torso.

Brody redirected his gaze to Morgan. It sucked he couldn't kiss her goodbye, but he'd promised her he wouldn't touch her in front of her brother—yet. He made a pouty face to make her aware of his disappointment.

"Logan," Morgan nearly shouted, not showing any reaction to his plight, "play nice with Brody or else."

Logan turned his head. "Or else what?"

She arched her brow. "Fuck around and find out."

He scrunched up his face like a toddler who'd been warned not to be naughty, then he winked at her.

"Okay, let's go." Drew pushed herself from Logan's hold and made her way down the porch steps.

Morgan gave him a little wave, then followed.

Just as he anticipated, once the women had driven off, Logan had questions. He settled back in the rocker. "What did you do to my sister?"

"I haven't done anything. Okay, I did kiss her." Brody held up his hands. "But that's it. I've been nothing but respectful. Ask her."

That might not be the truest statement he'd ever made, but it was close enough. Logan didn't need to know he'd handcuffed her to his headboard, or smacked her ass, or got her so riled up she stripped in front of him to prove a point.

"That's not what I mean. She's different. No, that's not accurate." Logan rubbed his head and groaned. "She's not different. She's…"

"Happy?"

He shot him a look, then pulled a face like he'd been told something awful. "What the fuck, man?"

"You don't want your sister to be happy?"

"Of course, I do."

"Just not with me?" Brody asked. "Or do you expect your sister to be alone because you're more comfortable with that?"

Logan pulled out a cigarette and lit it. "It sounds really fucked up when you put it like that."

"I have a little sister, so I get that knee-jerk reaction to your sister seeing someone. I know better than to interfere, though. As long as she's happy and safe, it's up to her who she spends her time with." At least, that's the way it'd be once Hope was allowed to date.

"I think it's fucked up that you asked her to be your partner, and now you're trying to get in her pants. Bet you thought you'd hit the jackpot when you saw her, huh?"

Brody wanted to punch him, but that wasn't going to help the situation. "I'm going to let that one slide because you're her brother."

"Do the job and keep your hands off her."

He flexed his fingers. "Why the fuck do you think you get any say in what happens between me and her?"

"She's been through enough. I don't want her hurt again."

"I'm not hurting her. Look around, Logan. I'm the only one in her life who is being part of her peace. With what she just learned, she's handling it damn well, don't you think?"

"Oh, so you get the credit for that?"

"No, she does. But it's a hell of a lot easier to process something like this when you've got unconditional support, instead of people trying to control how you react."

"I try to control how she reacts?"

Brody shrugged. "Why didn't you call before you showed up?"

"Because I was only a few hours away and I didn't want to talk about it on the phone."

"You could have given her a heads-up."

"She'd have told me not to come," Logan said, missing the point.

"I don't think that's true, but it sounds like you didn't want to take the chance on it happening, so you took that control away from her."

"You know what? Fuck off, Brody. Morgan and I have a great relationship. You think she doesn't need her family? First, you act like Uncle John is toxic. Now me." He laughed, but neither of them found any of this amusing. "You trying to isolate her is a huge red flag."

"Isolate her? Have I told you to leave? No. Just like I told John, you are welcome here any time, as long as it's okay with her. Secondly, I'm not calling anyone toxic. I see how much she's loved by her family. But if I think your actions are going to upset her, you're damn right I'm going to get in your way. I don't give a fuck if you like me."

Logan stayed quiet until he finished his cigarette. He stubbed it out in the unused sand-filled pail he'd put in the corner for Morgan's cigarette butts. Then his hand flew to his back pocket. "She stole my wallet."

"Morgan?"

"No, although I'm sure she was an accomplice. She and Uncle John thought it'd be hilarious to teach Drew to pick pockets and I'm her favorite victim."

Brody grinned. That was kind of funny.

"What are you smiling about?" Logan squinted. "They probably hit you too."

Brody pulled his wallet from his pocket and held it up. "Nope."

Logan tilted his head. "Picking pockets is child's play to my sister. You got a safe?"

His heart sank to his stomach. She wouldn't steal from him. Except, she already had. His bomb. "I'll be right back."

Logan's chuckle followed him into the house.

He took the stairs in long strides and rushed into his bedroom, going straight for the safe in his closet. After putting in the combination, he swung the door open. Right there on top was a little piece of torn paper with I.O.U. written on it.

"Fuck," Brody muttered, more confused than anything. He stuck the piece of paper in his pocket, then checked his cash. One of the banded stacks of bills was gone. Five hundred dollars.

When he returned to the porch, Logan said, "She got you, didn't she?"

"Yeah, but I don't understand. What are they up to?"

He shrugged. "No idea."

"You aren't worried?"

"Nah. Morgan's smart and capable, and Drew's not gonna do anything that could get her in legal trouble."

If Logan wasn't stressed about it, he wasn't going to be either. "Alright, then, let's go blow shit up."

44

That Hot Farmer
Morgan

MORGAN PULLED A PINK floral dress from a rack and held it up. "What about this?"

Hope tilted her head side-to-side. "I don't know about that color with my red hair."

"I've got options," Drew said, coming from the other side of the boutique with several dresses draped over her arm. "I even found something for you," she told Morgan.

"We're not shopping for me."

"You are going to come to the dance, aren't you?" Hope asked.

"Why would I?" she stuck the pink dress back where it'd come from.

"To be Brody's date."

Drew nodded. "You should go."

"He's chaperoning, not going for fun."

Drew handed off the dresses to the girl working the boutique, who gestured for them to follow.

Morgan plopped onto an upholstered bench in the dressing room area and leaned against the wall.

"Get up." Drew grabbed a short white dress from the group hanging on a hook inside the dressing room. "Try this on."

"I don't need a dress, Drew."

"But *I* need to see you in it."

"This shopping trip is about Hope. She's the one going to the dance." They'd left Brody's and gone straight to his parents' house. She'd been nervous, unsure whether Gia would trust Morgan with her daughter. It wasn't like she knew her well. But Hope had been ecstatic, and Gia seemed relieved. Drew was the ace up her sleeve. What better person to go shopping with than a fashion designer? Morgan knew Drew would do an exceptional job at helping Hope choose a dress and accessories.

"I know Brody's going to ask you to go with him," Hope said. "Are you going to turn him down?"

Her mouth opened, but she had no defense, so she snatched the dress from Drew, went into the other dressing room, and swiped the curtain shut. With the form-fitting dress on, she evaluated herself in the mirror. It had cap sleeves and a neckline that came to the base of her neck. For a dress, it was super simple. Mid-thigh length. No embellishments, nothing fancy at all. And yet...it was the perfect mix of girly and sophisticated. And it fit her like a glove.

She pulled back the curtain.

Hope had on her first dress and Drew was fussing over her, pinching the fabric in places, probably seeing where alterations could be made. They both froze when they noticed Morgan.

Drew covered her mouth with both hands.

"You look gorgeous," Hope said.

"Me? That dress is so pretty on you."

Hope's dress was sage green, had spaghetti straps and an empire waist. She did look very pretty, and Morgan wanted to get out of this dress that she had no occasion for and focus on her.

"I'm not sure if we've found the perfect dress for Hope yet, but *that* is the dress for you," Drew said.

"I don't have anywhere to wear it."

"The dance," Drew and Hope said in unison.

"I'm not going." The event was for teenagers. Making a chaperoning gig into a date would be weird. She wouldn't know anyone there, and Mr. Manners would feel obligated to keep her company, thereby not giving all his attention to watching the kids.

There was also the fact that she couldn't afford to buy it. She no longer had a steady paycheck. Those bills kept on coming, though. She needed to be careful with her finances.

Drew shooed Hope into the dressing room. "Try the blue one next."

Morgan headed to her dressing room, but Drew maneuvered around her, blocking the entrance. She pointed at the trifold mirror a couple yards away. "Get your ass over there, missy."

Only one person on this planet was more stubborn than the Cashes, and she was engaged to Logan. She loved that for her brother.

When Morgan didn't budge, Drew grabbed her arm and tugged her along to the trifold mirror. She put her hands on her shoulders, turning her and forcing her to look at her reflection. "You don't want that hot farmer to see you in this dress?"

Morgan rolled her eyes. He'd seen her in less. Drew didn't need to know that, though. Not today, anyway. She didn't want Brody to be her dirty little secret, but things between them floated in a strange, ambiguous state. Until she had a better understanding of what they were, or weren't, she'd keep it to herself. "He's seen me in a dress before."

Drew gave her a stink face in the mirror's reflection. "Not this one."

"I don't know, Drew. I'm not sure this is the right vibe for a barn dance."

"It's the right vibe, period. If you don't want to wear it to the dance, I bet he'd take you somewhere fancier."

"Can someone zip me up?" Hope asked, poking her head out of the curtain.

"I've got you," Drew said.

Morgan scurried back into the dressing room. She left the dress hanging in there and went to see Hope's next pick. It was a Cinderella blue sundress with a swishy skirt and bows on the shoulders.

"I like that one," Morgan said, coming to stand next to Drew.

Drew pursed her lips. "I don't know. It's cute, but not a showstopper."

"It's kind of scratchy inside," Hope said pulling at the top.

"Then, it's a definite no. Next!" Morgan sat on the upholstered bench. She'd wait while Hope tried on a thousand dresses if that's what it took. Lucy had been so patient whenever they had gone dress shopping. Those memories made her heart ache, but instead of pushing them out of her mind, she let them wash over her in wave after wave.

It took exactly twenty dresses before Hope found a turquoise boho maxi dress. The sheer fabric was plentiful, falling in tiers to the floor, the gold dots accenting the fabric shimmering under the light. Everything about it was perfect.

What Hope didn't know was that the dress was only the beginning.

45

I didn't like you enough, already?

BRODY

THE SUN HAD STARTED to dip by the time Morgan and Drew returned. Hanging out with Logan turned out to be not that bad. Like his sister, he was a fun person to be around. Even so, after three hours, it got awkward. What a relief that they weren't staying the night. They'd booked one of the cottages at Taylor's bed and breakfast, and first thing in the morning, they'd head back to Savannah.

A car door slammed, followed by another. Brody stopped loading the dishwasher, rinsed and dried his hands, then went to the porch.

Logan had gone out to smoke. He leaned against the railing with both forearms, and he was giving Drew a hard time about buying the entire store as she walked to the porch with several shopping bags.

Morgan walked up the steps empty handed. Her gaze tracked between him and her brother. "You two didn't kill each other?"

"Disappointed?" Logan asked.

"Kinda." She grinned, and fuck, why did he want to kiss her so bad after she'd joked about his murder? Her lack of bags had him suspicious, so he chose to focus on that.

Finding out why she'd needed that five-hundred dollars was more pressing. Maybe. Okay, it wasn't, but it *should* be.

"Want to see what I got?" Drew asked Logan.

"Is any of it lingerie?" he asked.

"No."

"Then, no."

Brody's phone buzzed in his pocket. As he fished it out to see who was calling, Morgan slipped inside the house. Seeing it was Hope, he hit ACCEPT, and held it to his ear. She probably wanted to beg him to take her shopping again. He supposed he'd have to bite the bullet and do it. "Hey, Hope."

"I'm calling to say thank you. Dressing shopping with Morgan and Drew was so fun," she said with pure joy in her voice. "So, thank you for asking her to take me, and also, thank you for paying for everything."

So, that's where the money went. And Morgan had given him credit for all of it. "Uh, you're welcome. Glad you had fun and got what you needed."

"Okay," she said, and he could tell she was ready to get off the phone. She probably wanted to call her friends and tell them all about it, but his parents had raised her right, so he wasn't surprised she'd called him first to express her gratitude. "Talk to you later."

"Bye." He stuck the phone back in his pocket and went into the house. He couldn't understand why Morgan had been sneaky about doing something nice for his sister, but he was going to find out.

She had the fridge door open and pulled out two bottles of beer. She looked over when he came toward her.

"What? I didn't like you enough, already? You had to go and take my sister dress shopping?" Hard to love? Nah. Too fucking easy to love.

But even if he could wrap his mind around it and acknowledge it to himself, he was certain it would send her running if he admitted his feelings ran that deep.

Brody took the bottles from her, set them to the side, then backed her up against the cabinets. Grabbing her waist, he lifted her onto the counter.

Morgan gasped, eyes going wide. "You sound mad…"

He curled his hand around the back of her neck. "The only thing I'm mad about is you, Morgan. You drive me crazy in the best fucking way." He sealed his mouth to hers. The kiss wasn't gentle or sweet. He didn't have that in him at the moment. But at some point, he was going to have to find it in him because it was what she deserved.

Impatient for her to open her mouth to him, he pressed on her chin with his thumb. When her lips parted, he swept his tongue inside. He flattened his palm across her lower back and urged her closer until her body was flush to his.

With a kiss-muffled moan, she wrapped her arms around his neck and her legs around his waist.

He slid his hand from her knee upward, creeping under her skirt, gripping her thigh. He slanted his mouth across hers over and over, not even close to getting enough of her and the little noises she made in the back of her throat.

Her hands drifted down his chest, grabbing fistfuls of his shirt.

Distantly, in the back of his mind, the sound of the screen door squeaking registered, but he couldn't bring himself to stop kissing her to see who'd come in.

A hand landed on his shoulder and tugged him backward. As his body lost contact with Morgan's, he braced himself. As expected, Logan's knuckles connected with his face. He took the punch and breathed through the sting.

"Logan!" Morgan slid off the counter and put herself in front of him. "What the actual fuck?"

Brody broke into a wide grin. She was being protective. *Of him.* Siding with him over her own flesh and blood.

Drew burst through the door, her gaze bouncing between the three of them. "What happened?"

"Logan punched Brody," she said, still staring him down.

"Oh my god," Drew muttered. "Logan! What the hell is wrong with you?"

"You didn't see the way he was kissing her. Like he—like he —"

"Don't even try to finish that," Drew said. "Calm the fuck down. My brothers saw you kiss me, and they didn't lose their shit."

Logan rubbed his forehead. "That's different. They're not in a relationship."

"You're delusional." Drew snorted. "Neither were we at the time. We were just fucking. Mind your own business, 'kay?"

Well, damn. Granted, Brody hadn't had a real conversation with Drew, but he'd have never guessed she'd get so salty. That was good, though. Logan needed that.

Morgan laughed. "Ouch. Burn."

"She's perfect for him," he whispered in her ear.

Her shoulders shook, probably trying to hold in her laughter.

Logan's gaze snapped to his sister. "What are you laughing about?"

"Nothing."

His gaze shifted to Brody, then back to her. His brow lowered, like the impossible had happened and his world no longer made sense. "Morgan, I know you think you want—"

"Not-uh," she said, effectively cutting him off. She jabbed her finger in his direction. "You do not get to tell me what I want. My life, my choices. I can take care of myself."

"I know you can," Logan said, head down, then glanced up at her with a sheepish expression. "I really did come to see how you were dealing with the Lucy stuff, and because I missed you. Not to check up on you."

"Aww." Morgan walked to him and gave him a hug. "You really know how to dig yourself out of a hole, don't you?"

46
Call Your Mom
Morgan

"DREW, GET MY FIRST aid kit from my room, and take care of Brody," Morgan said. "Logan and I are going for a walk."

Drew shook her head as though she'd been asked to perform open-heart surgery. "You're the nurse, not me."

Brody grabbed her around the waist and pulled her close to whisper in her ear. "You're *my* nurse, remember?"

She pushed up on tiptoe and poked at his cheek. "It's swelling, and you have a cut. We need to get antiseptic on it."

"I'll live."

"At least put some ice on it."

"Yes, ma'am." He pecked her on the lips.

She shook her head at him. What happened to him not touching her in front of Logan? Oh well, she supposed the cat was out of the bag.

She led Logan outside. A couple steps into their walk, she said, "I can't believe you did that."

He groaned. "I know. After what Eric did to you, I just...*rage* even thinking about you with any man. But that's my hang up, and I need to get over it. You deserve to be happy."

She linked her arm through his and continued to the pond. "Thank you."

"So, you really like him?"

He had no idea how much she liked Brody. Brody might not even know how much. "I really do. A lot."

It was as if each minute spent with him led her closer not toward the person she'd been, but toward the person she was meant to be. Being around him felt right. Even though he always found fun—or made it when there was none—his calm soothed her chaos.

"He better be good to you." He pulled his pack of cigarettes out and offered her one.

She shook her head.

"You quit?"

"Yeah. You should too."

He sighed and lit one up. "I know, but today's not the day."

Fair enough. Quitting was hard, and it had to be the person's decision. Being pushed into it was counterproductive.

"Maybe you could quit before your wedding. When's that going to be, again?"

"Ask Drew. She's the one avoiding it."

Morgan frowned. "Too busy with her new career?"

"Maybe. I don't know. I think it's probably got something to do with her mom not being there for it."

Logan wouldn't rush her. Besides, they already lived together, and Morgan didn't think either of them were in a hurry to start a family. Getting married wouldn't change much for them, if anything.

"Look, Drew said I should keep my mouth shut about you working with Brody, but I'm not gonna leave without telling you to be careful."

"I know what I'm doing."

"It only takes getting caught one time to end up dead or in jail."

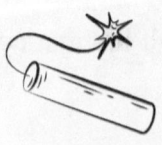

Morgan pulled a bag of frozen peas from the freezer and wrapped it in a tea towel. She walked over to the kitchen table where Brody sat and pressed it against his cheek. "Hold this."

"I already iced it," he said, even though he did as she ordered.

"And it's still swollen, so you're going to keep icing it."

Logan and Drew had left, and she was oddly nervous to be alone with Brody. Especially since he was being so handsy. His fingers trailed up the back of her thigh, sending shivers through her. She wanted Brody, but she got a lump in her throat whenever she thought about doing anything more than kissing him.

She flipped open her first aid kit and pulled out antiseptic and butterfly closures. "Why did you let Logan hit you? You're fast. You could have dodged it."

"He needed to get it out of his system."

Out of his system? What the hell did that mean? She turned with the supplies in her hand. "What are you talking about?"

"It's an older brother thing. You wouldn't understand."

Morgan rolled her eyes. "Speaking of siblings, why couldn't your mom take Hope dress shopping?"

He stayed quiet for a few beats. "She's afraid to leave my dad."

"Why?"

"Because the last time she left him for more than twenty minutes, he had an episode. Hope was with him, and she didn't know what to do. It was bad. So, now, she doesn't go far."

She didn't know what to say. She could understand the fear, but she didn't see why Brody or even a home health nurse couldn't stay with his dad from time to time so his mom could get out and do things, most importantly, making memories with her daughter.

The second she moved back within reach, Brody's hands were on her, this time her waist, urging her closer until his knee was between her legs. She pulled the bag of peas away from his face.

"What's wrong?" he asked. "You look like you're contemplating something awful hard right now."

"I can't stop thinking about Lucy." The shopping trip had really done a number on her emotionally. "I keep imagining how she must be feeling right now. Her relationship with Uncle John is wrecked, and she probably thinks I'm never going to talk to her again."

"Call her."

"But—"

"Baby, that's your mom. I don't care what anyone thinks or what the government has documented. She's your mom. Call her."

"Aren't you getting tired of my family drama getting in the way?" She swiped at the small cut on his cheek with an antiseptic wipe.

He winced. "A little bit, sure. But I'm not free from family drama. I live right next to them, and it will bleed over into this at some point. As long as you and I are good, and don't have drama between us, I can handle the outside nonsense."

"And if we do have drama?"

"Then I'll handle you."

A little gasp slipped out before she could stop it. His knack for knowing what to say to elicit an unexpected turned-on reaction was not fair.

He grabbed her wrist, took the wipe from her, and tossed it on the table. Speaking of fast, he put his hand under her knee and lifted, moving it to the outside of his leg, and forcing her to sit on his lap before she could so much as shriek.

She grabbed his shoulders. "Brody!"

He grinned at her and tugged at the hem of her skirt. "You have about thirty seconds to finish what you're doing, or you won't be calling Lucy until the morning."

Her chest grew tight. She tore open the closure package. "About that…"

"Calling Lucy?

"No." She secured the bandage over his cut, pulling it together where the swelling had separated his skin. "You and me…"

"What don't you want to say? You and me…having sex?"

Her shoulders sagged. She opened another closure. "Yes."

"Is this where you tell me you're not ready?"

She shrugged. She was and she wasn't. Whenever he touched her or kissed her, she wanted more. So much more. But she was also still riding the aftershocks of the emotional earthquake her family had unleashed.

"I can wait."

She looked at him, her heart beating fast. "You can?"

"I have a feeling it will be worth it."

47
Say You Understand
Morgan

IN BABY BLUE PAJAMAS Lucy had given her for her last birthday, Morgan crawled under the covers and laid on her side. She opened her laptop and took a deep breath. If she did this, she was going to cry. They were both going to cry.

She hit the button to video chat Lucy, then rested her head on the pillow while it rang.

Lucy's face appeared. She raised a finger while she fiddled with her phone. "Sorry. I had to figure out how to turn the microphone on. Can you hear me now?"

"Yeah, I can hear you." And it was so nice. Lucy's voice was the balm she needed.

"I'm glad you called." The screen went fuzzy for a minute before Lucy lowered herself onto her favorite chair and propped her phone up on something—probably the stack of novels on her side table. She would have just been getting home from work, but she wasn't dressed like she'd been at the office. That was the gray sweatshirt she wore when she cleaned the house. Her face lacked makeup and her strawberry blond hair was pulled up on top of her head rather sloppily.

"Are you okay?"

"That's what I'm supposed to be asking you."

Morgan rubbed her forehead. "You know what hurts the most?"

"What?"

"That you and Uncle John hid it from us. I'm not mad about any of it. I don't care that you didn't legally adopt me. I don't care that you and Uncle John had feelings for each other. I only care that you hid such a big part of your life from me."

Lucy hung her head and wiped at her eye.

"But maybe that's what we do," Morgan said softly. "I'm a hypocrite because I never told you everything that happened when I was in Savannah." *God, this was hard.* "Eric messed me up, Lucy. Not physically, but…I'm still struggling."

She'd glanced up while Morgan was talking and knit her eyebrows. "It's okay to be different after things destroy the version of yourself you knew."

Her heart squeezed and her nose stung. She scrunched her face, fighting back a sob. Why was it so emotionally overwhelming to have someone know exactly what she'd been struggling with and give her the permission to accept what she thought she shouldn't accept.

They spent the next two hours talking. Lucy was also a survivor of psychological abuse and had endured other types. She didn't go into great detail, but it helped knowing that even the strongest woman she knew had been susceptible to having her mind warped.

Morgan learned that when she'd started school, Lucy tried to bring up adopting her and Logan with John. She'd changed her mind, but he refused to discuss it.

She told Lucy about Eric. And then about Brody. "He kissed me."

"How was it?" Lucy leaned forward and propped her elbow on the arm of the chair, her fist tucked under her chin.

"Explosive."

"Ah, well," Lucy said with a smile, "that makes sense."

They both laughed.

"Thank you," Morgan said quietly as she ran her fingers over the stitching in the quilt.

"For?"

"Him."

"Honey…" If Lucy had been there, she'd definitely have pulled Morgan in for a hug.

She shook her head. "I was irritated with you for meddling, but the more I thought about it, the more I started to unravel it. You wouldn't have risked your relationship with Uncle John simply because you thought Brody and I would be cute together."

"If John and I were meant to be…in twenty-five years, we would have figured out how to be. I'm not happy unless you're happy, and after I got to know Brody, *I knew*. The only way to make it happen was to defy John's rules, so I did what I had to do."

"You don't think things will ever be good between you two?" It hurt her heart in the worst way to think they'd never all be together again. Holidays would be tough.

"Your uncle is a very stubborn man." Lucy sighed, then flashed her a *it's just the way things are* smile. "He sounded contrite when he showed up here to say that he'd told you, but I'm not going to make it easy on him. I want a proper grovel." She winked.

Morgan laughed. Oh, what she wouldn't give to see her uncle try to win Lucy back. By the time they finished their call, her eyes were drooping, and the next thing she knew, it was morning.

Brody had already gone off to do his farmer thing, so she'd had coffee while playing with Buster, took a shower, and put her vision of Gill's floor plan to paper. She was on the couch, organizing the photos of the equipment she'd snapped at the party, when he came in the house.

He went into the kitchen first and turned on the faucet. After a few minutes, he came into the living room and dropped onto the other end of the couch.

Her gaze wandered to him. "Hey."

He gave her a goofy grin, then bit into the green apple he held. As he chewed, he kept staring, his eyes shining with mischief.

"What are you up to?" She set her tablet on the coffee table and told her stupid pulse to stop racing. At times, she felt so relaxed around Brody, but just as often, she felt breathless and antsy.

"Nothin'." His grin stayed locked in place.

She leveled him with a stern gaze, letting him know his attempt at innocence was wasted. "Out with it."

"I'm not up to anything. I was going to ask you if you'd ever been to a county fair, but then I started imagining all the baby animals you'd try to talk me into bringing home."

Despite trying to not smile, she failed. "No, I have not been to a county fair."

He took another bite of his apple and wiped the juice that ran down his chin with the back of his hand. "You have plans for tonight?"

Her forehead wrinkled. "Um, no..." The only person she knew in the area was Brody, and she had no idea what there was to do around here.

"Do you want to go to the fair with me?"

"Like a date?"

He set the apple, which was now only a core, on the coffee table, and put his arm on the back of the couch and scooted closer. "Our *first* date, actually. And then tomorrow night, there'll be rides and carnival games at the fair, so we could do that for our second date. For our third date, I'm taking you to the dance."

"The dance for teenagers that you're chaperoning?"

"That's the one."

"It's a dance for teenagers, and you're chaperoning."

"Uh-huh," he said slowly, tucking her hair behind her ear and placing a soft kiss on her neck. "You gonna be my date or not?"

Heat flooded her body. She wet her lips. "It doesn't seem appropriate for a chaperone to take a date."

"Then we'll be inappropriate," he said in a husky whisper before taking her earlobe between his lips.

Morgan shivered and held back a moan. It filled her with the warm fuzzies that even though ninety-nine percent of the time, Brody was well-behaved, if she was by his side, he had no qualms about misbehaving. "So, you're asking me on three dates at once?"

He kissed her jawline. "Yeah, but if I have to, I'll bring out Bossy Brody to *tell* you that you're going."

She shoved him.

He didn't budge.

"I will go to the fair with you, but not the dance."

Brody cleared his throat, swept his arm under her knees, and the next thing she knew, she was on her back on the couch and he was hovering over her. "Baby, at six o'clock the night of the dance, you're going to be standing on that porch in a dress. Say you understand. And let's not forget, it's already been proven that you can't outrun me."

She reached up and put her hand on the back of his head, lifting her own to press her lips to his.

He pulled back. "Say. You. Understand."

Her stomach flipped. It was truly unfortunate she got so flustered when he dropped his voice like that that. "You don't want to kiss me?"

For several heartbeats, each one slamming so loudly in her chest he probably heard it, he stared at her. Then slowly, he lowered his head, brushing his mouth over hers. It wasn't much of a kiss, so she wrapped her arms around his neck and nipped his bottom lip.

His hips lowered, and she instinctively spread her legs for him. As if she'd somehow stripped him of his ability to resist her, he groaned and dove into kissing her. He tangled his hands in her hair as he slid his tongue against hers. The grinding of his pelvis against hers sent ripples of pleasure through her.

She shuddered when his hand traveled under her shirt, covering her breast. No regrets going braless for her. The rough texture of his palm and fingers against her nipple made her clit throb. The nerves she'd been feeling about having sex with Brody switched teams. Every part of her was firmly in the *do anything you want to me but do it right now* camp.

The sound of the backdoor opening vaguely registered. It wasn't until Brody jerked back and the heat and weight of his body left hers, that she fully realized that meant they had company.

He pushed off her and stood, subtly adjusting himself.

Morgan sat up and turned her head.

Nick stood between the living room and kitchen, grinning his head off. "Is this a bad time?"

"Yeah. What do you want?" Brody asked.

"I got invited to come to the stadium tonight for the game. I get to bring a guest and sit in the dugout."

"No way. That's awesome."

Nick's gaze darted to Morgan, then back to Brody. "You'll go with me, right?"

Brody looked at her.

"You should go," she said, pushing off the couch. Their first date, if it could even be considered that after all the time they'd spent together, could wait.

He looked like he had no idea what to do.

Morgan huffed. "I really didn't want to go out with you anyway, so this works out."

She headed for the stairs, but he caught her round the waist, and held tight.

"When do we need to leave?" he asked Nick.

"In thirty minutes, and"—Nick cringed—"they booked us a room so we can go to breakfast with the coaches tomorrow morning."

All her squirming did nothing to loosen his hold on her, but that detail had her motionless.

Brody stiffened. "Uh..."

Nick frowned. "If you've got other plans—"

"He's going," Morgan said. "Pick him up in thirty minutes. He'll be ready."

He squeezed her. Neither of them said anything until Nick left.

"We're not finished," Brody rasped against her ear. "Say you understand, Morgan."

"What is it I'm supposed to understand, again?"

He nipped the tender spot where her neck curved into her shoulder.

She hissed. "Okay. I understand."

"What time?"

"Six."

"Where?"

"The porch."

"Wearing?"

"A dress."

"Good girl." He released her.

She bit her lip so she wouldn't make any embarrassing noises. It was bad enough her nipples hardened with those two little words. "You better get ready. You only have a half hour."

He grabbed her by the waist and pulled her against him, this time chest to chest. "I can get ready in ten minutes. That leaves twenty minutes for this." He kissed her, this time slowly and sweetly.

Her toes curled into the rug.

He backed up, taking her with him, then eased onto the couch.

She'd only just straddled him when her phone vibrated on the coffee table. She bent backward, bracing herself with one hand on his knee and the other reaching for the phone.

His fingers dug into her side, his other hand flat against her stomach and sliding upward. "You *cannot* bend like this in front of me when I have to leave."

She righted herself and smirked. Then she checked the phone screen. "It's your sister."

"Oh, fun. See? I told you my family wasn't going to be shy."

She put the phone to her ear. "Hi."

"Hey, Morgan. I have a hair appointment today and my mom was wondering if you'd be able to give me a ride."

She stared at Brody while she listened, and then said, "I'd love to. Could I talk to your mom for a minute, though?"

His eyes wrinkled at the corners as he squinted at her.

"Hi, Morgan," Gia said through the phone a minute later.

"Hi," she said. "I was thinking that maybe instead of me taking Hope to her appointment, you could take her, and I'll stay with Theo."

Brody opened his mouth, but she covered it with her hand.

"Oh, that's okay," Gia said. "I don't think—"

"I'm a nurse," she said. "I'm qualified to deal with anything that could happen, although I'm sure we'll be just fine. You should have a day out with your daughter. Make some memories."

There was a short silence through the line and then, "Thank you. We'll be leaving in an hour."

"I'll be there." She ended the call and set the phone on the couch cushion.

Brody rested his head back on the cushions and released a long breath. "It doesn't feel right for me to be off having fun while you take care of my dad. I should be doing that."

"You're doing what your dad would be doing with Nick if he could." She ran her finger down his front, catching on his belt. "And, not to hurt your feelings, but who do you think your dad would rather hang out with?"

He laughed loudly, then cupped her face and brought his closer until their noses touched. "Will you be okay here by yourself tonight?"

"I think I'll survive."

"Call me if you can't sleep."

Her breath caught. She'd never get used to his thoughtfulness. Maybe she didn't want to.

48

Back the Fuck Up

BRODY

The instant Brody's foot hit the dirt in his driveway as he stepped out of Nick's car, he had to force himself to walk at a reasonable pace. Talking to Morgan through text messages was nice and all, but not as nice as being able to touch her and smell her and be near her.

He went in through the back door and dumped his duffel bag on the floor.

His dad sat at the kitchen table. Fishing lures and various tackle covered the surface.

"What are you doing here?" Brody asked, trying to sound curious and not like he wanted him to leave immediately. He scanned the kitchen, his gaze landing on Morgan in the corner, mixing something in a big bowl.

She set down the bowl and wiped her hands on a towel. "He's going to teach me to fish."

"You don't seem very happy to see me, son." His dad snickered and picked up a pair of needle nose pliers.

This was his house. Coming home and kissing her shouldn't be an awkward event. So, he wasn't going to let it be. He strode across the kitchen, cupped her face, leaned down, and kissed her.

She leaned into him, soft and smelling good and perfect in his arms.

More. That's all he could think about.

More skin.

More throaty noises.

More—

His dad cleared his throat loudly.

Brody smiled against her lips. "Hi."

She dropped her forehead to his chest and giggled.

"So, you're going fishing?" he asked, nudging her back and putting space between them that would hopefully extinguish his burning need for her.

His dad had been homebound, aside from doctor's appointments, for the past two years. Brody often felt guilty for not finding ways to get him out and about but doing so meant getting over two hurdles–the first being his mother. Even though Brody had bought his dad a reliable, portable oxygen tank, his mom's anxiety about his dad's health prevented it from getting much use. Arguing with her about it was a lost cause. Apparently, not where Morgan was concerned, though. She'd found a way to bust through all her what-ifs and get his mom to concede to accepting help.

Morgan had a big heart, but he didn't want to take advantage. Being a nurse didn't make her obligated to be a stand-in caregiver. This change of scenery and company was probably great for his dad, though.

The other obstacle was Brody's workload. He had to keep the farm running. He'd committed to stepping into his father's shoes—big shoes to fill—and even though he'd stumbled, and would continue to stumble, he wasn't giving up. For now, he could only do his best, and hope to make up for anything he'd failed at once they'd finished the Gill job.

She turned around and resumed mixing. "We're going to have a picnic lunch by the pond, and yes, *hopefully*, catch a fish."

"Just one?" He shifted on his heel to shoot a grin at his dad. Try as he might, he couldn't picture Morgan baiting a hook or reeling in a fish.

"Keeping our expectations low," his dad said.

"Do you want to join us?" she asked.

"Can't. Got too much to get done." He kissed her on the forehead. "Don't wear yourself out fishing. We're going to the fair tonight."

She muttered something about being bossy under her breath.

Somehow, he found the control to resist grabbing her and showing her what bossy really looked like. The surprise in her eyes whenever he switched from easygoing to pushy thrilled him. He wasn't sure if her surprise was because she didn't see it coming *or* because her involuntary reaction was so out of character.

He got lost in his to-do list, appreciative of having Nick home, which helped him get back on top of things much quicker than if he'd had to tackle it alone. It didn't hurt that Nick was just as anxious to finish so he could go to the fair too. He wouldn't admit to it but having plans with Taylor motivated him to get shit done.

When Brody called it quits and returned to the house, Morgan was descending the stairs in ripped jeans that hung low on her hips and a gray tank top.

"How was fishing?" he asked as he stripped on the way to the laundry room, save for his boxers.

"Awkward for me, entertaining as hell for your father." The smile she gave him said she had no regrets, then her face sobered. Her gaze swept over him as he stood in the doorway of the laundry room. "Wha—what are you doing?"

"Putting my filthy clothes in the laundry before I take a shower."

She fidgeted, her finger hooked into her neckline, moving back and forth along the edge of the fabric.

He had about ten seconds to get out of her presence before his dick got hard enough that there would be no hiding it. "Are you ready?"

Her eyes seemed to be glued to his stomach. "Oh, um, I know the other night I said I wasn't, and at the time that was true, but now—"

Brody pinched the bridge of his nose. "Morgan. Please, god, stop. I was asking if you're ready to go to the fair."

"Oh..."

"I need you to go stand over there so you're not within my reach on my way upstairs, or else my fantasy of making out with you on the

Ferris wheel is going to stay a fantasy, and I was really looking forward to making it a reality."

She bit her lip and stayed right where she was.

He took a step toward her. "This is not the time to try me, baby. We're going to have a memorable first date and it's happening tonight. Do you understand?"

Her lip popped free of her teeth. She nodded.

"Then, back the fuck up."

An hour after they got to the fair, Brody already knew this was the best first date of his life. No topping the way Morgan cooed at the lambs and piglets, or getting to feed her cotton candy and taste the sweetness on her tongue afterward.

With a strip of tickets, they headed toward the area of the fairgrounds where the carnival had been set up. Laughter and screams of delight mingled with the sounds of the games. The smell of popcorn and funnel cake floated in the air. For a summer night, it wasn't too hot and as the sun set, a breeze swept through.

"Are you good at these games?" she asked as they passed the balloon dart toss.

He wrapped his arm around her waist and pulled her closer. "Feeling competitive?"

"Always."

He pulled her over to the dart toss and paid the attendant. Morgan popped the same number of balloons as he did, but he won because he hit a balloon with a red star underneath it. He let her choose a pink octopus stuffed animal as the prize.

At the goldfish-ping-pong-ball game, he bought thirty balls and set the

basket between them.

"I'm better at this one." She grabbed a ball and arced her wrist. It landed straight in a fishbowl.

"Do it again," he said, handing her another ball.

With the same grace as before, he watched her sink ten consecutive balls. "Well, hell, don't stop now." He gestured toward the basket.

Of the thirty balls, she sank twenty-three, including hitting the center bowl. The attendant told her she could pick any fish she wanted, but she said she didn't like having fish as pets any more than she liked catching them on a hook, so they headed for the Ferris wheel fishless.

He spotted Nick and Taylor at the strong man game, and guided Morgan over.

Nick swung the oversized mallet and lit up the entire column of lights.

Whistles sang, but Taylor only gave an unimpressed glance in his direction.

Nick's face fell.

Brody tried not to laugh. If he wanted to win Taylor over, his usual tactics were going to need an upgrade. They'd known each other since childhood. Showing off his athleticism was not going to work on her.

After he'd introduced Morgan and Taylor, Nick asked, "Hit up the tractor showcase, yet?"

The showcase was a mix of antique and brand-new models. Normally, it was Brody's favorite part of the fair, but he didn't think it would interest Morgan.

"Nah. We're on our way to the Ferris wheel."

"Have you seen the line?" Taylor asked.

He swiveled his head. Damn. That was a long line.

"If you want to go check out the tractors, I can hold our place in line," Morgan said.

"Believe it or not, I have seen a few tractors in my lifetime." This was their first date. All that mattered was making sure she had a good time, and that he got to kiss her on the Ferris wheel.

"Go ahead," Taylor said. "I'll wait in line with Morgan."

"Come on." Nick put a hand on his back and pushed him. "She's not going to vanish if you take your eyes off her for a minute."

With the three of them ganging up on him, he relented, but that damn line better move fast because when he got back, he was making out with her whether they were on the ride or not.

49
Taylor Tells All
Morgan

TAYLOR HAD THE DEEPEST brown eyes Morgan had ever seen. With her long brown hair, brilliant smile, and legs that went on for days, it wasn't a surprise Nick found her attractive. But once Morgan had a conversation with her, she'd realized Nick was in way over his head.

Taylor's personality was fabulous. She was down to earth, funny, and took no shit—especially from Nick. It was highly entertaining to see how he hardly took his eyes off her, yet couldn't catch her eye, try as he might. It wasn't lost on Morgan that even though Nick was a huge flirt, all that confidence and charisma disappeared in Taylor's presence.

"I heard you own a bed and breakfast," Morgan said as they got in the line for the Ferris wheel. Drew and Logan had stayed there for the night, and they'd been impressed with the place itself and Taylor's hospitality.

She nodded. "My great aunt left me her house, which is actually a mansion. I sank my college savings into renovating it and having three tiny cottages built on the property. Most of my income comes from weddings and events, though. People don't seem to be into the whole bed and breakfast concept anymore."

"My brother's fiancée had nothing but wonderful things to say."

"I put them in one of the cottages near the beach to give them more privacy. Hey, you should come by. It gets pretty boring during the week."

"I'd love to."

The line moved faster than she'd expected, and before long, they were only four people ahead of them.

Morgan spotted a glimpse of familiar red hair in the line for the swings. "There's Hope."

Taylor swiveled her head. "And she's with a boy—who has got to be at least three years older than her. She better get on that ride before her brothers see."

She laughed. "I'll distract Brody, but you'll have to handle Nick."

"I've been handling Nick since we were in preschool." Taylor smirked and tossed her hair over her shoulder. "I love how protective of her they are, though. Anyone who says blood is thicker than water, hasn't met the Lewis siblings."

"What do you mean? Is Hope adopted?"

Taylor wrinkled her brow. "No, Nick and Brody are. You didn't know that?"

Morgan shook her head and tried to breathe through the uneasiness bubbling inside her.

"Crap," she muttered. "It's not a secret or anything. I assumed Brody would have mentioned it."

She'd noticed the lack of resemblance when she'd met his parents. How hadn't she put the truth together sooner? More importantly, why was Brody keeping it from her?

"Fuck." Taylor smacked her head. "Brody's a great guy. I don't know why he didn't say anything about it. Maybe he never found a time where it made sense to mention it."

Right. Like all the times they'd talked about Uncle John adopting her and Logan, or the very recent time when they'd learned Lucy had passed on the opportunity to adopt them.

"Yeah, that's probably it," Morgan said.

Strong arms circled her, and heat coated her back. "Miss me?" Brody whispered in her ear.

Nick slung his arm around Taylor's neck. "Should I go get us ride tickets?"

"I'm not getting on that fucking thing," Taylor said, pushing his arm off her. "Here, I'll hold your octopus while you ride."

"Afraid of heights," Nick said to Morgan as she passed the stuffed animal to Taylor.

The line moved up as the attendant opened the gate and let the two teenage girls in front of them through. Out of instinct, Morgan moved forward, but she didn't want to go on the ride anymore. She didn't even want to be at the fair.

Too bad she had nowhere to go. Maybe she could stay at Taylor's bed and breakfast.

She was trying to figure out what move to make, when the gate opened, and Brody nudged her through. Getting up on the platform and settled into the Ferris wheel car was an out of body experience. Too late she realized she was stuck in a tiny space with a man she'd just learned had been keeping big secrets from her.

Maybe Taylor was right. Maybe he hadn't found the right time. With all she'd been going through, it could be that he hadn't wanted to make things about him. If the perfect opportunity presented itself, would he fess up? Time to find out.

"Having fun?" Brody asked as the ride moved, raising them farther off the ground.

"Do you want to have kids?"

He put his arm around her. He probably thought this was a normal question for the beginning of a relationship. "One day."

"Would you consider adopting?"

The way he tensed sent off alarm bells in her brain. "What brought on this line of questioning?"

"Don't you think we should talk about it?"

He sighed. "I *thought* you and I were beyond this. If you have something you want to know, you don't need to play head games."

"Oh, I'm playing head games?" She scooted as far away as she could, which was only about two inches in the tiny Ferris wheel car with this big jerk. She couldn't wait until they reached the bottom, and she could tell the attendant to let her off. "Fuck you, and your stupid nice guy act."

The wheel came to an abrupt stop. Their car rocked at the very top.

"I didn't intentionally hide it from you."

"Then, why did I find out from someone else? The entire time we've known each other, you've known I wasn't raised by my biological parents. Why the hell wouldn't you have told me you're adopted too?"

"Because I don't like talking about it," he said quietly. "I know I've had plenty of opportunities to tell you, but I kept telling myself there'd be more and that I'd take the next one."

She swiped at the tear that rolled down her cheek. Damn it, why wasn't this ride moving?

"My story isn't like yours, Morgan." His voice, although calm, was thick with pain. "The only information I have about my biological parents is what I remember. It was a closed adoption, and I don't even know what happened to them."

"You could have told me that."

"I didn't want to. I don't want to talk about it right now, either. Every part of me wants to shut down because talking about it means I have to think about it, and that hurts." He huffed and pulled off his hat. He scratched at the top of his head, then pulled it back on. "That's not fair to you, though. I fucked up. Please, let me fix it."

"Fix it?" This all sounded too familiar. Too much like the lies she'd been fed in the past. "Unless you have a time machine, you can't. It's too late."

50
Soul Ache
Morgan

"Get out of my way." Morgan tried to skirt him as he met her on the passenger side of his truck.

He stepped to the side and watched her go into the house. Fuck. He'd never considered that she might hear it from someone else. His family never talked about it, so he hadn't worried one of them would tell her before he had the chance. He'd thought he had more time.

He'd expected her to be up in her room with the door closed when he came in the house. But that was not the case. She was standing in the kitchen, leaning against the sink, arms crossed, waiting. Waiting to fight with him.

Alright. Fine.

She was pissed, and rightly so, but she needed to get that out of her system so she could be receptive to what he had to say.

He stopped several feet from her. "Go ahead. Let me have it."

Her eyes widened and she gulped air. "That's what you say to me? How about sorry? How about—"

"Excuses?" he said, cutting her off. "Is that what you want, Morgan? For me to make up a bullshit story to tug at your heartstrings when the truth is that I should have taken one of the countless opportunities I had to tell you, but I didn't?"

Maybe that was what she expected. It was probably what she was used to. But that's not what she was going to get. Not from him.

"No, that's not what I want," she said, raising her voice and flinging her arms out. "You're not the person I thought you were. I don't trust you anymore. Nothing you say will make what you did okay. It's too late."

"No, it's not. If it was too late, you'd be upstairs packing your shit."

Her lips pinched together, and her eyes narrowed.

Shit. That might have been too far. He wanted to help her work out her mad, not damage her pride. Besides, there was no way he was letting her leave tonight. Come tomorrow, if that's what she wanted to do, he wouldn't stop her. It wasn't going to come to that, though.

Because he'd spend the entire night begging her not to give up on them if he had to.

He pulled out a chair and sat at the table. "I'm sorry I hurt you, Morgan. You shouldn't have had to find out from someone else, but I wasn't keeping it from you because I didn't want you to know."

"Regardless, you kept it from me. That's the part I'm hung up on. I've told you my darkest secrets," she said, barely above a whisper. "I should have left with Logan and Drew."

"Baby…" He ran a hand through his hair. "Sit the fuck down and stop saying shit you don't mean."

"Don't tell me what to do," she shouted.

"Fine. But let me point out that you only have two options. The first is we work through this because we're damn good together, but neither of us are perfect. We're going to make mistakes. The other option is you walk away from this, from me, and we never see each other again. And for the record, the mere thought of you choosing that option makes my soul ache."

She shifted her stance, her gaze pinned to the floorboards. "If you want to talk, I'm listening."

It taxed him beyond measure to not go and pull her into his arms. The last thing he'd ever want to do was hurt her, but he had. He'd been trying to be her rock, and now he was the one responsible for her pain.

He swallowed, so freaking uncomfortable with what he was about to confess. The guilt sat in his gut like an anchor. "A couple years ago, I tried to find my biological parents. Or find out what happened to them. But I didn't get anywhere with it, and then my dad got sick, and I felt like shit for looking, so I gave up. No one else knows that. You're the only person I've ever told."

She glanced up. "Why are you ashamed of that?"

"They went above and beyond to be good parents. I don't want them to think it wasn't enough, or that I didn't appreciate it."

"It's normal to want to know about your biological parents when you're adopted. It doesn't make you ungrateful. They told you that you were adopted, right? They didn't hide it?"

He released a short laugh. "I was five when they adopted us."

She gasped softly, like it was all falling into place, and she was starting to understand the differences in their experiences. "You remember your parents?"

He nodded slowly. That also felt like a sin, like somehow Theo's and Gia's love should have washed away any memories of his life before them. "I remember little things. My mom tucking me in at night. I remember my dad throwing me high in the air and catching me. Getting a puppy for Christmas. Going to the hospital when Nick was born."

"Does he remember?"

He shook his head. That part really sucked. His brother couldn't relate to him at all on this. No one could. Even Morgan. Like Nick, she'd been far too young to have memories of her mother, and she had no desire to meet her father. "He was too little."

"You could have told me. I might not understand exactly what it's like for you, but aren't you the one who said our situations don't have to be identical for us to commiserate?"

"I don't *want* to commiserate. I want to focus on the time I have left with the man who raised me and taught me everything I know."

Morgan wiped at her eyes. "Even when my world was falling apart because I found out my family was built on lies? You couldn't have gotten over your guilt, so I didn't have to feel so alone?"

"I did my best to be there for you. I got you out of Las Vegas when you asked. I held you for hours. After all that, you still felt alone?"

"I didn't then, but I do now."

That hurt more than an ax to the heart. "I convinced myself that it'd be self-centered to bring it up while you were going through that. It was the perfect excuse to get out of doing the thing I didn't want to do."

She walked closer, her expression neutral. "If you can lie to yourself that easy, then what hope is there that you won't lie to me?"

He hated that this had happened at all, but especially on their first date. "You asked me to promise I'd never lie to you. I don't think you'd have asked that if you didn't think I couldn't follow through."

They kept slipping, sliding backward. He wanted her to trust him, but he could only go so far. She was holding herself back.

"If you're not ready to make our relationship physical, I can wait, but I don't want to wait on your heart, Morgan. I swear, I'll catch you. All you have to do is let go."

51
The Queen of DTSS
Morgan

MORGAN BLINKED BACK THE tears stinging her eyes and sniffed. Up until she'd found out Brody was adopted she'd felt so good. Being with him came easy. He smiled all the time, which made her smile. The way he looked at her sometimes, though…it made her knees buckle.

Kissing him. The feel of his hands on her skin. How he held her. She didn't want to lose any of that. But she was terrified, and she didn't know what to do with the feelings she'd been having.

Squeezing her eyes shut was supposed to stop the tears, but it didn't. They flowed down her cheeks.

Chair legs scraped against the floor, and then big hands cupped her face.

She opened her eyes as Brody wiped her cheeks with his thumbs.

"I'm sorry." He shook his head. "I'm mad at myself right along with you. If anyone else made you cry, I'd whoop their ass, at the very least."

She put her hands on his wrists and squeezed. "I don't want to forgive you now and have you hurt me worse later."

"That's not going to happen. We're probably going to fight from time to time, though. I can't promise you a fairytale."

"I don't want one. I just want someone who shares themself with me as much as I share with them."

"That's reasonable." He held her face and stared. She probably looked like a blotchy, snotty mess. "I want to give you everything, Morgan. Everything you want. Everything you need. Things you didn't know you needed."

"You can't be everything for everyone, Brody." They were in this situation because he was great at supporting everyone, except himself. She pulled his hands from her face and shook her head. "Putting other people first and ignoring your own problems doesn't make them go away. You say I'm not alone, but I've been walking through a hell that you refuse to step foot in."

His shoulders sagged. "So, what now?"

She put her hands on his chest, leaned in, and stared up at him. "Kiss me goodnight, then start working through your damage."

She was his, but that didn't mean she wasn't going to uphold boundaries. This was a setback, not the end.

He palmed the back of her head. "You're going to let me kiss you goodnight?"

She raised her eyebrows and grinned. "We both know I'm the queen of doing things I shouldn't."

His top lip curled. "You shouldn't sleep in my bed tonight, either."

Morgan rolled her eyes. "Subtle."

He took his time leaning in, skimming his lips over hers. Just when she thought that was the extent of the kiss, he pulled her in tighter, pressing his mouth to hers like he meant it. Something happened inside her, like confetti exploding from a party favor.

She rubbed her tongue against his and reveled in his deep groan.

When she started coming up with reasons why sleeping in his bed wasn't such a bad idea, she pulled away. She took a staggering breath and backed up until her searching hand connected with the banister. One foot on the stairs, she bit her lip, then turned and went up to her room.

She'd half-expected him to chase after her, and when she hit the second-floor landing and no footfalls followed her, her heart sank. Which was stupid because this was what she'd told him needed to happen. A little space from each other might be a good thing too. Clearly, all it took was two seconds of his lips on hers to turn her mind to mush.

The next morning when she came downstairs, there was a glass jar filled with wildflowers and a black paper bag with twine handles on the table. She peeked inside. White fabric filled the bottom of the bag. She grabbed it and pulled it out.

The dress.

The one Drew had wanted her to get. That sneaky bitch.

She fixed her coffee and walked onto the porch, then dialed Drew.

"Hello?"

"Thank you for the dress."

"Does that mean you're going?" Drew asked.

It still didn't make sense for a chaperone to take a date, but she wanted to see Hope having fun, and Brody had made it clear she had to go. If it was that important to him, fine.

"I guess."

"Oh, you guess?" Drew laughed. "You better let that man take that dress off you tonight."

Morgan groaned. "I'm not talking to you about this."

"You like him, and he seems really nice, but in a hot *I'm not always this nice* way. What's your hang up?"

"We're still figuring things out."

"You're always going to be figuring things out. That never stops, trust me. Don't waste time you could spend figuring out how to make each other—"

"I'm hanging up on you," Morgan blurted out before Drew could finish.

"Happy. I was going to say happy. Have fun tonight. Get someone to take a pic of the two of you so I can taunt your brother with it."

She kept busy until the afternoon—playing with Buster, going for a run, packing up her hair and makeup tools to take over to help Hope get ready for the dance.

With an enormous bag and her cosmetics case, Morgan knocked on Brody's parents' door.

The door opened and Brody stood there, blinking. "Hey," he drawled out, snapping out of it, a grin stretching his face. He glanced at the bag hanging from her shoulder. "You ditching me and moving in with my parents?"

"I'm here to help Hope get ready for the dance."

Instead of welcoming her into the house with the manners his parents surely taught him, he took her case and bag, grabbed her hand, and tugged her inside. With the door closed, he set her things on the floor, then pulled her against him, and settled his mouth over hers.

He kissed her until she was throbbing in all the places she didn't want to be throbbing while around Brody's family. He tipped her chin up. "Hey, Cash."

"Brody," she said, her voice hoarse. "You can't kiss me like that just… whenever you feel like it."

He smirked. "Why not?"

"Because. I have things to do."

"So do I. If you don't want me to kiss you, don't come around looking so pretty."

Pretty? Right—In capri-length sweatpants and a cropped T-shirt, messy curls pulled into a sloppy bun, and zero makeup.

He pulled at the rolled waistband of her sweats, letting it snap softly against her stomach. "This is all your fault."

Her jaw fell.

He put a finger under her chin and lifted, effectively shutting her gaping mouth. "I didn't think I was going to have a chance to see you until tonight."

"Me neither. What are you doing here?"

"Just had lunch with my dad."

"Did you talk to him about…?" She raised her eyebrows. They both knew what about.

He slowly shook his head. "No. I'm still working things out in my head."

She wasn't rushing him. There was no deadline. His word that he was contemplating how to move forward with talking to his parents was good enough for her. When she'd woken up this morning, she'd no longer been upset about him not telling her. Brody had issues, just like every other person in this world. Finding out he didn't have it all together endeared him to her even more. It made him more real, more attainable.

"I'm glad you're here," Brody said. "Hope is having a meltdown. She doesn't want to go to the dance."

"What? But she's the president of the dance committee."

"Her date changed his mind about going with her."

"What?" This time she said it so loudly she swore the house shook. "What is that little asshole's problem? Do you know where he lives?"

He grinned, then shook his head. "Put away those claws, baby. Can you talk to her? None of us have been able to get through to her."

"I can try." Her pulse thumped. She didn't want to fail at this, but she also didn't know what she could possibly say to convince Hope to go to the dance.

Brody lifted her bag and makeup case. "I'll carry these up for you."

At the base of the stairs, he stepped out of her way and waited.

She shook her head. "Maybe, sometimes, I should get to be the one who enjoys the view."

He sighed dramatically, then marched up the stairs.

Morgan followed with a smile. But when she reached the landing, a sob and a "just leave me alone" erased her joy.

Brody led her to the closest door to the stairs and knocked lightly with one knuckle before opening it. "Morgan's here."

Hope lifted her face from her pillow and sniffed, then promptly resumed crying, much harder this time.

Gia, who'd been sitting on the edge of the bed, rose and walked to the door.

"What happened?" Morgan asked as she got close enough to Hope to place a hand on her back.

"My parents are ruining my life!"

She swiveled to look at Brody and Gia.

Gia shook her head and left.

Morgan turned her attention to Brody, and tilted her head, as if to say, "Well?"

He set her things down, leaned into the door frame, and crossed his arms. "Her curfew is ten, and her date didn't like that."

"Are you kidding me?" she blurted out. "That tiny-dick, pimple-infested maggot."

Brody's hand flew to his face and covered his eyes. He squeezed his temples.

She winced and turned back to Hope. "I mean…don't waste time being upset over him. He's clearly a selfish individual who is not worthy of your time."

"I'm going to be the only one without a date to the dance." Hope wiped at her face with her hands.

"No, you're not," she said, moving Hope's hair back so she could see her face. "You know, going stag to a dance is way more fun."

"Yeah, right," she muttered, sniffling. "I'm sure you never went to a dance alone."

She smiled. "I have, and not by choice. He was supposed to pick me up and never showed."

"Really?" Hope rolled over and wiped at her eyes.

"Because of him, I missed half the dance, but I still went because there was no way I was letting that…stupid boy ruin my night." Morgan glanced at Brody.

He winked at her, then left, softly shutting the door behind him.

"That boy did you a favor," she said. "You're going to have way more fun without him. I promise."

"All my friends are going to the bonfire party after the dance. I don't know why my parents have to be such jerks."

"They want what's best for you. We all do, and I know you're not going to like hearing this, but going to a party where there's probably going to be drinking and no supervision and having to depend on an immature boy if you decide you want to leave is not smart."

"All my friends are going."

"I bet they aren't. I bet you're not the only one pouting because their parents won't let them. Now, are you going to keep lying here feeling sorry for yourself, or are you going to go wash your face and let me do your hair and makeup, put on that fabulous dress, and make that boy regret cancelling on you?"

Hope sat up and wiped her cheeks. "You're going too, right?"

"Yes, but you better not point him out to me. Your brother will be very upset if he has to bail me out of jail."

52
Luck and Lipstick
BRODY

WHEN BRODY CAME IN from the field, Morgan wasn't at the house. They had to leave for the dance in thirty minutes. Even though he'd made a vow to himself not to track her unless he was concerned about her safety, he pulled out his phone and saw she was still at his parents' house.

She'd sent him a message earlier to say Hope had changed her mind and was going to the dance. With any luck, that was still true.

He ate leftovers, took a shower, shaved, and put on nice clothes—jeans that didn't have rips or stains and a plaid western shirt—then checked the time. Five minutes until six. Once he stepped outside his bedroom, the sound of the sink running in the bathroom next to Morgan's room alleviated most of his anxiety.

It wouldn't be the end of the world if she didn't go to the dance, but it'd be disappointing. Yeah, he had to keep an eye on the kids, but having her with him made everything more enjoyable. Not to mention, he'd be distracted all night wondering what she was doing on her own.

He went out to the porch to wait. At five fifty-nine, the screen door swung open. Brody stood, forgetting how to breathe for a second, as he took her in.

A short, white dress hugged her body. Curly hair that made him want to tangle his hands in it. Deep red lips. Sexy black high heels. Damn.

"You look nice," she said.

Only then did he realize he'd been gawking at her when he should have been telling her how beautiful she looked. Or at least said hi. He moved until she was within reach, gave her one last appraisal, then dipped down and tossed her over his shoulder.

"Brody!" she shrieked as he went into the house and took the stairs. She whacked him on the back with her little purse. "What are you doing?"

He froze halfway up. "Oops. Sorry. I lost my mind a little bit seeing you in this dress and forgot we had somewhere to be besides my bed." He eased her to her feet on the step above his and grinned.

"Later, Brody." She patted his chest, then moved around him and headed down the stairs.

His heart lurched and he spun. "Really?"

He didn't want to get his hopes up. All day, he'd been consumed with wanting her. But even if she said yes now, that didn't mean something wouldn't go wrong like it had on their first date. And technically, this was only their second date, so even though they'd been dancing around their mutual attraction for a while now, he hadn't properly put in the time and effort Morgan deserved. As difficult as it was going to be, he wasn't going to set any expectations.

"Unless you chicken out," she said over her shoulder before walking out the door.

He caught up with her by his truck and grabbed her hand. He spun her back into his arms. "All jokes aside, you look stunning, and I'm a very, very lucky man."

Her lips moved into a faint smile, but it was easy to see a bigger smile was under the surface. She pushed up on her toes and pressed her lips to his.

He did his best not to consume her. They had a dance to get to, not to mention she had on a pristine white dress that he was nervous he'd get dirty somehow, even though his hands and clothes were clean. But he was a sucker for those little humming noises she made. He liked how she

kept trying to get closer to him too, even when their bodies were pressed tightly together.

He pulled her bottom lip between his teeth, then released it, and moved his face away from hers. He smirked at the mess he'd made of her lipstick, then put his thumb to the corner of her mouth and wiped where it'd smeared. He wasn't qualified to fix her makeup, but her mouth transfixed him.

Her tongue slid across her top lip and that did not help his case at all. Fucking hell.

She opened her purse and pulled out a tissue. He didn't even think about her lipstick being on him until she wiped at the skin around his mouth. "Sorry."

"I'm not," he muttered, then kissed her again.

She laughed and pushed him away. "A chaperone showing up to the dance with lipstick stains is probably not the best look."

"When they see my date, they'll understand." He eased her out of the way and opened the truck door.

She climbed into the truck, then turned to him. "Brody?"

"Yeah, baby?"

"Nobody's luckier than me."

He smiled, and even though he wanted to kiss her again, he didn't because kissing her again would turn into kissing her again and again and again.

She fixed her lipstick in the mirror while he got in on the driver's side and pulled down his visor to check his face. It wasn't that bad. The bad part was that while he rubbed at the red marks around his mouth, his damn dirty mind got an idea of another part of his body where he'd like to see the color.

On their way to the dance, he pointed out different businesses and points of interest in the community. There were so many beautiful sites in the area, and he hadn't shown her any of them yet. As his mental list grew longer, it occurred to him how desperate he felt to convince her of the benefits of living here. He needed to knock it off. It was too soon to start thinking about forever.

When they arrived, he was glad to see Hope smiling and laughing as she set out refreshments. Her earrings sparkled, even from all the way across the room. Brody glanced at Morgan, then back at his sister.

"Are those your diamond earrings my sister is wearing?"

"They're just on loan."

"What if she loses one?"

"She won't. They have screw on backs, but if she does, so what? I told her it's against the rules to wear that big of diamonds without radiating confidence, and if it works, then it'll have been worth it to me, even if she loses them both."

Brody stared at her, and the gravity of how much he loved her slammed into him. His head spun as he tried to talk himself out of it. Too soon. Too much. He couldn't tell her. A confession like that would scare her off.

He leaned down and kissed her cheek, then whispered, "You're an amazing person."

She sank her teeth into her bottom lip and if they'd been alone, he'd have pulled it free and kissed her until she stopped him, or until they were naked and exhausted.

He took her hand and led her to Hope to find out what they could do to help, but Nick cut them off.

"Dang, Morgan. You look hot."

Brody scowled. "Nick, I'm only going to warn you once."

He didn't need to say what the warning was for. He loved his brother and he'd put up with a lot from his goofy ass, but there'd be no more flirting with Morgan as a means of tormenting him. She was his. People were going to look at her. He could live with that. Other men telling her she looked hot? Nope. He wasn't putting up with that. Anyone else touching her? He'd maim the first person who tried.

Nick smirked. "Does that mean I can't ask her to dance?"

"You can't play baseball with busted kneecaps, Nick."

Morgan elbowed him in the side. "Settle down. Save that energy for when you watch your sister dance with a boy with wandering hands."

"That better not happen," he muttered.

"That's a good way to lose a hand, or some fingers at the very least," Nick said.

She rolled her eyes. "Check the murderous rage, boys. We're supposed to be helping."

She slipped away from him and walked over to Hope.

"You're going to marry her, right?" Nick asked.

His brother never held punches. Hopefully, one day he'd turn that on himself and own up to his feelings for Taylor.

"Gonna try."

53
Give a Girl a Goat
Morgan

"Ah, so, you're Brody's girlfriend."

Morgan turned.

The boy who'd given her Buster stood next to her.

"Hi. Josh, right?"

He nodded and took a sip from a plastic cup. "And you're Morgan. How's the goat?"

"I named him Buster. He's good. I'm not sure he knows he's a goat, though." She was pretty sure he thought he was Brody's second dog, the way he followed him around whenever he was out of his pen. "Trying to work up your courage to ask someone to dance?"

"More like trying to talk myself out of it."

She snorted. "Which one is she?"

His face turned as red as his hair. He hesitated, then sighed, and pointed across the room.

Her gaze traveled to where his finger indicated. There was only one girl. Hope. She was adjusting the balloon arch she'd had Brody and Nick install around a photo backdrop where the kids could stand to have their picture taken. "Hope?"

"She hates my guts."

That didn't make sense. He seemed like a genuinely nice guy. She doubted *he* would have canceled on Hope at the last minute because of her curfew. "Why?"

Josh shrugged, continuing to stare at her from across the room. "I spilled chocolate milk on her on picture day in first grade."

"And she's never forgiven you for it?"

"She probably would have if I didn't hit her in the head with a floor hockey puck in third grade. Or if I didn't ruin her first kiss."

"How'd you do that?" she asked, fascinated by their childhood history, especially since Josh clearly had a crush on Hope.

"I drove by her and the guy on an ATV and splashed mud all over them."

"On purpose?"

He turned his head toward her and stared at her for a beat, then gave her a guilty smile and shrugged.

Interesting. She probably shouldn't be consorting with him. For all she knew, Josh had done something far more awful than the things he'd admitted to. Hope could very well have good reason to hate him. But her instincts said he was a good kid and those times had been accidents. Well, except for the last one. "She's in a pretty good mood right now. Maybe she'll say yes if you ask her."

Just then Hope spotted them. Her face morphed into a frown.

"Still think I've got a chance?" he asked dryly.

Morgan swept her gaze around the room, looking for Brody.

He stood by the exit, leaning against the opening of the barn door with his arms crossed, looking like a bouncer. That's pretty much what he was. Once kids left, they couldn't come back in. He marked their hands with permanent marker once they walked out. As if he'd felt her watching him, he looked in her direction. He grinned, and her stomach flipped.

In the beginning, she'd butted heads with Brody. A lot. He'd done things to purposely irritate her. But now, he got her worked up in other ways. Better ways. Ways that she needed to stop thinking about while she was at a dance for teenagers.

If she and Brody could get past the things they'd done to each other, she didn't see why Hope and Josh couldn't. But she wasn't getting in it. As tempting as it was to play matchmaker, she'd be doing exactly what she got mad at Lucy for doing.

Although…

She couldn't be mad at Lucy anymore. Not when Brody made her this happy.

But no, she would not interfere. Hope had plenty of time to find the one.

Wait. Was Brody *the one*?

She swallowed hard. She didn't hate the idea of Brody being her forever person. Panic flooded her system, but in a good way. Was there a good way to panic? Shit. Her brain wouldn't do its job and make freaking sense.

Shaking off her freak out, she turned to Josh. "Do you remember how you suckered me into taking Buster home?"

"Yeah," he drawled out, dropping his gaze to the floor.

She laughed. "I'm not holding it against you. I brought it up because that's what you need to do with Hope."

"Give her a goat?"

"No." She shook her head, smiling. "Tell her some outlandish story that suckers her into dancing with you. Don't take it too far, though, and make sure it's obvious before you dance with her that it was a ploy, okay?"

"She's not gonna go for that."

"You're not getting anywhere lurking over here in the shadows talking to me. And she didn't go for anything else you've tried." Because, Jesus, boys were stupid. "So, how important is it that you dance with her?"

She walked away because she didn't need a response. Josh needed to answer that question for himself.

A little guilt nagged at her for not sticking to her vow to stay out of Hope's love life. But she liked Josh and he seemed to need direction.

She'd intervened much less than Lucy had. All she'd done was give him a little push.

She headed over to Brody, unable to stop smiling, powerless to his devilish grin.

His hands landed on her waist when she came within reach. "Does it set a bad example if I kiss you right now?"

"If you kiss me like you usually do, then yes." Because his kisses were never just kisses. They were lust-filled, mind-scrambling events.

"Damn," he whispered, then let her go and approached a boy coming into the dance. He made sure he didn't already have marks on his hand and explained the rules before letting him pass by.

When he turned back to her, his lips pinched together, like he was holding back from saying something he shouldn't.

"What's wrong?"

"That's the kid who canceled on my sister."

She swiveled her head, searching the room.

Hope was with Josh. She glared up at him, but then her lips pulled into a grin, and she rolled her eyes. Before long they were slow dancing. Good. Maybe she wouldn't even notice the other boy.

Morgan faced Brody. "I think she'll be okay."

That held true for one and a half songs. Then all hell broke loose.

Hope's ex-date walked off the dance floor with another girl and attempted to leave.

"If you leave, you're not coming back," Brody said to them. "No exceptions."

"Whatever. This dance is mid."

"Why are you always screwing everything up for me!" Hope looked like she might slap Josh, so Morgan rushed over and put an arm around her.

"Come for a walk with me. Tell me what happened." Morgan pulled her along.

In the ladies' room, Hope spoke between sobs. "Levi changed his mind, and he was going to apologize when he got here, but Josh made me dance with him, and then Levi saw. He thought we were here together, so he asked Deana to dance, and now, they're going to the party."

Morgan pulled tissues from a box on the sink vanity and handed them to Hope. "You said, Josh *made* you dance with him?"

"Well, not like forced me, but he tricked me into it. I hate him so much."

"How did he trick you?" Oh no, this might be all her fault.

"I don't know. He was like…being funny, and no one else had asked me to dance yet, and I temporarily forgot what a jerk he is."

She put her hand on Hope's shoulder and wiped her tears, glad she'd used waterproof mascara when she'd done her makeup. "That sounds like he flirted with you, and it made you feel good, so you said yes to dancing with him."

"Why are you taking his side?"

"I'm not. I'm one thousand percent on your side. But I care about you enough to be honest with you when you're not thinking clearly because you're upset. Levi proved earlier today that he doesn't care about you. He made you cry once already. Then, he had the audacity to think he could show up late to the dance and make assumptions about you and Josh and retaliate by using another girl to make you jealous."

"But if I hadn't been dancing with Josh, Levi would have asked me to dance and—"

Morgan shook her head. "You consented to dancing with Josh. It was a choice you made. You don't have to like Josh. You don't have to ever dance with him again, or even talk to him for that matter, but the only thing he's guilty of is wanting to dance with you."

Maybe if someone had been that honest with her, she'd have wasted a lot less time on the Levis of the world. Hope wouldn't have to go through that if Morgan could help it.

"It doesn't matter how much you wish for a guy to be different and treat you like you want, he's either capable of it, or he's not. Everybody makes mistakes, Hope, but how they choose to fix them, or if they choose to fix them at all, will tell you all you need to know about who they'll put first—you or themselves."

"But I like him so much, Morgan."

"You like the idea of him. You're caught up in a fantasy where the older guy chooses you over the girls his own age. The problem with that is that I bet he's either burned through all the girls his age, or they've all rejected him."

For a second, she worried maybe she'd been too harsh with her, but Hope wiped her face and without sobbing, said, "I'm too embarrassed to go back out there."

"I don't think you have to stay. I'm sure one of your brothers will take you home. But you worked hard to put this dance together. It seems like a shame to miss out on it."

"It's not like I'm going to have fun now."

"Really? Levi has that much control over your emotions?"

Hope shrugged.

"I told you, if you're going to rock three carat diamond earrings, you gotta do it like a badass. Badasses don't let fuckboys prevent them from having a good time."

"I'm not cool like you. Everyone will know I'm faking it and I'll look stupid."

"If that's your attitude, then you're probably right." She rubbed Hope's back. "I'll go talk to Brody. I don't think it'd be appropriate for three of the four chaperones to leave midway through the dance. Maybe I can drive you home in Brody's truck, and we can hang out until they get back."

"Wait." Hope grabbed her arm. "Is my makeup a mess?"

"Not a bit." It wasn't. Luckily, Hope had only dabbed under her eyes

and not rubbed them, so her eyeshadow and eyeliner had stayed in place. She had flawless, porcelain skin, and Morgan knew better than to mess with perfection, so she'd skipped foundation. "Do you want to stay here while I talk to your brother and then we can figure out how to sneak you out, so you can avoid seeing anyone?"

Hope took a deep breath. "I might stay."

"It sounds like they're doing some line dancing out there." She opened the door so it no longer muffled the sound. "Do you know this one?"

She nodded.

"Can you teach it to me?"

Her eyes got big. "You're going to line dance?"

Morgan put a hand to her chest. "Oh, girl, you have no idea. I have some serious moves. I've never danced to country music, but I can adapt."

Hope grinned. "Okay, let's go."

54
Don't Get Me Wrong
BRODY

BRODY COULD WATCH MORGAN dance and have fun with Hope and her friends all night. Her exuberance was contagious and changed the whole energy of the dance. At one point, every single kid was on the dance floor.

He was addicted to watching her move. When she forgot the steps or did the wrong thing, she'd laugh at herself and get reset to try again. It was cute as fuck. By the time the dance ended, and they'd finished cleaning up, he was so anxious to have her to himself that the second he had the chance, he grabbed her hand and pulled her out the door.

He didn't even wait to get in the truck to kiss her. He helped her into the cab, but kept her facing him, pulling her legs toward him, bringing her eye level. "You were incredible tonight. Thank you for doing that for my sister."

She put her arms around his neck and rubbed her nose against his. "I did it for you too. I know it's important to you that she gets to experience normal teenager stuff."

He brushed his knuckles across her cheek, unsure of what to say. If he said what came to mind, everything might implode. Even though she was showing him how much she cared, he didn't think she was ready to say it out loud, and he didn't want to risk messing up what was building between them.

She tilted her head and pressed her lips to his.

This was not going to be a short and sweet kiss. Grabbing her ass with both hands, he brought her even closer, her stretchy dress bunching on her thighs. He welcomed her tongue into his mouth with a groan. Hands were everywhere. His. Hers.

He froze with his fingers hooked in the lace sides of her panties, then tore his mouth away. "Let's go home."

"What?" She shook her head. "Why? We're the only ones here."

"I love that you're willing to let me have you here and now," he whispered, "but I don't have a condom."

"Oh." Her arms slid from his neck and her chin dropped.

"I can make *you* come, though, if that's what you want." He unhooked his fingers and slid one hand between her legs and the other behind her neck.

Those bright eyes of hers flickered shut. Her lips parted.

He hid his face in her neck, planting kisses from her ear to her collarbone. Pushing the little strip of fabric out of his way, he slid his fingers through her heat. So wet. So slick. A groan he was unable to suppress crept up his throat. The wait to touch her had been so long his want for her disintegrated rational thought. His only care was pushing her to the edge.

He'd push her over that edge, eventually. First, he wanted to see her desperate and at his mercy.

"Brody," Morgan said through a gasp. "Home. I think we should go home."

He stilled his fingers and lifted his head to meet her gaze. "What's wrong?"

"I need all of you. I need to feel your skin on mine. I need you inside me."

That's what he needed too. Badly.

After taking a deep breath, he stepped back and waited until she'd pulled her legs inside the truck to shut the door. The drive home would

give him time to get himself settled down.

Neither of them said a word until they got home and to the top of the stairs.

She paused in front of his bedroom and looked back at him.

"Are you seriously questioning where you're sleeping tonight?"

"I'm freaking out a little bit."

He lifted her chin and looked into her eyes. "It's a big step."

If she asked him to wait, of course he would, but he wasn't going to suggest it.

"Maybe you should kiss me."

"You'll never have to suggest that twice." He leaned down and kissed her, making out with her in the hallway until she relaxed into his body.

With his fingers laced through hers, he guided her inside his room, stopping to turn the lights on and dim them, then led her to the bed. He dragged down her bottom lip with his thumb, entranced by how her lips had plumped from his kisses. He leaned in again, tasting her, swiping his tongue across her swollen lips.

She melted into him again, sagging against his body as he kissed her slow, teasing her, dragging out every movement.

Gradually, he turned her, walking her backward to the side of the bed. He guided her arms around his neck and whispered against her lips. "Hold on to me."

She held on tighter.

"Good girl," he rasped against her ear. Hands on the backs of her thighs, he lifted her and laid her on her back, following her down but keeping his weight off her.

He shifted slightly to the side and ran his hand over her breast, her hard nipple tempting him beneath her dress.

Morgan arched off the bed, gasping.

She deserved to be worshipped and that's exactly what he was going to do.

"Is it okay if I take off your dress?"

Her lips pressed together. She nodded, then slipped out from under him and sat up.

He moved around to her back, but there was no zipper. He ran his hands over it just to be sure. "How do I get you out of this thing?"

"You're an engineer. You build intricate explosives, but you can't get a girl out of a dress?"

He grinned and kissed her neck. "When it's this dress and you're the girl? Not a chance."

She reached for the side of her dress and tugged down a barely perceptible zipper, then shimmied the dress up her thighs.

Brody grabbed the hem, pushing it up, following her curves, taking the fabric over her head. The strip of white lace across her lower back, disappearing between her ass cheeks, amped up his arousal.

He placed featherlight kisses down her spine.

She whimpered and tried to turn, but he placed one hand across her pelvis and the other on her shoulder.

Holding her tight to him, he trailed his hand up, cupping her breast. He leaned forward, gazing down her body as he ran his thumb across her nipple.

She turned her head to the side and moaned, one arm reaching behind her, looped around his neck.

"Baby, don't get me wrong, you looked hot when I saw you naked before, but I have never seen anything as sexy as you while you're stretched out like this."

He slid his hand from her shoulder to her panties and skated his fingers between her legs, rubbing along the lace, then slipping beneath, twisting it around his finger, tightening the string enough to cause a little friction.

"Brody," she said in a shaky voice.

"Does that feel good?"

She nodded and released a shaky breath.

Her thong string rubbed down her pussy and then he brought it back up, the string sliding around his finger and dragging along her flesh. She was so wet, and he was so turned on that he untangled his finger from the string and plunged it into her opening. She squirmed in his arms, and he let go of her breast and wrapped his arm around her like a belt.

He withdrew his finger, then took his time sliding it back in, stopping every inch to withdraw and start over.

She moaned. "Brody, please."

He'd pushed the limits of his control far enough. He slowly dragged his finger out of her and down her inner thigh, then loosened his hold on her. "Turn around."

When she faced him, her forehead wrinkled. "You need to get naked. Fast."

He put his hand on the back of her head and crushed his mouth into hers. While he took from her lips like it'd been months since they'd kissed instead of minutes, she pulled his shirt out of his pants and worked on the buttons.

He stopped kissing her, shrugged out of the shirt, then pulled her against him. Feeling her smooth, warm skin against his, he didn't think he'd ever needed anything as bad as he needed her.

55
Filthy-mouth Brody
Morgan

THE SENSATIONS CAUSED BY Brody's bare skin against hers shook Morgan.

And yet, she needed more.

She reached for his belt, but he covered her hand and dragged his mouth away from hers.

The intensity in his eyes paralyzed her as he pulled the covers back and laid her on the sheet, letting her head land gently on the pillow. He scooted off the bed, shucked his pants, then slid under the covers, and positioned his body over hers.

He supported his weight on one forearm and brushed a stray curl away from her face. "You're so beautiful."

She gazed up at him, the sincerity in his words hitting her deep. She needed this man. Always, but especially right now. She pushed at the waistband on his boxers.

He worked his way out of them, then grabbed a condom from his nightstand.

She tugged her thong down and kicked it off, losing it somewhere in the sheets and not giving a damn if she ever saw it again.

Brody settled himself between her thighs and placed a soft kiss on her lips. He trailed his lips down her neck and across her chest, swirling his tongue around her nipple.

Morgan turned her head into the pillow to muffle the sounds that tumbled from her mouth.

He stopped, hovering over her, not speaking until she gave him her full attention. "Who are you trying to be quiet for?"

Her blush burned, and surely showed, even in the dim light. She covered her face with her hands.

Brody circled her wrists and pinned her hands next to her head. "I want to hear you. I want to know if you like what I'm doing to you. Also, it's hot as hell."

She started to smile, but he lowered his mouth to hers and ground his pelvis against her. Morgan moaned into his mouth and shifted, trying to feel more of him.

Him rubbing his length against her *right there* made her brain cells scatter. His mouth and hands always compromised her ability to think coherently. Oddly, she didn't mind at all. Not when it was only the two of them. Being alone with Brody was the safest place she'd ever known.

She tugged her wrists, trying to free them. The need to touch him stirred a frenzy inside her.

He held his grip and lifted his head.

"I'd like to be able to use my hands."

He stared at her, dark eye lashes rimming his brown eyes. "Are you going to use them to hide from me?"

She shook her head and wet her lips.

His gaze dropped to her mouth. With a grin, he moved so that the tip of his dick pushed inside her, but pulled back out before she could lift her hips and take more of him.

She gasped and her eyes drifted shut. "Brody."

"Open your eyes, baby," he said, his face close to hers and his tone sugary.

She blinked up at him.

"Keep them open." He let go of her wrists and slowly slid inside her, filling her with such intense pleasure that her chin tipped up and her eyes rolled back. Brody tucked his hand behind her head and lifted, then swept his lips against hers.

She wrapped her arms around his neck and forced her eyes open, wondering why he was so still.

The softness in his gaze unlocked a part of her that she'd been unaware was lurking in the depths of her soul. A part that existed only for Brody. Or maybe it was that in this moment, it only mattered that she existed to be with him.

She trailed her fingers from the back of his neck to his cheek.

He turned his head and kissed her palm. Then his eyes were on hers and he was moving, taking away what he'd given her, just to give it back. Over and over.

He sought her mouth, and his tongue passed over her lips, sending a rush of warmth through her. The layers of pleasure blurred together, and nothing made sense, but it didn't need to.

Every time she shifted, trying to get closer, he adjusted his hold, a silent threat to never give her back the space she'd forfeited. He held her hips off the mattress, rolling his pelvis, hitting a spot inside her that pulled a loud moan from her.

She cried out as he repeated the movement. Her thighs quaked, her feet dangling in the air as he lifted her, strong hands squeezing her hips, sliding her up and down along his cock, meeting his shallow thrusts. It took effort to open her eyes but she was rewarded when she did by him meeting her gaze, the desire more than she knew what to do with.

He slowed the pace so much that she worried he'd stop. Need replaced that worry with the lengthening of his strokes, the tip popping out on each downstroke. The movement teased her, spinning her into a needy, begging mess. "Please, Brody. I'm—" *Coming* died in her throat, drowned out by sounds she couldn't control as she came hard, pulsing around him.

"Morgan," he groaned, then tucked his face into her neck as he shuddered. He continued to move, keeping the slow pace, but thrusting forcefully, prolonging her orgasm, stretching it on and on until they both collapsed.

He pressed his lips to her shoulder, then her jaw. Using a gentle touch to turn her face toward his, he kissed her long and hard. When he released her, he eased his cock from her and rolled onto his back, pulling her against his side.

Her lungs heaved for air, the rest of her body either tingly or on straight fire. "That was…"

His breathing was no less labored. "Yeah, it was."

She snuggled in closer and draped her leg across his.

Placing his hand under her knee, he pulled her leg higher, the crisp hair on his muscular thigh stimulating her hypersensitive clit.

Suppressing her whimper was a fail.

He rubbed against her again, this time intentionally.

"Brody," she whined, resisting the urge to rub back.

"I can't help it." He ran his hand up her side, moving in to cup her breast. "You're making me hard again already."

"I'm not doing anything." She wasn't even sure he could hear or comprehend her, as she was nearly incapable of speech while he touched her.

He lightly ground his thigh against her while pulling her nipple between his fingers. "I'm going to get rid of this condom, then I'm going to make you come again."

"What? No. I need a minute." Her body was still buzzing from the first time.

"You can have one." He held up a finger, then slipped away from her and out of bed. While he disappeared into the bathroom, she pulled the blankets around herself in a feeble attempt to replace his warmth.

When he returned, he stood next to the bed and stared at her while rubbing his jaw. He was hard.

Morgan swallowed, equally turned on and anxious. She was too

sensitive to handle any more right now, but instead of the pulsing between her thighs subsiding, it built back up.

He crooked his finger.

She raised an eyebrow.

Raising his eyebrows back at her, he flipped the covers off, and crooked his finger again. "I was going to bring you a warm cloth, but then I had a better idea."

Morgan stayed put, covering her breasts with her arm, and pressing her knees together. "What idea?"

"I'm going to wash you up in the shower, then I'm going to go down on you until you can't stand."

Her eyes widened and heat crept up her neck. "Aren't you tired?"

He gripped his cock at the base and stroked upward. "No."

A powerful, urgent need pulsed between her legs. She flipped over onto her hands and knees and crawled across the bed.

With his hand behind her neck, he guided her up to a kneeling position and brushed his mouth over hers. "Do you have any idea how hot it looks when you do that?"

He opened his nightstand and grabbed a condom. Then he scooped her up, cradling her. He carried her into the bathroom, then adjusted her in his arms while he reached inside the shower to turn it on.

"You can put me down."

"I don't want to." He kissed her intensely, turning her mind inside out with his tongue.

She got so lost in his kisses and touch she didn't know he'd stepped into the shower until the warm spray hit her skin. It sluiced over his shoulders, down his chest, pooling between their pressed-together bodies. She shifted and the water splashed around their feet.

Slowly, he turned his body, moving her into the stream of water. He lowered the arm under her legs, easing her to her feet. Hands cupping her face while he kissed her, he walked her backward, letting the warm water flow over her hair.

Morgan let him erase all her thoughts and inhibitions as he shampooed her hair and tenderly washed her body. She was so relaxed by the time he'd rinsed her clean that she didn't even tense when he leaned her against the wall and dropped to his knees.

She ran her fingers through his hair and held onto his shoulder as he lifted her foot onto the built-in shower bench. Her head fell back with the first suck Brody planted on her inner thigh. Scorching heat shot up her body. Her nipples hardened, tightening to the point that a water droplet sliding down her chest created a ripple of ecstasy.

His tongue rolled over her clit so lightly, she chased after it with her hips, silently begging for more. He didn't seem to be in the mood to be rushed, though. At first, she thought maybe he was just missing the mark and needed some guidance, but it became apparent he was purposely tormenting her by sucking on and flicking at the flesh around her clit, but never directly on it.

She groaned. "Brody."

He dipped his finger into her opening, then dragged it to her clit where he rubbed a tight circle, then pinched it between his thumb and forefinger. He lashed his tongue against her, causing her to jerk her hips.

He tugged at her clit, flooding her with pleasure. He dragged his finger to her opening and added a second, pumping them inside her. His tongue and lips had her bowing away from the wall. She'd probably have fallen on her ass if he hadn't been holding her in place as he relentlessly devoured her.

All at once, an orgasm plowed through her, and she moaned uncontrollably, bucking against him.

As the pleasure-filled pulses subsided, he kept going, but it was all too much. Morgan gasped and pushed his head from between her thighs.

She sagged to the bench, stars dancing in her vision.

Brody kissed her lips, then her chin, then her neck, working his way to her breasts.

"You have to stop," she said, panting. "I can't take anymore."

He lifted his head and pressed his forehead to hers. "You have to"—he ran his hand from her throat, down through her cleavage—"because I need more of you."

She licked her lips and shook her head tightly. "Stand up."

He did so, grabbing her arms to pull her up with him, but she stopped him and spread her legs wider. He froze, staring at her as she gripped his thighs.

She leaned in, sticking out her tongue and running it up the underside of his hard cock.

He jammed his hand in her hair. The other flattened against the shower wall.

His shuddering breath brought out a new dose of confidence. Morgan took him into her mouth, wrapping her tongue around him as her lips moved toward the base.

He moved his hips in time with her mouth, his grip on her hair tightening. "Look at me."

She opened her eyes and stared up at him, her mouth full, saliva dripping from the corners.

"Fuck," he muttered, his body tensing. Slack jawed, he groaned loudly, pulling himself free from her mouth and coming on her breasts. His chest rose and fell heavily. He pulled her up, turning her so her back was to his chest.

"You have no idea how much I want to rub my cum all over your tits and play with your nipples," he whispered against her ear. "But I'm pretty sure that would end up with both of us wanting to come again."

Her entire body flashed so hot she got lightheaded. She could not handle a filthy-mouthed Brody.

56
Only Brody's
BRODY

B<small>RODY REACHED ACROSS THE</small> bed, grabbed Morgan's arm, and tugged her back into bed. He wasn't pleased to be waking up to her sneaking out, but his rational side said he should give her the opportunity to explain why she'd leave his bed in the middle of the night. Maybe she had to use the bathroom or needed a drink of water.

She made an *oof* as her back hit the mattress.

He covered her body with his own, irritated with himself for making her go to her room and get a nightgown before they'd gone to sleep. He'd put on boxers too. No chance he'd be able to rest with her in his arms with her naked body so accessible. He sure didn't like it now, though. "What the fuck, baby?"

"What do you mean, what the fuck?" she asked, in a tone that said *have you knocked your head?*

Being fully awake before reacting to her departure would have given him the opportunity to mull over how to ask her a question without it sounding like an accusation. In the future, he'd try to remember that. "Where were you going?" he grumbled and rubbed his eye.

She pushed up on her elbows, bringing her face closer to his. Light spilled in from the moon to cast shadows on her features. "Are you always this grumpy when you wake up?"

"Maybe…"

"I was getting up because I can't sleep."

He threaded his hands through the wild, tangly mass of her curls and gently pulled, tilting her head at a better angle for him to place a soft kiss on her sweet lips. "If you can't sleep, you wake me up. Understood?"

"You have to work early. You need to sleep. It's fine. I'm used to being awake and alone. I don't mind it."

"I mind it." It pissed him off that he'd waited this long to have her next to him all night, only to have it snatched away, but more than that, he hated that she couldn't sleep, even though she had to be worn out after the night she'd had. Sex and line dancing would do that to a person.

She draped her arms over his shoulders and trailed her fingertips up his back and neck. "I'm kind of into this grumpy, sleepy thing you have going on right now."

"Yeah?" If his grumpiness got her hot, he wasn't going to complain. He nuzzled her neck while pushing her nightgown up around her hips. It was a silky black thing that inspired fantasies of coming home and finding her laid across his bed in it.

"Yes, but you should go back to sleep. You have to get up in a few hours."

It was funny she thought he'd be able to fall back asleep now. "We both know I'm not going to do that. Spread your legs."

She moved, trying to open her thighs.

Brody repositioned himself between her knees. "Since you can't sleep, do you wanna play Tensies?"

Her little laugh made him smile. "I guess your grumpiness is subsiding."

"How am I going to stay grumpy when I'm between these thighs?"

"So, if you're ever in a bad mood, I just have to spread my legs to cheer you up?"

"Wild having that much power, isn't it?" He loomed over her, grinning.

"I don't feel very powerful right now."

He could fix that. Brody pulled her hips up off the bed and flipped over, taking her with him. He positioned himself so he was somewhat reclined against the headboard.

"How about now?" he asked, sliding his hand up her thigh and under her nightgown. With her straddling him, he reached over to turn his lamp on the dimmest setting.

"After you just tossed me around like a pool noodle?"

He pulled the strap of her nightgown off her shoulder. "Morgan, flames could be licking these sheets and unless you moved, neither would I. If that's not power…"

She smiled and rolled her eyes. "You're ridiculous."

"It's only a small exaggeration." He gripped her hip and laid a kiss on her collarbone. "I need you, Morgan, so bad that I'd do *anything* you asked if it meant I could have you."

He slipped his hand inside the neckline of her nightgown. Her tits were perky as hell and her nipples were the perfect color, something he'd learned in Vegas and had thought about every day since. He'd never get enough of her body.

Her head fell back. "You don't have to do anything. I'm yours."

"I like hearing you say that." He trailed his hand from her hip to her inner thigh. "Say it again."

She rolled her hips, closing the distance between his hand and her body.

He slid his fingers through her slick heat, stroking her clit. "Say it."

"I'm yours, Brody," she said on a shaky breath. "Only yours."

He fisted her hair, then crushed his mouth to hers.

She moaned, opening her mouth enough to let him deepen the kiss.

He let the way she moved against him guide his pace. He wanted her to shatter when he sank inside her. While he worked his fingers between her legs, he let go of her hair and brushed his knuckles against her nipple through the fabric. She jerked, then whimpered into his mouth.

Discovering her nipples were crazy sensitive made playing with them extra fun. One day, he wanted to see if he could get her off by stimulating them exclusively.

He teased her with his fingers until she tore her mouth from his.

She sucked in air greedily. "Brody. Now. Please."

He leaned over and grabbed a condom, then lightly smacked her ass so she'd lift her hips and give him enough room to shed his boxers. He'd barely finished rolling on the condom when she put her hands on his shoulders and lowered herself.

He grabbed her hips, squeezing as she took him inside, surrounding him with her searing heat as she moaned. He stared into her eyes. "So impatient."

Her blue irises glimmered. "You're too patient."

He didn't feel the least bit patient. The intensity with which he wanted to feel her tight pussy gliding up and down his throbbing cock almost outweighed his ability to resist flipping her over and fucking her through the mattress.

She reached for the headboard, lifted while chewing her lip, then sank down.

He shimmied her nightgown up and over her head, then spread his palm across her back, and took a long look at her body. "I wanna watch you."

She blushed all the way to her nipples. So fucking sweet. And so fucking his.

He rolled his hips into hers. "Let me see what your gorgeous body looks like when you're fucking me like this."

She leaned back, letting him support her with the hand on her back, and pushed her hips forward. Her tits jutted out as she arched farther, placing her hands on the bed next to his thighs.

"That's my good girl, giving me a show while you ride my cock." He used his free hand to coax her closer to orgasm, watching his fingers as he dipped them into her slippery folds, obsessed with how his big, rough digits contrasted with her sweet, soft body.

Pleasure blanketed him as her hips rose and fell, sliding along his cock. He dragged his fingers up from her swollen clit to her stomach, creating a slippery trail to her nipple which was so hard it fit perfectly between his thumb and finger. He pinched and rolled, nowhere near as gentle as he'd been at first.

She released a rumbly moan and adjusted the tilt of her hips.

Brody used the hand on her back to bring her closer and dropped his head to her chest. He licked the space between her tits, then moved to her nipple, insanely turned on by tasting her pussy somewhere other than her pussy.

He ran his tongue back and forth in untamed licks. He flicked his gaze upward and found her watching him. He wasn't the only one who liked to watch.

"Brody," she said, her voice thick with lust. "I think—" Her ragged breathing prevented her from making coherent speech.

"You think what?" he asked, hand on the back of her neck, pulling her forehead to his. "You think you're going to come? I think so too. I think you're about to come all over my cock." He dragged his hand to her stomach and dipped it down farther, groaning against the slippery smooth skin and how she pumped herself up and down faster.

Feeling her pulsing around him as her movements became shallow triggered his release. He thrust up, guiding her hips down, pressing deep into her, wishing he was filling her with his cum. He couldn't stop thinking about how good it'd feel to put his cock in her tight, wet pussy bare.

She melted into him, wrapping her arms around his neck, and resting her head against his shoulder.

He tried to regulate his breathing while running his hand up and down her back. Once he'd come down and calmed down, he eased away from her, hit the bathroom to throw away the condom, then brought her a warm rag.

"I can do it," she said, trying to squirm out of his reach as he pulled the covers back and touched the rag to her thigh.

He sighed and pushed her knees apart. "Do I really need to remind you that I do things for you because I like doing them, not because you're incapable?"

He slowly ran the cloth down, gently swiping it over her swollen pussy—and yep, he should have let her do it. It was too tempting to drop the rag and finger her. He wet his lips as he remembered what it felt like when she came on his tongue.

She snatched the cloth from him. "Do I really need to remind you that you need sleep?"

This time, Brody let her get away, flattening out on his back as she went to the bathroom.

Ten seconds later, she curled into his side. "You can't stay up with me every time I can't sleep and still get up and take care of the farm."

She might be right about that. "I want you in my arms while I sleep—not that I expect you to lie there awake and be my security blanket." He tugged her down next to him and rolled to face her.

"Our schedules don't work well together, do they?"

"No, but so what?" He tugged at a bouncy curl. "We don't have to figure it out right now."

"I'll lie with you while you fall asleep. Just don't freak out and grab me if I get up."

He breathed deep. "I'll try."

They got situated under the covers and she turned her head on the pillow to face him.

"I don't want my issues to interfere with what you need to do. Your dad thinks you're doing too much already. What happens if you don't get enough sleep?"

"Nick has been helping." His dad always worried. Everything was handled, though. Maybe just barely but handled all the same.

"He's worried about you taking on too much, and not just farm work. You're a stand-in parent for Hope. Your dad said you and him always had coffee together until I showed up. Now, you miss coffee sometimes, but you still visit every day, except when we were gone, and you video chatted him instead. That's what you were doing when you didn't text me back, isn't it?"

He smiled at her and pulled her closer. "Nothing gets by you, huh?"

"That's me not even trying. I think I could probably…get your adoption records if you want them." She tensed, her body rigid against his, like she was waiting for him to yell at her. The offer wasn't subtle, but it didn't matter. He wouldn't be taking her up on it.

"Get them?" He leaned back and looked at her. "As in, steal them?"

"If you want to go slapping labels on everything, sure, we can call it that."

He shook his head. "No."

"Okay." She pulled the blanket to her chin.

"Thank you for being willing to do that for me," he said softly and kissed the top of her head. "But I've accepted that there was a reason the adoption was closed and that I'm better off not knowing what it was."

"You're okay spending the rest of your life wondering?"

He tucked her hair behind her ear. "I'm pretty certain my biological parents died. Knowing why they're gone isn't going to change that they're gone."

"But it could give you closure."

"I've got enough going on right now, as you've already pointed out. It's not one of my top priorities. Baby, please, just let it be."

"I'm not trying to talk you into it, but I want you to know that I'll help you if you decide to pursue it."

"Noted."

She snuggled into him, quiet. Too quiet.

Brody rubbed her back, sensing she wanted more from him. When he'd said he wanted to give her everything she needed, that included non-tangible things like trust and being vulnerable with her, having hard conversations. He didn't want her feeling alone or that she gave more emotionally. "I've always had my dad to lean on. He makes things okay, even when they aren't, just because he's there. And I don't know how much longer I'll have that."

"You'll still have it if you look for your birth parents. You won't be any less worthy of having him for your dad. It shouldn't be something that separates you from him. If you talk to him about it, it could bring you closer."

"I'll think about it, but first, I want to get this job out of the way." He wished the job were already over. He wanted it all behind him so he could focus on his family, and now…Morgan.

57

Don't Play With Me

BRODY

HE WAS GOING TO be one of those guys.

The kind that had to double-check the forecast because he'd been in a daze the first time he'd checked. The kind that had his truck plow through the barn because he'd gotten lost in his thoughts and accidentally put it in neutral, not park. The kind who went to buy a new oil filter, only to get there and have no idea what he'd come for.

He'd used to think those types of men were careless, but now he realized they cared a lot—about whatever naked woman they'd left in their bed before sunrise.

And *his* woman was ruthless.

How the fuck was he supposed to remember how much oil he'd mixed with fuel for his chainsaw when she was sending him sexy selfies?

The first one she'd snapped before she ever got out of bed. Wild, curly hair spread across the pillow, the blankets cocooning her. He'd stared at it for a number of minutes, remembering the scent of her hair, the taste of her skin, the funny feeling in his chest when he woke up with her snuggled into his side.

The next time he checked his phone, he fumbled it when he saw the message asking when he'd be back and the accompanying photo of her legs, feet propped up on the porch railing. No sign of clothes that he could see. Nothing but skin.

When he told her he wouldn't be done working for a while, she'd turned things up a notch.

I'm busy working too.

A photo of her with her hair somewhat tamed and piled on top of her head, and a pen pressed to her lips, followed the message. She sat at his kitchen table with her knee pulled to her chest. No fucking pants. Just panties and a skimpy little shirt. She held the camera out to the side to capture not only her sultry pose, but all the paperwork on the table. Lots of pencil drawings and eight-by-ten photographs.

He called her, and when she answered, said, "I think you might be violating company dress code."

"I'm my own boss. I decide the dress code."

"If you want to strut around my house naked, that's up to you, but I'm stuck out in the field fixing a piece of equipment." He didn't want her to think he didn't want to go straight to the house and put his hands all over her because that's exactly what he wanted. But it could take hours to fix this.

"Are you coming in for lunch?" Morgan asked.

"I can't, baby." Even though having Nick help would make it faster, every minute spent working on it was a minute they fell further behind.

"You aren't going to eat?"

"We have a cooler with sandwiches my mom made."

"Your mom still packs your lunch?"

"Pretty awesome, huh?"

She laughed and the sound pulled a smile from him. "So, I'm not going to see you any time soon?"

"No, probably not. Not until after dark."

"Bummer."

"I'm not happy about it, either. The selfies aren't making it any easier. Take mercy on me, please." He couldn't believe he was begging her not to send him sexy selfies.

"I'm going to be honest and let you know that there's very little probability that I'll be able to behave myself for such a long stretch of time."

He groaned and Nick glanced his way and raised an eyebrow. Brody waved him off, then turned his back. "I'm not going to check my phone."

"Yes, you will."

He rolled his eyes. "Love the confidence."

"Thanks. It was a gift."

"From?"

"You."

A relentless smile that made his cheeks ache overtook his face. He took off his ball cap, wiped the sweat from his forehead, then replaced it. "The word con artist is derived from the word confidence. I don't think I can take all the credit."

"That type of confidence is an act. How I'm feeling right now is legit."

"Probably because you know I'm wrapped around your finger."

Nick whistled, then made a *wrap it up* motion.

"I've gotta go before Nick has a hissy fit."

"Okay…"

"I'll see you later, Cash," he said, lowering and deepening his voice.

He hung up, tucked his phone back into his pocket. Time to get back to work. Hopefully, when he called it a day, he'd be able to stay awake longer than it took to shower and eat. Exhausted or not, he wanted to do so many things to her.

An hour—a very, very long hour—later, Brody caved. And was immediately sorry.

One video message waited for him.

He glanced around to make sure Nick wasn't nearby, then tapped the screen. The camera was up somewhere by her shoulder. He could see her bare stomach and a pair of tight, gray running shorts. Her hand was under the fabric and her hips rolled as she touched herself. It was a short clip, but enough to get him hard.

> Get a condom from my nightstand and put it in your pocket.

> Why?

> Because I'm going to fuck you where I find you when I get back.

> When will that be?

> Wouldn't you like to know?

Three dots appeared. Then disappeared. Then appeared again.

> I warned you before, don't play with me, Morgan.

58
Morgan's Lesson
Morgan

MORGAN JOGGED UP THE driveway and stopped next to the porch. She swept the curls that had fallen out of her bun off her neck, enjoying the breeze against her flushed skin. As the day turned to evening, the temperature and humidity remained brutally high, but the wind picked up, cutting down on the misery.

"Hey." Brody's deep voice startled her. He leaned over the porch railing, forearms draped across it, and a big smirk on his face.

"Hi," she said, her voice squeaky. She bent her head and walked to the steps, then sat so she could unlace her shoes. The intensity of her heart pounding made her breathing more labored than her five-mile run.

A shadow fell over her, cast from Brody's body blocking the porch lights. "Don't stop with your shoes and socks. Take it all off."

She glanced over her shoulder. "I'm sweaty and gross."

"You're not gross. Come here."

She set her shoes to the side and stood. She stared up at him, taking note that while he wasn't sweaty, he *was* dirty. But rather than being turned off by it, or wanting to wait until after they'd both showered, it thrilled her. "You're filthy."

"Baby, you have no idea." He ran his knuckles across her cheek. "I did wash my hands, though, because I'm going to put them all over you."

"That was thoughtful."

He smirked, then put his finger inside the waistband of her shorts and tugged. "Are these the same shorts you had your greedy little fingers down?"

Her face heated. It was the first time she'd ever sent anyone a video like that. She'd almost chickened out. "Yes, but not the same panties."

He hooked a finger from his other hand inside her shorts and used both to pull them down far enough to reveal her underwear. He leaned away, angling his head to get a better look.

Her face got even hotter. Her peach print undies were comfortable for running. She thought she'd get back before he did and have the chance to freshen up and put on sexier undies. These were cute, but not what she'd choose to wear, knowing he'd be taking them off.

"I need to shower." She pulled her shorts back into place as his hands slid up her sides, creating goosebumps on the bare skin between her shorts and sports bra.

"No." His stern tone sent a rush of nerves through her. "I told you I was going to fuck you where I find you. I meant it."

"But—"

He lifted her, guided her legs around his waist and pressed her against the post. He squeezed her ass with both hands. "You wanna play games, Morgan? Send me naughty pictures while I'm operating heavy machinery?"

"Sorry?"

His hot breath tickled her skin as he rubbed his nose beneath her jaw. "You don't sound sorry at all."

She held onto his biceps and licked her dry lips. "Are you going to make me sorry?"

He ground his hips into her. "I was going to make you come, but on second thought, that's probably not the best way to discourage you from doing it again."

"Probably not," she said in a breathy voice as his lips on her neck dragged her into a trance.

"You're supposed to be my good girl," he whispered.

And now *this* pair of panties was officially soaked.

"I'm trying," she whined.

His shoulders shook. "No, you're not. Not even a little bit."

She ran her nails across his shoulders over his shirt. "Is that really what you want? A good girl?" Hopefully not, because she'd never be able to pull it off outside of the bedroom.

He lifted his head. He took one hand off her ass and smoothed back the chaotic frizz the humidity had blessed her with. "Nah, I've always liked flirting with trouble, so it makes sense that I like flirting with you."

Her gaze landed on his mouth. He hadn't kissed her yet today. She hadn't even seen him since she'd fallen asleep curled up to him. She needed his mouth on hers more than she needed oxygen.

Brody met her halfway, their lips colliding. He pressed his hips into hers.

Ecstasy buzzed between her thighs. She shifted, grinding against him. The wetness in her panties added a heady sensation as his denim covered erection rubbed against her.

He pulled his mouth from hers. "Where's the condom?"

"I didn't have pockets."

His eyes widened. "Morgan, baby, I'm about to spank the hell out of you."

"It's on the table," she blurted out.

He set her on her feet. "Don't move."

She stayed rooted in place, the throbbing between her legs almost more than she could bear.

"Take off your bra," he rasped against her ear when he returned.

"We're outside."

"Yeah, at my house, with no neighbors and a half mile driveway. Take your bra off so I can play with your nipples while I fuck you."

Her heart beat quickened, but she grabbed the edge and pulled it over her head.

Brody kissed her, then spun her. He took her hands and guided them to wrap around the post above her head. He leaned in, his lips brushing her ear. "Say you're mine. Tell me you trust me to do whatever I want to you."

"I'm yours." She swallowed. "I trust you. Do whatever you want, but please, do it *now*."

Brody yanked down her shorts and panties, leaving them bunched around her knees. "You better be so wet you're dripping the way you've been begging for this all day."

Over her shoulder, she could see him stripping out of his shirt. Then his chest was to her back, warming her skin. He tucked his hand between her thighs and slid it up, reaching her slick pussy. His fingers felt so much better than her own.

The rough texture of denim skimmed her thighs as he dropped his pants.

She wiggled her hips, desperate to feel the hard cock pressed against her ass sliding against her pussy.

Brody gripped her hips, stilling her. "Are you on birth control?"

"No."

"Then don't fucking do that. Getting a taste of how you'd feel without any barriers would ruin me."

Morgan added it to her mental to-do list to research birth control options. She'd never had sex without a condom, but she'd also never trusted anyone this much. She wet her lips as the sound of him tearing open the condom package stood out amongst the breeze rushing through the cornstalks and the crickets chirping.

Brody grabbed her hips again, pulling them back toward him. Without hesitation, he thrust inside her.

Pleasure rocked her body. She gasped.

He pulled back, slipping out. "Fuck. You're so wet I can't even stay inside you."

The sensation of him rubbing the head of his cock against her clit tore a whimper from her throat. He surged back inside her. When he withdrew, he did it slowly, until only the tip was still in. He groaned and clutched her hips tighter as he sank deep inside her.

He slid his palm from her hip, up her body, to tug at her nipple. The calloused tips of his fingers incited shockwaves. They rushed over her body, pushing her closer to the place where she no longer cared about anything but this. Them. This connection.

She lowered one hand from the post and put it between her legs to rub her swollen, slippery clit. She moaned and pressed her forehead to the post.

"That's it, baby, make this pussy clench around me. Use those fingers to make yourself come all over my cock."

Morgan groaned, his dirty words propelling her toward climax.

Brody's thrusts quickened. He groaned loudly, pressing deeper inside her and staying there.

Her shaky legs threatened to give out.

He pulled out, then wrapped his arm around her middle, holding her against his chest. He kissed her ear, then her shoulder. "I hope that taught you a lesson."

59
The Sweetest Morning
Morgan

DEW COLLECTED ON THE rubber toes of Morgan's shoes as Brody led her to the back of his parents' property past outbuildings, alongside a field of wheat with fog rising above it as the sun crept up to the horizon. She'd watched the sunrise plenty of times, but never like this. Being woken up by a handsome man shaking her, telling her to hurry up and get dressed so he could show her something with the enthusiasm of a kid on Christmas morning was new and exhilarating.

She'd gotten dressed, then tried to get to the coffee pot, but Brody had intercepted her and held out an already-filled travel mug.

His refusal to tell her where they were going intrigued her.

She kept trudging along, not paying much attention to walking while she looked around.

Brody turned and waited for her to catch up—not because he was too fast to keep up with, but because she'd been paying so much attention to her surroundings, she'd gotten off track. His ball cap obscured his eyes, but his smile sent a *swoop* through her stomach. It said he had all the patience in the world for her.

He reached for her hand and led her to the structure farthest from the house. It appeared to be the newest and largest building on the property. A big sliding door on the side was open and inside, bales of hay were stacked high.

Once she entered, she could see the building was filled with hay. Not exactly her idea of something worth getting out of bed at dawn for. She glanced at Brody and tilted her head.

He let go of her hand and wrapped his arm around her shoulders so he could guide her to a small space tucked in the corner, then pointed at the ground.

With her travel mug clutched to her chest, Morgan shifted her gaze to the spot he indicated.

A cat laid there, feeding four tiny kittens. Two orange, two black.

Her mouth fell open and she glanced at him over her shoulder.

He winked at her, then lifted a hay bale off the top of a shorter stack and set it on the floor, creating front-row seating.

While he sat and drank his coffee, she knelt and watched the kittens, barely able to handle their cuteness.

"How old are they?"

"I don't know. A couple days. Four, at the most. I found them first thing this morning."

And he came to get her. Because he was excited to show her. That made her ridiculously happy.

"Which one do you want?" he asked.

She turned, still on her knees. "I can have one?"

"It'll be a few weeks until we can separate them from their mama, but it never hurts to have a barn cat to catch the mice."

Suggesting they adopt a cat together indicated a talk about their future was impending. Her stomach fluttered. A future with Brody sounded as wonderfully exceptional as it sounded scary.

"I have Buster."

He leaned forward, forearms on his thighs and gave her a pointed look. "You're telling me you don't want a kitten?"

"I do, but…"

He took a sip of his coffee while she tried to find a way to say what

she was feeling.

"Are we living together?" she asked.

"We've *been* living together."

"Things have changed, though. We've blurred all the lines. Moving in with you and staying at your house because we're working together are very different concepts."

"The only concept I understand right now is getting to see you every day and going to sleep with you in my arms every night. If you need me to drive to Savannah or Las Vegas and move all your shit here…baby, I will. Want a house key? I'll give you a copy today. You wanna decorate? Do it." He crooked his finger at her and when she came closer, said, "I'll do whatever I have to do to make you comfortable. Just stay."

"And the job?"

"I know you've been doing all the heavy lifting. I need a few more days to get caught up with farm work and then we can sit down and go over the plan."

She'd feel a lot better when the job was over, and she had a few million dollars. Having the freedom to go wherever and do whatever she wanted would put her at ease. She hoped it'd never be the case, but if she had to deal with a broken heart, she didn't want to do it while trying to find a new job, a new place to live, a new plan.

She stood and brushed off the knees of her jeans. "Can we get two?"

"Two?" He blinked and set his coffee by his feet. "Two *kittens*?"

She nodded and swayed. "They can play together and keep each other company."

His lip curled. "Do you expect me to tell you no?"

She shook her head, grinning. About something like an outside cat? No. He'd never. When it came to requests that he knew would make her happy, as long as they weren't unreasonable, he wouldn't deny her.

"Yes, you can have two if it's okay with Hope. The mama belongs to her."

She flung herself at him, knocking him backward.

He did a slow fall, slinging one arm around her waist and the other behind him to brace himself from hitting the ground hard. He landed with his legs bent over the hay bale and her on top of his chest, straddling his pelvis.

She ignored the not-so-comfortable position and kissed him, trying to avoid banging her face on the brim of his ball cap.

He took his hat off and tossed it out of the way, then cupped the back of her neck, rubbing his thumb against the base of her skull as he led her into a deep, soul-wrecking kiss.

They stayed there, on the floor, unable to get enough of each other. Brody didn't try to take things beyond kissing, though. His hands stayed on her neck and her lower back. Making out on the floor of a hay barn wasn't anything remotely close to how she'd ever expected to spend a morning, but she liked it. A lot.

Morgan pulled back, her palms flat on the floor next to his head. "I want a puppy."

"Okay." He squeezed her waist.

"Seriously?"

"If that's what you want, but if you get a puppy, you're getting zero kittens, and it has to stay outside."

She huffed, then made a pouty face.

He dragged her down for a soft kiss, then stared into her eyes, keeping his hand on her neck to keep them nose-to-nose. "Two kittens and I'll take you out for pizza—final offer."

"I'll take it."

60
Bang, Bang, Bullshit
Morgan

A LOUD THUD RATTLED THE windows.

Morgan sat up straight in bed. Pulse racing, she turned to Brody's side of the bed, but he wasn't there. She checked her phone. One A.M.

She grabbed the first piece of clothing she could find—his flannel shirt—and slid her arms into the sleeves. She buttoned it as she went down the stairs.

"Brody?" she called out, her pulse speeding faster and faster.

When he'd come back to the house at the end of the day, she'd been asleep on the guest bed on top of the floor plans she'd spent hours sketching. He'd found her, scooped her up, and carried her to his room.

She'd fallen back asleep as soon as he'd tucked her in. She didn't know what he'd done while she slept. It was unusual for him not to be sleeping at this hour—unless he was keeping her company.

A red glow through the window caught her attention. She flew out of the house, heart in her throat.

The far end of the barn no longer had a roof. Small flames licked at the beams that remained standing among the debris. Buster was freaking out, making all kinds of frantic, high-pitched noises from his pen, but he'd been far enough from the explosion that he wasn't hurt. Just scared.

Like she was.

She fought her tears as she raced toward the structure, calling out for

Brody. He didn't answer but she found him on his stomach, a good ten feet from where the door on that end of the barn had once been.

She knelt beside him and called his name, unable to keep her hysteria out of her voice.

He groaned and winced.

"Brody," she said with a woosh of relief.

His body was covered in grime and blood. He rolled onto his back and scrubbed his face with his hands. "Fucking hell."

"What happened?"

He sat up, looking at the damage the explosion had done to his barn. "I was tired. I made a mistake."

"Are you hurt?" She tried to assess him for injuries, but it was hard in the dark.

"I'm fine." He stood and wiped his hands on his pants.

She rose, trying to catch up as he went into the non-destroyed part of the structure, not at all okay with how he was minimizing the situation. "You could have been killed!"

"Baby, I'm fine," he said a second time, a fire extinguisher in hand. He leaned down to kiss her, but she turned her head. "Morgan…"

"What would I have told your family?" Her eyes tingled with unwelcome tears, and she couldn't catch a decent breath. "That you were building a bomb so that we could steal diamonds from a lunatic?"

"I know it must have been scary for you—"

"Shut up, Brody! Just…shut up!" She pushed away and took off for the house. Inside, she pulled her first aid kit off the top of the fridge and set it on the table.

She watched from the back door as he put out the small fire.

When he came in, he stared at her like she was the bomb that was about to explode.

"Imagine how you would feel if you woke up in the middle of the night and found me lying on the ground like that." She pointed to one of the chairs at the table. "Sit down and let me clean those cuts, or you're going to get an infection and die."

He peeled off his shirt and sat. Shallow gashes and scrapes from landing in the gravel covered his body. "I'm sorry. I shouldn't have been out there messing around. I just…" He shook his head.

"What?"

"I feel like I'm behind on everything, most of all our job, and I came in and saw all your work, and that only made me feel guiltier."

"So, it's my fault you blew yourself up?" She chucked a roll of gauze at him.

He dodged it. "No. It was my stupidity."

She opened an antiseptic wipe and swiped it across the gash that ran the length of his upper arm.

He hissed and jerked away. "Hey."

"Don't blow yourself up and then you won't have cuts that need cleaning."

The rumbling of an engine traveled through the screen door. There was a slam, then feet beat up the porch steps.

Nick pushed the door open and looked between them. "What happened?"

"Your brother decided to play with bombs instead of going to bed when he should have."

He looked at Brody. "You alright?"

"I'm fine. Scraped up, that's all."

"We heard the boom. It shook the windows," Nick said. "Everyone is worried. Are you sure you're okay? It might be worth a trip to the ER to make sure."

"Just go tell Mom and Dad that I'm fine."

Nick looked at her. "You're a nurse. Do you think he should go to the hospital?"

"He might have a concussion, but he doesn't appear to have any broken bones, and I don't see any wounds that need stitches. I think he'll be okay, but I'll keep an eye on him."

"Are *you* okay?" he asked.

She probably looked crazy, standing there in only Brody's shirt, with bedhead and a tear-stained face.

"Get out of here, Nick," Brody said between clenched teeth.

"Okay, okay. Glad you're alright."

Once Nick had left, Morgan tried to get through first aid as quickly as possible. She was barely keeping herself together and needed a little time alone.

"Morgan," Brody said, his voice soft. "It won't happen again. I promise."

"Has it ever happened before?"

He stared at his lap.

"Great." She picked up the trash from the wipes and tossed them.

"When it happened before, I wasn't tired. I was inexperienced."

She huffed and hugged herself. What Brody did in his barn had never been a secret, but she hadn't put much thought into the consequences of it. He built bombs. That was dangerous. So dangerous.

No. Of everyone she'd ever been romantically involved with, Brody's special interest was *the most* dangerous. Motocross stunts and cave diving seemed tame in comparison.

Wonderful. Here, she'd thought she'd broken the cycle and found a guy who wasn't anything like her usual type.

But Brody was exactly her type.

She just hadn't seen it until now.

Fresh tears spilled down her face. Of course, he was too good to be true. She'd seen what she wanted to see. With her back to the wall, she slid to the floor, dropping her forehead to her knees as sobs shook her body.

Brody tried to suppress his groan as he lowered himself to the floor across from her, but she didn't miss it. He could play down his injuries all he wanted. The fact was the blast had lifted this big man off his feet and flung him through the air like a stuffed animal. Minor incident? Yeah, okay.

He spread his legs and scooted closer, caging her in. "Can I touch you?"

She shook her head without lifting it from her knees.

He sighed. "You're right. If the tables were turned, I'd be losing my shit."

She sniffed and turned her head to the side, staring at the screen door. "You need sleep."

"I'm not going to bed without you."

"Do you really think I'm going to be able to fall back asleep?"

"Baby," he said in a tone she'd never heard from him. The underlying torment wasn't the biggest leap, but the helplessness in his voice...that wasn't the Brody she knew. The Brody she knew took charge. He fixed things. "I don't know what to do."

"There's nothing you can do. This is who you are. You build bombs."

"That's part of who I am," he said softly. "But it's only one part. Morgan, please, look at me."

She slowly lifted her head. Seeing the red mixed with dirt and soot all over his body, she burst into tears again.

"It's killing me not being able to hold you."

"I guarantee you it doesn't compare to how I'm feeling right now realizing that if one little thing goes wrong, I'll lose you forever. And for what? Money? Some stupid kink you have for explosions?"

"You have every right to feel the way you're feeling, but I don't think we should have this conversation while your emotions are running this high."

She glared. "Do you honestly think that my emotions are ever going to not be high when I think about you dead?"

He frowned.

Morgan stood and stepped over his leg. "You're right. There's no point in us talking about this while you're exhausted and I'm freshly traumatized."

He stayed sitting there, knees up, arms draped across them, head hung.

"Go to bed. You need sleep, and I need to be on my own so I can think."

"I know I should give you the space you're asking for, but I've never wanted to do anything less."

"I can't trust my own judgement. The right words and a few kisses could sway me into forgetting about this. Until the next time it happens."

He looked at her, brow furrowed. "What is there to think about? It's not like you just found out what I do. We met because you stole my bomb. We're planning a heist together. I'm not the only one putting myself in dangerous situations. You thought nothing of offering to steal my adoption records. If you think you can help someone you care about, you'll put your neck on the line without a second thought for your own wellbeing. Hell, if someone pisses you off bad enough, you'll retaliate without giving a damn about the risk involved. You're good, baby, but you've also been lucky. Just because nothing has happened to you so far, doesn't mean it won't. You're not invincible, either."

He wasn't wrong. About any of it. But it wasn't the same. "There's a difference between ending up in the back of a police car and ending up in the morgue."

He pushed up from the floor, wincing while holding his middle.

"You probably bruised your ribs, you dumbass."

He smirked. "If being mean to me makes you feel better, then do it. Yeah, I'm beat up, but I'm not dead. After we do this job, I'll never touch anything more explosive than fireworks, okay?"

She shook her head. "What if you get hurt or killed during the job? What if both of us do? You're right. I went into this knowing what you do is dangerous, but it hits a little different witnessing it firsthand. I need

time to process this."

He rubbed his face and sighed deep. "I'll leave you alone for now, but in the morning, we're working through this."

She didn't know how.

They were who they were. Brody would make promises and Morgan would believe them. Life might be hectic now, but when it slowed, he'd get antsy. He'd probably try to entertain himself with his hobbies, and maybe even pick up a few more. She'd be on edge until he caved.

Not only that, but she couldn't expect him to give up engineering explosives without promising she'd stay on the straight and narrow. She'd spent her whole life honing her skills. The only outcome would be one of them breaking their promise, or they'd grow to resent each other.

time to process this...

...asked her...? In a sudden. "I'll leave you alone for now, but I'll be waiting for you." ...run through the...

...she didn't know how...

They were somewhere deep... ...still many provisions and... ...up inside... ...hunting... ...she'd learned how to... ...some skill she'd tried to... ...shoot... ...herself, with the bow... ...and he'd each pick up a few... ...she'd scrape up the anting...

...explaining that... ...she would... ...together... ...square the mountain... ...vehicles within moments. She'd... ...to the slaughter and off into the... ...spot... ...hold the dinner... ...still... ...the surface would to one of... ...in the... ...the...

61
Punking Out
BRODY

BRODY WOKE UP WITH a gut feeling that something was wrong.

He rolled out of bed and went into the hall.

Morgan, who'd been coming from the guest bedroom, came to an abrupt stop, holding onto a suitcase and a duffle bag.

"Where are you going?" he asked. "Is it John? Why didn't you wake me up?"

She wouldn't meet his eyes. "Uncle John is fine."

He glanced at her luggage again.

It clicked. "You're leaving?" No wonder she hadn't woke him up. He shook his head. "No, you're sneaking out."

"I can't do this. We need to end it before we get in too deep."

Before? How could she not realize that it had already happened? At least for him. He figured Morgan would need more time than he would. He just didn't think she'd be far behind.

But here she was, copping out. Straight sneaking out in the middle of the night.

"You were going to leave without saying bye?" As the words left his mouth, the gravity of them settled. Anger so intense it made his hands shake grabbed hold. "What did I ever do to deserve that? Who the hell do you think you are, Morgan Cash?"

"Someone who's not strong enough to plan your funeral."

"You want to leave? Here, let me help you." Brody yanked the suitcase and bag from her. He turned and went downstairs and out the back door. When he reached her car, he set them down and popped the trunk. He put them inside, slammed the hood, then turned to find her standing there.

He brushed by her, heading for the house.

"Brody."

He stopped.

"I'm sorry. I tried to be better for you."

"I said I'd give you everything you wanted," he said without turning around. "This is me keeping my word. You wanted to leave without saying goodbye, so do it. I have nothing to say."

He walked to the house, so hurt and pissed off he couldn't think straight. His temper didn't get the better of him often. It took a lot to push him over the edge. Having her sneak out on him was by far the most hurtful thing anyone had ever done to him.

Either she'd drive for a while, realize her mistake, and come back, or she'd break his already-eroding heart.

62
Goat Custody
BRODY

BRODY NEVER WENT BACK to sleep. Instead, he stared at his phone screen, watching her avatar getting farther and farther on the map. When he lost hope that she'd turn around, he shut off his mind and focused on farm work.

On his way back to the house for pain killers because he was stiff and sore and miserable, a truck rumbled up the driveway. Josh Murphy, the boy who'd ticked off Hope at the dance, jumped down from his wannabe monster truck.

"Hey, Brody." Josh gave him a once over. "What happened to you?" He peered beyond Brody. "Um, what happened to your barn?"

He was a little scraped up, but the barn was worse off. After assessing the damage, he concluded it'd be better to demolish the whole thing and build new. "Long story. Nothing to worry about. What are you doing here?"

"Morgan asked me to come get Buster."

It was a knife to his gut. "No."

Josh's eyes widened. "If you want to keep him, that's fine. I don't have anyone lined up to take him. She said she couldn't bring him where she was going, and she didn't want to burden you."

This kid knew more about Morgan's plans than Brody did. How fucked. "Did she say where she was going?"

He shook his head. "She didn't tell you?"

"We didn't part on good terms."

"Really?" He frowned. "She seemed so chill."

That's not the first word he'd pick to describe her. But he wasn't going to discuss their falling out with a sixteen-year-old.

"So, dealing with girls doesn't get easier as you get older?" Josh asked in a defeated tone.

"I guess not. Does the girl giving you trouble happen to be my sister?"

His ears turned red. "I thought she wasn't allowed to date until she was sixteen, so I didn't ask her out." He shook his head. "But she's going to hate me forever now. Which tracks. Every time she starts to warm up to me, something happens, giving her another reason to add to her grudge."

"Are you looking for work?" Brody asked, because if this kid was going to keep pining away for Hope, he wanted to know what he was about. They also needed help and Josh could probably take a tractor engine apart blindfolded. His dad owned the local farm equipment dealership, but for some reason, Josh refused to work there, despite his four older brothers doing so.

"Always."

The hum of a motor progressively got louder. Nick stopped the UTV next to them and climbed out. "I need a post digger." He looked at Josh, then stuck his hand out. "Hey, man. What are you doing here?"

"I came to get the goat."

Nick swiveled his head and raised an eyebrow at Brody. "Are you making her get rid of him?"

He crossed his arms. "She left, and she called Josh to come get him."

"But Brody wants to keep him."

Nick stayed quiet, looking around for a long moment. "Morgan's gone? Like...gone, gone?"

"Yes," Brody snapped. He looked at Josh. "You can start tomorrow morning if you want. Be here at five."

Josh shook his hand, then got back in his truck.

Brody stomped to the house and flung the door open. He grabbed a bottle of pills from a cabinet and swallowed two.

Nick came into the house. "What's going on?"

He pulled the milk from the fridge and drank from the jug. "She got spooked by what happened last night and dipped out."

"Why didn't you stop her?"

With his jaw clenched, Brody shook his head.

"Call her," Nick said, like it was no problem at all. "How far do you think she got? Tell her to get a room and rest. I'll go with you to get her, and you can drive her back in her car."

"I'm not doing that." He dropped into a chair and tilted his head until he could see the ceiling. He stretched his neck side-to-side.

"Is this a pride thing or is there more to it that you're not telling me?"

There was so much more. Every moment he'd spent with her. Every laugh. Every blush. Her melting into him. Holding her. All the vulnerability. The deep, dark parts of themselves they'd let each other see. Thinking about his future and only seeing her.

There was no way to summarize that so someone else could understand.

He'd been patient while she dealt with her past, and even though he knew she wasn't done struggling, her doing this hurt like hell. He wasn't going to chase her and beg her to come back. It wasn't pride. He'd do anything to be with Morgan, except play into the unhealthy patterns she'd learned from the men who'd come before him. He'd fight anyone who'd dare to stand in his way—except her.

63
Candlelight Counseling
Morgan

CRYING HERSELF TO SLEEP in a motel bed in the middle of Indiana was an all-time low. Morgan wanted to believe she'd done the smart thing. Cut her losses. Bailed before she proved to herself and everyone else all over again that she was only drawn to men with the ability to rip her heart to shreds.

Brody wouldn't do it intentionally.

But it'd still happen.

And it'd be so much worse because she'd never truly given her heart to anyone before him. She'd figured that out as she put mile after mile behind her.

That's why she couldn't stay. The higher her bet, the more she stood to lose, and she'd lost enough of herself already. If she invested the last little bit of her heart she'd been clinging to, what would be left if the worst happened?

After a few hours of sleep, she drove the rest of the way to Las Vegas alternating between numbness and agony.

She hadn't called to say she was coming, so when Uncle John opened the door, he gasped. "What are you doing here? What's wrong?"

"Can I stay with you for a while?"

He took her suitcase and bag from her. "You don't have to ask that."

Obviously. She wouldn't have driven 2,500 miles if she'd thought he would turn her away.

She curled up on his sofa, pulling the throw blanket off the back and wrapping herself in it. She had to tell him something, but she didn't know what or how.

"I made stuffed salmon. I'll fix you a plate."

She rested her eyes while he set up an entire meal at the coffee table, complete with a lit taper candle and cloth napkins.

He placed a glass of amber liquid next to her plate and sat with an identical glass in his hand. Whenever she'd had a bad day, from the time she was old enough to remember, he'd let her eat dinner in the living room, and he'd always set it up ultra-fancy, including a vase of flowers. She wasn't a little girl anymore, and yet it was still comforting and made her feel the tiniest bit better.

"Do I need to make a trip to Maryland?" He crossed one ankle over his opposite leg, swirling his drink.

She shook her head and reached for her own glass.

"Don't touch that until you've eaten at least half of what's on your plate."

She grumbled but put the plate on her lap and picked up her fork. Just as well. It'd be a disaster getting drunk while she was feeling so raw.

"Tell me what happened."

"He got hurt and…" She pulled in a shaky breath. "I just can't do it. So, I left."

"Do what?"

"Lose him."

His eyebrows drew down. "So, you left?"

She sobbed, put her plate on the coffee table, and curled into a ball. "It might not seem very logical, but I don't want to spend my time waiting for him to blow himself up again."

"You'd rather not be with him, than be with him and have anxiety about something that might not even happen?" That *do you even hear*

yourself tone was the worst.

"It's not anxiety." She grabbed a tissue from the box on the end table and wiped her face. "It's choosing not to put my heart in a high-risk situation."

"Because he *might* die."

She nodded. "Yes."

"I hate to break it to you, kid, but he could be in a car accident or develop a terminal illness. Maybe he'll die of old age. We're all going to die. It's the how and when that's the mystery."

"I thought you didn't want me with him?"

He took a sip of his drink, never taking his eyes off her. "I'm not trying to talk you into going back."

"Then, what are you trying to do?" she asked.

"I'm trying to make sure you see it from every angle before it's too late to fix it, if that's what you decide you want to do." The tone he used sounded a lot like the one she'd used when she'd spoken to Hope at the dance. She'd been stern because she didn't want Hope to make the same mistakes. Was this Uncle John's attempt to guide her away from making the mistakes he'd made with Lucy?

"It's already too late. I tried to leave without saying goodbye, but he caught me."

Uncle John sucked air through his teeth. "How did he react?"

"He put my bags in the car and basically told me not to let the door hit me in the ass on the way out."

He pressed his lips together and turned his head slightly.

She gasped. "Are you laughing?"

"Lucy said he wouldn't put up with you being a brat."

She hoped her glare scorched his eyebrows. "A brat? Are those your words or hers?"

"Mine," he said. "You've always let fear blind you. You can't see beyond escaping the pain, so you power down your sweet, compassionate nature and throw a carefully calculated tantrum to distract others from seeing you're scared to death."

She stared at the candle flame. Avoiding feeling awful seemed like a standard response to icky emotions. "So, what?"

"It's not a problem as long as it doesn't affect anyone else."

Her chest ached. She reached for the drink and took a gulp before he could tell her not to.

"You feel in control right now, but only at the cost of someone else's. And you're trying not to think about what kind of person that makes you."

"Oh, I know what kind of person I am. A dysfunctional one. Brody dodged a bullet."

"I'm sure he doesn't see it that way."

"He didn't try to stop me, so he must not be too pressed."

"Did you want him to stop you?" He furrowed his brow.

She huffed. No. That's why she'd tried to leave without alerting him. He'd have talked her out of it. "I didn't want him to, but I expected him to."

"When you stomped out of brunch, he told me there was no use in talking to you until you'd calmed down. Maybe he's giving you time to sort through your feelings."

That wasn't it. She'd never seen him angry like that. The look he'd given her when he'd realized why she had her bags packed felt like a hot poker to the chest. It felt as though he'd finally accepted how messed up she was. That look changed everything between them.

Brody wasn't going to come after her. She'd been gone for over twenty-four hours, and he hadn't called or sent a single text.

Shit. He could track her. She pulled out her phone and hovered her thumb over the option to turn off her location sharing. He probably already knew she'd come to Las Vegas. Although, he probably could have figured that out even without a smart phone. Turning it off would send the message that she didn't want him to find her.

She couldn't do it. A small part of her ached to see him again. She wanted Bossy Brody to grab her, say she was his, and drag her back to Maryland. But he wouldn't be satisfied with her choice if it wasn't made freely. He gave a lot, but he also had standards for how he expected people to treat him.

And she hadn't met those standards.

64
Her Move
BRODY

BRODY HELD HIS BREATH as he picked up the phone from the table next to his rocking chair and flipped it over. Of course, it wasn't her. It'd been three days since she left, and she hadn't tried to reach out at all.

The caller wasn't Morgan, but maybe the closest thing.

"I'm sorry, Lucy," he said with the phone held to his ear.

"I called to see if you're okay. Not for an apology."

"No, I am not okay. Is she?"

"No."

"No? That's all you're going to give me?" He stood from the chair and paced the length of the porch.

"She starts crying out of nowhere. She's barely eating. She's been sleeping a lot, which she probably needs, but her sleeping patterns are erratic. Is that what you wanted to know?"

Of course, he didn't like hearing she was unhappy.

He missed her. Not seeing her, not getting to talk to her or touch her had been absolute hell. But she'd made her choice and stuck with it. He couldn't convince her to love him as much as he loved her. She cared. Just not enough.

"I'm not coming after her, if that's what this call is about." He hadn't done this. If Morgan asked him to, he would leave on the next plane, but she had to do it. Not Lucy.

"You're giving up?"

"*She* gave up on us, not me. Did she tell you she tried to sneak out without saying goodbye?"

"Yes, I'm aware. But it seems stupid that you're both sitting on different sides of the country with broken hearts when you don't have to be."

"That's her doing."

"I know she broke both of your hearts, but please remember, she's never had an example of what a healthy romantic relationship looks like. John and I didn't exactly set her up for success in that part of her life."

"I can empathize with her and still be angry she walked out on me." It killed him that she was hurting, but he couldn't change that. He was the reason for it—even if it hadn't been intentional. He should have never gone out to work in the barn that night. Then they'd still be happy.

Until they inevitably hit another hurdle and she punked out.

She might not want to live in fear that he'd have a fatal accident, but he refused to live in fear that he'd come home one day, and she'd be gone. The future he wanted with Morgan didn't include her running when things got heavy, instead of coming to him. He needed to be able to trust that he wasn't going to have to go after her. Again. And again. And again.

"I thought you two would be great together. I really did," Lucy said. "I'm sorry it turned out to hurt you."

"Lucy…" He squeezed his forehead. "You weren't wrong and I'm not sorry I met her. I do want her to come back, but that's got to be her choice."

"Do you think she knows she can come back?"

"If she doesn't know that, then she didn't pay attention to who I am and how I feel about her. I wasn't shy about it."

"That's where you stand, then? It's her move?" Lucy huffed, white noise crackling across the line.

"Yeah. It is."

"Brody," she said firmly, but softly, "she's not in a place where she's capable of realizing that's what she should do."

"Maybe someone should tell her then, but it's not going to be me."

"What about the job?" she asked.

"I don't know. I'll pivot somehow." When the hole in his chest scabbed over enough to think about those kinds of things. Without Morgan, he'd probably end up doing a bunch of smaller jobs.

"If she knew what you need the money for—"

"No. I don't want her to know." He didn't want her pity. He didn't want her guilt to be her reason for coming back.

"Haven't seen you in a few days," Brody's dad said once he'd gotten situated on the porch in a rocking chair with his oxygen beside him. His mom had dropped him off, like it was a routine occurrence, but the only time his dad had been to his house since shortly after Brody had finished building it, was when Morgan had brought him over. He'd rather spend time with his dad than just about anyone, but it was easier to go to him.

"I wouldn't have been very good company," Brody said.

"You wanna talk about it?"

He shook his head and reached for the bottle of whiskey by his boots. "Nope." This was the fifth day without her. She wasn't coming back. He couldn't say he'd lost her because it had become very apparent that he'd never really had her. "I know how much you like her, but I can't handle you telling me to go after her right now, so just…don't." That's why he'd stayed away. His dad thought the world of Morgan. They had that in common, but he didn't need to hear how wonderful something was when it was so far out of his reach.

"I didn't come here for that."

"Right," Brody muttered. "What'd you come for, then?"

"I came because you're my son and you're hurting. I came to sit with you because I love you. If we sit here and don't talk that's okay with me."

Brody held the bottle out to him.

His dad took a swig, then handed it back. "Broke out the good stuff, huh?"

"Seemed like as good a time as any."

He took another drink, then stared out at nothing.

His dad didn't say a word but kept rocking in his chair.

They sat there until it got dark. Brody broke the silence. "I thought I could be what she needed. I didn't think I'd be the reason she left."

"I don't know what happened, but I know you, and I have trouble believing you'd hurt her intentionally."

"Either way, she's gone, and she's not coming back."

"And you don't want to go after her?"

He shook his head. "Maybe I should want to. Everyone seems to expect me to. Maybe I'm not the right person for Morgan, because I don't know what to say to her at this point."

"Have you told her you love her?"

"That's not going to fix anything."

"You didn't answer my question."

"No," Brody said. "I never told her. I didn't want to scare her off by saying it so soon."

"Well, there's no risk of that now. Tell her. What do you have to lose?"

"My self-respect and feeling like a fucking idiot when she doesn't say it back."

His dad laughed. "You don't feel like an idiot right now?"

"Yes, but I'm an idiot with my self-respect still intact." He took another long swallow and winced as the burn trickled down his throat.

"Do you think hers is still intact?"

"What?" What a fucked-up question. Her self-respect hadn't been intact in the time he'd known her. She had principles she stood by, but the shame she carried for what she'd failed to protect herself from weighed her down.

"In the time I spent with Morgan, I learned that she believes listening to her heart is dangerous. If you're waiting for her to come back because she's made a mistake, you're probably going to have to wait until she forgives herself for making the mistake in the first place. I'd imagine she's being particularly hard on herself considering how highly she thinks of you."

"What are you saying? She was following her heart when she decided to leave, so I shouldn't hold it against her?"

"No." His dad shook his head. "I don't think she made the decision with her heart. That's what I'm trying to get through your thick head."

"Dad." He rubbed his forehead. "What happened to us not talking about this?"

"I didn't bring it up, you did. But as someone whose primary interest is seeing you happy, I'm warning you that if you want her, you might have to do something besides sit here on your ass and get drunk."

He could see her second guessing what her heart wanted, wondering if she was setting herself up to be torn apart by her own decisions. She'd learned to protect herself by analyzing situations and choosing what was safest, even if it was the opposite of what she needed emotionally.

His dad let it drop. They discussed the farm and Nick's baseball career. His mom came to get his dad and Brody finished off what was left of the whiskey, then pulled out his phone and looked for airline tickets. He was about to purchase a one-way ticket for the first flight out in the morning but decided to check her location. If he landed in Las Vegas, only to find out she'd gone back to Savannah, he'd not be very happy.

The app alerted him that she'd stopped sharing her location hours ago. Either she'd just remembered it was on and didn't want him to find her, or he'd missed his window.

Brody chucked his phone into the yard, then went to bed.

65
Poker and a Proposal
Morgan

MORGAN STUCK A PIECE of tape over the string of the paper bat garland that would hang over the entrance to the common room. She looked forward to coming to her new job each day. She didn't so much look forward to going home after work though. Uncle John and Lucy invited her to do things—separately, of course—and she'd gone out with a group of old friends once. But she was going through the motions, nothing more. Just like before she'd met Brody.

Until recently, she'd forgotten this feeling existed. Even when he was poking at her in the beginning, she'd been irritated. But not bored. Going to Savannah to celebrate Halloween with Logan and Drew would help temporarily, at least.

The past five weeks hadn't been easy, but she'd gradually pulled herself out of her hole of despair. She'd been hired for this job almost three weeks ago. Soon, she was going to look for her own place and figure out what her future looked like.

"He bought her a huge house and renovated it, and kept the whole thing a secret so she could focus on her career?" Dottie, the elderly lady on the bench of her walker, handed Morgan another piece of tape.

"Yes, and he's throwing her a surprise housewarming party." Morgan climbed off the chair. As the new activity coordinator at the assisted living community, she'd planned an entire day of Halloween festivities before finding out she couldn't be there for it because she'd be at Logan and Drew's housewarming. She was excited about the party, but also sad to miss something she'd put a lot of energy into and seeing the joy on the faces of the seniors she'd quickly come to care for.

"You must have some high standards for men with a brother like that," Dottie said.

A sharp laugh burst from her lips. "Not exactly."

"You're still single, aren't you?"

"Not because of my standards, that's for sure." She moved her chair so she could tape the other end of the garland.

"It can't be because of your looks," Henry said from a table in the middle of the room where she had him checking a string of candy-corn-colored lights she'd found in the back of the storage closet. Only half of them lit up when plugged in, but he'd said he'd take care of it. With how he'd hunched over the table, he'd seemed to be absorbed in his task, but it was no surprise he was eavesdropping.

"That's one heck of a hearing aid you've got," Morgan called out.

He grinned without looking up from the lights.

"Why is it the older people get, the more worried they become about younger people's love lives?" she asked, as curious as she was annoyed.

"Because the closer you get to the end, the more you understand that love is the only thing that matters in life." Dottie cut off another length of tape and held it out.

"And you regret that you wasted time on anything else," Henry chimed in.

"Young people today get so hung up on doing this and that, having fancy photos to post on their Intercam—"

"Instagram," Morgan said.

"Whatever it is." Dottie waved her hand dismissively. "They don't realize life isn't about what you do, it's about who you do it with. I was with my first husband for three and a half years before he got into a construction accident that took his life. We didn't have much money, so we couldn't travel, and we rarely did things like going out to dinner at a restaurant. My second husband was wealthy. I got to see the world. I met famous people. I went to extravagant parties. We had a good time and I loved him very much. But when I look back and think about the best days of my life, what comes to mind are always the ones where he didn't go to his construction job because of weather. We'd stay home and paint one of the bedrooms or play cards. I never laughed as much as I laughed with him. He was playful. Life never got boring with him."

Morgan stepped down from the chair. It was useless trying to avoid the residents projecting their regrets on her. But it was a lot easier to nod and smile when their lectures didn't hit so close to home.

She'd come to like rainy days too, and she'd choose making out in the hay over a kiss in front of the Eiffel Tower any day. Staying away from Brody was the hardest thing she'd ever done. She'd never find another person or place that felt as much like home as he did, but she was going to have to learn to be okay with that. He might be good for her, but she was no good for him.

Uncle John was right. She'd let her anxiety overrule her compassion. She'd chosen to hurt him so she could escape her own pain. And it hadn't even worked.

She didn't want to change Brody like Eric had changed her. He deserved someone whose head wasn't all screwed up. Someone who didn't impulsively leave in the middle of the night because she couldn't work through her emotions in a healthy fashion. He deserved far better than she'd ever be able to give him.

She spent the rest of her afternoon setting up decorations and showing the staff how the various games worked. She was checking her phone as she made her way to the parking lot, but a voice stopped her.

"Is this your way of finding a rich husband?"

Morgan turned and scowled at Charlie. "What are you doing here?"

"My grandpa lives here."

"No, he doesn't."

He flashed her a grin. "I need your help."

"Nothing good ever comes after those four words leave your mouth."

"I helped you."

Damn it. He had her. At Gill's party, he'd noticed she'd slipped away a couple of times and confronted her about it. Once she'd filled him in on what she was doing, he kept watch for her.

"I'm leaving for Savannah tomorrow. I'm not going to be around for a few days."

"I'm going to Savannah too," he said. "But first, I have to go to Atlantic City for a poker tournament and I want you to come with me."

"You could have called. Why did you show up here?"

"Because I thought I should do this in person." He pulled a ring box from his pocket and dropped to one knee. "Morgan Cash, will you be my fake fiancée?"

She rolled her eyes. "Why do you need a fiancée?"

He stood. "There's a tournament I entered in Atlantic City and I'm tired of being swarmed by the gold diggers beforehand. It's affecting my game. When I took you to Gill's party, they left me alone."

"You want me to be a buffer?"

"Please? I was talking to Logan about it because he knows what it's like, and he thinks it's a good idea."

"But I'm supposed to go to Savannah to help him prepare for the party," she said.

"He said he's got it covered without us, as long as we're there by the day of the party."

"Let me get this straight…you want to fly to Atlantic City tomorrow, play in the tournament that night, and then hop on a plane to Savannah the next day?" Sounded like a Charlie plan, that was for sure. But while the risk of it turning out to be awkward or aggravating was high, she yearned for an adventure.

"I know it's tight, but you know we'll have fun. I'll pay for everything."

"Fine."

Maybe this would help her bounce back and figure things out. Like how to stop missing Brody.

66
Poker Wifey
Morgan

COLD AIR CHILLED MORGAN'S arms as she entered the crowded ballroom. Her job was to get on television looking glamorous on Charlie Chao's arm.

They didn't want rumors that Charlie was hooking up with Logan Cash's sister floating around the poker circuit, so she'd worn a wig and spent an hour on her makeup. The point of this was to settle drama, not give the press fodder for more.

Tonight, she was going by Amy and the massive rock on her finger hinted that her last name would soon be Chao. She'd worn a short black dress with a gold metal belt, and two strips of lace that ran from the halter neckline to the waistband, leaving her back mostly exposed. The wig was a few shades darker than her natural blond, and had bangs that helped disguise her face, and soft waves that brushed her shoulders. To everyone who didn't know better, Morgan looked like she'd spent the day shopping in high end boutiques and getting glammed up in an expensive salon.

Playing the part of Charlie's fiancée went smoothly, at least for her. He was so awkward it made her abs tired from holding in her laughter. As they passed through security, getting their VIP badges, she moved in close and put her hand on his arm, displaying the fake diamond.

"Relax," she said. "Go play the best game of your life. Let me handle the rest."

These places were always swarming with gold diggers, and he'd drawn a following. Having been in love with the same girl since he was sixteen, Charlie saw the attention as a nuisance, not a chance to score.

There was a schmoozing hour, which he hated under normal circumstances, and since he was the highest ranked player here, he'd be the center of attention. That's where Morgan came in. She'd play the part of soon-to-be poker wifey, making it clear Charlie was off the market.

"Do you want a drink?" he asked as they neared the bar.

"Not yet. Let's get drunk at the blackjack table later," Morgan whispered. "Afterward, we can cry over our pathetic love lives while we count our winnings."

It wouldn't be the first time they had drowned their sorrows in tequila while commiserating over their doomed fates. As Logan's protégé, he was like her surrogate little brother. Maybe she should start setting a better example.

Over the next hour, no one outright asked about her ring, but *everyone* noticed it. When the tournament started, Charlie went to his table, but she could only watch the game on a television with the other guests. Knowing it would be hours before the tournament dwindled to the final table, Morgan settled in at the end of the bar.

Pretending to be Charlie's fiancé for an hour took more out of her than she'd expected. A drink was in order. While the bartender prepared her martini, she pulled her phone from her bag and texted Logan to see if he'd been watching and to find out if the commentators had mentioned her and Charlie.

Lookin' good, Mrs. Chao.

She smiled. When Charlie had told him he needed a fake girlfriend to keep the ladies at bay, Logan had suggested he take it up a notch with a fake fiancé and recommended her for the role. Her brother having confidence in her to pull this off felt nice.

Warmth coated her back in the shape of a hand. A hand much bigger than Charlie's.

Morgan turned her head and came face to face with a brown-eyed hottie. Her heartbeat stumbled. "Brody."

"Hey, Cash." He winked and flashed her a lazy smile.

"How'd you recognize me?"

He shook his head like she'd insulted him. "Come on, it'd take more than a wig and fake eyelashes to fool me."

She stared into her martini, her heart slamming.

The slightest movement of his hand sent shivers through her as his calloused fingertips brushed over her back. He leaned close as he whispered, "Are you and Chao pulling a con, or am I right to be jealous?"

He smelled amazing. Like bamboo and soap.

Morgan wet her lips and ignored the nerves creeping up her throat. She lowered her voice. "I'm doing him a favor. It's a guise."

"I almost came across the room and kicked his ass when I spotted him with his arm around you."

"If you don't move your hand, you might blow it for us, and then I'll have to kick *your* ass."

He removed his hand and leaned against the bar with his elbows, staring out at the stretch of poker tables in the center of the ballroom.

Her gaze stayed on his profile, reverence and shame mingling inside her. "What are you doing here?" And how much faster could her heart pound without exploding?

"I was going to play poker, but I saw a pretty girl and got distracted."

Her lips twitched as she held back her smile. She'd missed his ridiculous flirtations and transparency. The ache had only recently dulled enough to where she didn't cry daily. Now, here he was, reviving that ache. "You're in the tournament?"

"Not anymore."

"You aren't going to play? Isn't there a ten-thousand dollar buy-in?"

He didn't say anything, so she turned her head. "Brody?"

He kept staring ahead while nodding.

She closed her eyes, processing that he'd thrown away that amount of money to talk to her. When she opened them, he'd turned and was staring at the ring.

"It's not real."

His gaze flicked to hers. "Real or not, do you know what it's doing to me that everyone in this room thinks you're his?"

"That's what they're supposed to think," she said, dropping her voice and subtly glancing around to make sure no one was listening. "I can't fuck this up. It would humiliate Charlie."

Brody's jaw twitched. He was trying to pull off relaxed, but she saw through it.

She grabbed her clutch and stood. "I'm going for a smoke."

Morgan felt dizzy as she walked away. Who had seen her with Brody? The touches? The tension?

When she reached the main floor of the casino, she glanced over her shoulder, then sighed. She dug her phone out and texted him.

> You're supposed to follow me, you big dummy.

He turned the corner moments later, his gaze searching.

She waited for him to spot her, then resumed her path toward the hotel lobby, passing the exit and moving into the shadows by a bistro that wasn't currently open.

He followed her into the space, a thick pillar hiding them from plain sight. "I thought you were going for a cigarette?"

"I haven't started smoking again. I said that because I didn't want anyone to think I was sneaking off with you."

He walked closer, and she instinctively took a step back, farther into the dark alcove. He kept coming, a wolfish grin stretching his lips.

Her back hit the wall. Her eyes widened.

He put his hand on the wall above her head. "But you are sneaking off with me, right?"

"I don't know *what* I'm doing."

His breathing was heavy as he cupped her jaw. "We should talk."

She nodded, then her gaze dropped to his mouth.

Brody lowered his head a touch and she angled hers, bringing her lips an inch from his. He stared into her eyes, then swept his lips against hers. He lifted his head and waited, giving her time to change her mind.

As impetuous as always, she threw her arms around his neck and pressed her mouth to his.

He roamed his hands over her body, bringing her closer as he did so. The hunger behind his kisses and touches pushed her ache for him deeper.

Thankfully, she had better sense and pulled her mouth from his, tilting her head when he moved his lips to her neck. "I can't be gone long. It won't look good."

"I need to be with you," he murmured.

"For a night?"

He froze, his shoulder muscles tensed. The look he gave her said that wasn't an arrangement he'd accept. "Is that all you're offering?"

She lowered her gaze, centering it on his chest. "I'm leaving in the morning." Her throat tightened and a terrifyingly unfamiliar sensation bubbled up inside her. A tear slipped down her cheek. She wanted more than a night with him. Far more. Seeing him again, her heart no longer believed the lies her brain had been feeding it. The idea of separating herself from him wrecked her.

He wiped her tears with his thumb. "One night might not be enough to work through all our problems, but it's long enough to remind you that you're mine."

A fresh stream of tears fell. "And then what?"

"Then you come home with me, and we work through the rest of our shit because we belong together."

"It sounds easy when you say it, but it won't be. Isn't what I did to you enough for you to finally understand how messed up I am?" She sniffed and wiped at her face. Her makeup had to be fucked to hell. "I was afraid of losing you, so I left you. That's how my mind works. I spiral and contrive plans that are reactive and selfish and illogical."

"You freaked out in a situation anyone would have freaked out in, Morgan. You shouldn't have left the way you did, but I shouldn't have let you. I don't care about any of that, though. I stopped giving a fuck the second I saw you."

Her breath caught. "Brody."

"I want to be with you—even if it's messy."

She didn't want it to be messy, though. She wanted it to be beautiful. Whether that was possible, she had her doubts. Right now, she needed to think, and she never could do that very well with him this close. "I have to get back to the tournament."

"For how long?" The edge in his voice made her heart feel like it was locking up.

"It'd look suspicious if Charlie wins and his fiancée isn't there to celebrate with him." She had to stay until the end. There wasn't any way of knowing when that'd be. But no matter what, they wouldn't have much time together and they'd be tired.

Brody closed his eyes. He inhaled, his chest expanded, then he released it.

"Maybe we should wait to figure this out until we don't have such tight time constraints."

He leaned in, taking up her space. "When is that going to be?"

Living on different sides of the country created a challenge she didn't know how to overcome. The farm kept Brody tethered to Maryland. Her freedom to travel would be hindered by her new job—not that she'd taken advantage of that freedom when it'd been wide open.

"I don't know," she said. "Tomorrow, Charlie and I are flying to Savannah. Logan bought Drew a house and he's throwing her a surprise housewarming party."

He lowered his brow. "Your brother doesn't even try to be normal, does he?"

She smiled and shook her head. "I'll be there for two nights, and then I'm heading back to Las Vegas. I have a new job and I really like it. Unless you can come there, I guess our only option is discussing this over the phone."

He rubbed his forehead. "I can come to you, but it won't be right away. I want to resolve this now."

"I didn't know you were going to be here. I have an obligation," she said, voice raised. "Wait a minute. How did you know about this tournament?" How did Charlie know about it? Sure, he came to Atlantic City to play, but a last-minute decision to join a tournament when he already had plans to go to Savannah for the party didn't add up.

"Nick wanted to take a trip, so I looked to see if there were any tournaments. Why? Do you think we're being set up?"

"What are the chances of us both being here at the same time, staying at the same casino?"

"I don't think it's that big of a coincidence. Charlie and I have played at a lot of the same tournaments, and if Lucy or anyone else from your family tried to get us together, they'd have needed Nick to be in on it."

Good points. Their families didn't know each other. And Logan and Charlie would also have needed to be on board.

Charlie liked to help, and he knew her breakup with Brody had left her devastated. He wouldn't have been hard to convince. But Logan? No way. Although…he'd been calling her more lately, and he'd come to Las Vegas to be there for her right after she'd left Brody.

Their families' only connection was Brody.

"You're in on it, aren't you?"

He grabbed her chin and forced her to look at him. "Stop. You have every reason to believe your family could be behind something like that, but I'd never do that to you."

She tried to shake her head, but he still held her chin. "No, it's not right."

"Baby, you're spiraling. Take a deep fucking breath and pull yourself out of it." He let go of her chin and tapped her temple. "It takes effort, but you can rewire your brain. One day, your first instinct will be to stay calm and talk through things with someone you trust. If you want that."

She squeezed her eyes shut. Her trust didn't extend to many people, but Brody Lewis would always remain at the top of that list. Even with everything that had happened, it wasn't her trust in him that had been damaged. It was her belief that she wouldn't ever be happy—didn't deserve to be—that'd been revived.

"You don't have to change for me," he said. "I'll take you exactly how you are. But if you want to work on it, I'll tell you when you're being rash. I'd rather you stay and take it out on me than run, but if that happens, I will come after you. I'm not going to make that mistake again."

Him and his words. A dozen emotions swirled inside her.

After she'd left, once her heart had stopped aching enough that she could get out of bed, she'd made a discovery. How she'd felt when she and Brody were together—stronger and whole—hadn't gone away. It wasn't for rent. It wasn't contingent on him being in her life. It belonged to her.

Her time with him had healed her in so many ways.

She believed him that he'd come after her. She believed he wanted her as is. She believed he wouldn't placate her. She believed that no matter how crazy she acted, he'd love her anyway.

He'd never told her he loved her, but when the dark cloud that'd hovered over her shifted, letting slivers of light shine through, and her memories of Brody crept into her mind, it'd been obvious.

Accepting her feelings for him was another story. Knowing he deserved better kept her from going back. But with him standing in front of her, she didn't care all that much if she was worthy.

She would be.

She'd spend every day trying.

But not yet. First, she had an obligation to see through. Letting Charlie down wasn't an option. She needed to fix her makeup and get back to what she'd agreed to do. Hopefully, her inability to stop thinking of Brody didn't screw it up.

"We're not going to get anywhere with this right now," she said. "We should both take time to think things over and then—"

He took a step back and held his arms out, palms up. "Five weeks, Morgan. You've had five weeks to think things over. Do you want me or not?"

She blinked, not sure how that was even a question. It wasn't a matter of her wanting him or not. There were so many facets to it, so many things to resolve. "It's not that simple."

"Why isn't it? Why is the only time you hesitate when it's about me?"

"Because it matters more." She pushed past him, her lungs tight and heavy. This was too much for her to deal with right here, right now.

He grabbed her around the waist and tugged her close, his chest flush against her back. He put his mouth next to her ear. "Go pretend for everyone else that you're with Chao. I'm not going to let it bother me because the whole time, you're going to be thinking about what it's going to be like when I touch you again. If I have to wait…that's more time for me to decide exactly what I'm going to do to you."

Well, of course, she was going to be thinking about it after he'd put it in her head. And why did her body have to wake right up when he said it?

He kissed her shoulder, then patted her ass, and nudged her along.

She turned her head and glared.

He had the audacity to wink.

67
The Next Five Minutes
BRODY

BRODY STAYED FAR AWAY from the tournament for most of the night. There was no way he could be in a room with her and not gravitate toward her. He met up with Nick by the roulette tables. They gambled and drank for a few hours. Before he went back to the room, he checked how many tables were left in the tournament. The answer was *too many*.

She wasn't getting out of there any time soon.

He spotted her on the other side of the room, with a group of women who chatted animatedly. It probably wasn't obvious to anyone else, but she wasn't enjoying herself. She wasn't contributing to the conversation, but if spoken to directly, she'd nod and smile. It was going to be a long night for her. He'd love to rescue her from it, but she was determined to uphold her commitment.

He dipped out of the room, writing her a text as he walked.

> I can't decide if I want you to come on my face or my dick first. What do you think?

> I'm in the mood to suffocate you, so let's go with your face.

He chuckled.

> I'm going to be here for hours. Don't be mean.

> Say you're going out for another smoke. I'll be real nice to you.

> I miss flirting with you.

He walked onto the elevator and typed out his reply.

> I don't hate hearing that.

> Gotta go. They're taking a break.

Nick was already in bed, looking at his phone like he hated it, when Brody got to the room. This trip was supposed to take their minds off women. Running into Morgan made it kind of impossible to do that, and Nick had been stalking Taylor's social media all day and night. She'd gone on her own trip. With a guy that was not Nick. He did not react well to seeing photos of her in a bikini with some dude draped all over her.

He'd tried to get it through Nick's thick skull that if he wasn't going to make a move on Taylor, he was going to keep going through this. When he'd mentioned a future where Taylor posted wedding photos, Nick shut it all down and said not to talk to him about it for the rest of the trip.

Brody settled in bed and turned his ringer volume as high as it would go, in case Morgan got bored and wanted to flirt, or sneak out and take a shot at suffocating him.

But that wouldn't happen. The chances he'd get to see her tonight were slim.

She might be hung up on resolving their issues first, but he could care less. He had every intention of fixing things. That could take a while, though, and at this point, he wanted her so bad, he'd fuck her in that dark corner she'd dragged him into and have no regrets.

He woke up to a pitch-black room, aside from the phone lit up on the nightstand, ringing. He snatched it and silenced it. "Hey," he whispered as

he held the phone to his ear.

"I can't sleep."

He sat up. "Where are you?"

She gave him her room number, then he scrambled around using the flashlight on his phone to find his clothes. It was after four. The hallway lights blinded him as he made his way to the elevator. He rubbed his eyes, trying to get himself more awake. The grogginess still lingered as he knocked on her door.

It opened immediately. Morgan put her finger to his lips, then waved him in.

Her hair was in a ponytail and her face was freshly scrubbed. No more wig, no more fancy dress or shoes. She wore a T-shirt and pajama shorts.

No more big ass rock on her finger.

At least, for now. He'd fix that.

He shut the door quietly, then followed her into a suite with a living room in the center and doors on either side, presumably to bedrooms.

She walked to one of the doors and went in, holding it open for him.

Once she'd shut it, she stared at him. "I'm leaving for the airport in three and a half hours."

"And you can't sleep."

A blush dotted her cheeks. "I'll sleep on the plane."

"What do you plan on doing for the next three and a half hours?" He couldn't be trusted not to touch her, so he kept himself several feet away.

"That depends on what happens in the next five minutes."

He raised an eyebrow.

She twisted the hem of her T-shirt in her fist and shifted from one foot to the other. "Sit down. I have something to say."

He took a seat on the loveseat by the window.

Her demeanor sent a prickle down the back of his neck. He didn't like seeing her anxious. Especially with what was on the line.

She sat next to him, feet on the carpet, forehead bunched. Then she turned toward him and pulled her knees to her chest. That lasted all of two seconds before she stretched her legs out and shimmied against the cushions.

"Morgan, what the hell are you doing?"

"I don't know. I thought I could do this, and I had a plan, but sitting here like this...I don't know. It doesn't feel right."

He rubbed his jaw, his gaze roaming her body. Without warning, he leaned over, hooked his forearms under her knees, and swung her over to straddle him. "Better?"

She slapped his shoulders. "You never warn me when you're going to do that."

He put his hands under her shirt, settling them on her waist. "You like it."

Her lips parted and she gaped at him.

He looked down, admiring her hard nipples through the thin fabric. He lifted his gaze and grinned.

She rolled her eyes.

"Say what you need to say." He moved his hands lower, resting them on her thighs. He spread the fingers of his right hand, sliding his thumb along the soft skin of her inner thigh, then dipping it under her shorts, wanting his finger slick from stroking her wet pussy. Instead, he took his time, moving inch by precious inch.

"Brody," she said in a voice that made him want to throw her on the bed and rip her shorts off so he could bury himself inside her.

Ah, fuck. He didn't have a condom. Not even back at the room and he doubted Nick did, either. This trip was for the boys. Because the boys needed to get their minds off the girls. So much for that.

He moved his hand back to her thigh and gripped it. "I'm listening."

Morgan took a deep breath. There was a shakiness when she released it. "Fuck it. I'm just going to say it. I love you."

She what? He sat up straighter, wrapping his arm behind her to keep

from dumping her onto the floor. "Run that by me again?"

"I love you, Brody."

He broke into a smile. "I love you too, baby."

Her smile, so bright and beautiful, made him happier than he'd been in a long time.

He leaned in and kissed her. And he didn't stop. Not until she shifted her hips and rubbed against his erection. "I don't have a condom. I basically sleepwalked here. I didn't even think about it."

"I don't have one, either."

"I'll go buy some."

She frowned and pouted her lips. "We don't have much time together and I don't know when we're going to see each other again. I don't want you to leave, even for five minutes."

They both knew it'd take longer than that to find a store open this early in the morning.

He rubbed his thumb over her bottom lip. His desire to sink into her, to feel her body under his, was hard as hell to suppress. But he was going to because he'd give her whatever she wanted. "I'm not going anywhere, then. I can still make you feel good."

"I know, but…"

He choked back his laugh. "But what? You want the D?"

Her face reddened. She bent her head.

"I'm going to give it to you real soon, Morgan," he whispered. "But for the next three hours, you're not going to be thinking about my dick because you won't be able to hold a thought in that pretty head of yours."

68

Groggy, Grumpy Brody
Morgan

MORGAN WOKE UP WITH Brody's palm flat across her pelvis and his warm breath coasting over her bare shoulder. His deep breathing indicated that he was still asleep. And hard. His erection rubbed against her, the tip gliding through her slick thighs, not inside her, but all she'd have to do to change that was angle her hips differently.

She didn't do that, though.

Before they'd fallen asleep, too exhausted to even think about putting on clothes, he'd made her come twice. She'd gone down on him after that, but in the short time it took to get him off, she'd gotten so turned on she'd been throbbing. One more orgasm later, she closed her eyes and was out.

"Brody," she said softly.

He mumbled something, then slid the hand on her pelvis lower.

She moaned and arched her body as he dipped his fingers between her legs. "Brody."

He grunted and flipped her onto her back. His body covered hers, his hips settling between her thighs.

This was that groggy, grumpy state she found both sexy and endearing. It was the only time he wasn't fully in control of himself.

She gasped as he entered her. Her eyes fluttered shut, the sheer ecstasy of him inside her without a condom overwhelming.

His loud groan sent shivers through her. He slowly moved in and out, his face tucked against her neck. Then he went still.

She squeezed his hips between her thighs. "Don't stop."

"Christ, Morgan, don't ask that. Fuck. What am I doing?"

"Just be careful. I trust you. Please."

He lifted himself and gazed down at her. "You don't play fair."

"I never claimed to."

He kissed her, then rocked his hips.

The pace was slow and sweet, but it pushed her to the brink just the same. He made love to her slowly, but intensely.

Her thighs shook and she sought his mouth, needing his kisses to keep her from waking Charlie with her moans.

Brody grabbed her under one knee. "Baby, I can't keep doing this. If I feel you come, I'm going to come."

But she was so close. She needed it. Was desperate for it.

He pulled out, almost.

She wrapped her legs around him and used her heels to pull him back.

He cupped her breast, swiping his thumb against her nipple.

That did it. She shattered, whispering, "Oh, my god," over and over.

He dropped his forehead to her shoulder and shuddered.

The haze began to clear, and she tensed, weighed down by the gravity of what they'd done.

He lifted his head. His face showed his guilt. "I'm sor—"

A loud knock drowned out his words. "Morgan, we need to leave in ten minutes," Charlie said through the door.

"Shit." She pushed Brody away and scrambled out of bed. "I overslept," she yelled. "Just give me a minute to pack."

She grabbed the T-shirt and shorts Brody had taken off her the night before and stuffed them into her suitcase. Before heading into the bathroom, she glanced at him.

He laid on his side, propped up by his elbow. "Stay. I'll go to Savannah with you. We'll get a later flight."

"I can't. I need to get there early to help Logan set up. But if you can get a flight, you can be my date to the party." She went into the bathroom and turned on the sink. While waiting for the water to get warm, she took her hair tie out and turned her head upside down, smoothing her hair into a less chaotic bun. She washed her face, cleaned up the cum dripping down her leg—which turned her on a little bit—then went to dig clothes out of her suitcase.

Brody was dressed, sitting on the end of the bed. He watched as she pulled on clean panties, then wiggled into jeans.

She put on a tank top, tugged a sweater over it, and grabbed her things from the bathroom, then tossed them into her suitcase.

"This fucking sucks," he grumbled.

After zipping the suitcase and setting it upright, she moved in front of him. "Agreed."

He put his hands on her hips. "Will you call me when you land?"

She nodded.

With a sad smile, he pulled her down for a kiss, then stood, and grabbed her suitcase.

She braced herself for Charlie's reaction, then opened the door.

Leaned against the arm of the couch, he glanced up from his phone. A slow grin spread across his face.

She'd told him last night that she'd seen Brody, but at that point, she wasn't sure if she was going to try to see him before she left or not.

Charlie shook Brody's hand, and to her surprise, didn't say anything to embarrass her.

The three of them walked to the elevator, but Brody held her back when she tried to step into the elevator.

"We'll get the next one," he told Charlie.

Charlie wiggled his eyebrows at her as the doors closed.

Her pulse quickened. Five minutes ago, she'd had Brody's cum running down her thigh, and now she was nervous about being alone in an elevator with him. She couldn't make it make sense.

Brody, however, had no such nerves and the second the doors shut, he pressed her up against the wall. "I love you, Morgan. It'll make me feel a lot better about letting you go if you promise we're going to be together again soon. I can't handle the torment of a long-distance relationship."

"I don't want that, either."

"Then, come back to Maryland and keep your ass there."

69

The Motive

Morgan

ANOTHER FIVE WEEKS.

Morgan didn't want to abruptly quit her job. It was only right to give them proper notice, especially after how she'd left her last job to become Brody's partner. She'd offered them two weeks, and they'd counteroffered with four weeks and to nearly double her wages for that period.

Brody hadn't been happy to hear about the offer, but ultimately, he told her it was her decision. He'd visited once for a long weekend, but it'd been three weeks since then.

It was her last day of work and they'd given her a little going away party—which was very generous considering she'd only worked there three weeks before resigning. In two days, she'd get on a plane to Maryland, and Brody would pick her up at the airport.

She didn't know what was going to happen after that, but she looked forward to finding out.

While digging in her bag for her keys to Uncle John's condo, she almost bumped into someone. She glanced up.

Brody grinned down at her. He held out a gigantic bouquet. "Hey."

A smile so big it hurt spread across her face and she took the flowers. "What are you doing here? I'll be in Maryland the day after tomorrow."

He kissed her. "I missed you."

"Let's go inside." She handed him back the bouquet. "I have to find my keys."

"It's unlocked. John let me in before he went to Lucy's."

They went in and she kicked off her shoes, dropped her bag, and went to get a vase.

"So, you missed me?" she asked skeptically. "And you couldn't wait two more days?"

He frowned. "I have some stuff I need to take care of while I'm here, actually."

She waited.

He raked his hand through his hair.

If he wasn't here simply to see her, there was only one other reason she could think of for why he'd come to Vegas.

"You're here to do a job?" It came out loud enough for the neighbors to hear, but she didn't care. What the fuck?

"Can you try to keep your head on and let me explain?"

"Are you working alone?"

He shook his head. "I'm working with Benny, but if you—"

She crossed her arms. "What's the job?"

"Morgan, are you going to let me talk, or not?"

"Go ahead." She left the flowers on the dining room table and went to the bar. Uncle John's vodka would do.

"You know that my dad is sick. Well, there's this treatment, but it's in another country, and it's expensive. They'll take him as a patient, but he'll have to stay there for months, and if my mom goes with him, there won't be anyone to take care of Hope or do the bookkeeping. If I go with him, the farm will suffer, and after everything my dad has put into it, he's not going to want to go get treated, knowing what'll happen if someone isn't around to take care of it."

Morgan wrinkled her forehead and turned. "I can see how you'd need money, but what's your solution to Hope still having a parent and the farm continuing to thrive?"

"My mom and I will take turns. Hope will stay with me when Mom is with Dad, and vice versa. And I was thinking, I'll take Hope there for a week or so, if we can plan it around one of her school breaks. All that traveling is going to cost a fortune, and I also can't keep doing everything myself. I'm going to hire some workers and buy more equipment to make things more efficient."

"Was this your plan the whole time?"

"Yes, but you never asked, and I didn't want you to feel any additional pressure while doing the job." He slowly made his way to her. "This is the last time. I promise."

"What's the job?"

He dropped his gaze. "So, that's the thing I knew you'd be upset about but—"

"Our job?" she yelled, flailing her arms around, the bottle of vodka slicing through the air. "You're going to do *our job* with Benny?"

He pulled in a big breath and jabbed his tongue on the inside of his cheek.

She stood there, flabbergasted. "I planned that whole fucking heist, Brody. That's my intellectual labor. You didn't think to ask me to be your partner?"

"You'll get a third of the take, but I'm not putting you in danger."

"You were fine with it before."

"No, I wasn't. I didn't like you going to Gill's party."

"You think Benny can do what I do?"

"Baby, it's not like that, and you know it. You're hands down more skilled, but I'm not going to be on my A game if you're there. Benny and I have worked together plenty. We'll get it done and then, I swear, Morgan, I'm done. I'm going to focus on you and my family and the farm."

She was so mad she shook. The discomfort from clenching her jaw was nothing compared to the beating her heart was taking.

Brody reached for the bottle in her hand, but she twisted her body, keeping it out of his reach. "I have to do this. It means my dad lives longer, and more comfortably. I knew you'd be pissed, but I don't know what else to do."

"When is this going down?"

"Tomorrow."

"Why'd you even come to see me? You could have done it and told me after."

"Because I'm not doing it behind your back, and I thought it'd go over better if I told you in person."

She put the bottle back in the bar, then stomped into the kitchen. She needed coffee, not booze. She rummaged through the cupboard. All Uncle John's cups were uniform. High quality, but plain and boring. She grabbed one and walked to the coffee machine, which was even fancier than Brody's and could make espresso and froth milk.

Brody stood in the archway to the kitchen with his fist pressed to the frame. It annoyed her that he looked so sexy in his black T-shirt and jeans when she was trying to be mad at him. Maybe *that's* why he wanted to do this in person.

"You don't seem as upset as I thought you'd be."

"Therapy must be working." It wasn't. She didn't care for her therapist. This was the third one, and she was losing hope she'd find one she felt comfortable with. And Brody knew that.

"The fuck it is." He shook his head. "Holding it in is what gets you in trouble, so come on, tell me about myself."

"Fine." She threw the white cup on the kitchen floor. It shattered, the debris in the space between them. "You're stupid and I want my coffee mug back!"

70
How to Bait a Hothead 101
BRODY

BRODY LOOKED AT THE pieces of broken ceramic on the floor, then up at Morgan. "That all?"

"No." She crossed her arms. "Tell Benny you don't need him, or I'm not moving to Maryland."

He sagged against the door frame and huffed. "Morgan, this isn't to hurt you or undermine your skills. I love you, and I'm asking you to understand."

"I understand why you need to do the job. I don't understand why I'm not your first choice for a partner."

"I told you, I don't want to put you in danger."

"But you'll be in danger."

"I have to take the risk. You don't."

"You're at an even bigger risk with Benny, who has never even been in Gill's house. How dare you ask me to sit on the sidelines while you put *your* life in jeopardy?"

He walked around the broken mug fragments and pulled her into his arms. "If you don't want me to do it, then I won't. I'll find another way, but I'm not involving you."

"Another way? What other way? Play the lottery and wish for the best?"

"I don't know," he said, the stress of coming up with a new plan already weighing on him. "I'm not going to lose you over it, though."

Her eyes widened. "You're choosing me?"

"You're damn fucking right I am. I will always choose you."

"Over your dad?"

"I'll find another way."

She pushed his shoulder. "I don't want you to do that. Just let me help you."

"I'm not putting your life at risk. This isn't about your capabilities. It's about mine." The plan she'd come up with meant they'd be separated during the heist. He wouldn't be in the house with her. He wouldn't be able to see her and know she was okay. Even with an earpiece—which she'd already said she wouldn't wear because it would hinder her—if he kept checking on her, it'd distract her, and she needed to be as quiet as possible. "There's a good chance I'll fuck up if you're there."

"That's not fair."

"Agreed. It's not fair, but it's true."

"Whatever," she muttered. "Just do it with Benny, but I don't want a cut."

"You earned it."

"That's not what I want."

"You want something different?"

The mischief that flickered in her eyes put him on edge. "Let me get your adoption records. You don't have to look at them. But let me get them and we can keep them sealed until you're ready, when and if that happens."

"*That's* what you want?"

"Yes. I love you and I want to live a normal life with you, but I'm afraid you'll change your mind and not tell me because you won't want me to take the risk. So, you take your risk, I'll take mine, then we'll be done."

"Baby…" He pulled her in tighter and put his chin on the top of his

head. "Why are you so damn sweet?"

"I'm not. I'm a badass."

He laughed, and tipped her chin up and kissed her. "You're both."

Right back where he'd started, Brody walked up to Morgan's boat, floating in the same slip as the first time he'd seen it.

Movement up the dock caught his eye.

Logan walked toward him. "What are you doing here? Where's Morgan?"

Brody tried to figure out a delicate way to say that he'd pissed her off, and now, had no idea where she was, or what she'd done with his goddamn bomb.

"Where's my sister, Brody?" Logan asked again, teeth clenched. "You know, short little blonde, absolutely crazy about you, likes to prowl around at night. Remember her?"

"I'd also like to know the answer to that question."

Logan put his hand to his forehead. "What stupid thing did you do?"

"I told her Benny and I were going to do the Gill job."

"Oh, so, you've got a death wish? Do you know my sister at all?"

"We talked about it and came to an agreement. She was okay with me doing the job. That's what she said, anyway. Her actions prove otherwise." Brody shoved his hands in his pockets. "She stole my bomb."

"Wait. Again? A second bomb?"

He nodded. His ego was already bruised. Logan laughing at him wouldn't make any difference. He wasn't going to tell him about the little scrap of paper with I.O.U. written on it that she'd left in the bomb's place, though. He couldn't understand why she did it—why she'd prevent him from accomplishing what he needed to so he could help his family and have more time with his dad. He sure as fuck was going to find out, though.

Once Logan finished laughing, he asked, "It can't go off, right? It's not live or whatever? There's no chance of my sister getting blown up?"

"It wasn't fully assembled. She'll be fine. Until I get a hold of her, anyways."

Logan rolled his eyes. "Sure, tough guy. What are you gonna do? Kiss her to death?"

He shot him a warning look. "We should probably change the subject. Obviously, I'd never hurt her, but I don't think you want to know what I plan on doing to your sister when I find her."

He scowled and pulled out his phone. "I should push you off this dock, but I'm going to call Morgan and find out where she is so I can get rid of you." After holding the phone to his ear for a minute, he frowned and lowered it.

"She didn't answer?" Brody asked.

"No. Did you ask Lucy or Uncle John if they know where she is?"

He scratched the back of his head. "They swear she's okay but won't tell me where she is."

Logan made a *move over, I'll take care of this* face and pulled his phone back out. After a few seconds, he said, "Hey, Uncle John." He held up a finger, then walked away.

It took a good ten minutes for him to return. He didn't look happy. "Yeah…so…he wouldn't tell me."

"Why not?" Brody asked. "You didn't tell him you were trying to find out for me, did you?"

"No, I'm not a fucking idiot. I said I hadn't been able to reach her and asked if he'd talked to her recently. The next thing I know we're talking about what horse he should bet on." He shook his head. "I didn't realize he'd played me until we hung up. It's what he's good at, so let's not make an issue of it."

Brody laughed. "What about Lucy? Think you could get it out of her?"

He snorted. "Not likely."

"What about Chao? Would she be with him, or would he know where she is?"

"He's in Tokyo. I doubt she's with him."

Brody groaned. Nothing but dead ends. He pulled out his phone. She'd never turned the tracking back on, so that was no help. "She's reading my texts, but she's not replying to any of them."

"Say something that'll piss her off. That's How to Bait a Hothead 101."

"She's already pissed off."

Logan shrugged. "So, what do you have to lose?"

71
Her Man
Morgan

> Answer the phone.

Morgan took a sip of coffee from her polka dot mug.

The phone rang.

She sent it to voicemail.

Several minutes later, the phone lit up again.

> Morgan, just so you know what you're in for if you keep ignoring me...I am going to shove you against the nearest wall and fuck you so hard it leaves an impression of your body in the drywall. I'm not going to let you come, though. Not until you tell me you're sorry for how worried I've been for two fucking days. I want you on your knees begging my forgiveness. Then I'm going to fuck you again, and the only way I'm letting you come, is if you beg for that too.

The drywall part made her jaw drop and it stayed there as she read on. Eh, she didn't hate it. There would be no begging on her part, but she'd apologize for letting him worry. She couldn't help it. She needed the head start. But now, she wanted Brody home, and she was impatient as hell.

> Baby, I love you, but I'm not kidding. I promise you that I will in fact do all of that and a lot more. The longer it takes me to find you, the longer it's going to be until I let you come. Answer your phone.

Morgan went upstairs, laid in his bed, and took a selfie. She sent it.

The phone rang with a video chat request. She answered and held it above her.

Brody took up the screen, standing on the dock in front of the Gypsy. "Morgan, what the fuck? I've been trying to find you and you're at my goddamn house?"

She smiled and shrugged. "What are you doing in Savannah?"

"What do you think I'm doing?" Brody looked at someone off screen. "Found her. Gotta go."

He walked up the dock to the parking lot, the phone held in front of him. "It's going to take me hours, but you better be wearing that dress when I get there."

She ran her fingers from her cleavage, down to her belly, popping the buttons of her dress open along the way. She hadn't worn anything underneath. "What if I'm not?"

He groaned. "If I can't get a flight, I'm renting a car. However long it takes me to get there, I'm going to spend every second of it thinking of all the ways you're going to pay for this."

Her mouth opened and a little gasp slipped out.

He grinned devilishly, inciting a throbbing between her thighs. "Do you trust me, baby?"

"Yes."

"Remember that when I get there."

"Wait, wha—" The video disconnected. Shit. Now she was kind of nervous. And horny.

Her phone rang, abruptly pulling her out of her thoughts. She fumbled

and dropped it. Once she'd scooped it up, she saw it was Taylor.

She'd sent her a text earlier saying she was at the farm alone if she wanted to get together. She hadn't known Brody would be back today. Even so, it'd be late when he returned, and she needed a distraction. "Hello?"

"Hi," Taylor said. "Do you want to come over for dinner?"

She had to eat. "I'd love to. What can I bring?"

"You can bring the tea on you and Brody."

Morgan laughed. "What time?"

"Six? I'll text you the address."

"Okay. I'll see you then."

She fed Buster and Reese, then changed into jeans and a hoodie and got busy with the project she wanted to finish before Brody got home.

That evening, when she drove through the gate of the Van Belle Mansion, she worried she might have under dressed, but Taylor opened the door wearing yoga pants and a long-sleeved T-shirt. Her hair was in a sloppy bun.

"Come in."

Morgan stepped into a spacious, bright foyer thanks to the prism-y skylights directly above it. "Thank you for having me over. Wow. This is awesome."

"That's always been Nick's favorite part of the house."

Funny she'd bring him up. Morgan couldn't help her curiosity over whether Taylor returned Nick's feelings. He was still in denial, so she'd respect that and be careful about what she said. "He spent time here with you when you were younger?"

"Entire summers, just about. We'd swim in the pool and run around. It's twenty acres. Here, I'll show you." She led her through a series of stylishly decorated rooms, and out through large sliding doors. The bay was visible from the patio, the water stretching along the length of the property. No beach, but there was a dock and a rack with kayaks on it.

Closer to the water's edge were little houses.

"Those are the cottages," she said, pointing. "Some couples avoid bed and breakfasts because of the lack of privacy. They'd rather stay at a vacation rental."

It was cold out, so they went back inside, and Taylor gave her a tour. The house was massive and had a billiards room and a library. Throughout the house there were a variety of sitting areas.

"I saved my favorite for last," Taylor said, her hand on the knob of a door off the kitchen.

She opened the door to a walk-in closet, but not for clothes. It looked like a store. Floor to ceiling shelves with a variety of items and labeled bins. "I just got this organized and honestly, I get a lady boner every time I open the door."

She had all the travel-sized toiletries Morgan would expect and extra pillows, sheets, and blankets. But what struck her as odd was the section of the closet that had unopened products. She picked up an interesting plastic bottle. "Is this lube?"

Taylor laughed. "You'd be surprised the things I get asked for. I've got condoms, Plan B, yeast infection cream—"

She picked up a box. "Pregnancy tests?"

"Yeah, why do you need one?" Taylor laughed, but stopped when Morgan didn't join in.

She licked her dry lips. "Um. The last time I had my period was… *shit*." She grabbed the test. "Is it okay if I take this and replace it?"

"You don't have to replace it. Do you want to take it here?"

She nodded and Taylor showed her to the bathroom.

Her hands shook as she opened the package and read the directions. With everything that had happened in the past weeks, she'd forgotten they'd had unprotected sex in Atlantic City. And she was late. Two weeks late.

Damn it. She'd meant to pick up emergency contraception when she got to Savannah, but it'd been a whirlwind seeing Logan and Drew's new house and helping decorate it for a Halloween party.

She did the whole pee on the stick thing, then left it on the sink and set a timer on her phone.

Taylor was pulling a roasted chicken from the oven when Morgan returned to the kitchen. She set it on top of the stove, then turned around and gave her a smile. "Are you okay?"

"Yeah. I'm just waiting the twenty minutes the instructions said to before reading the result. Thanks for the test. I'm glad you had it."

"Girl, I've got everything. One time, I opened a package a guest had shipped here, not realizing it wasn't for me. Imagine my reaction when it's a box full of dildos."

"It was full of them?"

Taylor waved her off. "It was an assortment of sex toys, but I swear that man maxed out his credit card on that order."

"Who sends a package like that to a bed and breakfast?"

"In all fairness, he asked if he could have a package sent here, and I said I'd set it aside for him. I wasn't supposed to open it, but I'm not used to receiving deliveries for guests."

"Is it weird that people probably bang in all the bedrooms?"

Taylor laughed. "I try not to think about it. A lot of guests are couples looking to escape their children for a weekend so they can hump like bunnies."

"It'd be cool if there were places you could stay where beforehand you could shop a catalog of spicy items and order things that'd be waiting for you when you got there. Especially if it was a nice place like this and not some sketchy motel or something."

"I've done some honeymoon gift baskets but nothing like I think you're suggesting."

"It would take the weirdness out of going to an adult toy store. Is sex work legal in this state?" Morgan asked.

"I don't think so."

"It'd probably be breaking all kinds of stupid laws."

Taylor leaned into the kitchen island. "Even if it was legal, people in the community would be weird about it."

"Confidentiality and privacy would be important. You'd have to at least pretend to have a normal B&B as a front, and the other part be underground."

They continued discussing the concept, but Taylor wasn't sold on it. She was happy to be a wedding venue and a traditional bed and breakfast.

The alarm went off. Morgan stayed glued to her stool, gripping the edges of the counter.

"Are you going to look?" Taylor asked. "I could do it for you, if you don't want to."

"I don't need to look. I'm pregnant." She pressed her hand to her stomach and lifted her gaze to stare at Taylor with wide eyes. "Brody is coming home tonight."

And she was pregnant. With a baby. His baby. Their baby. *A baby.*

She sucked in air and shook her hands in front of her, trying to calm herself. Her emotions pulled her in two directions—nervous enough to puke and deliriously happy.

Taylor squinted and twisted her mouth. "Don't smack me for asking, but it's his, right?"

Morgan nodded. "What if he's not happy about it?"

"Sweetie, have you met your man?"

72

Out with a Bang

BRODY

BRODY TURNED INTO HIS driveway. He'd never been happier to be home than he was right then.

He parked next to a gleaming black Mustang. He eyed it as he passed by it on his way to the house. A pretty sexy car, for sure, but there was something much sexier in his house. And he was anxious as hell to get to her.

When he got inside, she was sitting on the steps wearing the dress, looking guilty.

He shook his head at her. "Do you have any idea how much trouble you're in?"

She glanced over into the kitchen.

He followed her gaze. On the table there was a sealed brown envelope, an iPad, and a black pouch the size of a cantaloupe. "What's in the bag?"

"Go ahead and look."

As much as he wanted to grab her and kiss her, his curiosity won. He walked to the table. As soon as he lifted it, he knew what it was. He could hear and feel the diamonds shifting around inside the bag. He whipped his head in her direction. "You've been busy."

She shrugged. "I'm retiring, but I wanted to go out with a bang."

"Is that supposed to be funny?"

"Yeah, and it is. Now, you can take care of your dad and keep the farm running. Does it matter where it came from?"

He stalked over and went up the steps until he was two down from the one she'd parked her ass on. "It does matter. You put yourself in danger, which was exactly the thing I was trying to prevent."

She leaned back on her elbows and stared up at him. "This was the least dangerous option for everyone. No bombs. No distractions."

He couldn't argue with that without her accusing him of doubting her skills. Fuck. He grasped the nose of the step on either side of her and leaned in. "Why have you been ignoring me for two days?"

She blinked up at him, then her gaze dropped to his mouth.

"Eyes up here, baby." Once she met his stare, he asked, "Why didn't you answer my calls or texts?"

"Because I needed time to do something."

"What's that?"

"Check the envelope."

He pushed away and went to the table. He released the metal clasp, then slid out the contents, not surprised to see it was a file from an adoption agency. Not wanting to look at it yet, or maybe ever, he set it down. "What's up with the iPad?"

"I didn't intentionally do it, but I saw the contents of your file. I wanted to make sure it was the right one. The info was right there on the first page. I couldn't not see it."

"Okay, so?"

"Are you sure you want to know?"

He sighed and rolled his shoulders. "Tell me."

"Your parents are deceased. The cause of death for both was a fatal car accident."

Brody nodded. He'd expected that. He still didn't like hearing it, though. "Anything else?"

"There wasn't much in the file about them. Names, ages. But with that info, I was able to find out where they went to high school."

"What? Why?"

"They were young. I thought I might be able to find people that went to school with them and find out what they were like."

"What does this have to do with the iPad?"

"They were estranged from their families, but I found their friends on social media, and they were happy to talk about them and some even had photos. I set up a virtual meeting with a few of them and recorded their stories. That's what's on the iPad."

He glanced at the iPad, then back at her.

"I know I overstepped big time, but I love you and I didn't want to give you that pathetic file and have you open it one day, expecting to learn about your parents and only find their names and cause death. Nick's file is upstairs in the safe, by the way. Maybe the two of you could watch the videos together."

"Come here," he said, his voice hoarse.

She pushed herself up and walked down the stairs.

He cupped the sides of her face. "I'm not mad at you. I agreed to let you get the records. The extra stuff you did…that's why I love you, Morgan. You have a beautiful heart."

"There's something else on the table I don't think you saw."

He let her go and turned. Next to the iPad was a plastic sandwich bag with something white in it. How had he not seen that? He picked it up.

Brody froze. Slowly, he thawed. "You're pregnant?"

She nodded with her lips pressed together.

He tried to read her face for some sign of emotion, but he couldn't tell what she was feeling. "How do you feel about that?"

"Not as freaked out as I probably should be. What about you?"

"More turned on than I probably should be."

"Brody!"

"To be fair, I've been thinking about what I want to do to you for hours"—he put his hand on her belly—"and hearing you've got my baby inside you might have pushed me over the edge." He felt so possessive of her right now, he didn't know what to do. He wanted to push her dress up and fuck her against the wall—especially now that he didn't have to worry about using a condom. The urge to do everything in his power to make her happy and take care of her and the baby consumed him.

"That's it? It makes you horny? We made a person, Brody. You aren't freaking out at all?"

He shook his head. "It's unexpected and a little scary but it's you and me. I don't care how daunting something is as long as you're next to me."

"I think I'm still in shock."

"When did you find out?"

"Tonight."

He pulled her into his arms and looked down at her. "Do you wanna do this?"

She nodded. "Do you?"

He smiled and nodded. He wanted it all with Morgan—all the good stuff life had to offer. This was a head start, that's all.

"Before you say anything else, I need you to know that I don't want you to propose because of this."

That was cute. Brody rolled his eyes. "I already bought a ring and asked John and Lucy for their blessing."

She gasped. "You asked them?"

He shrugged. "I was determined to marry you even if they said no, but I thought they'd appreciate being asked, especially John."

"How did he react?"

"Like a father coming to terms with letting go of his little girl. Pretty sure he cried a little, but he played it off."

"So...are you asking me?"

"This isn't how I planned to propose."

"I don't need a sunset or flowers or pretty words."

He tucked her curls behind her ear. "I don't have the ring on me.

Although, I'm glad I had the wherewithal not to hide it in the safe."

She laughed. "If you're not going to propose...then, this is kind of awkward."

"Is it?" He popped open the top buttons of her dress. "It doesn't feel awkward to me. Nothing ever feels awkward when I'm with you."

"You're not really going to make me beg for you to let me come, are you?"

"You think you're off the hook just because you're having my baby?"

"Yes?"

He laughed. "Okay, fine. But I've got two I.O.U.s and tonight...I'm collecting."

Epilogue
Morgan

THE WOOD CRACKLED AS it burned in the fireplace at the Van Belle Mansion. Snow had fallen the morning before and didn't stop until the next evening. It stuck to the windows, adding a nice touch to the cozy winter wedding Morgan wanted.

Taylor had made Morgan's vision a reality.

The entire mansion was a winter wonderland. The scent of balsam pine filled the air and boughs and wreaths and swags decorated the setting. Pinecones dusted with sparkly faux snow and white peonies mingled in each arrangement.

It was the most beautiful wedding Morgan could have imagined, but she was more enamored with the man she'd promised to love forever. She glanced across the room to where he stood, talking with the men in their families. The wedding was small, his family, hers, and the captain who'd married them. Taylor's father was longtime friends with him, and he often officiated the weddings she planned.

Brody was already looking at her, and when their gazes connected, he said something to Logan, then came straight toward her. He wrapped his arm around her waist, pulled her into him, and kissed her so thoroughly, she had to lean into him or else become a puddle on the floor.

"I'd so get you pregnant tonight if you weren't already," he whispered in her ear.

She laughed and leaned back to look at him. "I love you too?"

"I do love you, but that's not what I was trying to say." He brushed his lips against her ear and whispered, "I can't wait to bend you over and push up this fluffy-ass skirt, Mrs. Lewis."

Her breath caught. Having a fashion designer for a future sister-in-law was awesome. When she'd started talking about a wedding dress with Drew, she'd struggled to choose a silhouette. It was an intimate wedding. She didn't want a ballgown. But she also didn't want a form-fitting dress that would expose her small baby bump. Everyone in attendance knew she was pregnant, but she wasn't ready for anyone besides Brody to see the changes her body was undergoing. Drew had showed her dozens of silhouettes, but when Morgan, hormonal as hell, got upset because none of them appealed to her, the talented designer told her to stop thinking about it. The next day, she'd sent her a sketch of a tea-length gown with a poofy skirt and three-quarters length sleeves. And it'd been exactly what she didn't know she'd wanted. The fabric shimmered like snow in the moonlight, which made it the perfect choice for a winter wedding.

The best part was Brody's face when he saw her walking toward him, and how he'd rarely taken his eyes off her all evening. He'd probably have reacted the same way to any dress, but this one made her feel beautiful and confident.

Her *husband* looked extra handsome in a gray three-piece suit with a sage green tie and pocket square. His proposal and his earthy, ruggedness had inspired the color palette for their wedding. Days after he'd come home, an alarm on her phone had woken her—an alarm she hadn't set. A note waited for her on the nightstand, telling her to bundle up and go out to the pond. She hadn't even had to dig for warm clothes, which she had very little, because they'd been laid out for her. A long, white wool coat. Black, fleece-lined leggings. A camel-colored cashmere sweater. A hat. Gloves. Scarf. Even boots. Each garment had a Drew Miller label.

Drew wasn't the only one in on Brody's proposal, though. Hope had greeted her with a choice of coffee or cocoa and homemade glazed donuts Gia had made. Hope had been positively giddy, but kept her lips zipped about what was going on. It'd been obvious what was about to happen, but the anticipation of not knowing how sent her heart racing.

The second she got to the pond and saw Brody her heart nearly burst. Bundled up in a coat the same color as the tie he currently had on, he'd waited next to a crackling campfire. Huge bouquets of white roses, pinecones, and pine branches framed the area in a wide circle.

The words he'd used to ask her to marry him hadn't been fancy— they'd just been Brody. Direct. Honest. A little teasing.

They'd decided on a short engagement, wanting to have the wedding before Brody left with his mom and dad for his dad's treatments. Morgan was going to watch after Hope a week while Brody helped them get settled. They were going to work on the nursery, a distraction to make the time pass faster for her and Hope, who couldn't be more ecstatic about becoming an aunt.

Announcing her pregnancy to their families had opened doors to conversations that they'd needed to have. Brody had brought up his biological parents, telling Theo and Gia about the video interviews Morgan had collected. The entire family watched them, and she'd been thankful to be present so she could see Brody's reaction to the addition she'd made. One of the people she'd interviewed had taken it upon themselves to ask a distant relative of his biological parents to get baby photos of him and Nick. She'd never seen Brody with tears in his eyes before that and probably wouldn't again any time soon.

The Cash family was, of course, extra when it came to their reaction to the news. Uncle John had gone all nostalgic and pulled out her baby book. Every phone call since then had included him suggesting names. Logan was beside himself worried about her health—mostly her mental health due to their family history of postpartum depression. He tried to be subtle about it, but she saw through it. Drew had sent her a photo of Logan's bookstore haul. All nonfiction. All having to do with pregnancy. But he was cute about it too. He'd sent the baby gifts already. Her favorite was a tiny leather jacket. And Lucy…she couldn't stand it that Morgan and Brody had decided to leave the gender a surprise. She'd started making plans for the baby shower the second the bridal shower had ended. Introducing Lucy to Taylor may have been a mistake. Their intrepid personalities magnified when together. She'd overheard them talking about having her baby shower during the evening so they could have Brody set off fireworks.

*Tink*s filled the room as one person tapped a fork against their glass. Everyone joined in.

Brody gave her a smooch that was so quick she didn't have time to react. "Are you ready to get out of here?"

She nodded. They'd danced. They'd cut the cake and fed it to each other. They'd been congratulated personally by each of the guests. Time to start the honeymoon—which unfortunately, wasn't going to be anything more than a night in one of Taylor's cottages. There wasn't enough time for them to go on a trip before Brody left with his parents, but he'd promised to make it up to her before the baby came. She didn't really mind. She could be anywhere with Brody and be content. What she didn't like was how much she was going to miss him.

Goodbyes said, they escaped to the cottage, which had been decked out for their wedding night. A white velvet quilt covered the bed and flickering LED candles of various heights had been placed on every available surface.

Brody slid her coat from her shoulders and laid it across a chair, then added his coat and suit jacket to the pile. "Tired? It's been a long day."

"Why? Are you going to let me go to sleep?"

He laughed and spun her to face him. "No."

"Do you think you can get me out of this dress or is it too complicated a task for you?"

The grin he flashed her sparked a pulsing ache between her legs. "I'll get you out of it one way or another, eventually. But not just yet." He swooped her up in his arms, causing her to shriek.

She wrapped her arms around his neck, admiring how handsome he looked in the glow of candlelight. "You're pretty."

He set her on the end of the bed and knelt in front of her. "Pretty?"

"Mmhmm."

He shook his head, then unbuttoned his vest, shrugged out of it, and rolled his sleeves to his elbows.

Morgan leaned forward and grabbed his tie. She pulled until he was close enough to kiss, but as soon as it heated up, he pulled back. Tingles spread throughout her body as he lifted the skirt of her dress, pushing it up while his hands traveled up her legs.

His fingers hit the lace band of her thigh highs and his gaze shot to hers. "Maybe I do want to take this dress off so I can see everything that's underneath it."

She braced her hands behind her and leaned back. "You won't be disappointed."

The intensity of his stare sent waves of nerves through her. She couldn't explain why the heat in his gaze always flustered her, but she didn't hate it. She liked everything he did to her, every time.

"I'm sure I won't, Mrs. Lewis." The rumble in his voice made her thighs clench.

Although, she hadn't spent much time thinking about marriage before she'd met Brody, she'd thought a woman changing her last name to her husband's was a stupid tradition. Even he'd been surprised when she'd told him she wanted to. It was Lucy's idea. Uncle John had backed it. The reason had been to make her harder to track down. She didn't worry about her father finding her, but it put their minds at ease, as well as Brody's, for her to take the step. She'd have done it anyway, so their little family would all have the same last name.

Brody placed a kiss on the inside of her knee, then an inch higher, then another inch, until his mouth reached the lace of her panties. He flattened his tongue and ran it over the fabric.

She tilted her head back and moaned. "Take them off, please."

Without hesitation, he tugged them down her legs, but left them around her ankles. He slipped off her shoes, then removed her panties and tossed them aside. The teasing of his tongue against her clit had her thighs shaking in no time. One long lick and she was done, pulsing hard around his fingers as they slid in and out of her.

She had virtually no time to recover as he crept over her, the fluff of her skirt flowing around him.

He covered her mouth with his, his tongue tasting of her. While he drove her back to the neediness he knew exactly how to evoke, he braced himself with his arm next to her head, unbuckled his belt, and unfastened his pants.

Somehow, as he dragged her into a lust-induced trance, he got her out of her dress, then stripped out of the rest of his clothes, his gaze greedily taking in the view of her in thigh-high stockings and a white sheer bra.

"Fuck, baby." He settled himself between her thighs. "It's not fair for you to be this sexy."

"Even if you're allowed to do whatever you want with me?"

His smirk showed how much he liked hearing that. Brody might be super attuned to her needs, but she paid attention too. Reminding him she belonged to him and offering him unfettered access to her body was the fastest way to get him hot and bothered.

He shifted his hips, his hard length sliding against her.

Morgan groaned and lifted her hips. "Stop teasing me."

"It's our wedding night. I'll drag it out if I want to." But he must not have wanted to. He grabbed her hips and sank inside her.

Her eyes fluttered shut, the pleasure too intense to focus on anything other than feeling.

He rubbed her nipple with a featherlight caress. Pregnancy made her breasts and nipples tender, but Brody, being Brody, had adapted and his touches stirred nothing but bliss.

"Look at me," he rasped, his voice filled with emotion.

Morgan opened her eyes, and a slow smile spread across her lips. Exhilaration filled her chest with the realization that this man wanted to spend his life with her.

His mouth tipped up at the corner. "I'm so in love with you, Morgan."

She traced his bottom lip with her fingertips. "Good. Because I'm yours. Forever."

SUPPORT AN INDIE AUTHOR

If you enjoyed this book, please review it and tell your friends about it. By doing so, you'll be helping me spread the word, which means I can spend less time marketing and more time writing.

Sign up for my mailing list:
https://www.marycainbooks.com

www.ingramcontent.com/pod-product-compliance
Lightning Source LLC
Chambersburg PA
CBHW030849030726
47495CB00005B/1441